100

D1274621

Also by Daoma Winston
THE HAVERSHAM LEGACY

The Golden

DAOMA WINSTON

Valley

SIMON AND SCHUSTER ⋮ NEW YORK

Published by Simon and Schuster
Rockefeller Center, 630 Fifth Avenue
New York, New York 10020
Designed by Edith Fowler
Manufactured in the United States of America
1 2 3 4 5 6 7 8 9 10

Library of Congress Cataloging in Publication Data

Winston, Daoma.
        The golden valley.

        I. Title.
PZ4.W784Go   [PS3545.I7612]   813'.5'4   75-28323
ISBN 0-671-22165-5

For Murray

prologue

"The vultures," Maria cried, starting up from the pillows. "The vultures . . . Madre de Dios, I see them! I see them, I tell you. They're here, Doña Lupe!" Her hoarse voice broke and she sank back, fingers lax on the two hempen ropes that were attached to the posts at the foot of the canopied bed.

Her head dropped sideways and her hair, thick and black as polished jet, loosened from its white binding and fell free, veiling her face.

She drew a deep, choked breath, released it in a long panting whisper. The winter of 1875 was severe, and her whisper blended with an icy November wind that sucked and sang at the velvet-draped window. Then her panting murmurs became a scream, rising high and thin into a raw, ugly shriek.

Her dark eyes, gleaming with fever, opened wide, her pale lips contorted. Her body writhed on hot currents of pain that emanated from the great mound of her belly. Beyond it she saw vaguely two black shapes, a shadowed rippling movement. The scream died away and left behind in her throat a burning like that of swallowed fire. "The vultures," she murmured. "They hover over me with wide dark wings. I saw them once before, Doña Lupe!

They danced just so around the tiny bleeding body of an injured lamb. I know, I know . . . they wait for me to die."

There was a cool light touch at her cheek. Her eyes snapped open. "Doña Lupe . . . I know them for what they are, believe me. They're standing near the fire now and regarding me with avid eyes."

Her mother-in-law laughed softly. "Why, my Maria, how can you be so unkind even in your pain? You've known these two good women, Felicia and Ana, for long years, and you know they're here only to help you."

The midwife Ana shrugged bony shoulders, but Felicia frowned slightly, troubled by the fever that caused the delusion in Maria's mind.

"Then if these are Felicia and Ana, why won't they do something?" Maria moaned. "It's so long, so long. I can't bear it much longer, I tell you."

"I know you think so now," Lupe said. "It's what every woman has always thought. But when it's over you'll remember nothing of it."

"But I *do* remember," Maria retorted, her weak voice strengthened by anger. "I remember the others. Maria Santísima, how well do I remember!"

Lupe made sounds of wordless comfort, but sighed within herself. Perhaps that was the trouble. Three times before, Maria had been brought to childbed, and each had been followed by mourning for the new, innocent life ended so quickly. It might be that Maria was afraid to allow this infant to escape the protection of her body. Perhaps she clung to it and wouldn't let it go, lest it, too, be taken from her forever.

Lupe gestured to the two women and Felicia poured a steaming decoction into a silver goblet and brought it to the bedside.

Lupe held it to Maria's lips, whispering, "Now, niña, you'll take this. It'll make you rest and sleep. And when you waken, you'll be ready and then you'll have your son."

Maria sipped the brew until the goblet was empty. She roused herself to murmur "Thank you, Doña Lupe," and, the words barely spoken, she slept.

Lupe waited a moment before turning away. A good girl, this Maria. Lupe herself had chosen her to be Lorenzo's bride when it was time for him to marry, nine years before. But now Maria was nearing thirty and there wouldn't be too many opportunities. This time Lorenzo's son must survive.

She left the room saying softly, "Just call me when Doña Maria is ready. I'll go to Don Lorenzo now."

Lupe went slowly along the twilight-shadowed hallway. Many souls were brought into this world, she thought. And many were lost too soon. But this one . . . this one must be held here, here on this earth, to live and grow and love. Lorenzo must have his son. And she, she herself was fifty-seven years old. She wanted to hold her grandchild in her arms. Her fingers crept to the gold crucifix at her throat. Maria Santísima, this time, por favor . . .

The heavy carved door that led into the large drawing room called the sala made a faint sound as Lupe opened it.

Immediately her son, Lorenzo Martínez, raised his head and looked anxiously at her. "Is it time, Mamacita?"

"No, my son," she answered. "Not yet. But perhaps soon."

"It's the waiting that's so difficult," he grumbled.

"Yes," she agreed. But a small bitter smile touched her lips. It was always thus. The men spoke of the waiting while the women fought the pain.

Lorenzo sank back in his chair to stare abstractedly at the fire.

She moved to draw the heavy green draperies against the swiftly falling dusk. This time, there was no beef cooking slowly above the flames in an open pit. There were no huge vats of beans simmering over blazing fires, nor ears of corn steaming within their husks. There were no trays of empanaditas and bizcochitos sprinkled with sugar waiting to be served.

Lorenzo had wanted it so. Perhaps he had thought to ward off a fourth disappointment by neglecting the usual preparations.

There was one way, however, in which the old formalities were observed. She saw, as she looked out, that the people of the ranch were even now gathering in the snowy courtyard to await the news.

With a sudden start, Lupe turned. She had, until that instant, completely forgotten that a few hours earlier their oldest neighbor in the valley had also come to share their vigil.

Don Cipriano Diaz did not seem to mind that she and Lorenzo had neglected their duties as hosts. He nodded comfortably on the settle, his booted feet barely touching the floor. One arm was stretched along the back as if, even in his sleep, he reached out to protect the two small children who sat so still beside him.

She smiled at them, but didn't speak, lest in doing so she disturb the old man's nap.

The children gravely returned her smile.

She gestured at the tray of sweets she had set out for them earlier, and each took one and nodded a silent thanks.

She settled herself in a deep chair, thinking that they

were a sedate couple. Seven-year-old Josefa Diaz, with her long brown braids and round black eyes and too-white face, was Don Cipriano's only grandchild, orphaned at the age of four. The boy, Matthew, was perhaps five, with chestnut-colored hair, marked by a single white lock over his right temple.

Lupe looked down at her small withered hands. Don Cipriano had had some good fortune, at least, despite all the ill that had befallen him. For he had these two to moderate the cold of his aging years.

A small sound made her turn, and she saw her reflection in the mirror that hung on the nearby wall. The tortoiseshell comb, once her mother's and grandmother's, worn, it was said, by an early ancestor in Seville, rose from the thick round knot at the back of Lupe's head. From it fell the black folds of a delicate mantilla. There were wide wings of white in the darkness of her hair, and her nose, chin, cheekbones were sharp. Time's handiwork had marked her. Yet she believed that the outer skin meant nothing. It was the spirit within that mattered. And she wasn't done yet.

She rose as a wagon rattled to a stop in the courtyard and a horse snorted and stamped.

Lorenzo raised his head.

"It's probably Don Esteban," she said softly. "Will you welcome him, Lorenzo?"

Lorenzo pushed himself up. Standing, he was peculiarly diminished. He had huge thick shoulders and a round barrel of a chest. His arms bulged with muscles. But his legs were short. It was only seated that he looked like a giant. He nodded, tugged his spade-shaped black beard. "Yes. I'll bring him in."

As he left the room, Don Cipriano gave a single loud

snore and jerked awake. "Eh? Eh? What's that? Has it happened yet, Doña Lupe? What is it? A girl? A boy? Not that it matters, I say." He cast a loving look at the children beside him. "Either one is a blessing. Either one, I say."

"You made a noise like a mountain lion." Josefa giggled around the tip of her braid.

He uttered a sound of disgust, pulled it from between her lips. "Phaw, phaw, how can you do it, eating your hair again? You'll get balls of fur in your belly." He turned to Lupe. "What am I to do with her?" And then, recollecting, he jumped up. "Doña Lupe, tell me—what happened while I slept?"

"Nothing, my dear Don Cipriano. We all rested with you. And Maria's sleeping at the moment, too."

Lorenzo returned with Don Esteban Delagado, who came quickly to Lupe and, taking her hand, bowed over it. "Doña Lupe, am I in time?"

"Very much so," she answered. "We're about to have chocolate."

Lorenzo was more understanding. He smiled at his mother. "Mamacita, the brandy perhaps?"

"Brandy, of course," she agreed dryly.

"And here's Don Cipriano, with Josefa and Matthew," Esteban said, his thin face brightening with pleasure. He was fond of the children, of Don Cipriano too. He himself was alone on the ranch that his father had left him.

It was Lupe's judgment that he should marry. He was twenty-five, though he looked somewhat older; he had the beginning of a paunch and his very dark straight hair, worn slicked back off his forehead, was already thinning at the temples. Lupe would have been delighted to arrange a match for him, but there was no one suitable in the valley of Tres Ríos.

He took Josefa on one knee, and Matthew on the other, as the serving girl, Dora, appeared without summons from the direction of the kitchen. She carried a heavy tile tray framed in carved pine. It held a silver pot of foaming chocolate, small cups, a carafe of brandy, and glasses.

"You've taken the thought from my mind," Lupe said.

"The men will be chilled," Dora answered, grinning. "And the children don't like brandy."

Lupe looked at her guests, then at Lorenzo. It was something to think about that here in this room were the three great landowners of the valley.

Suddenly an anguished wail came clearly into the room, and a rush of quick footsteps sounded beyond the heavy door.

"Doña Lupe! Doña Lupe, now, now. We need you!"

Esteban drew his breath in sharply, and Don Cipriano sighed, then gave the children a reassuring smile.

Lupe turned to her son. "I'll come back as soon as there's word," she said, and hurried out, thinking of another November night when the same icy wind had whispered at the windows. Then it had been her own anguished cry that sounded through the house. And later, after much struggle, she had heard Lorenzo's first wail of protest, and she smiled before she slept. She prayed that it would be the same for Maria within the next few hours.

But Maria's face was dyed the color of saffron. Her eyes were dull. She made a whimpering sound when Lupe said soothingly, "Soon, niña. Very soon, child, I promise you."

Felicia took up the ropes, placed them firmly into Maria's hands and tightly closed her thin fingers around them. "These will help you, Doña Maria, but you must

13

make the effort. You, you alone can do this. We've been here and waiting and trying for you for fifteen hours nearly. Por favor, niña, you must make the effort yourself now."

"Already fifteen hours," Maria moaned. "Already so long, and I can't . . . I can't . . . it just won't come."

"It will. Only moments more," Lupe answered. She folded her withered fingers around Maria's, clasping the rope. "Try, my darling, try, my heart," she murmured. "You can. Just try." She knew how it was. She had lain thus in this same bed, staring through tear-burning eyes at the blue fringes of the canopy above her, while she labored to bring forth Lorenzo; and she had seen him become Don Lorenzo Martínez y Escobedo, sole heir, when her brothers died in an Indian attack on the hacienda, to all the Escobedo holdings. Martínez y Escobedo. That was how the ranch was called. It was for this that Lorenzo so desired a son.

Maria's hand jerked convulsively. "Doña Lupe . . . "

Lupe bent close, whispered, "Niña, think only of your son."

Maria's arched body collapsed and quivered, then began a slow side-to-side thrashing. "Help me," she wailed. "Madre de Dios, help me now. Mother of God, remember Your own travail and be kind."

Lupe fixed her eyes on the carved wooden figure above the bed. El Cristo hung on His cross, head drooping, eyes and mouth showing all the age-long agonies of man. Silently she prayed for His mercy.

"Ah, no," Maria screamed suddenly. "Ah, no, no, I can't. The vultures again . . . they spread their black wings over me."

"No, niña," Felicia whispered, her hands moving in

a slow rhythm on Maria's swollen belly. "No, niña . . . we three are here to help you, child. Pull the ropes . . . pull. . . ."

Maria strained to listen and obey. But no, no. She couldn't.

She was seized, shaken, then flung down.

There was brief surcease. Slowly she struggled from her daze and said, "Lorenzo will be happy to have his son, Doña Lupe."

"Yes, my Maria. Yes."

Maria was seized again. The pain was like silver daggers flashing into the core of her being, and then the core split, and there was more pain and searing heat, and at last Felicia's encouraging voice came crooning through swirling red mists, "Ah, yes, my Maria. You're a good girl. You're blessed, my Maria."

Maria had it on her tongue to say, "Let me see my son." But the words wouldn't form themselves. She had no breath. The ripped and burning core at the center of her body suddenly hardened and exploded outward. She screamed shrilly, and heard the thin terrible sound coming back at her as she sank into overwhelming blackness.

"Look!" Ana gasped. "Doña Lupe! Look!"

She held a tiny infant in her two trembling hands.

"Maria Santísima!" Felicia breathed, and raised from between Maria's limp and bloodied thighs another tiny body.

The two were bound together, entangled in the cords that had sustained them in their mother's womb.

"There are two," Felicia panted. "Two, Doña Lupe, bound together. It's the first time in all my years that I've seen such a thing."

"I see," Lupe breathed. "Yes, yes, Felicia, I see

indeed. But be quick. And you, Ana, hurry. Look after the infants at once. I'll attend to Maria myself."

Felicia touched the cross at her throat, spanked the infant she held until it gave a long howling shout. Then she cut the cord, knotted it. Slowly, holding her breath, she cleaned the tiny unmarked body.

Ana took up the second infant. She slapped its bottom, and it gasped and choked and mewed softly. When it was cleaned, she, too, crossed herself. A long narrow red mark lay along the base of the tiny throat, a scar left by the cord that had nearly strangled it.

"Quickly," Doña Lupe said. "Run, one of you, and tell Dora to bring word to Don Lorenzo." She bent over Maria, smiling. "You have your son, niña, and a daughter, too. You're doubly blessed for this night's work and suffering. In a moment you'll hold them in your arms and begin to heal again."

"A boy and a girl," Maria murmured drowsily.

"Lorenzo will be proud," Lupe said.

Moments later Dora hurried importantly into the torchlit courtyard.

Porfirio Romero, the ranch foreman, stood among the people. He was a man of forty-seven. Tall, broad-shouldered, with a shock of heavy black hair and almond-shaped black eyes, he had a certain presence that all his life had set him apart.

"Porfirio! Porfirio!" Dora touched his arm. Her breath made small white plumes in the cold air as she cried, "It's happened at last! Don Lorenzo asked me to tell you. He has his son at last, and a daughter as well. There are two infants. And Don Lorenzo says to break out a cask of wine!"

Porfirio grinned, a flash of white teeth against his

swarthy skin. "I'll do that!" As she darted into the house, he raised both his arms to make the announcement.

Within the room the air was hot, still. Even the sweet spice of the cedar boughs could not hide the odors of illness that seeped from the bed where Maria lay burning with fever.

She stirred, a dream of brilliant sun fading so swiftly that she couldn't remember where she had been.

Felicia immediately offered her water, but Maria shook her head, whispered, "The babies?"

"Don't trouble yourself, Doña Maria. They're fine. Each is perfection."

"The babies?" Maria repeated.

Felicia moistened a cloth and wiped the sweat from Maria's forehead. "Doña Lupe will bring them, niña."

Maria's lips curved in a thin smile. "You'll find a wet nurse for them?"

"Yes, yes, we will. Never fear."

"Though I'd give anything to feed them at my own breast . . . "

"As you shall when the fever is gone, niña."

"Will it go, Felicia?"

The midwife gave a brisk nod, then turned quickly away, relieved to hear Doña Lupe's light footstep just beyond the door.

Maria watched as the older woman came across the room, carrying an infant in each arm. Her eyes brightened and a touch of color rose in her cheeks.

Lupe leaned close. "Maria . . ."

"Beautiful," Maria whispered. "Hands like the petals of flowers, Doña Lupe. Lips like tiny buds." Her thin fingers stroked the black down of one tiny head, then the other. "And eyes . . . eyes like emeralds . . ."

"From their father," Lupe said softly.

17

"And he, he's happy, Doña Lupe?"

"You know he is, niña. And he'll be here again in a moment."

"Then I'm content." Maria sighed, traced the shape of two tiny chins, then allowed her hand to fall to the quilt. "I'm tired, Doña Lupe, and cold. Still so cold."

Lupe said nothing but Maria knew. She asked softly, "Doña Lupe, you'll raise them and care for them?"

Lupe swallowed, kept grief from her face, from her voice. "You'll do it yourself, niña."

Maria didn't reply. She looked once more into the tiny faces of the infants. Then she closed her eyes.

She didn't stir when Lorenzo sat beside her, nor when the infants cried and were quickly carried out of the room by Dora.

But toward dawn she opened her dark eyes and fixed them on the crucifix she held. Then her fingers loosened their grasp and her head slid sideways so that her suddenly empty eyes seemed to look at the door. Her breath came out in a long slow sigh, whispering, "The babies . . . the babies . . . " And then she was still.

1

The two horses moved sedately up the ridge through the thick stand of blue spruce. At the top, well screened from those censorious eyes that might have been watching from the ranch house below, Anitra reined in.

"Now," she said, her face alight with mischief and her green eyes glinting. "Now, my brother."

"Sometime Papa will see you, and then there'll be the devil to pay," Antonio answered, but even as he spoke, he climbed down to release the tied stirrup on her saddle.

"Sometime." She shrugged, freeing the wide circle of her tucked-in skirt. "But not today."

She flung her leg over the pommel and thrust both feet firmly into the stirrups, rising to stand tall with her arms flung wide. "Oh, Antonio, how good it is to be free!"

He remounted, reflecting soberly that it took only small things to give Anitra such a feeling, while he himself, in all their shared twelve years, had never known it. Unconsciously his hand crept to his throat to adjust his collar, lest any small part be revealed of the thin red scar that lay there.

The whole of the valley of Tres Ríos lay before them. It had been named hundreds of years ago for the three rivers that must once have crossed it. Signs of two of them remained only in those ancient Indian carvings he and

Anitra had found high on the canyon walls. The third river still ran deep within its timeless narrow gorge, a black ribbon that wound its way through the lowlands.

On all sides the mountains rose to meet the sky, bare defiles glistening in pink morning sunlight, shadowed with cedar and spruce and piñon, their ragged peaks still tipped with winter snows.

A few small rutted brown roads, some no more than wagon tracks, wended their meandering ways across the valley floor to a scattering of adobe houses, each with its own milpa of corn, each with a spiral of blue piñon smoke rising above it.

In the bluish distance, a huddle of buildings and the tall silvery limbs of cottonwoods lightly veiled in the green of early May marked the town of Tres Ríos.

There was a stillness here, and no sign of the blood that had spilled on the red earth. The valley and its village had been old when the Spanish conquistadores first saw it, their armor gleaming, the plumes dancing above their helmets. It had been old when they rode astride their horses and looked down at the golden plain from the mountain pass, seeing the shadowed rim of the river.

The Indians had lived here then, at the base of the mountains, among fields watered by springs that ran from their snows.

There had been battles, and bloody uprisings, and many a soldier lay moldering and forgotten in an unmarked grave. His own uncles had died protecting the land they called theirs, fallen beneath painted lances. Now, finally, in 1887, the lance throwers, who had learned to use guns, were withdrawn to the south, and the valley of Tres Ríos had found peace.

Antonio sat at ease in his saddle, dreaming of the

past and considering the present, but Anitra cried, "Antonio, come on!" and lightly flicked her crop at her horse. The bay leaped out, stumbled and caught itself.

Anitra wasn't one for dreaming, he thought. It was another way in which they were different. And through his mind there passed the memory of whispers around the outdoor ovens and the smell of baking bread, and mingling with it, his horror at hearing of the day he and his sister were born, entangled in their cords.

Hearing the same story, she hadn't shared his horror. She had flung back her head and laughed. "Why, I always knew it, Antonio. We're twins and closer even than twins!"

Now she cried again, "Come on! Let's ride!"

Antonio spurred his horse, but the animal sagged, badly off balance, and went down on both forelegs. The boy was jolted from the saddle, his feet losing grip on the stirrups, his hands torn from the reins. He pitched forward and hit the ground with a bone-jarring thud. Grasping wildly at the thick underbrush, but unable to stop himself, he spun away down the slope.

"Madre de Dios! Antonio! Antonio!" Anitra screamed. It was as if she felt within herself the awful force of his fall, the ripping and scratching bite of mesquite within her own flesh. She galloped after him, raising a cloud of red dust, and flung herself down beside him. "Antonio! Are you all right, my brother?"

He raised his dark head slowly, grinned. "I think so. But I wouldn't have wanted Papa to see that."

She sat back on her boots, smiling, her heart-shaped face alight with relief. "He didn't see it, so never mind. As long as you're not hurt."

"It's nothing, Anitra." He rose quickly, and a pebble

spun away from beneath his boots to drop soundlessly into a narrow cleft near his feet.

In the shadows there a thick coiled body stirred. A diamond-marked head rose slowly. Soft motes of golden dust trickled around it, and vibrations rippled through the dark. The coils tightened, loosened, tightened again. The head drew down and lifted, and lifted once more. This time it emerged in response to the sun's warmth and the stir caused by the movement of Antonio's feet and the impatient hooves of the horses. The coils tightened. The rattles sang. The diamond-marked head lanced forward.

Anitra saw and flung herself at Antonio, thrust him back as the flat fangs struck, spewed venom on his boot and leg.

She seized her quirt, and as the snake coiled once more, head rearing back to strike again, she lashed downward with the weighted end. Her deadly aim caught the flat head at its center and drove it low. But the coils re-formed. The flat head rose again, wicked fangs ready. She struck once more, then again. Slime spewed from the suddenly misshapen head. It fell, its long coiled body finally going still. She wiped the stained quirt clean in the dust and rubbed her bespattered hands dry of ugly wetness. Then, still breathing hard, she rose. "He didn't get you, Antonio?"

He looked at where trouser and boot covered his right ankle. A shiny black stain marred the fabric, and broken threads, too, showed where the fangs had caught. He shuddered within himself, fighting to keep what he felt from his face. He glanced only once at the crushed and broken thing she had left behind, and then looked away. Suddenly he was choked by the thick clot of despair that rose in his throat. It was he who should have killed the snake—he who should have battered it to death. But he had been frozen in fear while Anitra acted. At last he said softly, "It was close, I think. But no, he didn't get me."

She didn't reply—just stood, hands on her narrow hips, surveying the slope. The threat was gone and she dismissed it. Now she faced another problem. At the first sign of the rattler, both horses had panicked and fled.

"Come on, Antonio. Let's find the silly fools. Why are horses such cowards anyway?"

She started off, unaware of the rider who just then breasted the ridge above. Now he sat back in his silver-trimmed saddle, a smile narrowing his blue eyes, and deepening the dimple near his mouth.

He had ridden some eighty-five miles north from the city of Santa Fe, passing only a single wagon, several tiny villages, and innumerable wandering herds of sheep. Yet he already knew that his instincts had led him truly.

He looked up at the mountains and felt their power as his own. Such mountains made some men small, taught them their own weaknesses. But not him.

When he reached the pass and saw the valley spread before him, the mountains that encircled it, he rose up in his stirrups, filled with a heat and hunger that was almost sexual. He felt it in his flesh and muscle and in his bones. But there was no final release. His passion for the valley, for the mountains that surrounded it, became a part of him. This land would be his. The long wandering years were done with. Here was his future, his destiny. Here he belonged.

He rode on, filled with hot excitement. At the ridge he pulled up to watch Anitra and Antonio climb down the rocks toward a stream where their two horses were contentedly munching buffalo grass.

23

The girl, her long black hair blowing on her shoulders, belonged here. The boy stumbling after, his hand at his throat . . .

Leigh Ransome smiled more broadly. Oh, yes, these two were a part of the wind-scoured valley, just as he had once been a part of that steamy Eastern plantation which he hardly remembered.

His grin suddenly faded. Below him he saw Anitra approach the bay, saw the horse shy off and the girl tumble to the ground.

He raked his mount with quick spurs and galloped down the slope.

Even as he approached, Anitra was on her feet. "Stop it, you beautiful fool. The rattler's gone. It's me! It's me, I tell you."

"Anitra, wait!" Antonio shouted.

But she flung herself after the bay and grabbed it by the bridle. The horse reared, reaching for the sky. Anitra hung on, raised up with hair and skirts flying, shaken as if she were weightless, and finally, when the bay came down, slammed into the ground.

The bay's hooves flashed up once more, and Antonio yelled.

Leigh drove in, whipped the rampaging horse away as Anitra leaped to her feet, her cheeks red with anger and smudged with dust, and shouted, "Don't hurt my horse, you idiot!"

Leigh reined in abruptly. He looked down at her and grinned. "You'd rather be trampled into the dust than see your horse driven off?"

His accented Spanish, the Spanish he had learned in Texas, brought a lift to her dark brows. Now she noticed his blue eyes, the bronze curl that escaped from under the wide brim of his black hat. He's an American, she thought. But she said only, "I can take care of myself, señor."

"I noticed," he answered dryly. He had noticed more than that. Her emerald-green eyes were curiously adult, but she was much younger than he had thought her to be at first. She was hardly more than twelve or thirteen. And yet, plainly, she was very near to being a woman.

Antonio said quickly, "Señor, you must forgive my sister. It's only that she's upset. You see, a little while ago we stumbled upon a rattlesnake." His words were no more than an automatic courtesy to a stranger. He saw the look Leigh bent on Anitra and he didn't like it.

She cut in sharply, "But, of course, I thank you for your help."

Leigh's grin widened. There was a touch of mockery in his voice when he answered, "It's nothing, señorita. But may I suggest that you wander too far afield. What with snakes, and recalcitrant horses . . . "

"Far afield?" she retorted. "But we're not. This is our land."

"Your land?" Leigh asked softly.

"Well, this is common grazing," explained Antonio. "It belongs to all. Our ranch lies beyond."

Anitra ignored her brother's words. She eyed Leigh's fine black coat, his tooled leather boots, and narrow silk tie. She said, "It would appear to me that it's you who are far afield."

Leigh laughed openly. "Perhaps I am. And now, would you like me to get your horse for you and see you safely into the saddle?"

The bay stood across the stream, eying the group. Antonio's sorrel placidly waited.

"I would not!" Anitra flashed a single angry glance at Leigh, pulled up her skirts so that her slim ankles showed, and stamped through the stream in a great splash of silver spray. She approached the bay, hesitated, and then mounted, setting both feet firmly into the stirrups, thinking, Let him make of it what he likes.

Leigh allowed his amusement to show on his face. In a time when women rode sidesaddle it was a gesture of defiance to ride astride.

Antonio swung onto his horse, said, "Again, thank you."

"Por nada," Leigh replied. And then, "It's a beautiful valley."

"Yes, señor. Do you come from far?"

"From Santa Fe."

"Ah . . . " Antonio's eyes brightened. "Is it as busy and as beautiful a place as I've heard?"

"More busy certainly, but less beautiful than your valley, amigo."

"You're very polite to say it, señor."

"And I mean it," Leigh answered, and with a nod to Antonio, a lift of his hand to Anitra, he turned his horse and rode off.

He was more deeply sincere than Antonio realized. Leigh had been so long embittered by the loss of what had never actually been his that he had been successful at nothing in his life. He had never faced his failures but had always drifted away, leaving no mark behind. But now, within moments, between one breath and another, he had found meaning and faith where there had been none before. There was the valley, the mountains that watched over it. And there was the girl, slender, green-eyed . . . the girl whose name he didn't know.

Anitra watched until he had disappeared into the willow thickets; then she joined Antonio.

"You were rude to the stranger," her brother said.

"I didn't like his interference."

"He didn't intend to interfere. He probably doesn't know our ways. I wonder what he's doing here from Santa Fe. Did you notice his clothes, Anitra? Surely they weren't those of the saddle tramps that we've seen come and go."

"As *he'll* come and go," she said. "Regardless of his fine clothes, there'll be nothing for him in Tres Ríos, and by dark he'll know it."

"Perhaps," Antonio agreed. If it were so, it would be just as well. Americans, gringos, even if they spoke the language, weren't particularly welcome in the neighborhood.

Anitra didn't answer. She threw back her head, her face suddenly glowing. "Antonio, listen! Listen, do you hear it?"

Across the valley, from beyond the river gorge, came the long distant wail of a train.

"Let's go," she cried. "Let's ride. Maybe we can catch it this time."

He knew they wouldn't. They never had, although they'd tried many times before. But he followed when she leaped over the stream and went bursting from the trees at a full gallop and dashed down the narrow trail that led into the canyon. When they reached the rim of the gorge with the river beneath them, they saw that the tracks on the other side were empty.

She sat back, imagining that she could still smell the sooty billows from the train's smokestack. "Ah, never mind, Antonio. One day we'll see it. One day it'll stop here, waiting for us."

He nodded, and by unspoken agreement they sat silently, looking into the gorge below.

She sensed the slow settling of peace on Antonio's

spirit and was glad and regretful at the same time. It was always this way. When Antonio was separated from the ranch, from their father, he stood straighter, rode faster, looked about him with seeing eyes. But in Lorenzo's presence he became uncertain, torn between fear and burning anger. She sighed within herself. She found it hard to watch, although it had always been that way.

Antonio, feeling her gaze on him, turned and grinned at her.

She laughed aloud. It was a good morning. The rattlesnake had not struck Antonio. The interfering bronze-haired American had not spoiled it either. The thought of Matthew came into her mind. It would be a perfect morning if Matthew were here, too.

Increasingly in this past year she had found herself changing toward him. Whereas before she had always taken him for granted, now she had begun to see him with new eyes.

Her grandmother had told her how he came to Don Cipriano's. It was when he was perhaps three years old, though no one could be absolutely certain of that. As no one could be absolutely certain of his true name.

One day Don Cipriano had ridden past an Apache Mezcalero encampment on the far side of the river. He saw among the horses and dogs, six or seven small children, dirty, half-naked, with long unclean hair. Among those scampering savages there was one who looked up with a flash of pale-gray eyes. Don Cipriano reined in for a closer stare and noticed a white streak in chestnut hair and patches of pale skin glowing through mud-spattered cheeks. He climbed down from the saddle, and as he went toward the boy, the child ran to him, flung his arms around Don Cipriano's knees, and shouted, "Papa!"

It seemed the only word that the child knew, but it was enough for Don Cipriano. After several hours of barter, he bought the boy for three ponies and eight silver buttons. As he prepared to ride away from the encampment with the boy in his arms, a woman thrust into his hands an old and worn Bible. When he examined it later, he found that a last entry on the flyleaf was the name Matthew Britton, the date affixed some three years before then. He assumed this to have been the Bible that belonged to the boy's parents, and that the boy himself must be Matthew Britton. And so he called him Matthew Britton out of respect for the dead who had made him. But Don Cipriano loved the boy as if he were his own, and he had taken the place of the sons Don Cipriano had lost.

Now, at seventeen, Matthew was a man. He did a man's work and thought a man's thoughts. Of that Anitra was certain. He had a slow, deep voice, and a slow, warm smile, and he treated everyone with the same careful courtesy. It rankled Anitra that although the five years' difference between them had become as nothing in the past few months, he was still the same to her as he was to Josefa. It wasn't fair. Josefa was virtually his sister, after all. And besides, she was two years older. She wore her hair in a coronet of dark-brown braids. Don Cipriano allowed her whatever choice of dress she desired, just as he allowed her whatever else she wanted. Her pallid presence seemed always to bring out the hoyden in Anitra. It was no wonder that Matthew didn't realize she was now grown. Ah, but some day soon . . . some day . . .

It was as if she had willed it. There was a shout from across the meadow, and Matthew rode toward the gorge. She jerked her horse around and spurred ahead to meet him, conscious of Antonio following more slowly. She ran her fingers quickly through her long tousled black hair. If only her grandmother would allow her to put it up.

Matthew was, at first, no more than a familiar dark silhouette in the distance, lean body swaying with the rhythm of his horse's stride. Then the sunlight unveiled him. His big hat hung from his throat by a leather thong so that his chestnut hair was revealed, thick, springy, with crisp deep waves, brushed back from his forehead, and pierced by a wide white lock that angled upward from his right temple.

With a pang she wondered if that lock marked the place where he had been injured as a child, if he had come so close to sharing his parents' fate, so close to being lost to her forever.

His jaw was square, his mouth long and narrow. His light-gray eyes seemed to catch and hold points of sun, as if tiny stars were trapped in their depths.

Her heart gave a great leap of joy. Warmth spilled in quick currents through the whole of her body.

She reached again to smooth her hair. She was grown. She felt grown in her soul. Why did no one else see it? She touched the small shining curls at her ears and quickly tucked in the white bodice that had pulled out at her waist.

He didn't seem to notice the small feminine gestures. Instead, when they met, he said severely to Antonio, "I've been looking all over for you. It's Doña Lupe. She sent me."

"Because of my father," Antonio said, sighing.

Matthew nodded.

"He wanted me to ride to Coronado with him."

"Antonio!" Anitra cried. "You didn't tell me that. I'd have gone with you. I'd have . . ."

"I didn't want to. I simply didn't want to go. I didn't want to see it."

"But, Antonio, there's no need . . . why, if we went together . . ."

"It wouldn't matter, I tell you. I didn't want to see it." Antonio slumped in the saddle. "He wants me to be what I can't be."

"But what did he want?" Matthew asked quietly.

"Some poor fool there in Coronado had stolen a lamb. At least, that's the word my father had for it. He was set to punish him, with me as witness. I don't want to be part of such business."

"Anyway, your grandmother is waiting," Matthew said. "We'd better go back."

"Don Lorenzo is very angry," Dora murmured.

"I'm afraid so," Doña Lupe agreed.

"But it's hardly a crime that Antonio should ride in the valley with his sister," Dora protested. "And such a rage . . . Oh, if only Doña Maria had lived . . . may she rest in the peace of God . . . but if only she'd lived . . ."

Lupe closed her eyes, her small thin hands clenching into tiny fists. It was no good to think of what might have been.

The raising of Anitra and Antonio was Lupe's responsibility. Physically they were beautiful, her two grandchildren. Already tall for their years, arrow-straight, with good shoulders and long shapely limbs. Their black curls were alive with health, their green eyes sparkled. And yet . . .

Dora was asking anxiously, "But what shall I say to Don Lorenzo?"

"I've sent Matthew to look for the children. I'll speak

to Don Lorenzo myself," Lupe answered, and heard Dora's small sigh of relief.

Lupe sighed too. Always it devolved upon Lupe herself to make a fragile peace in the uneasy household.

She felt the weight of it. She was no longer young, and she yearned for rest. But unease dogged her days. In some deep and wordless way she feared for Anitra, for Antonio. The elder by only moments, Anitra was just slightly the larger, the stronger. She was quicker on her feet, more open with her feelings. She was first to learn to talk, and Antonio had followed. She was first to learn to handle a horse, and had then coaxed Antonio into the saddle. Though they both had Lorenzo's brilliant green eyes, the look was different. Anitra's were sharp, alert, burning with interest in everything, while Antonio's were shadowed with unspoken thoughts.

Lorenzo, too, saw these differences, and was angered by them. The son he had idolized as an infant had become a torment to him. The daughter he had largely ignored had become a constant irritation.

Lupe's gaze drifted to the window, where beyond the distant clump of Chinese lilac she saw the snow-capped peaks of the mountains. Soon the May sun would melt away the winter whiteness, the acequias, those life-giving irrigation ditches, refill, the peach trees blossom.

Lorenzo came into the room then. "And where's Antonio? Why isn't he here? He knows I expect him to join me!"

Dora edged quietly through the door as Lupe said, "I think perhaps he's forgotten, Lorenzo. He rode away several hours ago with Anitra."

Lorenzo's face hardened. A vein throbbed quickly in his temple. "Forgotten? Is that what you said? Then I'll make sure he never forgets again."

"I've sent Matthew to look for him, my son."

"It won't happen twice."

"Lorenzo," she began softly. "Antonio's still only a boy. You must try to remember."

But he cut in, "I won't have you lecture me, Mamacita. I know what's best for my son." He went into the courtyard, heavy shoulders square, thick arms rigid.

Here it was again, he thought. No matter how he tried not to see, no matter how he fought his disappointment, he was forced to admit that Antonio was lacking. The boy was timid when he should be bold, quiet when he should be rowdy. It was as if Anitra had taken from him, at the moment of his birth, all those qualities which by right should have been his. For Anitra was plainly all that her brother ought to have been. She was resourceful, demanding of attention, and receiving it no matter whether or not it was her due. She did not know how to be afraid, and neither yearned for heaven nor feared the fires of hell. It was she, Lorenzo was certain, who had led Antonio to this defiance today.

Lorenzo had doubt now that he could change her, but he was determined to fight what he considered to be the weakness in Antonio, to tear it out of the boy and replace it with what a man must be—what a Martínez y Escobedo must be.

He stamped across the courtyard to the stables. From a hook on the wall, he lifted down a long, coiled whip. He carefully ran it through his fingers, feeling its supple strength before he re-coiled it. He had just stepped outside when he heard a sound. Pausing, he raised his head, while his hand tugged thoughtfully at his beard. The sound came again. A clinking, another, then what could be identified clearly as a long, happy sigh of pleasure.

Lorenzo's face reddened. The cords in his thick neck

went taut. The whole of his short body hardened. He strode purposefully to the storeroom from where these suggestive noises came.

The air there was thick and sweet with the scent of fermenting grapes. It was dim, shadowed. But there was enough light to see the small man crouched at the wine cask, to see him fill the tin cup with the precious wine that Lorenzo himself made from grapes laboriously grown on his own land—wine made only for the use of the hacienda, and precious because there weren't all that many good years when the grapes would grow.

He rasped, "Patricio Sánchez, what do you think you're doing?" and walked into the shadows.

Patricio looked up, the whites of his eyes showing, his thin face suddenly wiped clean of joy and twisted with fright. The tin cup he held to his mouth slowly tipped, spilling purple in two small streams down the front of his patched shirt. "Don Lorenzo . . . " he whispered, "You see, Don Lorenzo . . . "

"Get up," Lorenzo yelled. "On your feet, man. Stand and explain yourself. Why do you dare to drink my wine?"

"You see," the gardener quavered, "I was . . . "

"Explain yourself," Lorenzo roared, stepping closer.

"It was there," Patricio muttered, "near the peach trees. I was working at the soil, and the warming touch of it gave me a great thirst. The sun burned me dry, and the warming earth sucked at my fingers, and I heard Satan whisper to me that here . . . "

"Leave Satan to Satan," Lorenzo cut in. "Do you delude yourself that I'd accept such a puny excuse? *You* steal my wine. Not Satan. No doubt you've done the same many times before."

"No, no," the small man said, his voice trembling.

"On my soul, I swear to you, Don Lorenzo, I've never crossed the threshold of this place before."

"And you won't again, that I swear." Lorenzo gestured with the whip he held.

Patricio stepped carefully around him and scurried, limping, into the sunlight. "I'll get back to my work, Don Lorenzo. You'll have no reason to be displeased with me, Don Lorenzo. The peach trees will bloom, and the grape arbors . . ."

His whispered gibberings died in a quick gasp of pain as Lorenzo lashed out with the whip, all the accumulated fury of the past few hours in the blow.

Patricio turned to run. He was agile in his middle age, but as a boy his left leg had been permanently damaged in a fall from a horse, while he was searching out a group of Don Lorenzo's lost sheep in the stony foothills. That left leg crumpled under him now, and he fell to the dust. When he tried to rise, calling on God to protect him, the whip brought him down again.

Lorenzo stood with his legs wide, his broad shoulders hunched. Over and over, with all his strength behind it, he wielded the whip.

Patricio groaned, covered his head, cringing in the dust, the patched, purple-stained shirt slowly reddening with his blood.

From the house, Dora and Felicia watched with frightened eyes.

Lorenzo was unaware of them. He was unaware that Anitra and Antonio had ridden into the courtyard with Matthew.

Anitra leaped from her horse, shouting, "Papa, Papa, what are you doing to Patricio?"

The whip flicked back, came forward.

The young girl lunged across the space between them, and threw herself at her father, clinging to his arm. "Papa, don't!"

He shook her off so that she almost fell. She staggered back, caught herself at the storehouse wall, and braced herself there, her head up and her eyes blazing with a green fire. "Why are you beating Patricio? Why do you hurt him so?"

Lorenzo gave her a contemptuous look and turned to the fallen man. Antonio was kneeling beside him, whispering, "Patricio, are you all right, amigo? What is it?"

"You'll do what I say," Lorenzo roared. "You'll do as you're ordered. Both of you. Both of you, now and forever. You'll do as I say!" He brought the whip down in a hard angry, whistling blow. It lashed across Antonio's thin face and Patricio's bent shoulders. The boy and the gardener shrank together in shared pain. Antonio made no sound, but Patricio yelped with anguish.

"No," Anitra screamed. "No, no, Papa!" Again she made a rush from where she stood. Like a small whirlwind, she leaped forward.

Lorenzo turned toward her, the whip raised over his head.

Matthew caught her first by the skirt, and hauled her back. Then he seized her wrists, holding them tightly in his big strong hands. "Don't!" he whispered. "Anitra, you mustn't!"

It was then that Porfirio came into the courtyard, summoned by Felicia.

The foreman seemed to glide from his horse in a single smooth movement. "Don Lorenzo!"

An anger as deep and burning as Lorenzo's own filled him. He was, among the people of the valley, the most powerful of men. His heart hungered now to seize the whip from Lorenzo and allow the man to have a taste of it himself. But here he must tread softly. He was no more than a foreman to Don Lorenzo, and he must consider the welfare of all those on the ranch—not only the welfare of Patricio Sánchez.

He said quietly, reasonably, "What's this, Don Lorenzo? What has Patricio done?"

Lorenzo flung the whip aside. "Take him away from here at once, Porfirio. Send him from the ranch. I don't want to see his face again."

"Send him from the ranch?" Porfirio repeated blankly. "But his home is here, Don Lorenzo. This is where he was born. Where shall he go?"

"It's no longer a concern of mine," Lorenzo rasped.

From where he and Patricio huddled together, Antonio made a protesting sound.

Lorenzo glared at him. "And you! What are you good for? Why do you look at me like that? You were to go with me to Coronado. And we'll go now. Get on your horse. Get on your horse, Antonio. You'll learn, no matter how you defy me."

Antonio rose to his feet, stood with his head down, not answering. A single drop of blood rolled slowly down his cheek, along his jaw, and spread into the red scar at the base of his throat.

Porfirio raised the gardener to his feet. Felicia would know what to do for these sorry wounds; but Porfirio himself would have to find a new place for Patricio. A place where he could earn his cornmeal and beans. Slowly, without another glance at Lorenzo, he led Patricio from the courtyard.

Lorenzo had already forgotten gardener and foreman.

He said once again, "We'll go to Coronado right now, Antonio."

Antonio shook his head from side to side. "I won't go with you. When a man's hungry, he must eat. What's one small lamb to you, Papa?"

"One lamb is all," Lorenzo retorted. "If you won't obey me, then go to your room and stay there. I'll deal with you later." He turned his back, stalked into the house.

"He has no understanding in him," Anitra said softly, her voice trembling, and turned her blazing green eyes up to Matthew's face.

He saw the quick pulse in the silken whiteness of her throat, and the rise and fall of her small high breasts.

In that moment, he fell in love with her.

2

It was dark in Tres Ríos.

There were no gaslights here yet. Leigh liked that. He liked the small dusty rectangular plaza with its few stone benches. He liked the strong scent of piñon burning. He liked the comfortable silence.

He had stabled his horse, taken a room in the town's only hotel. He had washed thoroughly with the icy water in the large white porcelain pitcher provided and had shaved carefully in the small square of flawed mirror. Dressed in fresh linen, his black flared jacket brushed spotless, he went into the hotel dining room.

He was received as what he appeared to be, a man of substance and gentility, soft-spoken and smiling, whose bronze hair seemed to turn on a light in the corner of the dim room. After dining on venison and baked squash and boiled onions, washed down with bitter black coffee, he went out-of-doors to study the town.

The stars hung low. The mountains thrust hunched shoulders against the silver sky. Lilac sweetened the still air.

He walked the small plaza, pausing before a two-story house. It was white clapboard and set well back from the road behind a white picket fence. The lower floor had a wide veranda and high windows. Lights flickered behind them and shadows moved, and from within there was the muted sound of voices.

But it was the veranda at which he stared thoughtfully, his eyes suddenly midnight blue and the dimple near his mouth suddenly gone. It brought back, in sharp detail, a memory of his earliest years. He was perhaps three then, and he sat on the lowest step, with his father, grim-faced, and mud-spattered boots sprawling, just above him.

There was a time, Leigh remembered, when his father had ridden off, blue eyes ashine with laughter, his red hair flaming under a wide-brimmed gray hat. Now, returned, with all joy gone from him, his big hands busy cleaning his guns, he was saying, "It's bad, and I don't know when I'll be back. But I'll be here. I'll come for you, for the both of you."

Leigh's eyes went to his mother and saw her shiver and nod. Soon after, his father rode off down the driveway where the live oaks hung thick with Spanish moss.

Leigh was nearly seven when he saw his father again— saw but didn't know him. The tall, once-laughing man came on foot, in tatters, gaunt and starved, with one arm gone at the elbow, and with more white in his hair than red.

By that time the white veranda was a fading memory, its pillars charred by fire. The plantation was ravaged, empty. Their slaves had all gone. Leigh and his mother survived on humid air, sour water, and whatever vegetables and roots they could scavenge.

Within days after his father appeared beneath the live oaks, the three of them were on the move. They settled in Texas—red-earthed, treeless Texas. Others prospered there, but Leigh's father sank into apathy, his mind always filled with what he had lost, until finally he died. Leigh's mother quickly remarried. At fifteen, Leigh was six inches taller and twenty pounds heavier than his step-father, and he hated the small bespectacled banker more than he'd hated anyone in his life. At eighteen he was set to reading law, against his will. At twenty he emptied his stepfather's iron safe of nine hundred dollars and stole a horse, and he rode away without looking back. For the past seven years he had been satisfied to drift from town to town, supporting himself however he could, plausible when he gave legal advice, with the sweet courtly manners of his father, the quick dimpled smile of his mother. . . .

Now more laughter spilled across the shadowed veranda. He smiled. These would be his first subjects. For he'd own this valley one day. It would all be his. They'd be his, too. He didn't yet know how it would happen. But it would.

He went on, past a small bank, a dingy general store, and, following the sound of music to its source, into a tiny cantina.

The noise of gaiety faded as he entered. Dark eyes stared him up and down, noting the light hair that showed below the brim of his black hat, the thick, high boots that gleamed with polish, the blue of his eyes, noting the height and breadth of his body that made each man there seem small.

He ignored the sudden silence. He stood at the bar with one foot on the rail and ordered a whiskey. He drank it slowly, and meanwhile conversation slowly resumed around him, most of which he understood.

Leigh had a second drink, then left to take another turn around the plaza. When he passed the white clapboard house, he grinned. He'd own that some day, too.

Small lanterns gleamed at him from the end of the block. He went that way and found a gambling casino, and when he stepped through the heavy wooden door onto the soft, thick floor covering, his dimple deepened and his brows lifted in surprise. Big round cartwheel chandeliers were lit, spilling golden light. Glasses and colored bottles lined the bar, and a tinted mirror covered the wall behind it. The card tables were well-polished blackjack oak, hand-hewn and pegged, and the roulette wheels with their spinning balls were surrounded by layers of marked green baize. He hadn't suspected that the huddle of small brown buildings that was Tres Ríos could offer the likes of this.

The usual looks came his way, but he made himself comfortable at the bar, ordered a drink, and soon had the bartender engaged in small talk.

Standing alone at the end of the bar was an elderly man in clean but rough working clothes. He was nearly bald, only a fringe of gray making a horseshoe around his head. His eyes were light blue and sunk in raddled flesh. He had a stringy body and large calloused stringy hands. In one of them he was juggling three big rough gold nuggets.

The bartender caught Leigh's glance and grinned. "They look pretty, don't they?"

"Not bad," Leigh agreed. "If they're real, that is."

"He's old Jake Heimer. Been around as long as I can remember."

"And his nuggets?"

"They're real, right enough." The bartender laughed. "He probably won them in a dice game. He sure didn't find them in Tres Ríos."

Leigh laughed too, but there was no amusement in his eyes. If the nuggets didn't come from the mountains around Tres Ríos, then where did they come from?

He finished his drink and went to one of the gaming

tables. In placing a bet he deliberately jostled the arm of another man standing there.

The two exchanged quick, smiling apologies, and then names. That was how Leigh came to meet Esteban Delagado.

At the Diaz ranch, Matthew was saying gravely, "I'd like a word with you, Grandfather."

Don Cipriano jerked his head up, pretending he had been reading the book he held in his hands, rather than dozing. "A word with me? What's on your mind, eh? Why do you look so troubled?"

Matthew's gray eyes regarded Josefa meaningfully. She sat near the window, her pale face tipped forward to stare dreamily at the rising moon, though her head was cocked to listen.

Don Cipriano understood. What Matthew had to say was not for Josefa's ears. Ah, he was a good boy, his Matthew. See how carefully he protected Josefa. Don Cipriano rose slowly, saying, "We'll have cigarillos in the patio, Matthew." And to Josefa, "Excuse us for a little while."

She nodded and leaned forward to watch a last sliver of moon slide over the mountain peak.

"And now," Don Cipriano said, when they were settled in the patio, their cigarillos haloing their heads in aromatic blue smoke, "what's on your mind, eh, Matthew?"

Matthew described, in a few quick words, what had happened that day at the Martínez ranch. He ended by saying, "Don Lorenzo would have beaten Anitra, too, I'm sure of it, if Porfirio's coming hadn't distracted him."

Don Cipriano scratched his gray beard. He was concerned by what he had heard. He was concerned, too, by the pain he saw in Matthew's eyes when he spoke of Anitra. She was growing up to be beautiful. He understood Matthew's feelings. But this was not what Don Cipriano had in mind. He thought of the nineteen-year-old girl sitting before the window, who no doubt had begun to chew her braid the moment he left the room. Her health had been suspect ever since she was a tiny child. It didn't improve. Josefa must be protected. Still, Matthew was a good boy, and always had been. He'd know what was right, and he'd do it. Don Cipriano brushed that concern aside.

"I'm sorry to hear this," he said at last. "What I can do about Don Lorenzo, I don't know. But as for Patricio . . ."

Thus, by the time Porfirio had decided to go to the Diaz ranch, Don Cipriano was prepared. He said, "Yes, all right, Porfirio. I understand. I'll take Patricio Sánchez. He'll have a small house, a bit of land for growing his corn. But we have no gardeners, as you know, and no use for them. We'll find something else for him to do. Let's not make too much of this, eh? It's settled now."

Porfirio understood that the less said of Don Lorenzo's actions the better. He went away relieved.

Yet the next evening, riding to the Martínez ranch with Esteban, Don Cipriano said, "I'm sorely troubled by Don Lorenzo's behavior. The time for the whip is long past, Esteban. Aside from all else, there are laws against it. Don Lorenzo seems not to realize that."

Esteban nodded agreement. Lorenzo Martínez saw himself as an hidalgo of old, a ranchero with his land, his flocks, lord of his holdings. It might have been that way once, but it was no longer so.

Lorenzo had been eleven years old when General

Stephen Kearny marched through the mountains and claimed all the Southwest for the United States.

He was thirty years old when both slavery and peonage were forever abolished in the territory. And that was just a few years after Kit Carson and Smith Simpson hauled the Union flag over Taos plaza, and guarded it night and day with loaded guns from those who threatened to replace it with a Confederate banner.

But Lorenzo was a man with a mind turned fiercely toward the past rather than toward the future.

So, perhaps, Esteban thought, he himself might be— except that he was younger, and heavily aware of the strong winds that blew threateningly from the East. What had begun as a trickle of mountain men trapping beaver had become a flood of traders and businessmen and ranchers wanting more and more land. The Americans were pouring into the territory faster every week. Why, just the day before, here in Tres Ríos, he had met Leigh Ransome, hadn't he?

Don Cipriano glanced over his shoulder at Josefa, who rode in the back of the buggy with Matthew. They had between them a month-old lamb they were bringing with them. Josefa had fastened a red bow around the silly beast's head, and now she allowed it to lick her face.

Don Cipriano said in a lowered voice, "There's much else Don Lorenzo doesn't realize, I fear. Antonio and Anitra are nearly full-grown. He refuses to see it."

Again Esteban nodded.

"I judge from what Matthew told me, and from the look in his eyes, that it wasn't a good thing that happened the other day." Don Cipriano sighed. "I don't approve of it, you know. I never took a whip to my sons. Nor to Matthew either. It's wrong, wrong."

"In that, as in other ways, Don Lorenzo remains old-fashioned," Esteban said.

"Old-fashioned, eh? No, Esteban, my good friend. Not old-fashioned. Merely foolish." Once more Don Cipriano glanced over his shoulder. "Lead with love, I say. Teach with love, I say." He chuckled. "Look at the two of them, Esteban. You can see I'm right. Just look at my Josefa. At my Matthew."

"Yes, Don Cipriano. And I agree with you."

"But Don Lorenzo wouldn't. He'd say I indulge the children. Well, what's wrong with that? How can a little indulgence hurt? And that—" Don Cipriano's voice grew lighter—"and that reminds me, Esteban. When next you go to Sante Fe, I'd like you to look around for me. Matthew fancies having a few good horses to train for racing, and I see no reason why he shouldn't. He's a fine horseman and loves the beasts, and how can having them bring him to harm? So see what you find of the right stock, and then we'll all go together and have a look."

"I'll remember," Esteban promised. "It's a commission I'll enjoy."

When they arrived at the ranch, Josefa and Matthew presented the small frisky lamb to Anitra.

She hugged him to her, her eyes shining. "Is it for me?" she asked. "Is it truly for me?"

"Of course," Josefa told her. "For as long as you want it, that is. Lambs grow into sheep, as you know, and while the one is a good house pet, the other is—is somewhat tiresome."

"I'll never be tired of Baa," Anitra vowed. She straightened up to look at Matthew. "How did you come by him?"

"His mother didn't want him," Matthew answered.

"But why?" Anitra demanded.

Matthew shrugged. "I don't know why, Anitra. Perhaps she had too many for her teats. Perhaps she didn't like the smell of him."

She said softly, looking at her father, "It seems unnatural to me that a parent shouldn't want his own child."

Later that evening after a large dinner of many courses served by Dora and Felicia, with Doña Lupe presiding at the foot of the long table, and with Antonio's empty chair a mute reminder that he was still confined to his room, Esteban sat with Don Cipriano and Lorenzo before the fire in the sala.

Lorenzo had brought out the brandy.

Esteban said, "I'm concerned that the newest pronouncements of the territorial government won't help us, Don Lorenzo."

The expression on Lorenzo's face was one of contempt. "And what are they?"

Past the older man's shoulder, Esteban saw Anitra raise her head to listen. She was sitting in a corner with Josefa while Matthew entertained the two of them with card tricks. Now, plainly, her attention had wandered.

Esteban sipped his brandy, went on, "The old village governments are dissolved. The alcalde and the ayuntamiento are no more."

Don Cipriano swore and then glanced apologetically at Doña Lupe. "How will the grants be governed without a mayor and a common council?"

"How indeed?" Esteban asked.

A cynical smile curled Lorenzo's lips. "They'll learn that in this territory their new laws mean nothing. We've older ones."

47

"Yes, yes," Don Cipriano agreed impatiently.

"You mean the Brotherhood of Penitentes," Esteban answered. He looked at the words burned into the dark wooden beam just over his head.

La Gavia guarda secretos de épocas muertas, de vidas que ya nadie conserva en la memoria.

It was a romantic way of saying that here were guarded the secrets of the past and of lives no longer held in memory. No doubt some early Escobedo had put the words there.

"Of course. The Brotherhood," Lorenzo was saying. "For all that the churchmen have tried to do, it exists, and it will continue to exist. The people need it. And it represents the will of the people. Be damned to padres, and the territorial government, too."

There was support even in Don Cipriano's silence.

Esteban understood how these two men felt. The Penitentes had been a lay order of the Church for untold generations. Most probably its first followers had come to the new world with the conquistadores. They believed in self-flagellation for purifying their souls of sin, and for atonement. They celebrated Santa Semana, that is, Holy Week, with enactments of the Crucifixion. In the period after Mexico's separation from Spain, when the arm of the government had shrunk to nearly nothing in the North and the strength of the Church was at ebb there, the Penitentes were the law and the bearers of the Cross. So they had remained.

Esteban had many times seen just outside the village the well-kept meetinghouse, known as the morada, with its single high window and austere wooden cross. He knew the morada was in use. He didn't know if Lorenzo or Cipriano went there, because he himself did not. He cherished his flesh too much, he supposed. In any event, he would make his confession to the padre in church, and seek absolution there as well.

Whether Lorenzo belonged or not, he shared the Penitentes' pride. In that he was one of them, if in no other way.

At last Esteban said, "I fear the Penitentes can't do everything, Don Lorenzo."

Lorenzo shrugged.

"Nor should they have to," Anitra said, rising to her feet. "Papa, Don Cipriano, Don Esteban, don't you see? If the mayor and town councils are no more, then there must be something to take their places. You must explain it to the politicos in Santa Fe so that they understand."

Lorenzo sent her a sour look. "You know nothing about it, Anitra."

She opened her lips to speak again, but Matthew took her hand, drew her down to her chair. She forgot what she had been about to say. She forgot everything but the quick excitement that burned through her at his touch. She looked up. Josefa's pale face was shadowed by lamplight. But her dark eyes seemed frightened. As Anitra watched, Josefa covered her mouth and began to cough.

"The Brotherhood will deal with it, you may be sure," Lorenzo was saying.

Listening as she served small cups of scalding black coffee, Felicia shuddered. Porfirio had told her nothing, as was usual. But she knew that he and the Brothers would meet sometime tonight. Her skin prickled. She hoped that she had done the right thing when she repeated to Porfirio what she had learned two days before from the girl Juana Rivera.

Porfirio stood at the door of his house, waiting.

He had been elected Hermano Mayor, that is, Elder Brother of the Penitente Brotherhood, just eight months before, and within his big scarred hands he held the responsibility for all of the Brothers who lived in the valley. All through the mountainous North, in every village, no matter how small, there were members of the Brotherhood. Each group was individual, having no connection with another, except as they would sometimes meet in long processionals during Santa Semana. Yet each group had the same rules, elected the same types of officials to guide them, and believed in the same precepts. From the beginning, nearly forty years ago, when the gringos had first taken the territory and made it their own, it had been clear that the people couldn't trust gringo law. Those in the city of Santa Fe knew nothing, and cared nothing, for the problems of isolated villagers. Thus had it fallen upon the Brotherhood to protect themselves—to punish the transgressor. A crime against the gringo was one thing, and not that important, for the gringo was able to deal with threat. But a crime against the Brothers was another thing. Too many of them were helpless.

Porfirio sighed. This Eustacio Rivera, now, what did one do with such a man? A man who had fallen upon his fourteen-year-old daughter in lust. At the meeting in the morada, after due consideration by the Brothers sitting in judgment, he'd been pronounced guilty. He'd been ordered to present himself for his punishment tonight.

Porfirio watched the moon rise. When it touched the mountain peak, he mounted his horse. He rode alone, but through the chill darkness he heard the sound of other horses. The faint clip-clop of hooves against stone. The creak of leather harnesses and saddles.

The Brothers converged on the morada at about the

same time. They didn't speak. It was unnecessary. Each knew his salvation lay in repentance. Each believed that repentance was rooted in punishment.

Within the simple building there were two rooms. In one there was a small altar covered with a black cloth. There was a long narrow bench in the other.

The men formed two lines inside the door of the dark room. A single candle flame lightened the gloom.

They stood waiting, silent, as Eustacio made his way alone through the clearing. His breath rasped in his throat. His knees shook. In all of his thirty-five years he'd never known such a fear.

He bore on his back the ritual scars of the initiation. They'd been cut into his flesh at the age of eighteen when he took the oath to abide by all decisions of the Brotherhood. He believed with all his heart in what he had sworn to then. But he was afraid. Yet if he didn't go to the morada now, the oath would be broken. He'd be cast out, no longer a brother. He'd be alone in a dangerous world. Were his small shack to burn down there'd be no one to help him rebuild it. Were he to be attacked by brigands for his goat and chickens, there'd be no one to regain for him what had been his. Were he to fall ill, there'd be no one to attend him. Were he to die, his flesh would rot where he fell and his bones bleach white in the sun, and there'd be no prayers for the repose of his uneasy soul.

He paused in the shadow of the cottonwoods, pressed trembling and wet palms to his shaking thighs.

He didn't yet know what the judgment had been. He had been unable to read the still faces around him while Porfirio questioned him.

"Is it true that you took your daughter, Eustacio? Did you despoil her, and hurt her, and sin in the eyes of man and Christ?"

He'd known it was useless to lie. The thought never crossed his mind. Truth was truth. "Yes, yes, mi hermano," he whispered. "I came home from the cantina half mad with loneliness. It was dark and my mind was dark, too. I couldn't bear the lot that's mine, mi hermano. She slept on her pallet, and I didn't know her. I swear to you, my brother. I thought she was my long-dead wife. I didn't know her."

He remembered only the soft warmth of female flesh and the pain of hunger in him. He saw disgust in the faces of the men around him. For a long moment no one spoke. Then Porfirio said, "You'll present yourself to the morada tonight."

Now Eustacio forced himself to go on. He crossed the clearing to where pale light flickered at the high window. He drew another deep rasping breath and slapped the closed door with a shaking hand.

"Who's there?" Porfirio demanded.

"I'm a penitent sinner. May I enter?" Eustacio whispered.

"Enter," Porfirio said.

The door swung open slowly.

Eustacio dropped to his knees, and on his knees he crawled across the threshold.

Slowly the door closed behind him.

Eustacio coughed, cleared his throat. Finally he asked in a husky whisper, "Hermano Mayor, will you forgive me for my grievous sin?"

In those long silent moments that followed, Eustacio saw in the shadowy corner an old solid-wheel cart, leaning forward and resting on its empty shafts. It was called the carreta de la muerte, the cart of death. Standing inside it was La Santa de La Muerte, the Saint of Death, called by some Doña Sebastiana, a figure carved of wood. The

Saint of Death, made in the form of an old woman, a white skull with glaring empty eye sockets, and a wide empty grin. A black shawl was wrapped around her bony head. Her bony hands held a bow, a red-tipped arrow set in it. The arrow seemed to point at Eustacio's heart.

At last, Porfirio said, "For my part, I forgive you, Eustacio. May God forgive you, too."

These words were a part of the ancient formula. Porfirio, the others, had known them since their manhood.

Before each one of the Brothers, Eustacio prostrated himself, repeating his plea for forgiveness. Each one of them replied in Porfirio's words.

Eustacio began to think, hope, that his terror had been uncalled for. Perhaps they understood and pitied him. Perhaps all knew what an animal lust makes of man. Relief made his muscles slack and brought tears to his eyes.

But when he reached the Corregidor, the administrator of punishment, the man, who was named Mundo Segura, said sternly in answer to Eustacio's now automatic question, "All the others have forgiven you, but I cannot and will not." He took from the wall behind him a black snake whip. It whispered as he ran it through his fingers. His mouth was stern beneath its thin moustache, and his small black eyes were hooded. He was filled with painful sympathy for the poor man prostrate before him. Mundo would do the duty to which he was elected, but he wouldn't enjoy it. Eustacio was a pobre, a poor man whose life had been made what it was by the ricos. It was a rico that Mundo preferred to have before him now. He drew a breath, said softly, "Take off your shirt." And when Eustacio didn't move, "Your shirt, my brother."

Eustacio's flesh crawled. The whole of his scrawny body tightened. He hardly managed to raise his arms to pull off his shirt. His dark hair fell forward, hiding his face, as he bent his head.

The first blow knocked him sideways. He fell hard, gasping with pain. Mundo waited until he had pushed himself up to hands and knees, until his head was bent, and the whisper of his prayer was clearly heard. "*Yo penitente pecador. Yo penitente pecador.* I am a penitent sinner," he was saying. "I am a penitent sinner. Forgive me."

The next fifteen blows, as agreed upon earlier by the members of the Brotherhood, came steadily, hard, and without pause.

A darkness swam before Eustacio's eyes. He was afire. His body burned, and his soul burned. But there was salvation. "Forgive me," he panted, weeping. "Forgive me, for I have sinned."

Later the Enfermero bathed his back with a brew of rosemary leaves, and when he was able to listen, Porfirio told him, "It's further decided, Eustacio, that your daughter won't live any longer in your house."

"But then who'll cook for me?" Eustacio asked. "Who'll light the candle at the window so I know the path home after dark?"

Porfirio shrugged. "You'll find a way."

"Who'll tend my goat and chickens when I'm doing the gardening work assigned to me at the hacienda?"

"You'll find a way," Porfirio repeated.

Eustacio looked into the eyes of the men who stood around him. He sighed, "Yes, yes, my brothers. My daughter will live where you say."

"I'm glad you agree," Porfirio answered, nodding at Mundo, who slowly coiled the whip and hung it on the wall.

3

The first time Lupe mentioned to Lorenzo that she wished to make a pilgrimage to the sanctuary at the small mountain town of Chimayo, he said impatiently, "Not now, Mamacita. I've too much to do here at the ranch for the present."

But she was determined. All her life she had wanted to make that journey. El Santuario stood upon consecrated ground, and she had set her heart upon praying there.

She bided her time patiently, and one evening, after she had made certain that Lorenzo had enjoyed his favorite meal, she said, "I've been thinking, my son . . . if you could allow Porfirio to accompany me, I'd take Anitra and Antonio, too. We might visit César Vargas and his family in Santa Fe. It's several years since I've seen these cousins of ours. Then the children and I could go on to Chimayo together."

Anitra stirred, then became very still, but her eyes slanted a look at Antonio. The glance they exchanged was of muted excitement, of cautious hope.

Lorenzo saw it as a look of complicity. He thought angrily that it had always been so. Ever since the day of their birth, when they had taken his gentle Maria away from him forever, they had turned to each other. And never to him.

Lupe saw his color heighten. She said softly, "Lorenzo, this is something I've thought of for a long time. And remember, por favor, I'm an old woman now. . . ."

A long moment passed while he fought his spleen, but at last he said, with a disgruntled look, "Very well, since you insist. It will be arranged as you wish. And I'll go with you to Santa Fe myself. I've some business there, which might as well be dealt with now as later."

They left on a morning at the end of May.

Lupe felt every jolt of the old-fashioned carreta in her bones as its uneven wheels tumbled from rut to rut, leaving behind a wake of drifting golden dust.

The air was sharp, tangy with the scent of wild flowers, spiced with sage. The hills were pink with early sun.

For a while excitement left Anitra wordless. Then she called, "Porfirio, how many people live in Santa Fe?"

On horseback next to Esteban, he leaned toward her from his saddle, grinning. "I don't know the number, chica. But many, many, that much I do know."

Lorenzo listened and frowned. There were too many people in the capital, and of the wrong kind as well. It was no longer the Royal City he remembered from his boyhood.

Then it had been a pleasant place, with a pulse that beat with the slow rise of the sun that brought day and the slow growth of the long dark shadows that foretold night.

Only at the plaza, which was the town's heart, did

one see crowds gather, hear voices raised, and it was there that life centered. The favored set up stalls that sold all manner of goods. Soaps made from amole root and scented with roses. Yard goods of every color and description brought by wagon from Mexico. Woven baskets and fans and parasols and paper flowers and paper lanterns carried by cargo ships across the Pacific and hauled from their docks by burro over badlands and mountains to ford El Río del Norte. The less favored spread blankets on the hard ground and offered pots of tin or pewter. Some sold gunpowder and flints, and herbs and unguents, and others sold bits and pieces of household goods. All these were offered from sunup until well after dark under flaring torches, accompanied by the cries of the vendors, bartering, making proposals and counterproposals. Day and night there were fresh tortillas for sale, and beans, and huge vats of fiery salsa in which everything was doused, and melting tamales. . . .

Once Lorenzo had been in the plaza when the cry went up, "Los Americanos!" and the great ox-drawn caravans pulled in, trailing clouds of dust. They had come as guests then, and friends, and there had been the quick singing of the fiddle and the guitar, and merrymaking in the streets as goods from Boston and New York and St. Louis were unloaded.

But later the Americans came as conquerors, and now the Royal City was changed. Lorenzo sighed. His frown deepened, and his fingers tightened around the reins.

The party stopped for refreshments at Tesuque. The usual tortillas and spicy beans and strong black coffee for Lupe and the children, and the same for the men, but mistela, too, a hot spiced brandy, to warm them.

A short while after they pressed on, the narrow road suddenly filled with a company of dragoons under a standard bearing the Stars and Stripes.

Lorenzo frowned as their leader directed the carreta out of the way. It was a symbol of the grudge he had cherished all his life. This country was his. His. Don Lorenzo moved aside for no man, no flag. Yet he was made an alien on the soil where he was born. He loathed the slow drawling voices that spoke in a tongue he didn't understand—nor did he want to. He loathed what that tongue stood for. In far away Washington City, by all accounts a place uncivilized and uncultured, men who had never seen the grandeur of the Sangre de Cristo Mountains, nor the mixed beneficence and misery they could bestow, men whose souls had never shrunk in their long shadows, made laws that took from him his peones, made laws that challenged those grants which had given him his land.

He ignored the friendly salutes of the passing soldiers. They were the enemy, he thought. They would always be the enemy. But the calendar couldn't be turned back, nor the past altered. He already knew in his heart that he would have to deal with them. That was partly his errand in Santa Fe—to discuss such matters with his cousin, César Vargas.

It was for the same reason that Esteban was making the trip. Though he said nothing now, his eyes narrowed with bitterness, and he sat stiff in the saddle. He was in dire trouble, and he knew there was only small chance of saving his land and his fortune.

Anitra, hearing the unfamiliar shouts, half rose. "Listen," she cried. "They're speaking to us. What are the soldiers saying, Grandmother?"

"I believe they're saying 'Good morning,'" Lupe told her.

"Good morning," Anitra shouted as the troops rode by, and for an instant she thought of Leigh Ransome, the tall bronze-haired man she had chided for trying to help her.

The hoofbeats of the dragoons faded away over the golden hills. The sweet dry air was a wine that sent the pulses racing, and quickened the breath, she thought. And then the city of Santa Fe loomed ahead. The Royal City of the Holy Faith, it had always been called. Always, until the Americans came.

At the plaza, the carreta was forced to stop.

A great mass of Indians was crowded into San Francisco Street. There were some five hundred of them, Jicarilla Apaches, mostly women and children. They were being moved from the reservation on which they'd been held in the South back to the Río Arriba country, which had always been home and hunting ground to them.

Slowly, while Lorenzo swore under his breath, and Anitra stared wide-eyed, the whole contingent rode by.

The women were on ponies and burros. They held blanket-wrapped babies in their arms. Tiny children were tied to the saddles, toddlers ran along beside. They were surrounded by dogs that yapped and snarled, and pack animals loaded with gourds and clay pots and more blankets.

Six Indians acted as marshals under the direction of three blue-clad cavalrymen. Black hair glistened in the sun. Teeth flashed in swarthy faces. Dark eyes gleamed from beneath lowered lids. They were going home, and even their bodies expressed their joy by leaning North. North to the beautiful mountains.

Anitra smiled, raised her hand in a friendly salute.

"Behave yourself!" Lorenzo ordered in a sharp undertone, seized her wrist and thrust it back on her lap.

Finally the last of the Indians cleared the plaza.

Porfirio waved the carreta on. Here, by night, magical lanterns fed by invisible fuel cast a yellow light, and beneath it the usual evening promenade would take place. Ladies in fine silk, with mantillas of lace covering their heads, would mingle with girls in red cotton skirts and tight white bodices wearing rebozos over their hair. They would all walk one way. Passing them in the opposite direction would be groups of men in fine suits of broadcloth, in wrinkled work clothes, in cotton pants and hand-sewn leather vests. Smiles and flirtatious winks would be exchanged. Assignations would be planned with a toss of a head, promises made with small gestures of the hand. A steamy heat would fill the air.

But now the sun burned on the white octagonal bandstand, where goats and burros once grazed, and where now, at twilight, the white-gloved band from Fort Marcy came to play. All around there were new two-story buildings with white railings and long verandas, and at the end of the street was the Cathedral of San Francisco. On the corner nearby was La Fonda Hotel, for so long the end of the Santa Fe Trail that began in Missouri.

Soon the large gates of the Vargas home loomed before them. They opened as the carreta drew up. Servants waved them on into the courtyard.

Lorenzo helped Lupe alight, while Anitra and Antonio jumped down, stared about. This was a city house, not an hacienda. Here the walls faced on hard-packed sidewalks, and within the walls there was a formal garden.

The door swung open.

Don César bowed low over Lupe's hand. "Doña

Lupe, my house is yours. Come in. You must refresh yourself after your journey." And to Lorenzo, "Welcome, my
cousin. And to you, too, Don Esteban. I'm glad you're
here." He grinned at Antonio and Anitra. "How you've
both grown! My son and daughter wait in the inner patio
to greet you. When you're ready, of course."

"Now?" Anitra asked impatiently.

"In a little while," Lupe told her, smiling.

Vicente Vargas y Escobedo was nineteen years old.
He had thick straight black hair that covered his head like
a burnished helmet and small deepset black eyes. He was
short and broad-shouldered, and he walked with a swag-
ger. He had not been pleased with his father's suggestion
that he stay at home that afternoon along with his
fourteen-year-old sister Carlota and help entertain his two
country cousins.

He was still scowling when the door to the courtyard
opened and César and Lupe swept through, followed by
the twins.

"So," César said. "We're together at last. Doña Lupe,
you know my two children. My son, Vicente. My daughter, Carlota."

"My dears." Lupe offered her cheek to each for their
dutiful kisses. And then, "My granddaughter, Anitra. My
grandson, Antonio."

Carlota smiled quickly. "Welcome to our house, my
cousins."

Vicente found himself rising from the stone bench,
bowing with his father's courtliness. "Anitra. Antonio."

"Doña Lupe, will you sit with us?" Carlota asked.
"Tell me about your trip through the mountains."

"Thank you, my dear. But I'm tired. I must rest for

our journey tomorrow," Lupe said, and returned indoors with César.

When the two adults were gone a small silence fell. Carlota hummed beneath her breath. Vicente stared sideways at Anitra. She was only a child, hardly older than a baby, in fact. Yet there was something about her—a boldness in her bright-green eyes . . . a composure in the way she held herself. He would have liked to be pleasant, but suddenly he was at a loss for words.

Anitra looked him up and down and found him lacking. She wished that Matthew had made the journey with them. She took a seat on the bench, turned her head deliberately toward Carlota and said, "That's a beautiful gown you're wearing. Who made it for you?"

Affronted, Vicente covered his chagrin and said heartily, "Antonio, my cousin, let's leave these girls to their chatter of gowns. I'll show you the Vargas property."

Within the house, César was saying, "We all have the same concerns. You in Tres Ríos. And those of us here in Santa Fe."

Lorenzo nodded over his small black cigar, and looked thoughtfully around the big room.

The velvet draperies were closed against the twilight. A large round chandelier gleamed overhead. César had done well.

"Yes, yes, it's so," Esteban agreed. "We do have the same concerns. You, Don César, and you, Don Lorenzo, and I, too. Every one of us who is of Spanish blood, these days."

"Concerns compounded by a bit of good fortune." César replied. "In your case, Don Esteban, and in yours, too, Don Lorenzo, I suspect that the railroad connecting Denver and Santa Fe has drawn attention to your valley, and brought Tres Ríos into the civilized world at last. And so the Americans have become interested in your land."

"Agreed," Esteban said with a bitter smile. "But it's also a matter of a few good years. They don't remember the years we stood each morning in the fields and stared at the clouds as they passed us by, always to drop their rain beyond the mountains."

"They believe that for them it will always rain and always be green," Lorenzo said bitterly. "Now that they're here, of course."

The others knew that by *they* he meant the gringos.

"I can't give up." Esteban leaned forward. "I'm pinched from all sides, Don César. Yet I can't give up. The land is mine."

"And the records, deeds, titles, grants. They were always kept in the Governor's Palace, of course, as they should have been. But so many of those legal documents have disappeared." César sighed. "We all know what happened. The American governor, William Pike, decreed that he needed the storage room and moved the old papers out. *Our* legal documents. They were burned, thrown away, used to wipe soldiers' backsides. How do we prove the land is legally ours in that case?"

What had happened in 1869 could hardly be repaired in 1887, Lorenzo thought dryly. But he knew why César mentioned it, how the man felt. Inside himself, too, something sickened at the thought of the fine old parchment, marked with the great seal of Spain, signed in the king's own hand, being misused in such a manner. Not to mention what the loss of those parchments meant in destroyed security. Without them any man's ownership to his acres could be challenged.

"Gold," Esteban said. He slid four fingers across his

thumb. "Gold. That's what it takes. For that, new papers can be made, so I'm told." He gave César an expectant glance.

César agreed. "If you know the right people."

"You do," Esteban replied. "And that's why I'm here."

Lorenzo deliberately stubbed out the ember at the end of his cigar. Then he looked up and smiled, stroking his beard. "All we can do is try, my friends. We've lost nothing yet, the three of us. But others have lost everything, so we're well warned. If the land office continues to accept these so-called patents as deeds, along with the bribes paid to obtain them, then we, like our compadres, will end with nothing."

"Unless we use the bribe, too," César said softly.

"Then see what you can do, my cousin," Lorenzo suggested, while Esteban slowly nodded his head.

4

The sky beyond the wall was pink when they went into the courtyard together.

Porfirio, armed with a rifle slung on his shoulder and a knife in his belt, was already waiting. His face showed none of the satisfaction he felt that the mission to Chimayo would provide him with an unexpected opportunity to accomplish a mission of his own.

Lupe climbed into the enclosed carriage provided at César's insistence for the journey. She settled herself between Anitra and Antonio with a sigh. Ah, yes, the padded seat was an improvement over the carreta.

Lorenzo made brief conversation with Porfirio, then stepped back. César and his children waved.

From the carriage sounded a long and plaintive bleat of protest. It came from Anitra's lamb, Baa, hidden in a basket at her feet. She had washed and combed him for the journey, and had tied her own blue ribbon at his throat instead of Josefa's red one. The evening before, she had saved bits from the late meal and, when all slept, had gone out to feed him and then moved him from the carreta to the carriage.

The Vargases grinned, and César said, "So you're taking a lamb on the pilgrimage, are you?"

There was no amusement on Lorenzo's face as he

jerked the door open, shouting, "What do you mean by such foolishness?" Ignoring Anitra's cry of protest, he seized the small woolly creature and flung it away.

It slammed into an adobe brick pillar and slid down it to lie with its four legs feebly kicking before they were still. The blue bow turned dark, shiny. The small tongue lolled.

Carlota whispered, "Oh, no, no."

Anitra evaded Lupe's reaching hand and leaped from the carriage. She gathered Baa into her arms, and turned to confront her father, screaming, "Baa's dead. And Matthew gave him to me. Baa's dead. And I hate you. I'll hate you as long as I live!"

"Be quiet," Lorenzo roared. "Get into the carriage and go, or there'll be no pilgrimage today."

Porfirio silently took the lamb's body from her arms. With soft little pressures of his hand, he urged her into the carriage. After giving over the small body to one of César's servants, he got in and drove out of the courtyard.

Anitra lay in Lupe's arms, choking on harsh dry sobs as they rolled past the plaza, where the first activities of the day were beginning. As the miles passed, Anitra became calmer. She straightened, smoothed the thick black braid that hung to her waist. But she murmured, as if to herself, "He shouldn't have done it."

Lupe folded one small hand over Antonio's, the other over Anitra's. "It was an accident, my children. Your father meant no harm to the lamb."

"But Baa is dead," Anitra murmured. "And I hate him for it."

"No, niña," Lupe answered. "You can't go to El Santuario with hate in your heart. You must forgive him."

Anitra didn't bother to answer. As her own spirits

eased, she saw how deeply Antonio was affected. "It'll be all right, my brother. Perhaps Matthew will find another unwanted lamb for us."

Lupe's heart expanded with sudden certainty. This was right, good. More than ever she was sure that the pilgrimage would be meaningful. She'd place these children under the protection of Santo Niño, the Holy Child, and He'd understand. He'd love them and teach Lorenzo to love them, too. She said softly, "Forget the past, my dear ones. Think ahead to El Santuario."

Anitra nodded compliance, but her anger stayed with her.

When at last they entered the tiny town of Chimayo, Porfirio leaned down to ask, "Doña Lupe, shall we stop here for a moment? It would be wise to rest and stretch your legs, and I'll have the horses watered meantime."

She agreed, and she and Anitra and Antonio alighted.

Porfirio led the horses and carriage around to the rear of a small shack. It was here he would dispose of the other contraband that had been in the carriage, secretly transferred, like the dead lamb, from the carreta the night before.

This had been his commission. To obtain for the Brothers of a morada high in the hills above Chimayo the guns they needed. Tres Ríos, being a crossroads, was a place where anything was available at whatever price men could afford. Briefly Porfirio wondered why the men of the distant morada should require rifles, but then he shrugged. A favor had been asked. It would be granted. That was the way of the Brothers.

A man came from behind the thick trunk of a cottonwood. They exchanged greetings. The guns were handed over quickly. The silver coin was passed in payment.

"Gracias. Con Dios," the man said quietly. "Go with God, hermano."

Porfirio nodded, "Go with God," and hurriedly led the horses and carriage to the front of the shack where Doña Lupe and the two children awaited him. There was, he saw, no suspicion in Doña Lupe's face when she smiled and said, "It was good to stretch, Porfirio, but now let's go on."

They resumed the trip. Stray sheep ambled along the road, ignoring a party of pilgrims on foot that the carriage soon over-took and left behind. After that a few turns of the wheels brought them to El Santuario. It was built within the shadow of Truchas Peaks. High on the red walls of those mountains were gleaming crosses of white snow, called ice glaciers by some, called the handiwork of Almighty God by others. The old adobe walls of the church nestled into the side of a hill covered by silver-gray willows. The sky above was blue, cloudless, and without end. The earth was washed in the glittering golden brilliance of the sun.

It was said that, only a few generations before, one day a man had been plowing his fields with yoked oxen when his small daughter, playing at his side, suddenly said, "Papa, hear the bell tolling!"

Her father heard nothing and went on with his work. But she insisted, "Papa, do you hear the beautiful bell calling from under the earth?"

At last he returned to her and dug, and his shovel rang on metal. He dug deeper. He used his hands to scoop away the red earth. An old sanctus bell was exposed to the sunlight. He crossed himself and smiled at his child.

She breathed, "It's beautiful, Papa, but dig more."

He couldn't refuse her. Again he used his shovel, but cautiously. In a little while, from under the place where he had unearthed the bell, he took forth a statue of Santo Niño, the Holy Child.

After that, many miracles of kindness to the needy were performed in the presence of Santo Niño, and soon the grateful people of Chimayo built the chapel in His honor. In a small room next to the main altar remained the same hole from which Santo Niño had been taken. No matter how much holy mud was removed from it over the years for purposes of cure, its size remained always the same.

The shrine was hushed, still, when Porfirio helped Lupe from the carriage. Anitra gazed around, her heart beating quickly. For a moment, she forgot what had happened in the Vargas' courtyard. This was an adventure to her. Unconsciously her feet moved in quick dancing steps.

Antonio walked more slowly, his eyes fixed on the building, its arched doors and windows opening into what seemed to him to be eternal darkness. He wondered now why he had come. What ill afflicted him that he should waste the time of the Holy Child, who wore out His shoes doing errands of mercy? His gaze moved to Anitra. Always they had been together, she one step ahead. Was that why the hard core of his manliness seemed lessened? Was that why his father despised him?

Lupe led the way through the door, paused at the font and touched her fingertips to the holy water, then genuflected as she moved toward the altar.

It was covered with a black cloth woven through with thin threads of gold. Behind it the statue of Santo Niño seemed to shine with the reflections of sunlight that had not actually penetrated the thick walls.

Lupe knelt, Antonio and Anitra on either side of her. Together, with heads bowed, the three of them prayed.

But as her lips moved with the words, Anitra saw again her father's anger-contorted face. She saw him seize the small lamb and fling it away. Even as she said the words of prayer she felt the sting of anger in her veins.

At last the three rose. They went through the small door near the main altar. Here it was dark. A single candle was only an ember of light in the hovering shadows.

Lupe took up a handful of mud from the hole at her feet. From here Santo Niño had come. From here all blessings would come, too. She held the mud, felt its strange pulsing warmth, and prayed once again. That Antonio's tenderness be tempered by strength. That Anitra's headstrong ways be ameliorated by experience. She had heard that a touch of the holy mud to the five points of the body on which Jesucristo had suffered His wounds would heal any ill. Now she lightly touched Antonio on these five symbolic points.

Tears stung her eyes as she rose. She pressed her lips to Antonio's cheeks, whispering, "You'll see, my Antonio." Then she turned to Anitra and carefully performed the same ritual.

They stepped outside into the brightness of sunlight, as if moving from one faraway and lost world into a newly found place. Antonio suddenly stopped, frozen, with El Santuario behind him, the small cup of the valley before him. He waited, but he felt nothing. He looked at his grandmother.

"Nothing happens in a moment," she said. "We'll go home now. It's a long way."

Anitra, climbing into the carriage, wondered at the luminous joy in Lupe's face. As the three drove away, the sun began to set, dyeing the red mountains an even deeper red, and spilling waves of carmine across the sky.

Twilight veiled the slopes with blue shadows, spread

70

a purple haze across the road. A light wind arose, stirring the sage. The wind grew stronger, swirling off the ridges in quick gusts. The purple haze became a darkening green. Far across the dry meadows, red clouds arose from the earth. The red clouds in the distance moved swiftly and three tall dust devils leaped from the slope and came spinning toward the carriage.

Porfirio covered his mouth and nose, ducked his head, nearly blinded. He hauled hard on the reins, cursing. They were in a narrow ravine and the roar of the dust storm covered the sudden thud of hooves behind them.

Too late Porfirio saw the two masked men burst upon them. Before he could pull his rifle, a shot threw him to the ground.

The carriage horses plunged at the sound of the shot, and the carriage tipped dangerously on its wheels as the horses reared. Lupe was flung first into Antonio, then against Anitra. She caught the girl and clung to her, and was torn away when the carriage righted itself and settled with a crash on all four wheels.

A man, faceless and more terrible for that, leaned from his saddle and caught a bridle. All was stillness for an instant. Then the wind roared again, and, raised against it, a hard voice said, "You, inside, stand down. We want your money!"

"Bandits," Antonio whispered through dry lips.

"Don't be afraid," Lupe answered.

The door jerked open and a masked face appeared. Lupe faltered, "What do you want, señor?"

"All that you have, old woman. Get down and let me see."

Antonio leaned forward, "You mustn't hurt my grandmother."

The masked man reached out, hauled the boy down,

and flung him sprawling to the ground. Lupe moved stiffly across the seat and to the door. "He's only a child," she cried, half-falling from the carriage.

Anitra leaped after her, swift and angry. "You don't have to hurt anybody. Take what you want and go. Take it and go, I tell you!"

Porfirio lay still, bleeding from the head, but under his body, his fingers twitched carefully at his belt.

Antonio pushed himself up, stood swaying beside Lupe. "Do as my sister says."

The masked man slipped from his horse. "Your jewels, old woman. And your money."

Lupe took her silver pin from her dress. She offered the reticule that hung from her arm, while the wind whipped her mantilla across her cheeks and tore at her clothing.

"That's all I have, señor," she said finally.

"No," he answered. "I see a gold chain at your throat, old woman, and I want it. I see a gold ring on your finger. And I want that, too."

She drew herself up. "These you may not have. I've worn the cross at my breast since I was only five years old. I've worn my gold wedding ring that my husband gave me . . ."

He seized her left hand.

She screamed as Porfirio jumped to his feet. Half blinded by blood, by wind-driven dust, he flung his knife. It made a silver trail through the air as it struck the second bandit's shoulder.

The man's rifle roared and Lupe fell, choking as a wave of sweet hot blood rose up from her chest.

The last sounds she heard were the drumming of hoofbeats, a man's angry curses.

5

Leigh was standing under a cottonwood tree when the wagon came slowly down the lane.

Porfirio sat on the front seat, the reins in his fist. A bandage showed under the brim of his hat. Anitra sat on one side of him, Antonio on the other, their hands linked across his spread knees. The back of the wagon was filled to the top with the cut lilacs that covered the braced and black-draped coffin. Lorenzo and Matthew rode to one side. Esteban brought up the rear.

Through Esteban, deliberately chosen for that casual meeting in the casino, and carefully cultivated thereafter, Leigh had learned the identity of Anitra and Antonio. Through Esteban, too, he had heard of what had befallen the Martínez family.

He looked up as the wagon passed.

Antonio's eyes were red-rimmed, his face pale. He remembered nothing about what had happened, just that the bandits had come like black shadows out of the dust storm.

Anitra raised her eyes as Leigh stared at her. Her small red mouth was set with pain. It was she who had insisted that the black-draped coffin be covered with lilacs, and thousands of tiny lavender stars now hid what lay beneath. But the scent had become bitter to her.

Only Matthew had not asked questions. He had lightly kissed her cheek when he met the wagon at the pass and said, "Anitra, I'm sorry."

And Anitra, heart full, had cried, "Matthew, my father killed Baa!"

Matthew said gently, "I'll find you another Baa, Anitra." And plainly he understood why she mentioned the lamb when she wept for her grandmother.

Now, still at his side, she looked down at Leigh Ransome. He gravely removed his hat, startled by the impact of her eyes. They were a clear, hard, and shining green, with an expression completely adult.

The party went on, but at Leigh's signal, Esteban hung back.

"If there's anything I can do," Leigh said, "be sure, I'll be willing, Don Esteban."

"Thank you."

"A terrible thing," Leigh went on. "The children look distraught."

"The suddenness of it all," Esteban answered, and hurried to catch up.

Leigh's blue eyes shone brightly as he walked slowly around the plaza. "Anitra Martínez." He said the name softly, tasting it on his faintly smiling lips. Anitra Martínez . . ."

He looked across the low flat buildings of the plaza to the tall peaks of the mountains beyond. They would never fail him. All was going as he planned. He knew now where Jake Heimer lived. He was certain that he had fathomed the old man's secret. It was only a matter of time, and not much of that, before he proved himself right.

A week later, an hour before daybreak, Jake Heimer checked the load on his two burros, the pick and shovel, the sacks of beef jerky and flour and salt. He pulled his ripple-brimmed hat down to his ears, covering his silver sideburns, and mounted his horse. He sat still, the lead in his gnarled hand, and scanned the horizon. Seeing no one, he set out, mumbling to himself, "Now then, Jake, let's go."

Some time in the latter half of the day a feeling of uneasiness settled on him. By then he was far above the town on a forested hillside. He stopped, listened, studied the terrain. He found no reason for his feeling. But it remained. There was a tension in his belly that wasn't hunger. There was a prickling in the hair on his arms. He doubled back, crossed his trail, doubled back again. He sidetracked, adding hours to his journey.

At twilight he set up camp, slept close by a small fire with his rifle at his knees. At dawn he was on the way again, the same sense of uneasiness still persisting.

"No reason for it," he told himself. "You're getting old. That's your trouble. You're just plain getting old." But he didn't really believe that. He felt the same man he had always been. A loner, strong and well able to take care of himself.

Still he remained careful and alert. He knew where he was going; he didn't want anyone else to know. What he'd found was his. He wouldn't stake it and file papers and start a gold rush. He'd use it until he died, and when he did, it would remain undisturbed. God's wealth, a monument to old Jake Heimer.

It took him three days when it should have taken one—such was his caution. And Leigh, trailing him, silent as a shadow, grinned to himself. All the old man's canniness would do him no good.

At twilight on the third day, Jake went slowly along a ridge, hugging the deep shadow of the blue spruce.

A rock suddenly spun through the undergrowth from somewhere out of sight. Jake pulled up. His burros nickered softly. There was nothing.

Looking down from above him, close enough to see the stains on the crown of Jake's hat, Leigh let his breath out slowly. He could have brained his horse for kicking that rock. They were almost there. They had to be.

Soon the old man stopped, making camp with the leisurely movements of a person settling in. There was a stream nearby—a good one that dropped like a small waterfall from the rocks overhead. Soon there was the smell of meat frying.

Leigh licked his lips. For three days he had forced himself to be content with water and hard biscuits. Now his stomach growled, but he made himself wait until Jake finished his meal and undid his bedroll before he rode down to the fire.

The old man reached for his rifle, but his hand wasn't fast enough. Leigh slid down from his horse and smiled charmingly. "Do you mind if I rest by your fire?"

Jake looked up at him and after a moment's hesitation said, "No, son, I don't mind at all. Come warm yourself. The nights are cold. And maybe you'd like some coffee. There's a little left in the pot."

Leigh's smile broadened. He dropped down to his heels, picked up the old man's rifle and threw it among the trees.

Jake set his teeth together. He should have listened to his feelings. He should have turned around and gone back to town. He'd given away the location of his mine. But the boy didn't know yet. He really didn't know. He coughed a little and forced a smile. "Just go ahead and help yourself, son. Whatever you want. I always believed in sharing."

"That's nice," Leigh said, but he didn't move. He was looking at a clump of bright-red wild flowers blooming at the edge of the stream. He saw the small tiny shape of a hummingbird drift over them. He got to his feet, moved soundlessly to the stream's edge and stood there a moment before his hand whipped out. When he returned and sat down beside Jake, he was holding the small, wildly struggling bird. "Those were some pretty good nuggets you had in the gambling house in town a while back," he said.

Jake let his breath out in a long sigh. "I knew I'd seen you somewheres."

"Tres Ríos isn't all that big," Leigh answered.

"Only you just drifted in one day."

"To remain for good," Leigh said softly. "And about those nuggets . . . "

"Oh, them? Nice, weren't they? I bought them off a high grader down to the Moreno Valley. He was hung over and hung up for coin, so he lost his judgment."

Still smiling broadly, Leigh said, "That's a silly story, old man. You got those nuggets yourself. You dug them up or washed them up, either one. You've got a mine stashed away. I want it."

"A mine?" Jake quavered. "Why, boy, you're crazy. Plumb crazy, that's all. If I had a mine, why'd I live like this? Why'd I be nothing but a poor man, with bills a mile long to pay, and . . . "

"And you always pay them after your little trips up here," Leigh said coldly. "Listen, old man, just you listen to me. They said in Tres Ríos you've been playing with those same gold nuggets for years. I knew better when I heard it. I just knew. Just like I know you're lying to me now. Don't waste my time. And don't waste yours. Where's the mine?"

"Isn't any," Jake said, thinking as fast as he could. "I steal the nuggets, and that's the truth."

"Where from?"

"From wherever I can, of course. And I come up here as a blind. Just in case anybody like you . . . " Jake's words faded. His eyes widened as he watched Leigh's big hand begin to close around the small fluttering bird. Jake didn't want to see, but he watched as Leigh's fingers closed and made a fist, and from the fist there poured a smeary dark fluid. He watched as Leigh at last opened his hand and shook from it a mixture of pulp and feather and bone. Then Leigh reached out and took Jake's hand. "I want to know, old man. You hear me? I want to know." With each repetition of the phrase, he tightened his hand around Jake's fingers.

The blood drained from Jake's face. His body crumpled, and he fell sideways, still unable to free himself, while the small bones in his hand broke, and the flesh split and became mangled pulp. Finally Leigh released him, and he lay on his side, nursing his destroyed hand. He'd never tell, he thought silently. He wouldn't tell. But when Leigh took hold of his other hand, Jake heard himself say, "I'm an old man . . . I don't know anything . . . I can't help you. . . . " And then he heard himself scream as Leigh's fingers tightened. "I'm an old man," he cried. "Let me go . . . gold in the stream . . . in the stream, I tell you. Placer mine . . . I pan for it . . . I won't tell. Just let me go."

Leigh released him, grinning, and got to his feet. "Stay there and don't move."

He knew the old man wouldn't dare. His spirit had broken along with his hand. He lit a torch and began to climb along the banks of the stream. When he found the marks of earlier work, he nodded, pleased that once again his instinct had proven to be right. He climbed swiftly to where the stream fell, and smiled when he found the cave behind the waterfall and the hollows laboriously dug out by Jake Heimer.

Jake moaned, watching Leigh return. He didn't dare move, lest more happen to him, as Leigh finally came and squatted down beside him, saying, "Thanks, old man." And then, "Why don't you stick your hands in the stream? Maybe that'll make them feel better."

Jake got up cautiously, fighting nausea. At the stream, he went down to his knees, as if he were praying, though there were no prayers in him, and thrust his broken hands into the icy water.

Leigh came up silently and asked, "How're you doing now, old-timer?"

Some threat in the silken voice brought Jake halfway to his feet before Leigh swung the fist-sized rock in his hand and clubbed him to the ground.

A thin rim of light brought to the mountain peak a clear and unblurred sharpness. Leigh rose to study the area. There was no sign left that an old man had camped by the stream under the spray of the waterfall. The fire had been cleared away, even the kindling buried and the ashes scattered. The packs, utensils, supplies were hidden under feet of rich earth, each fresh surface smoothed and covered with dry pine needles. Nothing was left except for the implements high in the cave above the waterfall, and the horse and the two burros. He'd need the burros, Leigh thought, and it was that certainty which made him careful. Later on he'd sell them in Sante Fe.

No, there was nothing here to show that an old man

had died. Except that he no longer stood in Leigh's way. It was the first time Leigh had killed a man, but it meant no more to him than the killing of the hummingbird. The gold was now his, and with that gold he would buy what he wanted.

He worked for hours, gently running his fingers through the graveled bed of the stream and gathering handfuls of pebbles to wash in the sieve he held.

The pale dawn became fiery red over his head, but he didn't notice. It was noon, with the sun straight overhead, before he stopped with a small sound of satisfaction.

Within the sieve, shining with the drops of water that still clung to them, were lumps of mud and gravel coated with the slime of the stream. But each of them emitted a glow, a brightness. Leigh slowly let his breath out. There it was. All his. Gold.

Three days later he came down from the mountain, leading the loaded burros. He avoided Tres Ríos and set out directly for Sante Fe.

He had it all planned. He wouldn't stake a claim because he couldn't claim the whole mountain. If he filed, there'd be a rush. The old man had known what he was doing. He hadn't been greedy. Leigh wouldn't be either. He'd see what he had for his three days' labor, and then he'd know. Once a month, for as long as the summer and weather held, he'd go on a hunting trip and bring back venison—some for Don Esteban, too. And he'd do a few small chores at the stream at the same time.

In Santa Fe, Leigh had the nuggets assayed. He'd been certain they were rich, and they were. He had, within moments, more money than he'd ever seen before in his life. But his only acquisition was made on the way back to Tres Ríos when he stopped for a meal in a Tesuque cantina.

A team of horses and a wagon were tied in front of the place. From the back of the wagon there was a wild chorus of yelps and snarls. Leigh took a look and saw a pair of caged dogs, a male and female. They were both black with rusty markings. Though still young, they exuded a sense of power with their deep chests and strong arched necks. He reached between the wire to stroke one, and sharp teeth raked his hand. The blood welled out and ran into his palm. He drew back, his eyes suddenly dark. He had to own them. Whatever they were, and he didn't know what, they had to belong to him.

He went into the cantina, licking at the torn spot on his hand, and asked, "Whose wagon is that outside?"

A man at a small round table looked up from his plate of burritos. "It's mine. And if those dogs got you, then you had your hand where it don't belong."

Leigh grinned. "I'm not here to complain to you. I just want to know what you're asking for them."

"What're you offering?" The man rose with alacrity, then looked crafty. "But they're worth a lot. I guess you know that. Doberman pinschers, they are, brought over from Germany just last year. I doubt there's another pair of them in the country."

"I don't care what they are," Leigh said. He took out a twenty-dollar gold piece, dropped it on the table. "I won't bargain for them."

The man stared at him, shrugged, pocketed the money.

Leigh went outside. He took the cage, strapped it onto the back of his horse. Cora, he named the female in his mind. He named the male Cal. He patted the top of the cage, and the dogs lunged for his fingers. He laughed and said softly, "Not yet, my sweethearts. Not yet. Soon you'll learn who's boss around here."

In the late afternoon he stopped at the pass and looked down into the valley. He had his gold. Soon the valley and the mountains, they'd all be his.

Smiling, he rode toward Tres Ríos.

6

Lorenzo said, "Antonio, it's past time that you learned to handle a rifle and gun. We'll begin today."

There was a silence at the big round table. At last Antonio said, "My father, I don't wish to learn about guns."

Lorenzo drew a deep angry breath, his eyes on Lupe's empty chair. It had been vacant for three months, and yet he expected to see her sitting there. It was the same for the children, he knew. He had thought to divert Antonio, but no matter how he tried, Antonio was determined to thwart his will. He said, scowling, "I've not asked for your feeling about it. You must learn to use guns."

"There are lessons today," Antonio said quickly.

"Be damned to your lessons. Some things come before others. As you'll learn one day."

"I hate guns," Antonio whispered.

And Lorenzo said, "Have you forgotten your grandmother so soon?"

"Guns didn't save her," Antonio said. "They killed her."

Anitra straightened. "But if we'd been armed, if Porfirio hadn't been shot . . . " Her voice hardened as she went on, "I'll learn. Listen, Papa, you teach me. Then Antonio will see it isn't bad to know how to protect one's life."

She had taught him to ride. Surely she could teach him to shoot. Lorenzo's face was growing red. His temper was rising.

Antonio refused to meet his sister's glance. "I'll not learn, Papa."

Anitra opened her mouth as if to speak, but Lorenzo gestured her angrily to be silent. "I won't discuss it any further. We go out in two hours. You'll learn what you must know."

Antonio remained silent, but Anitra begged, "Papacito, I want to know how to shoot. Let me come, too."

"You will not. You'll start to understand now that you'll not share every hour of your brother's day, as you'll not share every hour of your brother's life."

Anitra didn't answer. She and Antonio had always been together, always would be.

She watched as Antonio put his hand to the place at his throat where the collar of his shirt hid the long thin red scar.

It was later that same day. She was in her room. Uneasiness suddenly assailed her. She set aside her book, rose from her chair. It was, she saw by the clock, the time that her father had set for Antonio to go with him.

She tried to resist wandering outside, since her presence would only make her father angry. But at last she gave in to her feelings. She would cut some late flowers for the house.

Her ruse didn't deceive her father.

He stood near the trunk of a peach tree on which he had hung a target. His face was dark with rage. He was alone. "Where's Antonio?" he demanded.

"I don't know, my father."

"Find him at once."

She knew better than to argue. She searched through the hacienda, questioning the servants. None had seen him.

He was gone. He'd run away. Somewhere in the golden hills he leaned on a rock, and raised his face to the blue of heaven and prayed.

Suddenly certain, she was overwhelmed by tears.

The men were gathered in the courtyard, their horses stirring restlessly in the chill that followed the burning heat of day. Porfirio watched for Lorenzo's lifted hand, the signal that would send them out into the dark.

He thought, as he had thought many times in the past three months, that he'd sooner be dead himself than to have seen Doña Lupe lying in her blood in the dust. He blamed himself that he'd thought of morada affairs, wondering why the Hermanos of Chimayo had needed more guns, and thus he had been less than vigilant. To his sorrow, he'd learned why the Hermanos of Chimayo had needed those weapons. With bandits about, how else was a man to protect himself and his own? His back bore the marks of the disciplina with which he had flailed himself, seeking relief from guilt in the pain of contrition. Now there was another guilt to accept. For with Doña Lupe gone there was no one to stand between the angry father and the resisting son.

The boy hadn't been seen since the afternoon meal. It was hours since Porfirio had sent word to all the Brothers of the valley, while Don Lorenzo stormed about the house. At sunset Don Lorenzo directed that riders go to the other ranches.

Now Don Esteban trotted into the courtyard with his new gringo friend Leigh Ransome.

"Don Lorenzo, we came as soon as we heard. Here's

my friend, Señor Leigh Ransome, who was visiting when word reached me. He wanted to do what he could, so I asked him to join us."

Leigh smiled his most charming smile and leaned forward in his saddle.

Lorenzo stared at him, then turned away. "Thank you for coming, Esteban," he said and turned to Matthew, who had come in place of the ailing Don Cipriano.

Leigh allowed his big body to relax. Don Lorenzo would be sorry some day for the snub. At the moment, Leigh didn't allow it to trouble him. He was here, at the Martínez ranch, and his eyes scanned the darkness for the girl, Anitra.

But on Lorenzo's orders she was confined to her room. She peered out at the riders as Lorenzo raised his hand in a signal.

Even after the courtyard was empty she sat staring into the darkness. But she no longer saw the remaining torches, the hard-packed earth. She was remembering. . . .

She felt enwrapped in bitter cold. Her legs were cramped and her back ached. A wind blew with dry whispering breath around her head. The straight white-washed walls of her room became dark and curved, and the brown beams in the ceiling disappeared. Small quick bright eyes peered at her. There was the chittering of tiny animals. Over her she felt the weight of earth, red earth and gray stone.

She knew Antonio's hiding place.

Dora, who had come to wait with her, whispered, "Anitra, niña, what is it?"

She made no answer. She slipped silently from the room, caught up a warm shawl, and hurried into the now empty courtyard, carrying a lantern.

No one hailed her from the shadows. No one tried to

stop her. In the stables, there were only her horse and Antonio's sorrel, the latter contentedly munching feed, the sweat dried on him after the long run back.

She threw a blanket over her bay and mounted him. He knew her weight, saddled or not. He knew her touch on the reins whether she rode astride or not. He was ready to run.

She blew out the lantern and left it hanging on the hook.

Quietly she took the horse into the courtyard and then across it to the wide-open gate. Once they had passed beneath the arch, she gave the bay his head. She knew where Antonio was, but she didn't know if she could find the place again. The two of them had been there only once before.

As her eyes grew accustomed to the dark, the starshine became brighter. She saw the shape of the mountains against the blue of the sky. The horse raced toward them. She hung on, her wide skirts flying, her hair whipped back in silken black streamers.

She sped through a deep canyon, and as she broke into the open again, the silver of the moon appeared to light her way. Ahead she saw the tall palisades, striped with shadow.

Here, in this cliff, Indians had lived. They had cut small rooms into the stone, using what implements she couldn't imagine. They'd bred children, cooked, sewn, woven and died there, to be succeeded by the young who went on as their forebears had. Then one day, for no reason that could be guessed, they'd simply climbed down from their cliff dwellings and gone no one knew where.

But the small rooms remained. She and Antonio had once explored them.

Anitra began to climb, her feet steady and sure as a

burro's. She pulled herself up over a projecting ridge and lay still, panting hard. There were cuts on her knees and elbows. Her fingers were rubbed raw. She licked them, waited to catch her breath. Then before her she saw the black opening in the darkness of the mountain wall.

"Antonio, Antonio, are you here?"

There was no reply.

She made her way through the opening, ducking her head, her two hands outstretched before her. Silken strands of broken spiderwebs slid across her cheeks, and motes of acid dust brought burning tears to her eyes.

"Antonio!"

This was the place. He had to be here. She waited until her eyes were accustomed to the almost-dark. In a corner was a pile of bones. Skulls, long and broken joints, tiny chips that might have once been toes. Nearby there was a square of dust, perhaps a rug reduced to nothing but its shape. At her feet were neatly arranged cooking pots with smoke-blackened undersides. Yes, yes. These were all familiar. She and Antonio had speculated upon them.

Then where was he?

She made her way slowly around the walls, breath held. Antonio, she said silently, Antonio, my brother, tell me where you are. But nothing happened.

She made another slow tour around the room, and this time she found what she hadn't seen earlier.

A hole broke through the rough surface of the stone floor. A hole large enough to admit the passage of a man's body.

In perfect faith, she lowered herself into it, hung by her fingertips until the last moment, then let go.

She fell only a few feet into an unaccountable brightness.

The room in which she stood was impossibly silver with moonlight, even though it was deep within the mountain.

Antonio sat in that brilliance, his head haloed, his face glowing.

He looked up at her, but didn't speak.

She sank down beside him on the cold stone. "What are you doing here? Why did you come?" she demanded. And then, "What's this place, Antonio? We didn't find it before."

"It's an ancient kiva," he said, whispering almost, as if some invisible presence still lingered. "A place where long ago the Indians sought their gods."

She was suddenly irritable. "What have the Indians' gods to do with you? Why did you run away? Why are you hiding like this?"

"I didn't want you to look for me, Anitra," he answered. "You'll have to learn to let me be."

"Let you be? How could I? And you have our father and all the men of the valley out searching for you."

"I'm sorry," he said. "But you should have left me alone."

"You're sorry," she mocked him. "And what have you accomplished? Papa will hand you a gun and stand you up before the peach tree where he's nailed a target, and you'll learn to shoot, no matter what you say."

Antonio didn't answer her. But he already knew what he would do. He had come to the kiva in need, and he had been favored. He had seen his way. He *would* learn to shoot, learn to be all that his father wanted. But he would learn it on his own, and secretly. And when he was adept, then his father would see that he was a man.

Annoyed even more by his silence, Anitra snapped,

"Very well. Sulk, if you like. But will you come home with me?"

"What difference does it make? If I don't you'll stay with me, won't you? And if I go elsewhere, you'll follow."

"Of course." So saying, she rose, looked about her for a ladder.

He said, "The Indians' ladder must have rotted away long ago, Anitra. If you hadn't come for me, I'd have stayed here forever."

She pretended not to have heard, not to have understood his words. To have acknowledged them would have given them a reality she couldn't bear. She motioned him to stand on her shoulders so that he could reach the hole above their heads. He managed that way to climb out of the kiva. Then he lay flat on his belly and hung his arms down until he could grab at her wrists. Grunting with effort, he managed to pull her up after him.

They rode home on the bay, she astride, Antonio silent behind her.

From a stand of trees above the trail, Leigh, who had deliberately separated himself from the other men, saw them. He kicked his horse into a run and angled downhill.

"Is everything all right?" he called.

"Yes, yes, thank you," Anitra answered.

She rode astride, long slim legs clearly outlined by her skirt, her back very straight, her waist slim. Leigh flexed his hands on the reins, thinking how easily they'd span her. Her black hair, like the finest of silk, lay in loose waves upon her shoulders. Even now, disheveled by the long ride, she had an extraordinary presence for so young a girl. "Need any help?" he asked.

"No," Antonio said. "No. I'm all right, but thank you."

Anitra flashed a quick, bright look at Leigh. "You

appear very opportunely, señor. Not only once, but a second time, too."

His smile broadened. "And both times I find I'm not needed."

"But you came." Now her smile met his. "It was good of you."

"Where did you end up, Antonio?"

The boy shrugged, but Anitra waved vaguely in the direction of the distant cliffs.

When they reached the arched gate of the ranch courtyard, she slid down, saying, "Antonio, go in quickly. Dora will give you a hot meal and then you'd better go right to bed."

What she meant was that it would be wise to stay out of their father's path. Antonio understood. He went on toward the stables as she seized the bell rope, ringing out the news that her brother was safe.

Leigh stepped down from his horse. It didn't matter to him that Lorenzo had made it plain he wasn't welcome. Anitra drew him. She was the pulse of the valley. She symbolized its essence.

Standing behind her, he folded his hands around hers, pulling the rope with her. She felt the heat of his body against her own and turned to look up at him.

He saw the quick flash of her eyes and felt her movement against his flesh. She was only a little girl, years younger than he, he thought, but in that moment she was totally a woman, the woman she would soon grow to be. His arms tightened around her, his fingers clenched around her hands. The bell swung over their heads, tolled, tolled again. Vibrations flowed down the rope in quick hot currents. He wanted her. Child though she was, he wanted her.

As he moved closer there were shouts from beyond the courtyard, the drum of horses approaching fast.

The bell rang out once more, and then Anitra tugged her hands free of his, swung quickly away from him. She was confused by what she felt—an excitement she'd never known before, a fear she'd never known before. She saw the faint smile on his mouth, stammered, "Thank you, Señor Ransome," and ran for the house.

Watching as the heavy door slammed shut, he knew that some day she would be his, just as the whole of the valley would be his.

7

Looking ahead to the time when Lorenzo would return to the subject of guns, Anitra convinced Porfirio later that same week that he must teach her the handling of the rifles. When she had mastered the skill to a reasonable extent, she tried to show Antonio what she knew. He would neither watch nor listen. He was determined to learn on his own.

One morning, having made his plans, he went into the courtyard. When Anitra trailed after him, he said, "I don't want you to come. I'll ride alone today."

"But I'm going riding, too," Anitra answered.

Eustacio Rivera, squatting at his work, moved his fingers slowly through the hardening earth beneath the bare lilac bushes. He sighed, for the earth was growing cold now and going to sleep, and it would no longer speak to him when he touched it. Winter was coming, and there would be little for him to do here. Since Porfirio had set him to take over the garden after Patricio had been sent from the ranch, he had come to enjoy the place more than he'd ever imagined he could. The smiles of the two children made up for the loss of his daughter and blurred the memory of his terrible sin.

Stiffly he rose, dusted the soil from his hands. But

when he saw Anitra's expression, he stilled his usual morning greeting.

"Do as you please," Antonio was saying. "The valley's large enough for both of us." Then he strode toward the stable, leaving Anitra looking after him. She was still there when he cantered out of the courtyard.

He stopped first for only a moment at Porfirio's house, and then went on into a small and secluded canyon. There he climbed down, tethered his horse, took the gun Porfirio had lent him, and set to work, loading it with clumsy fingers. When at last the unfamiliar chore was done, he brought the rifle to his shoulder. He was concentrating so hard that he was unaware of the horseman riding up behind him.

It was chance that had brought Mundo Segura there that late September day. When he heard sounds from the clearing ahead, he pulled up. Then the blast came. He leaned over his saddle, his long thin face intent, his mouth narrowed into a mean line under his thin moustache. Peering through a concealing willow thicket, he saw the boy stagger under the hard kick of the rifle, saw him haul it up again, handling it so clumsily that Mundo chuckled aloud. The boy pulled the trigger again, then flung himself to the earth, rubbing his shoulder.

The chuckle soured on Mundo's lips. Antonio Martínez y Escobedo was trying to teach himself how to handle a gun. And not doing well. Pobrecito! The heir to a great slice of the valley of Tres Ríos didn't know the first thing about guns at the age of twelve.

But after all, what could you expect of the son of the ricos? Their blood ran thin, and had for generations. It was Don this and Doña that, but the work was done by the pobres. And always would be.

94

Mundo rode through the thicket, stopped and called down, "Hola, are you in trouble, amigo? Can I help?"

Antonio rolled over slowly, got to his feet.

"I will if I can," Mundo went on, with mock gentleness.

"There's no trouble, but thanks," Antonio told him, looking up with faint recognition. This was one of the men who worked the far ranges, overseeing the herds. He'd be back in the valley now that winter was coming.

Mundo slid down from his horse, tied it to a bush near Antonio's sorrel. Standing, he was nearly two inches shorter than Antonio. He was bitterly aware of the difference between them. But the smile beneath his moustache was casual as he squatted down on his boot heels and jerked a thumb at the rifle.

"They're mean to handle until you get the knack. They've a kick like an ox. The first time I put one against my shoulder and pulled the trigger, it knocked me off my feet, amigo."

Disarmed, Antonio laughed. "I didn't fall, at least. But it was close." He rubbed his right shoulder. "And I can still feel it."

Mundo rolled two cigarillos and casually offered one to Antonio.

Watching Mundo, imitating him, Antonio drew cautiously at the cigarillo, repressing the need to cough.

Mundo pretended not to notice. He said, "All guns are simple, amigo. Else who'd be able to use them? It's a question of feel." He hefted the gun in his right hand. "Feel it. Touch it. Hold it. You'll see what I mean."

Antonio accepted the gun, and Mundo leaned forward, speaking softly, explaining, and seeing the look of pleasure on the boy's face as he listened.

It was a few hours' sport for Mundo. He, a nobody, a shepherd, spoke with Antonio Martínez as an equal. He, the pobre, whose ancestors had starved to support such as this rico, proved he was the better man.

But later, in the plaza, what had begun as sport became something else. . . .

Don Cipriano leaned hard on his crutch with one arm and offered the other to Josefa as she stepped down from the carriage. She was very thin and pale. Her small hollowed face was made even smaller by the thick coronet of brown braids in which she combed her hair. Her dress was a pale green, beruffled at collar and sleeve and hem. The weight of the rich fabric emphasized the fleshlessness of her body.

She coughed into her handkerchief, then said, "Thank you. In two hours then?"

"Phaw, two hours wasted, my girl! When you could, the both of you, be doing something worthwhile. Worthwhile, instead of picking through that place, I say." He jerked his gray head at the general store. "But still—if that's what you want. A harmless occupation, if a foolish one." He bent a look on Anitra, "And you, too . . . so suddenly interested . . . I don't understand. Yesterday, a hoyden, and now—are you growing up on me?"

Anitra grinned at him. "Don Cipriano, if it hadn't been for you, I'd not be here at all. And you know it."

"Ah, well," he chuckled. "It did seem nice that my Josefa should have company. And your father saw that when I pointed it out to him."

"I'm grateful." She was even more grateful than she said. Without Don Cipriano's insistence, added to Josefa's gentle pleas, Anitra wouldn't have been allowed to go on this shopping trip in Tres Ríos. Here was an exciting peek at a world she'd hardly ever been allowed to see before.

Indians dawdled in the plaza under the cottonwoods, and across the way, tall, bronze-haired Leigh Ransome was tying his horse to a hitching post, and there at the end of the plaza was the gambling casino, and . . . She could stand like this for hours and feast her eyes. But her father didn't approve. She smiled at Don Cipriano. "Yes. I'm grateful to you," she repeated.

He patted her cheek. "It's nothing, niña." And then, "Josefa, if you tire, promise me that you'll ask the señor inside for a chair so you can sit and rest."

"I'll not tire, my grandfather," she answered, and once again she coughed into her handkerchief.

He squinted at it, trying to see. Was there blood this time? It was a dread he'd lived with for years. But he didn't ask. "And I've arranged with Don Esteban. He and Matthew will come for you."

"Thank you." That was Josefa.

"You could, Anitra, if you asked nicely, perhaps persuade Matthew to show you the new horses that Esteban found for him in Estancia," Don Cipriano suggested.

Anitra merely nodded and cast down her eyes, lest the others see in them a gleam of excitement. She was glad, now that she knew she'd be seeing Matthew, that she'd argued Dora into allowing her to wear this skirt and blouse. They fit closely, almost too small for her, and the pale blue seemed to brighten the green of her eyes. She permitted her cloak to hang open so that it wouldn't hide what was beneath. It would be perfect if Antonio had come into town, too, but he was riding with the men, at their father's insistence. She tried not to think of how he felt.

Don Cipriano was saying, "And you'll stay here at the store, and not wander off alone, should they be a few moments late?"

This was a delightful thought, and just what Anitra herself wanted to do—to wander off, to explore the town. But Anitra knew they would not do it. Josefa was so dutiful. Mealymouthed, Anitra called it. Josefa was nineteen, a grown woman, yet she obeyed every injunction. She could induce in Anitra a vast impatience, and usually did. An impatience concealed, because Matthew himself was plainly never disturbed by Josefa's demureness.

"Don't worry," Anitra said. "We'll do just as you say. You mustn't worry about us." She went dancing in a swirl of blue skirts and swinging cloak to the door of the shop and waited there while Josefa exchanged a last word with her grandfather.

There followed a long two hours. Or so it seemed to Anitra. She trailed Josefa, making suitable comments, while Josefa examined bolts of black lace and white and blond. She helped choose a dozen two-yard lengths of velvet ribbon. She decided on her own purchase, a width of scarlet silk, to which she already knew Dora would object, and which her father would forbid her to wear. But all the while she considered the slowness of passing time. It was as if there was to be a special meeting today between Matthew and her. Despite all the casual encounters they'd had before, this was to be a beginning of something new.

At last Matthew and Esteban pulled up before the store and the girls paid for their purchases and went outside.

"You finished when you said you would, Josefa," Matthew said, jumping down off the wagon.

"I always do," she answered gravely.

"And the cough?"

"Much better, thank you, Matthew."

Much better, thank you, Matthew, Anitra thought. Oh, what a simpering fool! Was that the way to talk to Matthew? But it was as if she had suddenly seen the two of them with new eyes. Josefa was the elder by two full years, yet Matthew treated her as if she were the younger. And there was something . . . something else changed as well. Anitra couldn't quite put her finger on it, but she sensed it there.

Matthew said to her, "And you, little one, did you enjoy yourself?"

She felt her cheeks burn. She shrugged.

"Aren't we speaking this evening?" he demanded.

"I'm thinking," she retorted. "I'm still considering a length of goods about which I couldn't make up my mind."

"Then come along. Don Cipriano will be waiting."

She was suddenly dispirited. Ignoring Matthew's proffered hand, she leaped into the wagon, wishing that she had come on horseback like Don Esteban. Then she could ride wildly away, leaving the others behind her.

Instead she was trapped here with them, and must put a good face on it. She tilted her chin, smiled fixedly.

But Matthew was no longer paying attention to her, she realized. He was staring across the plaza, watching a small involvement just outside the cantina.

Mundo stood with his bandy legs outspread, his long thin face agleam. He held a silver coin between his fingers and waved it back and forth before Patricio Sánchez' fascinated and bloodshot eyes. "If you want it, amigo, then dance for it," Mundo said, chuckling.

Patricio gave a wide ingratiating grin. "I'm thirsty, friend. You're so kind—and have a good face, too. Yes, yes. I'm thirsty. But I can't dance."

Mundo's long thin face grew brighter. "Sure you can, Patricio. Just dance a little and you'll drink all the wine you can hold."

Patricio swayed closer, licking his lips. He shuffled his feet, then grinned hopefully.

"More," Mundo ordered, aware of the crowd growing around him, hot with the same sense of power he had when he stood in the morada with the black snake whip in his hand. "More, Patricio. And kick your heels."

Again Patricio shuffled and swayed, and then leaned close.

Mundo thrust him back, the silver piece aglitter between his fingers. "Is that dancing? Hombre, surely you can do better than that."

"I'm a gardener, amigo," Patricio whined. "A gardener, as you're a shepherd. At least, a gardener is what I once was. Now—" he shrugged—"I tend Don Cipriano's horses. Nothing grows beneath my hands any more."

"All poor men have their troubles." Mundo laughed. "Dance, my friend. And then you'll have wine and that'll make you forget yours."

The crowd pressed closer. Other voices were raised.

"Dance, estúpido!"

"Show him, Patricio. Show him a fancy step."

"Kick your heels, hombre. He offers you silver. Earn it and we'll all drink with you."

The small man limped this way and then that. And with each shuffle, he yearned toward the silver in Mundo's hand.

Matthew pressed his way through the crowd. Hot

points of light glowed in his eyes. "Patricio, a word with you, if you please."

"Dance, fool," Mundo jeered. "Words don't fill the mouth with wine. Dance, I tell you." It was beautiful to feel this big and powerful. He was a rico in *his* world, was Mundo Segura.

Patricio wavered first toward him, then toward Matthew. Esteban, observing the disturbance from afar, had climbed from his horse to the wagon, not wanting to leave the girls unescorted, and had driven the wagon closer. He hesitated now, prepared to interfere if need be.

Josefa was deathly pale, but Anitra was leaning forward, her small hands clenched, her eyes burning. Even as he looked at her, she stirred. He reached to stop her, but she slipped away, disappeared into the group of men and burst through to stand at Matthew's side.

He said softly, but so that all could hear, "Only a monkey need dance for his drink. And you're not a monkey, Patricio. Here, here, take this coin and lead those who are your friends into the cantina with you."

"Who do you think you are?" Mundo demanded. "You've no right to stop my fun."

"You know very well who I am. But if you wish it confirmed, then I'll tell you. I'm Matthew Britton."

But the crowd had edged back. The men stared hard now at Mundo. Patricio was one of theirs. Why was Mundo humiliating his own?

Mundo sensed the change. He was suddenly small as always, the brief satisfaction that had filled him since his encounter with Antonio gone. His mouth thinned into a mean line under his moustache as he shrugged and turned away. Matthew Britton. Don Cipriano's heir, it was said in the cantinas. A rico . . . always it was a rico who deprived him of what was rightly his. It had been that way since his birth. The rich took from the poor, took all, including honor. Mundo had forgotten that he'd baited a poor man with money for wine. He remembered only the silent stares of the crowd that had been with him for a few moments and then turned suddenly against him. All because of the rico . . .

"You were wonderful," Anitra said as Matthew drove the wagon out of town. "Oh, Matthew, Matthew, I was so proud of you."

"You'd have been less so if there'd been trouble." Josefa's voice was a strange mixture of anger and fear. She had difficulty breathing; she gasped and finally broke into a fit of coughing.

Matthew said, "Josefa, it's nothing. Mundo Segura's not a man to be frightened of. He's a bully and no more. He'll only torment a man like Patricio, one he knows is weak."

"Patricio is a good man," Anitra put in. "He drinks wine when he can, but who doesn't?"

"Don Cipriano sees that he's not near the wine," Matthew said dryly. "Which is why he attends my horses, though he'd rather be a gardener, as he'll tell anyone who listens."

Josefa nodded, coughed into her lace handkerchief. Then, "Grandfather suggests you might like to show Anitra the two new horses, Matthew, that Don Esteban brought you."

"It's been enough for you today," he said briefly. "Another time, Anitra."

"One is a palomino," Josefa added. "So beautiful, with a pale mane and tail. And Matthew vows he'll grow to be seventeen hands high."

Anitra was hardly listening. She studied Matthew's profile and finally said, "Matthew, why didn't you knock Mundo Segura down? Surely he deserved it."

"It wasn't necessary," Matthew told her. "He understood, and without a beating, what I intended."

Josefa put her tiny, clawlike hand on Matthew's arm. Anitra caught the smile he gave Josefa and heard his whispered "All right now, Josefa? You needn't be frightened any more."

A coldness enwrapped Anitra. She sat back and firmly turned her head away so that she need not see how Josefa held onto Matthew's arm.

But it was only later, after Josefa and Matthew had been left at the Diaz ranch, and Anitra started for home, escorted by Esteban, that she understood her feelings.

Esteban said thoughtfully, "Josefa's not so well. Do you realize it, Anitra?"

"She hasn't been for a long time. I don't remember when she was truly well."

"Yes. But lately . . . "

Anitra slid a quick, bright look at him. "Tell me, why don't you marry her?"

It was a gross impertinence to a man old enough to be her father, and if her father had heard it, he'd have been enraged at her. But Esteban accepted the question with good grace.

He laughed and said, "Why, I couldn't do that, Anitra. I'm waiting for you to grow up, and it won't be long now, will it?"

She stared hard at him, saw the amusement in his eyes, and snapped, "Don't trouble yourself to do that, Don Esteban."

He answered as if he hadn't heard her, "And besides,

Anitra, it's decided, you know, that Josefa will marry Matthew."

She was suddenly without breath. The brilliance of the sinking sun brought tears to her eyes. She was silent all the rest of the way, spoke only once, hoarsely, to thank him before she went indoors.

Josefa and Matthew . . . it was not to be believed. Not to be borne.

"A fool for a son," Lorenzo was saying, his voice hammering the walls of the sala. "A fool! Who else would do such a thing?"

Putting aside her own anguish, she went to the doorway and looked in.

Lorenzo spied her, roared, "And you, where have you been?"

"But you know where, Papa. Don Cipriano himself asked you, and you gave your permission."

"Not to stay out until all hours. The two of you are a fine pair. You, running about in town as if you'd nothing better to do. And your brother—riding away from the men. He had his chores. Did he do them?"

Antonio said nothing. There was no way to explain. He had become separated from the others purely by accident. He'd spent an hour or two searching for them until Porfirio came upon him.

"No," Lorenzo yelled, his face red. "He hides from his rightful labor. What'll become of the ranch? What'll happen to all we own, to all that our forebears lived for, when I die? Who'll carry on for me?" His voice dropped. He sank into a chair near the fire. "Oh, get out. I don't want to look at either of you."

Anitra stepped back, waited for Antonio, but he brushed by. She hurried after him, whispering, "Wait, wait, where are you going?"

"Out for a little while."

"I'll come, too," she said.

"No." His face was white, strained.

"Please, Antonio, let me . . . "

He jerked away from her, ran down the hall, and into the courtyard where he mounted his sorrel and rode toward the small canyon in which he'd met Mundo. Before they had parted Antonio had the satisfaction of knowing he could shoot. He returned now in search of a comfort he couldn't find in himself.

Mundo grinned when he heard the sound of the horse and quickly rolled two cigarillos.

As Antonio dismounted, he heard, "Hola, amigo, I wondered if you'd come back."

"Mundo, is that you?"

"For certain it is," Mundo said. "Come sit down." But then, before Antonio could, Mundo was on his feet. He thrust the lit cigarillo at Antonio. "No, never mind. Let's ride a little."

"Now?"

"Why not?"

"That's right. Why not?" Antonio drew on the cigarillo as he remounted the sorrel and followed Mundo's lead. It was a good thing to have a friend.

They rode side by side, for several hours. Antonio did not notice that they had left Martínez land and entered Diaz property until Mundo said, "I hear Matthew Britton has new racing horses."

"Yes, and he's training them himself. Some day they're going to be winners, Mundo."

"Oh? I doubt that. What does he know of racehorses?"

"Matthew knows everything. And the two that he owns . . . " Antonio's eyes glowed. "They're so beautiful, he says. One has a blaze and is all black except for that.

Matthew calls him Star. And the other's a palomino. Matthew will allow me to ride them one day."

"Then you've not seen them yet?" Mundo said.

"Not yet," Antonio confessed.

"Let's go and look at them now." Mundo grinned.

"Now? Tonight? I can't, Mundo. Tomorrow perhaps . . ."

"Matthew Britton doesn't like me. He'd probably order me away from the place," said Mundo. "But you're my friend. You know I won't defile Don Cipriano's ranch if I pass by there in my boots."

"Of course not," Antonio cried.

"Then let's go, amigo."

Matthew's horses, separated from the other ranch buildings by a three-acre meadow, had their own rough training corral. Antonio didn't understand the need for stealth, but fell in with Mundo, both breathing lightly, not speaking as they tied their horses and peered at the dark stable.

There was a soft nicker from within, acknowledgment that their presence was noted. But no other sound came, no voice was raised in question.

Antonio sighed in relief. Patricio wasn't about. It wouldn't be necessary to explain his presence there with Mundo at this strange hour.

Mundo went ahead and silently opened the stable door. There was another gentle nicker.

"Softly," he said, going inside. "Softly, amigo." He caught up a lantern quickly, and waving away Antonio's protest, he lit it. "I want to see them, my friend. Now that I'm here, I want to have a good look."

The two horses leaned at their stall to return his stare, ears pricked forward, dainty hooves dancing. "Ah, yes. Yes, they're truly beautiful, amigo."

Only a rich man could own such horses, he thought. Only a fattener on the blood of the poor.

The stealthy approach, the whispering voice, had affected Antonio. He said urgently, "Come on, Mundo. Put out the light and let's go."

And at the same time there came a rich warm voice singing "Las Mañanitas." Patricio, making a wavering path through the meadow, bellowed to the stars the traditional words of the birthday song. "This is the birthday song, sung by King David, because this is your birthday, I sing it to you."

Antonio wet his lips, began to call a greeting. But Mundo moved with the speed of lightning. He clamped an arm around the boy's waist, a hand across his mouth. He lunged toward the door, and as he went, he deliberately nudged over the lantern, then kicked the barn door shut behind him. Still clasping Antonio in his relentless grip, he dragged the boy with him into the shadows of the corral and dropped to the ground.

A whisper of sound came from the stable. A sudden drum of horses' hooves, a nicker that became a neigh suddenly shrill with terror.

Strange light spilled between the chinks of the walls and at the single window. There was a puff of smoke, a gust of hot wind, and the whole building was ablaze. Flame poured from the exploded window.

"This is your birthday." Patricio approached, still singing, and then suddenly stopped. "Madre de Dios! Don Matthew's horses!" He threw himself forward, dragged the heavy door open, and disappeared into the inferno while Antonio writhed and fought in Mundo's paralyzing embrace.

The fire billowed up, danced along the roof. Over the terrible pounding in his ears, Antonio heard a long agonized scream. Then a black thing hurtled from the doorway clothing aflame; it staggered and fell, only yards from where Mundo and Antonio lay.

Mundo pulled Antonio to his feet, thrust him into the saddle of his horse and threw the reins around his neck. "We can't help him. And no one must know we were here. Else it's bad for both of us."

"Patricio," Antonio whispered dryly.

"It was an accident," Mundo said. "You can't blame yourself or me. The lantern exploded. If not tonight, then another night. Ride to the ranch, amigo, and forget you've been out."

The older man ached. He had not intended Patricio harm—it was Matthew Britton's horses that had been his object. Matthew Britton himself. Yet Patricio was dead. And it was Matthew's fault for offending Mundo Segura.

Stunned, Antonio made his way home, while Don Cipriano's bell echoed through the valley.

Anitra awakened, the breath of terror in her throat as she heard the distant ringing. Putting on a covering garment, she tiptoed quietly into the hallway.

The lamps were lit there. The heavy front door hung ajar. She heard the voices and horses in the courtyard. Her father, the other men of the ranch, were going to answer the frightening summons. She went slowly into Antonio's room.

He was still in bed, shrunken within its largeness. His eyes were fixed and dull.

"Antonio?" she said softly. "What's the matter? Why don't you get up?"

He neither moved nor responded, and after a long moment, she crept away.

Hours later, when the men had returned, when dawn filled the valley, she slipped out.

She found Matthew, as she had expected, near the ruins of the destroyed stable.

The body of Patricio had been carried away, the remains of the dead horses, too.

Matthew's head was bent, his cheeks were smudged, and there was a long ragged tear in his grimy shirt.

She sat beside him silently, put an arm around his shoulders, straining to encompass their breadth.

After a long moment, she felt the stiffness in him ease. At last he turned to her. "Only you understand, Anitra. Only you." And then, his arms enfolding her, drawing her to him, "My heart, how I love you. How I love you, Anitra."

Antonio kept to his bed for two days, burning and struggling with a burden of guilt that grew in him like a weed in rich earth.

Each time that Anitra drew aside the bed curtains and asked, "Antonio, what is it? How can I help you?" he turned away, mumbling, "Leave me alone. Leave me alone, that's all I ask of you."

On the third day, he rose, dressed.

When Lorenzo saw him, he said, "Ah, you've condescended finally to get up, have you?"

Antonio didn't answer.

"And will you condescend to hunt with us?" Lorenzo demanded. "Or will you stay here with your sister while the men bring back deer from the hills?"

"I'm going with you," Antonio told him. He was determined that he'd be what his father wanted. It would be his act of contrition. He could bear, and would, the pain, but only if he paid in pain for his part in Patricio's death. He'd not allow himself ever again to think of Mundo Segura.

But later, when the hunting party rode high in the hills above the ranch, Antonio sighted a buck, a big animal, sleek, proud, with gleaming antlers. Lorenzo gestured at him, and Antonio raised the rifle to his shoulder. Even as he fired, the buck became Patricio staggering from the barn with his hair aflame. The rifle jerked and the shot went wild.

Lorenzo turned away with a contemptuous grimace.

8

"I don't mean to hurry you, Don Esteban, and if you'd like another cup of coffee, I'll be glad to wait, but if you're done would you step outside with me for a little while?" Even as he spoke, Leigh folded his napkin and thrust back his chair.

Esteban followed suit, reflecting ruefully that it was just as well that he didn't want another cup of coffee. Following Leigh from the hotel and around into its rear courtyard, Esteban thought that the gringo, Leigh Ransome, was an unusual man. He'd arrived in Tres Ríos in May last. Now it was January. And he had worked at nothing. Though he lived simply, his hotel room hardly luxurious, his clothes elegant but not the most expensive, he still must have some independent source of income. But what it was Esteban couldn't imagine.

Now as they reached the courtyard, Leigh's dogs set up a loud barking. Esteban concealed his distaste. To him, the caged animals were mere brutes. But Leigh grinned affectionately at the animals.

"The children know that we're here." He pulled off his coat, thrust it at Esteban. "Please hold it for a little while. I always train them at this hour, but if you don't mind waiting, I'd like to show you something when I'm through."

Esteban shrugged. "I don't mind, of course."

But Leigh had already left him. Drawing off his belt, the gringo walked toward the cage. He held the belt doubled, folded once around his knuckles, with the big buckle fitted firmly into his palm and his hand closed into a fist. He flicked the lock on the cage and stepped back three paces.

"Come," he said softly. "Come, Cora. Come, Cal."

They'd grown quickly in the past months, chests deepening, legs lengthening. They surged forward, shoulder to shoulder, their ears laid back, their gleaming teeth exposed in their gaping muzzles.

"Come," he said once more. And then, tossing a bundle of rags to the end of the courtyard, "Kill, Cora. Kill, Cal."

The dogs streaked after the bundle, threw themselves upon it fiercely.

Watching, Esteban swallowed his revulsion. He had to watch what came next, even though he knew it would shock him.

The dogs ripped the bundle to shreds, ripped and tore at it ferociously until it was a mass of saliva-moistened pulp.

Leigh stood waiting. At last, he said softly, "Heel."

Cora's head lifted. She trotted a few steps, then turned back to join Cal.

"Heel," Leigh murmured, eyes darkening. But now he went to them. He seized Cora firmly by the muzzle and brought the belt down hard. The dog struggled, and Cal came running to lunge at his legs. He kicked Cal off, and brought the belt down again and again until Esteban felt the blows in his own flesh.

When Leigh stopped, Cora stood in shivering submission. He thrust her into the cage and turned his attention to Cal.

Esteban stood still, holding Leigh's coat, but closed his eyes so that he would not see. When he looked again, both dogs were back in the cage, cowed and quiet. Leigh allowed the closure to swing open.

"Come," he said, and they leaped out.

"Kill," he said, and they streaked for the shredded bundle at the end of the yard.

"Heel," he said, and this time they immediately came to lie at his feet.

He laughed, reached behind him into a barrel for two hunks of bloody meat, and sent them flying. "Kill," he said softly, and with long yowls the dogs leaped after the meat.

Leigh watched with satisfaction. Soon, with belt and bloody meat, they'd be trained to instant obedience. They'd kill on command. They'd retreat on command. His word, his voice, would be law. He waited until they had eaten, then put them back into their cage and returned to Esteban.

"I'm ready." He accepted his coat, grinning at Esteban. "You don't like my beauties, do you?"

"They seem dangerous to me."

"They're supposed to be," Leigh told him. Then, "Come. Now let me show you."

They walked together across the plaza, Leigh savoring his own hot excitement. He had managed to make six three-day trips into the mountains before winter set in. Each time he'd carried out bags of nuggets and had taken them all the way to Albuquerque to convert them. Now he had amassed a sound base for his fortune, all quietly banked in Santa Fe.

The old man had been smart, and Leigh was smart enough to learn from him. No one would know of the gold. For it was the valley that Leigh wanted, the land itself in all its richness.

He led Esteban past a row of small adobes, and finally stopped. "Here, Don Esteban, here's where I'll build my house. What do you think?"

Esteban looked at the wilderness of brush and tree. From the hard-packed road where they stood, out to the white-covered mountains, there was nothing but raw land.

"It's all mine," Leigh was saying. "As far as your eyes can see. I bought it today."

"You bought it?" Esteban repeated. "Now I *am* surprised."

"You didn't guess that I'm a man of some private means?" Leigh asked, his eyes alight with amusement. "Then how did you think I lived?"

"I never considered it," Esteban lied.

Leigh grinned. "I wanted to be sure I'd settle here before I made any move."

"You're certain now," Esteban said softly.

Through Leigh's mind there floated a picture of the valley in sunlight, and riding across its meadows, Anitra, her hair blowing, her skirts swirling around her tall slender figure. "Nothing could drive me away," he answered.

Esteban heard the passion in Leigh's voice, looked at him quickly, but then turned his eyes to the two old adobes that flanked Leigh's property. "It's too bad you won't be able to get those shacks at the corner. Then you'd have frontage right on the plaza. But I think the families that own them have had them forever, and won't let go."

"We'll see," Leigh answered.

The next day he hammered stakes and laid out the lines for the house he had dreamed of ever since he first saw Tres Ríos.

It would be nothing like the one on the plaza, its white clapboard and wide veranda so like that from which he had been driven in fear, looking back on its ruins with his vacant-eyed father and weeping mother.

Leigh's home would be hacienda-style, which suited the town and the mountains that guarded it. It would have two stories; it would be walled, with barred windows and wooden roof beams and two courtyards. And once built, it would stand forever.

The execution took longer than the planning. But Esteban was a great help to him. It was he who gathered the crew, a mixture of Indians and townspeople, that raised the frame of the house; he who brought in the adobe brickmakers and plasterers, and then the ironworkers to do the outside finishings and the high, curved inside staircase. It was Esteban who had found the furniture maker who built the trastero, the wardrobe, for him and the huge carved headboards for his beds.

Leigh himself designed and built the large wire pen for the dogs in the inner courtyard, and the small low door through which they could enter the house going directly into the room he decided to use as his office. He himself built the high gunrack just inside the front door on which he would keep his rifles, a practice no longer customary in the town, although it continued in the countryside.

A full year elapsed before he was able to move into the house.

That evening, with a tall whiskey in his hand, he

made his first tour as master of the place he had called El Castillo. He looked with pleasure at the whitewashed walls, the wide-boarded floors scrubbed to the sheen of satin.

The furniture was well polished and well placed. Two plush-upholstered heavy chairs with high carved backs had come all the way from Mexico City. The long mahogany table had bounced around in a wagon, crossing the Kansas plains. The tall black vase of baked clay had been made in one of the Indian pueblos, and the paper flowers that filled it had come from the Philippines.

As he examined each detail, he saw a woman before his fireplace, tall, slender, with silken black hair. Her face was heart-shaped, with high cheekbones, and her eyes were a deep clear green. He whispered her name aloud, "Anitra," and saw her smile at him from the tall curved staircase, and saw her rise to greet him from the plush chair. Soon she would be his. As the valley would be his.

That same evening, after the tour of the house, he went down the road to the shack closest to El Castillo. The broken door was opened by an old woman. Her thin gray hair was pulled back from her withered face and tied in a small bun. Her black dress was faded and darned.

Leigh introduced himself and stated his errand. He'd like to buy her house, he said, and though it was worth nothing, he'd pay her well for it, for now that he had seen her, he understood her needs.

Ignoring the bright charm of his smile, she flung an emphatic "No, señor," at him and slammed the door in his face.

That night, and the next, he sent Cora and Cal on two yowling strolls around the old lady's house. They scented at the windows, thrust their muzzles at the doors.

They scattered her meager pile of wood and knocked over her cherished pots of geraniums.

When he went to see her at the end of that week, she refused to open the door, but shouted through the window, "Go away, señor. You have the mal ojo! I'll not look into your eyes again!"

That night he set out a bowl of milk. When a stray cat had eaten its fill, he strangled it and threw it in the old lady's well.

She was gone in four days. He never saw her again. He bought her house and ground for cash from an intermediary.

He obtained the second house even more easily. He went there with the dogs and an official-looking paper he'd prepared himself.

He told the young pregnant woman who opened the door to him that she'd paid no taxes for three years.

"Si, señor," she agreed. "I know. But I have no money. My husband works in Albuquerque. He brings me what he can. But it's only enough to live on."

He explained to her that if she signed the document he proferred, he'd pay the taxes for her, and she'd only owe her rent to him.

What she signed was a bill of sale, but since she couldn't read, she didn't know that. She was evicted two days later, protesting that it wasn't possible. She hadn't sold the house. She and her children moved in with her parents. Leigh never saw her again either.

He built an adobe wall around the town side of his property, enclosing the two newly acquired lots. The land beyond the wall and all the way to the mountains was his, as well, but he didn't need fences there. It was part of his kingdom already.

He continued his friendship with Esteban, gambling with him at the casino, although Esteban could hardly be called a gambler. They rode together, hunted together, and gradually began exchanging small confidences. Those Leigh offered were more fiction than fact.

Esteban never guessed the depth of his friend's interest as he described the bribes he and the other local landowners had paid to try to verify their land grants. Finally he even confessed his need to make a good marriage.

Leigh listened and remembered and planned. He had been in Tres Ríos a full three years before he was ready to act, and when he did, it never occurred to Esteban to wonder exactly when his bad luck began.

One summer night, three hundred of his sheep went into a panic and raced blindly over a cliff to die on the rocks below. This was after Leigh had made a midnight foray into Delagado territory with Cora and Cal racing beside him.

It never occurred to Esteban to wonder why the mountain stream that fed his watering pond was suddenly dammed with boulders and logs. This was after Leigh spent three days doing an artful job of construction.

Esteban wasn't suspicious, but very grateful, when Leigh offered to lend him a goodly sum of cash to pay for replacing the lost sheep, to pay for the labor to clear the dammed-up stream.

When he stammered his thanks, Leigh just said, "Don't worry about it, Esteban. This is just one of the things friends do for each other."

9

In the spring of 1890 there were rumors of smallpox in the city of Santa Fe, whispers of hasty secret burials by candlelight with only the gravediggers as mourners. Thus Lorenzo wasn't surprised when César Vargas proposed that Vicente and Carlota visit Tres Ríos.

César had been successful in confirming Lorenzo's land deeds, even though the cost had been high, and Lorenzo was eager to welcome his kinsman and his family. On the afternoon of César's arrival the two men sat sipping chocolate and exchanging news. Vicente, now twenty-one, and invited to join the two older men, found his attention wandering. Beyond the window, Anitra and Antonio played like children under the white blossoms of the peach trees, while Carlota, prim as befitted her seventeen years, sat on a wooden bench, twirling a black curl around her finger.

It was Anitra that he watched. Although she was well past fifteen, her behavior was disgraceful. She ran, she shouted, she flung her skirts about. And Antonio wasn't a proper brother. He followed her lead, where he should have boxed her ears and made her behave. Vicente told himself that he pitied the man who eventually wed her. That one would pay dearly for her father's neglect.

The sharp breeze, slanting down off the distant mountains, molded her bodice to her breasts. High, round breasts. He could even see the sharp outline of nipples.

A hot twisting gripped his loins and he rose abruptly and excused himself.

In the courtyard Anitra and Antonio continued their game of dodge and tag as if he were invisible. Annoyed, he settled himself beside Carlota, who sighed. "Dios, it'll be a long, dull two months, Vicente."

"I'm afraid so."

"There'll be nothing for us to do. Look at Anitra and Antonio—children still." Carlota yawned, squirmed on the bench. "Vicente, tell me, has father mentioned to you who he thinks to choose for my betrothed?"

"No," Vicente replied. Privately he thought César would probably choose Don Esteban, whose holdings here in Tres Ríos were vast, and for whom César had, over the years, already done a number of favors. Esteban was much older than Carlota, of course. But that didn't matter. He'd provide a good trousseau and no doubt would prove himself an amenable son-in-law.

Carlota grumbled a further complaint about Anitra and Antonio.

"Don't look at them if they trouble you," he answered. For himself, he couldn't look away. Imagining himself part of their flailing play for a minute, he couldn't even rise. He bit hard on the inside of his cheek. At last he could move. He got to his feet and walked to the shadows of the peach trees where Antonio and Anitra now stood brushing blossoms from each other's hair.

He said, smiling in what he thought was a brotherly fashion, "What a pair the two of you make. And I'd heard such good of you! Why, it was told to me that you're as serious as a padre, Antonio. And that you, Anitra, you are . . . are . . ."

She burst into mocking laughter, green eyes agleam behind the thick fringe of black lashes. "I can guess what was said of me, my cousin. You needn't stammer so."

"Nothing bad has come to my ears, I assure you," he said pompously.

She was suddenly no longer the hoyden who had wrestled her brother only moments before. Her red mouth had a flirtatious curl and one black brow was raised teasingly. "Careful, Vicente, my cousin. Think of your immortal soul. Even one small lie, though meant as a kindness . . ."

She looked him up and down, slowly and thoughtfully. She didn't care for what she saw.

Vicente, smarting under her dismissal, turned quickly to Antonio. "Is there a riding trail you recommend? I'd like to see the country while I'm here."

"Of course, Vicente. Let's get the horses now," Antonio said.

Anitra put in, "And I'll come."

"But Anitra," Antonio protested, "you mustn't leave our cousin Carlota to sit alone."

She glared at him. Why did he want to ride off with Vicente and leave her behind? She turned to her cousin. "You'd like to ride, too, wouldn't you, Carlota?"

"In truth, I wouldn't." Carlota touched her curls. "I find the country frightening."

Antonio avoided Anitra's eyes as he led Vicente to the stables.

Anitra watched, her fists doubled at her side. Then a thought came to her and she turned to Carlota. "You said in your letters that you had learned to speak English. I too would like to know the new language of our country. Could you teach me?"

"I'd be glad to try."

"Let's begin now," Anitra cried, drawn to Carlota as she had never been before.

Her absorption was so deep that she suffered no distraction until much later, when Matthew rode into the courtyard. He was dressed for town in a trim brown riding jacket. His chestnut hair curled lightly on his collar, and his narrow sideburns framed his square jaw.

Carlota instantly preened, crying, "Oh, Matthew, how good to see you again," for she'd met him in Santa Fe. "And how is dear Josefa, and dear Don Cipriano?"

"Don Cipriano's not too well," he said. "And Josefa's as usual. Thank you for asking." He turned to Anitra, "Is your father inside? Don Cipriano has sent a message."

She looked up at him, her heart singing. The smile he gave her was a message, too. I love you, Anitra, his look said.

She returned both smile and look as she answered, "Yes, Papa's indoors."

As he went into the house, Carlota said softly, "Dios, I should like to have such a neighbor as that one in Santa Fe, I think."

What was begun that day continued through the whole of the summer. While Antonio and Vicente spent their time together, Anitra sat with Carlota and struggled with a strange new vocabulary. She learned quickly. Soon she had trained her tongue to say, "Thank you," instead of "Gracias," and "You're welcome," instead of "Por nada." Soon she knew all the words for the clothes she wore, the furniture in the hacienda, the scenery beyond it. Her father had frowned when he heard of the lessons, but since Carlota was a guest in the house, courtesy kept him from exploding into open rage. With Carlota's departure, Anitra knew, she'd have to answer to him for the hours she'd spent studying.

At August's end, Vicente and Carlota departed for Santa Fe, and Esteban went with them. He'd had adequate opportunity during the summer to observe Carlota. She was young, pretty, and dutiful, he thought. He supposed she'd bear him several sons to warm his old age. And to have César for a father-in-law was no mean thing.

Those left behind at the ranch settled down to the business of preparing for winter.

Porfirio saw to it that the woodpile grew higher and higher with fresh-cut piñon. The ristras of chile, dried red by the summer sun, were now hung in the storeroom. Long strings of dried beef and mutton were put up on high roof beams. Barrels of dried beans, onions, peppers lined the walls.

One afternoon as Porfirio rode in, Antonio galloped up to join him. "Porfirio, a word with you, if you please." The boy hesitated, then continued in a rush, "I've thought it over carefully through this summer, and I wish . . . would you be so good . . . surely, you, of all people, would know to whom I must speak. Porfirio, I'm thinking of the Brotherhood."

Porfirio's face gave nothing away. He shoved back his big hat and rubbed gnarled fingers along his jaw. "Yes," he answered gently. "Yes, I do know, Antonio. But why do you ask?"

"I want to become a Brother, Porfirio. I must become a Brother." There was green fire in Antonio's eyes, and even though his hands trembled, he was suddenly no longer a boy.

But Porfirio said, "Think on it a little longer than a single summer. You're so young yet. You've time."

"I'll be sixteen in November," Antonio retorted. "Only weeks away. I'm old enough even now."

It was true that he was old enough, Porfirio thought—though not so many boys joined at that age, and it wasn't encouraged. The oath was taken for life, after all, and mustn't be assumed lightly. Still . . . "Why do you want this?" Porfirio asked.

"It's necessary to me," Antonio answered, his voice hoarse with emotion.

"And what of your father? You'll need his permission."

"I'll receive it, I promise you. This time he'll listen to me. It's what I must do, Porfirio. So be my good friend as always. Tell me to whom I must speak."

"You've already done it, Antonio. I'll take you myself to the morada," Porfirio said gently.

Through the months of that autumn, through winter, spring, and summer, for the whole of twelve months, Antonio took instruction, and though it was usual for a novitiate to make his vows during Santa Semana, Holy Week, he pleaded with Porfirio to permit him to embark on his entrada early in the winter when the year was completed.

One morning Antonio arose before dawn. He trudged the long miles from the ranch to the morada beyond Tres Ríos, a light snow falling upon him.

He was wet through, and his dark hair glistened with a powder of white, when he knocked at the morada door.

From within a voice demanded, "Who's there?"

"God knocks at this Mission's door for His clemency," Antonio intoned.

Several voices answered him, "Penance, penance, which seeks salvation."

Antonio whispered, "San Pedro will open to me the

gate, bathing me with the light in the name of Maria, with the seal in the name of Jesús. I ask this confraternity, 'Who gives this light?' "

The voices within spoke together, "Jesús."

Antonio asked, "Who fills it with joy?"

"Maria," came the reply.

"And who preserves it with faith?"

"San José," the Brothers answered.

And then, with Antonio murmuring along with them, the Brothers said, "Thus it's clearly seen that always having contrition, we keep in our hearts Jesús, Maria, and José."

The door opened onto a shadowy darkness wherein a single candle flickered.

Antonio was led inside and taken to the inner room of the meetinghouse.

There, surrounded by the Brothers, Porfirio said, "We've spoken before between us of those duties you wish to take upon yourself, Antonio. I'll mention them to you once more. There's obedience, remember. And the faithfulness in carrying out all of our rites. Loyalty to one's self and one's ideals, and to all the Brothers. Once taken, the vow of secrecy is binding forever." He drew a slow breath. "And for salvation, the mortifying of the sinful flesh through willing and humble self-punishment."

Antonio nodded. "Yes, Hermano Mayor, I remember all of this and I've come to Jesucristo to perform my devotion. I ask the forgiveness of the Brothers if I've offended any of them."

The Brothers answered together, "May God pardon him who is already pardoned by us."

Kneeling, then slowly moving first from one brother to another, Antonio kissed the hands and feet of each.

At last he rose and stood waiting. His heart beat hard

against his ribs. He was frightened now, not so much of what was to come, but that he mightn't bear it as a man.

"You'll remove your shirt now," Porfirio said softly.

Antonio pulled it off, laid it aside, then at Porfirio's gesture, he leaned over, bracing his body with both hands. The long red scar at the base of his throat seemed to burn in the shadows.

Porfirio glanced at him, remembering the night of the boy's birth, then looked at the Sangrador, the one called the blood-letter, whose job it was to inflict the seal of obligation.

Having served as Corregidor for three years, Mundo Segura had been elected to his new post only the previous Santa Semana. He held in his hand a flint sharpened to knife's edge. At Porfirio's nod, he leaned forward. His eyes met Antonio's. They had been brothers in guilt for three years. Now they would be brothers in salvation. Mundo cut into Antonio's back on both sides of the spine, three horizontal gashes. The incisions were deep enough to leave on the tender flesh scars that would last as long as the flesh adhered to the bone. Still, none of the muscles beneath were damaged, and the wounds bled cleanly and freely.

Antonio felt the pain. The small room seemed to spin around him and his eyes burned with tears. But he cried in an exultant voice, "For love of God bestow on me a reminder of the three meditations of the Passion of Our Lord."

The Sangrador raised the disciplina, a whip made of tough yucca fiber. He brought it down, once, twice, three times, over the fresh cuts.

Antonio's arms weakened, his frame quivered. "For love of God bestow on me the reminder of the five wounds of Jesucristo."

The Sangrador glanced sideways at Porfirio, seeking permission. For himself, though he still hated the ricos with all his heart, he felt something for this boy. He was ready to stop.

Porfirio hesitated briefly. Antonio had taken enough. He had proved himself. Yet he asked for more. It was his wish. Porfirio forced himself to nod once again.

The Sangrador brought the disciplina down in five quick hard strokes, then in five more.

Antonio gasped, "Thank you, my brothers," and his arms turned fluid as water. His throbbing body fell forward, and the dimness of the candlelit room faded away into nothing.

He was lifted gently, carried into a corner. His wounds were bathed with a brew of rosemary leaves. There were rounds of prayers. Hymns were sung.

When he returned to consciousness, he joyfully added his voice to the others. Later, he and Porfirio walked together into the fading night.

10

It was Christmas Eve.

Lorenzo alighted from the carriage and turned to help Anitra down. She waited stubbornly for Antonio to join her before allowing her father to take her through the snow and into the courtyard of the village church.

She'd had no chance to speak with her brother since his return from his three-day disappearance. After he had returned home, he avoided her deliberately. He disappeared with Porfirio on unexplained errands. Anyone who came to the ranch he used as a shield to hold between him and herself. He made a distance between them that she couldn't bridge. What she knew of his feelings she knew only by what showed in the unusual lightness of his step, in the straightness of his shoulders, in the voice with which he spoke to their father.

She felt alone. A part of her was gone. . . .

When Antonio finally joined her, she went on toward the church, where Lorenzo took the seat of honor on the first of the plain wooden benches.

Josefa and Matthew, accompanied by Esteban and Leigh Ransome, were close by. Lorenzo ignored Leigh and asked after Don Cipriano. He was ailing still, Josefa said softly, and didn't go about any more than he absolutely had to these days.

She was very pale, as usual, but there were faint tinges of pink in her cheeks, and her too-big eyes seemed to glitter. Nearly twenty-two years old, she was still slight, childlike in form and manner. She sat close to Matthew, her shoulder touching his, Anitra saw.

After one quick hungry look at his face, Anitra turned away. They had ridden together a few times, but he'd never again taken her into his arms, never again kissed her. Still she knew he was unchanged and that one day she would belong to him. Contentment filled her. Soon, under the altar, a group of villagers prepared to perform *Los Pastores*, the religious play passed down word for word through generations.

The play began, but Anitra paid no attention. She felt Antonio stir beside her and looked at him. His eyes were fixed unswervingly on the shepherds who took their places. His hand adjusted his collar, made sure that it covered the long red scar at his throat.

The play went on. The voices of the shepherds rose, fell. The Angel appeared, and Lucifer, too.

Anitra hardly heard the words she'd loved all her life. She looked at Antonio, willed him to turn his head to her. He didn't.

His lips moved. Though she couldn't hear him, she knew that he was whispering along with the actors' chorus. "For He was born for our good. The King of the infinite Heaven! A Virgin pure and chaste, Has given Him birth in Bethlehem!"

A message of hope for mankind . . .

She sighed, turned back to the players, and at last gave herself to the words.

But much later that night, when the hacienda was still, she slipped into Antonio's room. He was standing in the shadows near the window, shirtless in spite of the chill. At the first sound she made, he swung quickly about, to stand silently, staring at her over the candle light.

"I must talk to you," she said.

"It's late, Anitra. I want to think about *Los Pastores*." She came closer. "What's wrong, Antonio?"

He said nothing. It was hard to arm himself against her. For all his efforts in the past four years, he still found the struggle unbearable.

"You've changed," she said softly. "I feel it."

"You think so?" he asked. He was pleased, but he tried not to show it. He moved backward carefully as she approached, until his shirtless body was well hidden in the deep recess of the window.

"Where did you go?" she asked. "What did you do?"

He pretended not to understand.

She smiled at him. "Do you think you can fool me? Where were you when you disappeared for those three days?"

"It's really not your affair." His tone was gentle, reasonable, very adult, and just because of that, it was intolerable to her.

"It is my affair," she snapped. "You're my brother. You ran away into the snow before dawn. You were gone for three days."

"It was something I had to do, Anitra, and wanted to do. Be content with that."

"You say nothing," she cried.

He didn't answer.

"Why are you ashamed? Why is there a secret between us?"

"There's none, I tell you."

She smiled impishly, returned to the attack. "Then where did you go?"

How hard it was to explain, he thought. Though he denied it, there was a secret between them—the vow he had taken. At last he said, "You must accept what I tell you, Anitra. I'm not a part of you. I'm not even like you in any way but face and form. For all the closeness between us, I think my own thoughts, feel my own needs."

"Of course," she said. "Still, tell me what's happened."

He shook his head.

She came closer still, her fingers clasping his shoulder.

He pulled away, and in doing so he half turned, revealing the red scars on his lower back.

She cried out wordlessly, her eyes widening in disbelief. She'd known of the Brotherhood all of her life, had taken it for granted, but it had not directly touched her. Now, quite suddenly, the Brotherhood was her enemy. It stood between her and Antonio.

He said nothing, but his eyes shone proudly. He had, as was required, requested his father's permission, and for the first time in his life, Antonio had seen his father look upon him with respect as he asked, "Do you know what you do?"

"I do, my father. It's what I wish."

"You realize I'm no member myself, Antonio."

"I understand, my father. It's for each man to decide."

"Yes," Lorenzo said. "For each *man*." Then, "I'll not stand in your way. You have my permission. But if you shame me, Antonio, if you take your oath and violate it out of weakness, and bring dishonor to the Martínez y Escobedos, then I'll destroy you with my own hands."

"I'll bring no dishonor on us, my father," Antonio had said softly.

After that there'd been many long talks with Porfirio, who had been good enough to assume the role of his godfather. He'd listened, learned, understood. He'd known at the moment of his initiation the contrition that gave him relief from the pain of Patricio's death.

He didn't suppose that Anitra could understand. She'd never known such guilt as his, nor the glory of relief when it came.

He had returned home purified, having prayed and scourged himself after the symbols of his joining had been applied, and having spent those days afterward in service suggested to him by the Hermano Mayor. His hands were calloused with the work he had done for the old man who could no longer cut the piñon he needed to sell for his food.

Now Antonio knew how he would live the rest of his life. He was of the Brotherhood, and he'd give himself to it. When he was needed, he would go. He'd forever be a part of his people.

At last Anitra said, "Antonio, you can't! You can't!"

"We won't talk about it."

"The order is banned, and has been for a long time," she said sharply. "What would the padre say?"

"He'd say nothing; he'd just look the other way. As he's done for years already."

"Who brought you to it?" she demanded. "Who was your sponsor and who taught you?"

He said nothing.

"Was it Papa? Was it for him that you joined?"

"I've taken a vow of silence."

"I don't care for your vows," she burst out.

"But I do."

"What good are they?" she demanded bitterly. "They're just decaying reminders of the past. Old ideas, old ways, the same that brought our grandmother to her death. The pilgrimage to Chimayo—if we'd not been on that road . . . "

He answered softly, "This'll do no good. I'm sorry, Anitra, but it's no concern of yours."

"No concern!"

She turned away from him, hurt, confused. But she didn't truly believe, even then, that he could separate himself from her. They shared blood and flesh and bone, and had been bound together at their single birth. She didn't believe it was possible for him to deny what was between them.

11

The new year, 1892, was welcomed throughout the valley by the tolling church bells.

A sudden thaw melted the snows in February.

Later on, March winds brought tumbleweeds skimming across the meadows, and the drying earth crumbled, then re-formed as tiny dust devils.

In April the cottonwoods were misted with green.

Don Cipriano gazed longingly out the window. He wanted to ride with his men. It was a busy time on a sheep ranch. But he knew he would ride no more. He thanked God for Matthew, always his strong right arm.

The old man was shrunken and small in the wide bed. He turned his head from the window and sighed, looking at Josefa. "Phaw, what a sour face. And you're such a pretty girl when you smile."

"You must rest, Grandfather," she whispered reproachfully.

"Rest! Rest! There'll be time enough for that. Come, Josefa. Lean closer to me. I want to see you clearly."

She eased herself down, her slender weight hardly disturbing the feather mattress. She forced the curve of a smile to her pale lips. "Now you can see me, Grandfather."

He cupped his hands around her cheeks, frowning. They were warm. Always she was too warm. And her eyes

134

were too bright. He feared for her, but there was nothing he could do. Nothing but this one thing that lay so heavily on his mind. He said gently, "I believe I've done you an injustice, Josefa. I could long ago have arranged a good marriage for you, but I selfishly kept you with me."

"I'd not want to leave you and Matthew," she quavered. "I won't think of it. Who'd take care of me then?"

He went on, "Even so, I had expected to have another year—which would give me time to be certain of your happiness. But I think now I must not wait. Always it was in the back of my mind. Which was a second reason for delaying to look elsewhere for a husband for you. I shall wait no longer. I know how I feel. I must be sure of you, my child. Will you marry Matthew?"

"I've loved him since you first brought him home to us," she said simply. "And he's always taken care of me. He always will, Grandfather."

Don Cipriano sighed. "It relieves me. Now send him to me, Josefa."

When Matthew entered the room, the older man seemed to be sleeping. Matthew stood silently beside the bed. Don Cipriano was the only father he had known, the only family. He was old now and sick, and Matthew feared for him. But when Don Cipriano awakened, Matthew smiled easily. "You wanted me?"

"Closer," the old man said. He patted the quilt. "Here, where I can look at you." Matthew seated himself and Don Cipriano continued. "Why, when I was your age I had two sons. You're a man now. For that, and for my love of you, I ask you, Matthew, will you marry Josefa? Will you be good to her and care for her?"

A heavy weight pressed on Matthew's heart. He loved Josefa, and always had. But as a good and sweet sister.

His body had hungers, strong and driving ones that kept him restlessly turning through the night, but those hungers were never directed toward her. He had a moment's vision of Anitra, which he forced himself to bury. He told himself he had known, unwillingly, for a long time that it would come to this. For this was what Don Cipriano had always wanted. And all that Matthew was, the whole of his life, he owned to Don Cipriano.

"Speak only the truth, Matthew," said the old man. "I won't force you nor beg you. It must be as you wish."

Matthew said, smiling, his voice steady, "It's just what I want. You know that." And it was the truth. For if this was what Don Cipriano wanted, then it was what Matthew himself wanted, too.

Don Cipriano released his hand, sighed. "Then it'll be within the week."

The padre mumbled over the words.

Josefa's voice trembled on her responses.

Matthew spoke with his usual firmness.

Standing between her father and Antonio, Anitra raised her head proudly. She'd allow no one to guess that her heart was breaking. No one, no one must know what she felt.

She wore a gown of gay yellow, and yellow rosebuds in her hair. No one must guess that she'd wept all through the morning, and having finally forced herself to dress, that she had gazed at herself in the mirror and imagined that she wore a white gown and a white veil, and that soon she herself was to be Matthew's bride, soon to lie in his arms.

But he didn't want her. He had chosen Josefa instead.

The padre droned on, and Don Cipriano lay on his pillows and smiled.

136

Anitra closed her eyes. She couldn't look. She remembered too well what had happened three days before when her father had told her of the wedding.

She refused to believe it. She rode wildly to the Diaz ranch and found Matthew, and when she looked into his face, she knew the truth. Even then she refused to believe it.

She said softly, "Matthew, it's not so, is it?"

He nodded.

"You can't marry Josefa!"

"Go home," he said.

She curled her fingers tightly into his vest, and pressed close to him. "But you love me," she cried.

A wave of color moved into his brown face and then receded, leaving a dull pallor behind. The points of light faded from his eyes. He took her wrists and tore her fingers loose from his vest and repeated softly, "Go home, Anitra."

She'd watched as he turned away, left her to stand alone, trembling, but believing at last.

In moments now, the padre would say the words that joined them, and Matthew would be lost to her forever. He would belong to Josefa.

Anitra could bear no more. She took a step back. No one noticed. She took another step. Her father was looking at Don Cipriano. Her brother was looking at the floor. She took another step, and held her breath as her shadow moved across his boots. He didn't stir. The door was just behind her now. She eased it open and slipped out.

In the courtyard she looked wildly about her. Don Esteban's horse was nearby. She climbed into the saddle and galloped out, leaving a rising trail of dust behind her, and the shocked servants whispering in fear.

Tears burned her eyes, but she refused to shed them.

She had wept once for Matthew. Those terrible hours would have to do. He was lost to her. She was almost seventeen years old, and she was through with love.

Josefa was a pale puling thing who never had two words to say. And Matthew was a fool to choose such a bride. Certainly the marriage had made him Don Cipriano's heir. But he'd have inherited the ranch anyway.

Her gown billowed around her, a cloud of yellow sunlight. A curl broke loose from her bound-up hair and slid down to her cheek.

The drum of the horse's hooves on the road was like the drum of her heart. She gave no direction; she let him run. He chose the trail to town, and she hardly noticed until they were suddenly at the plaza. The horse moved to the hitching post before the bank and waited for her to do something. She climbed down, tied him, and went to sit on a stone bench in the plaza.

The sun had lowered by then, had slid behind the mountains, and blue shadows lay across her face. By now, Josefa and Matthew were man and wife. Soon they would lie close and warm in each other's arms. Josefa would hold Matthew . . . and he would be hers.

Anitra's small hands became fists. It wasn't fair. Ah, Matthew, Matthew, you belonged to me. . . .

A voice broke into her reverie. A voice that was deep, rough, yet lightened with laughter. It asked in English, "Ma'am, ma'am, can you tell me the name of this town?"

She looked up. A buggy had pulled to a stop beside her. It was bright yellow with high red-and-yellow wheels, far too light for the bumpy roads of Tres Ríos, and far too light for the man who rode in it.

He was huge, red-faced, with hair so blond that it was almost white. Anitra saw his clothes were covered with a layer of fine dust.

"The town is Tres Ríos, señor," she said.

"Tres Ríos? And where's that?"

"You're very lost, aren't you?"

"I must be. I never heard tell of Tres Ríos." He grinned. "But never mind. I've come a long way today, and Tres Ríos'll do me as well as anyplace else." He stepped down from the buggy and mopped his face. "Ma'am, do you mind if I sit awhile, and you tell me how come you talk the language? I noticed that not many around these parts do."

She nodded, and when he had seated himself, she said, "I'm learning. One day the others will learn, too."

"I'm glad to hear that." He grinned at her and switched to Spanish. "But I could have spoken to you anyway."

She smiled at him, not answering.

"Of course," he went on, "we talk the lingo different in Texas. But at least we try."

She was suddenly stiff. He was a Texan. It was bad enough, in the eyes of the town, that he was a gringo. But to be a Texan, too . . . What on earth was he doing in the territory?

"And I do pretty good, don't I?"

His Spanish, in fact, was terrible. But it would have been rude to tell him so. She contented herself with another smile, and then said, "Talk English, if you don't mind, señor. I enjoy the practice."

"My name's Leonard. How's that for a start?" He grinned. "Leonard Brooks, that is. And, as I told you, I'm up here from Texas." He paused. When she said nothing, he went on, "And as you already know, I'm a stranger in town. But I'm very pleased to make your acquaintance. Or at least I would be, if you'd tell me your name."

"My name is Anitra Martínez," she said.

"Anitra . . . beautiful," he breathed. "I never heard a name like that before. In Texas the girls are all named Mary Lou. And they aren't any of them as pretty as you are."

"You have a pretty tongue," she told him.

"A thirsty one." He leaned closer. "Listen, where can a man get a drink? And somebody to keep him company too? As I said, I'm a stranger, but I'll be staying at least for a while."

She inclined her head toward the casino at the end of the plaza. Its lights flickered against the deepening shadows. It was the safest place in Tres Ríos for a Texan. Rafael Ortiz, a friend of her father's for as long as she remembered, would allow no trouble.

Leonard was saying, "Now I don't mean a broken-down cantina. I mean someplace nice. Where a girl like you could go. And don't worry about money. I'm loaded with silver dollars. I just want to have a good time."

She turned her head, deliberately looked him up and down. She'd never been to the casino, but she saw no reason to tell him so. She said, "It's a nice place, only for very nice people."

"Then you'll keep me company, won't you, chiquita? And tell me about your town?"

A flicker of caution touched her. Her father, her brother . . . The casino was frequented by people who knew her. Within hours word would spread that she'd gone there with a stranger, a gringo. But then she thought of Matthew in Josefa's arms, and she thrust caution away impatiently. She'd show them, show everyone. What did it matter if people talked? She rose, smiling. "Mr. Brooks, I'll be glad to go to the casino with you."

They walked the half block together, he towering

over her. At the threshold, he whistled softly. "Well! I sure didn't expect a place like this. Make the people bigger and blonder and I'd think I was in Fort Worth!"

No one was playing yet, for it was early, and the place was very nearly empty. The few who were there turned and looked as Anitra, with a deep breath, led the way inside.

"We'll take that tidy little table over in the corner," Leonard said.

Rafael Ortiz himself came to stand beside them, his face impassive, though there was a glint of disapproval in his eyes.

It didn't occur to Anitra that it was unusual for the manager of the casino to serve drinks. But he felt it his obligation. He knew perfectly well that she was the daughter of Don Lorenzo.

"Now I'll have me a long tall whiskey, and don't spoil it with water," Leonard said expansively. "We don't like too much water down in Texas where I come from. And you, little lady," he said to Anitra, "what about you, honey?"

"I'll have a . . . a whiskey, too," she told him. "But not so tall, perhaps, and with water, if you please."

The disapproval in Rafael's eyes was sharper now. Old memories flickered through him. The assaults by Texans against the New Mexico Territory . . . the border killings . . . At the same time, he was amused at how well Anitra carried herself. Oh, well, Rafael thought, I'll keep an eye on these two, and get them out as soon as I can.

When he had served the drinks, Leonard took up his glass, hitched his chair closer, and said, "Now here's to you, little lady. You're just what I needed, and just what I came for. So here's to you."

She smiled, hesitantly touched her glass to her lips. The fluid was amber, like liquor, but what she tasted was bitter tea. She shot a quick look at Rafael, but his head was turned away. She didn't know that he watched her in the tinted mirror.

"That's what I came for," Leonard was saying. "A pretty Mexican lady like you."

"I'm not Mexican," she said. "I'm an American."

"Oh, well—" he grinned—"you know what I mean."

"You don't have pretty ladies in Texas?" she asked.

"Not like you."

His face was even redder now, and there was a sheen of sweat on his cheeks. He wrapped his fingers around her arm and leaned even closer, so she was pressed back against the wall. "A senorita . . . that's what I've been wanting. Hot Mexican blood and hot body to warm my cold bed. And what I mean is you, little lady. You're what I've been looking for all my life."

His glass was empty and he waved for another, a gesture repeated with extraordinary frequency in the next hour.

The casino gradually filled. Smoke hung over the tables. Groups of men laughed together, and women circulated, spreading smiles and banter. Yet everyone there was intensely discomfited by his presence.

Anitra sat silently beside him. She neither heard his words nor saw her surroundings. She simply sat, the yellow rosebuds wilting in her hair, waiting in quiet desperation.

An hour later, Leigh entered the casino and went to a gambling table. He placed a bet, then turned to survey the room. When he saw Anitra, his eyes turned dark, and the dimple near his mouth disappeared. Very deliberately he set down his drink and, hands empty at his sides, he crossed the room.

"Pretty little girl," Leonard was mumbling, his hand on Anitra's arm. "Hunted for you all my life. Now I've found you. One more drink and we'll go. You take me wherever you want to. Whatever you want, just say so. I've got plenty of money. Just whatever you want . . . "

Leigh stood at the table, his face stony.

Anitra looked up at Leigh, a mute appeal in her eyes.

He said quietly, "Good evening, Anitra. I'll see you home now."

She half rose, but Leonard held her. "Hey, hey, wait. Where do you think you're going?"

"I must leave you, Mr. Brooks. And I thank you for a pleasant time."

"Leave me," he growled. "Leave me! Hell, we're just getting started. I've been telling you all along what I'm going to do for you. Leave me!" He stopped, for the first time noticing Leigh. Then he grinned. "Sorry, compadre. I can't say as I blame you, but the girl's mine."

"No," Leigh said softly. "No. She's not."

"Say, who the hell are you? What do you want anyway?"

Leigh put his hand on the big man's shoulder. He leaned hard, bracing all his weight on it. At the same time, he reached over, deliberately removing the big man's hand from Anitra's arm. "I'm Leigh Ransome," he said softly.

Anitra rose in a single fluid motion. A yellow bud fell from her hair to the table.

"Hey, what the hell?" Leonard shouted.

Leigh leaned harder. "I'm taking Señorita Martínez home. I'd advise you to sit still and have another drink."

143

"Mister whoever-you-are, I didn't ask for your advice." Leonard pushed Leigh's arm away and got to his feet, wavering. "Now where'd she go, damn her eyes? Where'd she go? I'll teach her to run out on me."

"Damn your own eyes first," Leigh told him. He caught the big man by the shirt and flung him into his seat. The chair tipped back. Leonard went sprawling.

Leigh took Anitra's arm and led her from the casino.

Leonard, shouting curses, got to his feet again. A chair was thrust under him and he fell into it.

A small dark-haired girl put a drink in his hand, sat near him, and cooed, "Señor, don't you like this place? Isn't it nice? Tres Ríos is proud of its casino, you know."

Her name was Margarita Valerio, and she had worked three months for Rafael. He had signaled her to join the big ugly Texan, and she had obeyed. Rafael would have preferred to throw the man out, but considered it safer to keep him here until Anitra and Leigh were well away from the plaza. Margarita would divert him nicely. That would be better than having a brawl in the place.

"Thank you, Señor Ransome," Anitra was saying. "A thousand thanks. I can't tell you how . . . "

He touched his fingers to her lips. "Don't. It doesn't matter. I'm glad I was there. Now I'll take you home."

"Oh, no, it's not necessary, I assure you. I have my . . . I have Don Esteban's horse."

"I'll see to that as well." He smiled down at her. "Don't argue. I'll take you to the ranch."

She drew her yellow skirt around her. "I'll ride back and . . . "

"You're a very argumentative young lady," he said, his smile broadening, and added, "just as you were an argumentative little girl."

"Still, I do know my way home."

"No matter." He led her to his buggy and helped her inside.

She was suddenly giddy with relief. She said, "Oh, did you see his face?"

"I did. He wasn't pleased to lose you, was he?"

"Pleased to lose me indeed! Why, he never had me."

"He considered otherwise."

"I ought to explain."

Leigh grinned at her. "No. You oughtn't to."

She was silent for a long time. They left the faint lights of town behind them. Sheep bleated in the meadows. A dog barked and was answered by a long yowling chorus. Finally she said, "It's good to be free, with no need to answer to anyone."

"Of course it is. But you say that as if you're just finding it out, Anitra."

"I am," she said defiantly.

He put his head back and laughed. "Do you expect me to disapprove?"

They were near the ranch when a long wailing whistle floated across the still air.

She raised her head, her eyes glowing. "Oh, listen—a train."

"The Denver and Rio Grande, going to Espanola."

"My brother and I, when we were children, used to ride together and try to catch it." Her breath caught in her throat. It seemed so long ago. "Oh, we did it many times, flying like leaves on the wind, but always we were too late. The train was gone when we reached the gorge."

"And you've never seen a train then?"

She shook her head.

"I'll show you one, Anitra. One of these days, I'll take you down to Santa Fe on the Denver and Rio Grande."

It would never happen, she knew. Her father would never allow it. But she demanded fervently, "Do you promise?"

"One of these days. Yes, Anitra. I promise."

When they reached the ranch, she insisted that he leave her at the big gate to the courtyard. He helped her down from the buggy and they stood together under the big bell, where five years before he had held her in his arms while they called in the men from the search for Antonio.

"Good night," she said. "And thank you for everything."

He couldn't have stopped himself then if he tried to. He'd waited a long time for her. He'd wait a little longer. But he'd have at least this much. His arms closed around her. He held her close to him, feeling her sudden stillness.

She stiffened. She thought of Matthew and Josefa. They'd been together now for hours. Man and wife for hours.

Leigh thought he had frightened her. "It's all right," he said softly, and bent his head and gave her a light kiss on the lips. Then he let her go.

She fled, as she had fled once before, into the silent house.

He turned in at the gate to El Castillo, and hearing a noise in the road, stopped to look. A yellow buggy went rattling by, with Leonard Brooks lolling drunkenly on the seat. Leigh went in, closed the gate behind him, and forgot the Texan.

Inside, Leigh looked at the narrow black iron stairway that led to the second floor. He could imagine Anitra coming down to meet him, floating in a gown of red silk. He could imagine her holding her slender arms out to him.

The dogs barked, hurled themselves at the closed door of the room he used as his office. He went in, talking to them. "That'll do, Cora. Enough, Cal. The two of you get outside now."

They slipped through the small door that allowed them entry to their courtyard cage and hurled themselves against the wire mesh that held them prisoner.

He lit a lamp and sat at his desk. Opening a drawer, he dropped into it a single wilted yellow rosebud.

Then he spread before him a map of the valley. The acres surrounding El Castillo were colored in red. Here and there across the valley there were other red areas. Soon the valley would all be filled in with his color.

He leaned back in his chair and smiled.

12

The yellow buggy continued on the road that led out of town, while Leonard sucked broken knuckles and wiped sweat from his eyes and grumbled, "It's just one hell of a town, that's all. Why anybody'd come here, I don't know, and why anybody'd stay, I don't know. And that's why I'm going, I guess. Just a stinking hell of a town."

He didn't notice the three riders that followed him, moving not along the road, but through the adjacent meadows. He didn't see the three shadows merge into one, finally forming a single barricade on the road before him.

The buggy suddenly jerked to a stop, and he sat forward, shouting at the horse, "Damn you! Get on with it!" Then he saw the men. "Hey, what's that? What do you want?"

"You, señor," Porfirio said softly. "We want you." His face was aged, hollowed like wood shaped by the carver's tools.

"Me?" said Leonard. "Go away, hombre. You don't want me for anything. I've seen your town and I'm leaving it. And leaving it the way I found it, too."

"Not quite, señor."

Leonard scarcely remembered what had happened after Leigh took Anitra away. It was a quick, drunken blur

148

in his mind. The girl had been smiling and sweet, but he was no longer sure that she was the same girl he'd spoken to in the plaza. They'd spent a while, he didn't know how long, sitting at the corner table. Then, staggering on whiskey-weak legs, and taking the girl with him, he'd left a stack of silver dollars behind him.

"And now I must return to the cantina," Margarita had said when they reached the chill air outside. "I've my job to do, señor."

He laughed thickly, "Oh, forget the job. What're you talking about? I've been waiting a long time. I've been waiting all my life. A hot little body to hold to me, a greaser body slick and sweet, that's what I came here for, and that's what I'm going to have."

She looked up into his face, and answered with dignity and pride, "Señor, I drank with you and laughed with you. Because that is my job. But I won't go anywhere with you. I'm not that sort. Perhaps I made a mistake to see you safely out here."

He grinned. "No, you never made a mistake in your life."

She turned swiftly, her skirts flaring. The casino was only a few steps away.

He caught a fold of her skirt in his big fist and hauled her back to him and slapped a hand over her mouth. He half dragged, half carried her into the thickets of the plaza. When he tried to kiss her, she cried out. He slapped at her mouth, and she bit his hand. She kicked and clawed, and he forgot what he had wanted before. His hand became a fist and he hit her hard enough to knock her free of his grasp. When she fell, he threw himself on her and hit her again and again. She was still beneath the hammering blows, only moaning softly. Her face blackened with blood, eyes closing beneath folds of swollen and torn flesh.

After a while he got up and staggered to his buggy, and still grunting that all he wanted was a soft sweet Mexican girl to love him, he set out on the road out of town.

"You're not leaving Tres Ríos quite the way you found it," Porfirio said again.

The three had been chosen by straws after a quick meeting.

Eustacio Rivera had found Margarita after Rafael, concerned that she hadn't reappeared, had sent him to look for her. She lay where Leonard had left her an hour before, bleeding and torn and hardly able to gasp out the few words needed to tell what had happened.

The short straws were held by Porfirio, Antonio, and Mundo Segura.

This wasn't a task that Porfirio enjoyed. But it was necessary. Who else would protect the people from predators such as this man? Who, if not the Brotherhood?

The April moon spilled light through the trees, and Leonard saw clearly the implacable faces before him. They were unmasked, and he knew he would recognize them if he saw them again. But suddenly he was afraid. He brought his whip down hard. The horse reared in his traces, but the weight of three bodies, leaning hard into their grasp on the bridle, held him.

"What do you want?" Leonard bellowed.

Mundo seized the whip from his hand, hauled him over the edge of the buggy.

When he hit the earth, he was at the bottom of a mass of bodies. Six fists smashed into his face, six arms held him, six legs clamped him into helpless submission while the stars spun overhead.

A black mist covered the sky, and knives flashed through it. He felt their sting and yelled, and yelling he died.

The three men rolled him quickly into a thick Indian blanket, put him over a horse's back.

Antonio took charge of the yellow buggy. Within an hour, it would be dismantled and buried.

Porfirio and Mundo rode into the mesa, across it to the river gorge.

There they took the big, heavy body down and dragged it to the edge of the cliff. Mundo removed all the money from the body and handed it to Porfirio, who said, accepting it, "It will go into the poor box tomorrow."

They shoved the body to the edge of the cliff where it caught on a yucca spike, and they had to tear it free. Finally they sent it spinning over. It bounced from rock to rock, caught and pulled loose, and plummeted into the river to be sucked down and disappear forever.

"One less, Hermano Mayor," Mundo said to Porfirio. "One less to trouble us, amigo."

"Yes, but there'll be more and more to take his place. Always there'll be more of them, I think," Porfirio answered tiredly.

13

Lorenzo slapped his hand on the table so hard that the cups danced in their saucers, and a splash leaped from the spout of the coffeepot, staining the cloth.

Dora backed hastily from the room. She had seen the storm coming for the past ten days and didn't want to watch it break.

Lorenzo shouted, "You'll do as I order, Anitra. First you'll go to Don Esteban to apologize for taking his horse. Then to Don Cipriano for your wicked abuse of his hospitality! And then to Josefa and Matthew, for your intolerable rudeness to them! Antonio will accompany you to make sure you follow these orders to the letter."

Anitra sat straight in her chair, looking into his red face. Anger seemed to bloat the whole of his body. His gray-streaked beard was thrust at her like a weapon. "Do you hear me?"

"Yes, Papa. I hear you."

"And you'll go this very morning. To slip away during the nuptial service . . . "

"I'll go," she said unwillingly. "But Antonio needn't accompany me."

Lorenzo flung himself back in his chair. "He needs, and he will. You're no longer a child. You can't run about as if you were. You're seventeen and a woman, I'll thank you to remember. And I'll thank you to remember who you are as well." His gravelly voice dropped. "Besides, you know yourself what happened. You've heard about the girl, right there in the plaza . . . beaten so badly . . . "

Anitra dropped her gaze to her hands and folded them together. She didn't want her father to read the shame in her eyes. She'd heard a bit here and there and had been able to figure it out for herself. Soon after she left Leonard Brooks, the girl in the casino had joined him, and they'd left together. And then . . .

"And you were there yourself! With some gringo! Don't think I don't know!"

She rose quickly. "If I'm to go, then it should be now. Will you excuse me?"

He was irritated at having been interrupted in his tirade, but he nodded. Since the day of the wedding he had ordered her to remain at the hacienda until he allowed otherwise. And remain she did—until today.

Antonio followed her out, glad, too, to escape his father's presence. The memory of Leonard Brooks's death weighed heavily on him. No matter that justice was done, with Porfirio and Mundo at his shoulder—he still found himself reliving those moments too often.

"In the courtyard?" he asked Anitra.

"A moment only. I'll change to a riding skirt." There was a brightness in her eyes and he wondered if it were the excitement of going out at last, or if the humiliation of the coming interviews were troubling her.

But he saw, when they reached Don Esteban's hacienda, that she was not humbled at all.

She accepted his welcome coolly, seated herself, and said, "My father sent me to apologize to you for taking your horse from the Diaz ranch. I'm sorry."

He grinned at her. "No matter, Anitra. And the horse was returned the next day. As you probably already know."

"I didn't. But I'm glad to hear it."

Antonio stirred restlessly. He was relieved that his father wasn't here to witness this. There was a strangeness about Anitra.

She was saying, "You've known Señor Ransome for a long time, Don Esteban."

"I've known him for . . . now let me see . . . ah, yes, for nearly six years." Now it was Esteban's turn to stir restlessly. His eyes sought the blackened fireplace in the corner. It would have to be whitened. And the walls around it, too. He sighed. The whole room needed a white-washing. How was he to bring Carlota Vargas y Escobedo to such a place? And what of her trousseau? He supposed he must buy her fabrics for not less than seven gowns—though perhaps five would do, if he were pinched. And he would be—unless Leigh would help him again. Of course, the debt owing was already a large one. Yet Leigh had always been generous. The man's private income must be truly substantial.

"And I have known him as long," Anitra was saying, "though not well."

The tone of her voice caught Esteban's attention. He stared at her. "Your father . . . " Esteban's voice trailed off. He didn't know what to say.

Antonio, too, was staring at her. She was up to something. He knew that glint in her eye. He got to his feet and said, "Anitra, we should be on our way."

She ignored him. "Don Esteban, your friend, Leigh Ransome, he's well received in Tres Ríos, isn't he? Except by my father."

"Well enough," Esteban answered uneasily.

She shrugged, rose. "No matter. My father has a closed mind."

Esteban didn't reply. He also rose, grateful that the conversation was at end, although he didn't know why.

But the conversation was not at an end for Anitra. After she and Antonio had bidden Esteban goodbye and set out for the Diaz ranch, she continued, "Papa lives in a dream. He, and the others like him, they immerse themselves in the past. The real world lies beyond the panels of their carved doors, Antonio. Beyond their thick adobe walls and enclosed courtyards."

"You exaggerate," Antonio protested.

She gave him a look of open contempt. "My brother, you live in a dream, too. You, with your meetings by night, your whisperings by day. You and your Brotherhood, you're a part of the dream world, too. It's been almost fifty years since the American flag was raised over Santa Fe. What purpose is there in dwelling upon what was before then? It's gone, done, finished."

"No," he said. "No, Anitra. Never. We remain ourselves."

"It's finished for me," she told him.

Don Cipriano still lay upon his pillows. He smiled when Anitra entered the room alone. She made the sun seem brighter, he thought, and had there not been Josefa to think of, he'd have welcomed her as his own daughter.

Once again, as she made her apologies, there was nothing humble in her manner. She said, "Don Cipriano, my father insists that I tell you that I regret that I left the wedding ceremony as I did, and that I ask for your forgiveness."

"Phaw, what foolishness is that? Forgive you for what,

my Anitra? Womenfolk always cry at weddings, don't they? And if you sought privacy for that, why should you apologize?"

"You're very kind, Don Cipriano. You've always been so."

"And why not? I sat with your grandmother, with Doña Lupe, bless her memory, on the night you and Antonio were born." He drew a ragged breath. "Matthew and Josefa were there too when you came into this world. And so I ask you, my Anitra, be good to them. They'll need you as a friend."

"I will," she said softly. But there was a coldness in her. She never wanted to see Josefa and Matthew again.

Moments later, she did.

Josefa was ensconced on the sofa, a lace handkerchief in her thin hands. When Anitra repeated what had become the familiar words, Josefa cried, "No, no, I don't want to hear! What does it matter, my friend? You were faint from the warmth, perhaps. Or the padre spoke too long, loving the sound of his own voice as he does." She glanced at Matthew, "He does, Matthew. You said so yourself."

Matthew nodded, smiled easily. "It was too much for Don Cipriano as well. In place of an elaborate ceremonial, the padre made all the speeches."

Anitra rose, not looking at him, but Josefa seized her hand, drew her close. "Anitra, you must come to me often. We'll have good times, you and I and Matthew."

"We will," Anitra agreed, and still she didn't look at Matthew.

Returning across the meadows, she didn't speak to Antonio. She dismissed Matthew from her mind, thinking, I'll show him. I'll show them all.

Then her imagination was filled with thoughts of Leigh Ransome.

Late that same afternoon, Lorenzo watched as Antonio rode off.

He shrugged, turned away. In the past he had lost Antonio to Anitra. Now it was the Brothers who called and who were heeded. Again Lorenzo shrugged. It was what Antonio wanted. And he, himself, he felt some pride in that. Yet always he was afraid that the boy's weakness would finally shame him.

Soon Lorenzo went in search of Anitra, meaning to ask her how she had found Don Cipriano.

She sat in a chair before the small fire in her room. The lamp at her elbow was high, a brightness falling on her hair and face, on the magazine in her lap. An American magazine, he saw immediately. In a new surge of fury, he forgot the question that had brought him there.

"What's that you're reading?" he demanded.

Her fingers closed tightly around it. "You can see," she said coolly.

"English," he snorted. "You waste your time, your eyesight."

"I don't think so. And even you might be interested. It's *Harper's Weekly* for July twelfth, 1890. Yes, 1890. It's two years old. But what does that matter? I'm reading about Las Vegas in the New Mexico Territory. You might learn from it—if you knew English."

"I've forbidden you such trash in the house," he roared. "You defy me again. And I won't countenance that."

He seized the magazine, dragged it forcibly from her clasped hands and lashed it hard across her face. "I'll put a stop to it if I have to flog Porfirio. He's to bring you no such stuff from the city of Santa Fe. I won't have it!"

She sat as if frozen. Slowly her face reddened. "It wasn't Porfirio who brought it to me."

"Then who? I demand to know. I order you to tell me."

"It wasn't Porfirio," she lied again. "And I'll not say who. I'll not be the excuse for you to use your whip."

He flung the magazine at her and stalked from the room. His temples were throbbing. He felt a flicker of pain in his throat. He dropped into the chair in the library and buried his head in his hands.

Alone, Anitra picked up the magazine that had fallen to the floor. She closed the door her father had left ajar and went to the big carved chest that stood at the foot of her bed.

She smoothed the rumpled pages, then put it carefully away with her other English materials—all sent to her by Carlota, all carried by Porfirio, usually wrapped in lengths of yard goods. She lowered the chest lid gently, turned to the window.

Beyond the walls of the courtyard she saw the tips of the mountains. A buzzard wheeled there, making lazy black circles against the fading afternoon light. Suddenly she couldn't bear to remain indoors. She wanted to feel the wind on her cheeks, to outrun the violence of her feelings.

She went to the stable, ducking under the kitchen windows to avoid being seen by Dora. The air was crisp, now that the sun was lowering in the west. She tightened her thick woolen cloak, drew on heavy gloves.

The bay nickered as she saddled him and she said, "Oh, yes, you're like your mistress all right. You want to.be free, too."

She mounted quickly and rode through the court-yard into the road, kicking the bay into a gallop.

Leigh, some distance away, riding on one of his frequent surveys of the valley, drew up and watched.

Her cloak blew out behind her, as she lifted her face toward the sinking sun.

Deep hot hunger stirred in him. She hadn't been out of his thoughts for a moment in these past ten days. He wanted her as he wanted the land that spread from mountain edge to mountain edge before him.

He watched until she disappeared into a grove of cottonwood trees, her silhouette dark against their bare white trunks. Then he set out after her.

She slowed as she entered the stand of trees, listening, her eyes searching the dried brush. It was very still here. No birds sang, no leaves whispered.

Her hands went slack on the reins when she saw the morada in the clearing. A single window seemed to glare blackly at her, warning her away.

This was the place to which Antonio had come. It was here now that his heart, his mind, belonged.

She slid down from the saddle, let the reins trail. The bay stamped and snorted. She gave him an absent pat, then took a step toward the morada. There was no one about. The clearing was empty. The sky arched twilight over the bare trees.

There was a sudden flicker of movement in the brush. She saw it from the corner of her eye and turned her head. An old woman stood still, regarding her. Then behind her there was another woman. Five small dirt-stained sheep gathered to nudge each other in the clearing, and oversee-ing them were two young boys with tall staffs.

No one spoke. No one made a sound. But she felt a

hard, cold animosity seep into her from those who faced her. She finally said, "Good evening? How are you?"

There was no response. The two women glared at her as she moved slowly back until she reached the bay. He put his head down when she remounted. His neck muscles quivered, and his shoulders grew rigid. She whispered to him, flicked the reins. He tossed up his head, took two steps, and stopped.

The others remained unmoving. But the clearing had darkened, the shadow seeming to emanate from the morada itself.

Again she urged the horse on with her reins, and once more he took two steps. That was when Leigh rode into the clearing.

Even as she knew relief, she knew joy, too. For Leigh was why she had ridden this way, to the edge of town, to where, she had thought, his property began.

He didn't look at the morada. He seemed not to see the two women frozen in their places in the brush. He ignored the sheep and the two boys.

He came directly to Anitra, touching the brim of his big hat. "Has your horse gone lame on you?"

"Yes," she said. "I think so, Señor Ransome."

"I'll have a look." He swung down from the saddle, examined the bay's rear right hoof briefly, then nodded.

She kept her eyes firmly fixed on his face, but knew the others were watching. By full dark, word would have spread through the valley that she had come to the morada. Word would have spread that she'd met Leigh Ransome, the gringo. By morning, even her father would know.

She lifted her chin. Let her father rave and imprison her in the hacienda. She didn't care.

Leigh said, "Come with me. I'll have your horse reshod for you."

"Thank you, Señor Ransome. You seem always to be doing me a favor these days."

He grinned, taking up the reins of her horse and leading her through the clearing and over a small wooden bridge that crossed an acequia.

She followed without looking back, but knowing that the two of them were watched until the clearing was left far behind.

They went together across the fields.

"My house," he said, gesturing ahead.

"I've heard of it from Don Esteban. And of course, it's the talk of Tres Ríos."

"And now you'll see El Castillo for yourself." He led her through the back gates and onto the patio.

Cora and Cal instantly set up a howl, flinging themselves against the wire that penned them.

She shuddered.

"They can't get at you," he said laughing. "And if they could, they wouldn't hurt you. Not with me here."

"I've never seen such dogs," she told him.

"Not many have." He went on, "I've bred them, and they've given me a litter for my trouble. See?" He pointed to a smaller pen, where five puppies yelped and clawed the wire around them.

As she looked at them, he turned the horses over to a stable hand, directing that the bay be reshod. Then he went toward the house, but Anitra didn't follow.

She was suddenly without strength. El Castillo loomed before her in the bare and uncultivated patio like a prison, though its ironwork window bars were wrought in beautifully molded vine leaves.

He touched her arm and asked, "What's wrong, Anitra? You're trembling."

"I don't know," she said.

"Tinita will fix you a cup of coffee. And we'll talk. You'll feel better then."

He led her inside to a small parlor where she sank gratefully into a comfortable chair before the hearth. Leigh looked at her joyfully. He'd imagined her sitting there, just like that, a hundred times.

"Did you visit the morada for a reason?" he asked.

"Oh, no," she cried, thinking of the silence of the clearing, the suddenness with which the women and boys had appeared. It was as if they'd been waiting there for her. But they couldn't have been. No one had known she'd go that way. Not even she herself.

"Have you been inside it?" Leigh asked.

"Of course not." She glanced sideways at him. Then, "You know what it is?"

"I've made it my business to know. It's on my land."

"On your land? Why don't you burn it to the ground then?" she demanded. "Why do you allow it to be used as it is!"

"There's no reason to stop it." He paused while Tinita served the coffee and withdrew.

"I don't approve of the Penitentes," Anitra said stiffly.

"Nor do I. But that's something else again."

When Tinita returned, saying that the horse was ready, it was too soon for Leigh. He wanted Anitra to stay. He wanted to brush his lips lightly against hers as when he'd last seen her.

But she made ready to leave. He put both hands on her shoulders and turned her face up to his. "Anitra, say my name. Say 'Leigh.' Say it once."

"Leigh," she said softly, as if rolling it along her tongue to taste its flavor. Then again, "Leigh."

He bent his head, and his eyes were dark. When he spoke his voice was harsh. "I'm going to have you, Anitra. I'm going to have you, and soon. You're going to marry me, you know. You're going to be mine forever."

She felt the need in him, the passion.

"Soon, Anitra. But it must be right and joyful and proper. I'm going to court you and everyone will know it. And then I'm going to marry you."

She thought of Matthew and brief pain flickered through her. She looked up at Leigh not knowing how to answer.

Leigh said, "Don't say anything now. You don't have to. I don't expect it. I just want you to remember. You belong to me."

He bent and kissed her cheek, and then her lips, his arms tightening in possession, and she pressed closer to him, her arms going around his neck, her mouth opening under his in surrender.

By next morning, Lorenzo had heard from three different sources that Anitra had ridden into Tres Ríos alone. Worse, that she had met with Leigh Ransome and gone to his house.

Over breakfast he said in an even voice, "I've told you that you're not to go away from the ranch alone. And you have. I've told you not to consort with that gringo Ransome. And you have."

"Everyone else likes him," she answered.

"I've no interest in everyone else's opinion."

"I realize that," she retorted.

"And you keep a civil tongue in your head," Lorenzo yelled. "You'll not see the man again. That's final."

But in mid-July Don Cipriano died.

Leigh was at the funeral with Esteban. At the graveside she smiled at him, sensing that Lorenzo stirred beside her.

She saw him again later at the wake called the velorio, where the mirrors were covered with black cloth, and black crepe lay at the feet of the bultos of the Virgin of Guadalupe and San José and Santo Niño, and the men of the ranch walked around the bier, chanting prayers for the repose of the old man's soul.

Matthew had stood stiffly beside the weeping Josefa and Anitra had cried, too. She had loved Don Cipriano, and he had always been good to her. If only he'd been her father, everything would be different now.

She was about to speak with Leigh, but Josefa threw herself into Anitra's arms, crying, "Oh, you must come and visit me. Oh, I need you so, Anitra. It's terrible to be alone. I have no one now, no one but my Matthew. You must come, Anitra."

"I'll come," Anitra whispered. "I promise you, I'll come," and over the weeping girl's black-clad shoulder she saw Leigh watching, saw the hunger in his eyes, and knew his passion again, and thought, If only you were Matthew. . . .

14

She was virtually a prisoner at the ranch.

When she left, it was only to go to church or to visit Josefa, and even then Antonio rode with her, or else Lorenzo himself accompanied her.

But her visits with Josefa held little joy, for she must then see Matthew and remember the pain of her loss. To avoid that, she thought of Leigh. Beside him, she told herself insistently, Matthew was no more than a boy.

So the visits to Josefa, though an escape from the hacienda, were begun with dread, and ended always in a vast impatience. Josefa, growing paler by the week, lay on the big settle in the sala hour after hour, coughing into her handkerchief.

On this day in early August, however, Josefa had insisted on dining with the others, and had asked for wine at the noonday meal. She had had three glasses of it, though Matthew, laughing, had warned her against the last, and then, yawning, she had taken to her settle again.

Antonio and Matthew went out, and Anitra, relieved of Matthew's presence, had watched the wine overtake Josefa and the easy tears begin to gather.

"I'm so afraid," Josefa said at last, "to be alone. Who'll care for me?"

"Alone?" Anitra asked impatiently. "You have your husband. Whom else do you need?"

"He's so restless, Anitra." Josefa's black eyes were big in her pale face. "He walks the floor at night. I hear him . . . I hear those footsteps. And always they seem to be going away, going away from me, Anitra. And then what will I do?"

"You hear them?" Anitra demanded. "*Hear* them?"

Josefa's pale cheeks grew pink, and tears glistened on her lashes. "It's not as if I can be everything to him," Josefa said. "I'd want to be, but it's not possible, Anitra. I . . . we are as brother and sister. No more. We'll never be more. Don Cipriano never realized that I couldn't bear it. Nor could I bear it should Matthew leave me."

"He won't," Anitra said. "You seek for things to fear."

"If you could help me," Josefa whispered. "I'm so dull. We see each other every day. When you come, oh, it's like laughter has come into the house. He's different after you've been here. I see it, feel it. If only . . . ah, Anitra, if only I could be sure that what I fear won't happen. That some day he'll no longer love me as a brother, no longer love me, and leave me alone in this empty place to die."

Anitra jumped to her feet. "What talk is this, Josefa? You're not going to die. You're young and there's nothing wrong with you. You've only to move about more and ride in the good sun and air. You've played at illness all your life, and now it's second nature to you. But all you need do is get up from that settle and throw away that damnable handkerchief and swallow that damnable cough, and then you'd be well!"

A drowsy smile lit Josefa's face. "How simple you make it sound, Anitra." She raised her head. "They're coming. Antonio and Matthew. I hear them in the courtyard."

Anitra reseated herself, spread her skirts demurely around her, relieved that the confidences were over. Matthew had never held Josefa in his arms, and never would. He'd married her, but he had no love. Anitra felt contempt for him crowd her throat.

On the way back to the ranch, she was caught in sudden hilarity. She laughed and laughed until the tears poured down her face, while Antonio frowned at her.

It was only three weeks later that Don Lorenzo seemed to relent in his strictness and suggested the trip to Santa Fe for Carlota's wedding. At last Don Esteban had managed to organize his finances and make the necessary arrangements.

During the whole of the wedding party Anitra moved in a dream. She was sensible of the silk of her pink gown where it stroked her body and clasped her breasts in delicate folds. She heard the rustle of the many petticoats beneath, whispering against the curve of her thighs. She felt the weight of her hair, drawn up at the back of her head in a tiny circlet of pink roses from which the pale lace mantilla fell in perfect folds. She had expected an argument from her father over the grownup headdress, and she braced herself to remind him that she was only months from her eighteenth birthday. Oddly, there had been no argument. He'd looked at her and nodded his approval. Even that seemed part of the dream from which she must soon awaken.

It seemed to her that Santa Fe's most brilliant society had been invited to the wedding, but she didn't listen to the conversation around her. She heard only the sweet strains of music and the rise and fall of soft teasing laughter. She saw only the bright patterns of color made by the gowns of the women as they danced by in the arms of dark-clothed men. She breathed only the rich warm scent of the roses that hung like trailing golden nuggets along the adobe walls.

Lorenzo said, "Carlota is a comely bride."

Antonio nodded, turned to Anitra. "You'll be happy to have her live in Tres Ríos, I think."

Anitra agreed enthusiastically. Until a few hours before, she had actually been indifferent to this prospect. But Carlota had arranged a few moments of privacy while she was being gowned. She had hugged Anitra, laughing, "Oh, now we shall soon begin our English lessons again, my cousin. Although I confess to you there was a great noise in this house a month back when my father had read what your father had written to him. Dios! I gather Don Lorenzo was irate and didn't mind saying so! And my father did speak sharply to me for sending you books and papers. But then I reminded him to have a look at our guest list with all the Americans on it. If he and I and Vicente knew no English, how would we fare? And then I drew myself up and reminded him I'd soon be a married woman, and he laughed and agreed, and said after today my husband would have to take the responsibility. And I know Esteban . . . he'll not stop us."

So there were to be English lessons again, and plainly Carlota would prove to be a help in circumventing Lorenzo's strictures—if she could manage Esteban. And Anitra thought she could.

"Carlota may not be so happy about Tres Ríos herself when she knows it better," Lorenzo said thoughtfully. "After all, in Santa Fe, she knows everyone. The Governor himself is here, and with him three members of the Territorial House, and one of the Senate. Esteban can offer her no such company in Tres Ríos."

At that moment Carlota stepped from the house. A wave of applause swept the lantern decorated patio. The dancing stopped and the music faded away into a fanfare of trumpets.

This was the third gown Carlota came out to display. She had seven, given to her by Esteban to celebrate their marriage. It was the custom to wear each one for a little while and then to change to another. For herself, Anitra considered it foolish to spend one's wedding party putting on a gown, then taking it off to don another, all to prove a new husband's generosity and wealth.

The music began, and Anitra hummed with it, while her eyes searched for familiar faces at the small candlelit tables set up along the walls.

Matthew and Josefa had come down alone, and Leigh had ridden with Esteban. Lorenzo frowned when he heard that the gringo had been invited, but it was, as he said sourly to Anitra, César's house. Their cousins could invite whomever they pleased.

Vicente was talking with a group of men only a few feet away. As soon as she saw him, she averted her gaze and half turned to present him a slim powdered shoulder. But she was too late.

He came immediately toward them.

She tugged Antonio's arm. "Perhaps we could dance?"

And then Vicente was asking, "Don Lorenzo, may I have the pleasure of this dance with Anitra?"

She would have refused, but Lorenzo smiled broadly. "Of course you may, Vicente. Anitra will be delighted."

She wasn't delighted. But she had no choice except to step forward, to allow Vicente's arms to close around her.

He remembered that even as a twelve-year-old she

had caught and held his eye. But now—now she was beautiful. It never crossed his mind that she made no attempt to flirt with him only because she was indifferent. Instead he felt a growing heat in his body as he looked at her. If he were to have his way, her future would be settled soon. He had already spoken to his father, who'd promised seriously to consider Vicente's request and had seemed, judging by his manner, to be willing enough. Often he'd mentioned that Vicente was delaying his marriage overlong. Vicente foresaw no opposition from Lorenzo either. To the contrary, all signs were encouraging.

He smiled at Anitra. "Are you enjoying yourself?"

"Yes, thank you." She looked past him and saw that Josefa and Matthew had come into the patio.

Josefa was so small—doll-like almost. Her face seemed deathly pale in the glow of the golden lanterns. She was still dressed in mourning for Don Cipriano, so that the gown that floated around her ankles was black and unadorned. In spite of the warmth of the August evening, she was closely wrapped in a heavy black cloak. For the first time, Anitra saw her as ill, not just indulging herself in ladylike vapors. And Matthew, tenderly holding her arm, was breathtakingly handsome. In contrast to Josefa he seemed bursting with life, with virility.

And what a false picture he presented, Anitra thought bitterly. His virility was a fraud. He was a husband, but he had no wife. And it was to have no wife that he had taken Josefa and had turned his back on herself.

Aching, she watched the two seat themselves, lean their heads together to speak. She heard Vicente murmur but didn't understand the words.

"I'm sorry?" she asked absently.

"I say, Anitra, that Carlota's marriage to Esteban is a

good thing. For I'll have an excuse now to visit Tres Ríos more often."

"Yes, of course," she agreed indifferently. And then, "Vicente, I'm tired. If you don't object, I'd like to go and speak to Josefa."

In truth, she didn't want to speak to Josefa or to go anywhere near Matthew. But she could no longer bear Vicente's arms about her.

"Of course, Anitra, whatever you wish." But there was a faint flush suddenly in Vicente's olive cheeks. He cursed himself for a fool. He'd somehow frightened her. She was still hardly more than a child, no matter how she looked. And she wasn't used to the ways of society. The thought made him smile with indulgence. He would not have wanted her to be worldly. He led her over to Josefa and in response to a signal from his father excused himself.

"How was your journey down?" Josefa asked.

"Dull," Anitra answered. "I had no company but my father and Antonio, neither of whom were interested in conversation."

Josefa said, "We had errands in Santa Fe, else Matthew and I would have joined you."

"Are you well, Josefa? Have you done as I told you? Have you been going out a bit to take the sun and air?"

"Oh, yes, I have, and I do think it improves me, Anitra."

"And Matthew?" This was courtesy only.

Josefa smiled. "He's coming right now. You must ask him yourself. And . . . and ask him to dance, too, oh, please do, Anitra. I know he'd like to. But I truly can't."

Matthew heard only the last few words, "What is it that you can't do, Josefa?"

She looked down, shrugged her thin shoulders.

Confound the girl and her awful confidences, Anitra thought. She's made it impossible for me to behave with any sense toward Matthew. At the same time, she was asking hastily, "Will you dance with me, Matthew?"

It was what he'd wanted from the moment he saw her in Vicente's arms. He had felt longing flood him. She was like a lovely pink rose, and he yearned to hold her. But he glanced sideways at Josefa. She was nodding, smiling. A beloved sister, as always. She wanted him to have this pleasure that she couldn't give him. Would she want him to have that other pleasure, too, that she felt she couldn't give him?

A year ago he had given Don Cipriano his promise, and then gone to find Josefa. She was alone in the sala, her hands folded in her lap. "Is he happy now, Matthew?"

Matthew nodded. "He knows it will be, as he wishes, and that pleases him."

"But it'll always be the same, won't it, Matthew? I mean . . . for you . . . for me. We'll be as we were before?"

He saw the fear in her dark eyes, and his heart clenched within him. But he said steadily, "Of course, Josefa. Nothing will change."

She had coughed hard into both hands, and then said, "He won't know, will he?"

"No, Josefa." Matthew paused, then forced himself to put her meaning into words. "No, he won't guess that we remain brother and sister even after we become man and wife."

Now he hid his bitterness, said only, "If you'll excuse us for a few moments, Josefa, I will dance with Anitra."

She waved him away as he led Anitra to the center of the patio, near the lantern-lit fountain. To hold her thus fed the need of a man who had known hunger too long. He found that he couldn't talk to her.

For Anitra, just to be held by him and move with him to the music was a pleasure so intense that knowing it couldn't last was made unbearable. Allowing herself this brief painful joy only increased her hurt. Well, she thought, if she was to be hurt like this, then she would deliver hurt in return.

She tipped her head back, her eyes suddenly sparkling. "Matthew, dear friend, you must tell me what it's like to be married."

"You'll know soon enough," he said soberly. "I'm sure of that."

"Then you're more sure than I am," she retorted. "I know no one that I'll marry. I may remain a spinster all my days."

"I doubt it," he said dryly. "And if you know no man you'll marry, then you'd best be careful how you smile, Anitra."

"How amusing! I believe you're accusing me of being a flirt. But what's in a smile?"

"It can be a promise." He knew he was saying too much. The old friendly relationship of their childhood was gone. He had no right now to the jealousy that made him speak.

"A smile's not a promise from me. Not tonight. Tonight I'm just happy." She looked away from him, let her gaze travel around the patio. It was true. The scene was so beautiful to the eye, the music sweet to the ear. And she was in Matthew's arms, even if only briefly. "Besides, as I said," she went on, "I've not met the man I shall marry."

"What of your cousin Vicente?" Matthew asked. "To judge by how he held you . . ."

"Vicente!" Suddenly her father's smiling amiability to her since their arrival in Santa Fe began to make sense. A hot fury swept her. "I'll not choose him. Nor will I be forced into a marriage I don't want. I'm not like some I know ... I don't have ... "

"Anitra," Matthew said softly. "Please ... please ... "

"I won't even think of it." She saw, as he swung her around, an open gate, and as he moved her past it, she pulled sharply away and whirled through, still as if completing a square of the waltz.

It was a small garden, dark, so that no one could see the sudden tears in her eyes. Empty so that she could beat her small fists against the adobe wall, venting an anger that only Matthew must be permitted to witness.

He asked, watching her, "And will that help?"

She swung to face him, her eyes blazing. "Oh, I don't care! I don't care if it helps or not! What does it matter? No one, nothing, can change my mind. Carlota allowed her father to make her marriage for her, even encouraged it, and now she's the wife of an old man. And you, you yourself, permitted Don Cipriano to choose for you. Else why did you marry Josefa? What could she have meant to you?" It was on the tip of Anitra's tongue to shout out what she knew, what Josefa had told her. He wasn't a true husband. He wasn't a man. But she held back, wishing she didn't know it herself.

Matthew said stiffly, "Anitra, you know that Don Cipriano wanted the marriage. You know he was every-thing to me." Not everything, Matthew thought—Anitra was everything. But Don Cipriano had been able to force Matthew to a duty he hadn't wanted.

"And why should Don Cipriano have been everything to you?" Anitra demanded. "Why didn't you find your own love? Why didn't you fight for it?"

"I'd found my own love, and you know that," Matthew said quietly. "But I owed him peace of mind in his last days, even though you may not understand."

"All he did for you, he did out of love. You owed him nothing, Matthew."

"It was so he'd know Josefa is cared for." Matthew swallowed hard, thinking of the mockery of marriage in which he and Josefa were engaged.

"If you weren't weak you'd have made him accede to your wishes, not you to his," she said contemptuously.

"Perhaps. And perhaps I was wrong in doing as I did. But I'm not sorry. Josefa is very ill, Anitra."

"Yes, yes. She has always been. From my first memories of her I recall that. And always she leaned on your arm, Matthew."

He hesitated; then, not allowing himself to think of his reason for telling Anitra, he went on, "She coughs blood daily now, and only yesterday the doctor said she must eat well and rest well."

"Well, there! It's what I said. And that's what she would do if only she'd listen . . . "

Matthew went on, without expression, "He didn't say such a regime would help her."

Anitra's eyes opened wide. "Do I understand you to say she's really seriously ill? Is that what you mean?" He nodded soberly. Anitra cried, "Oh, Matthew, I'm sorry. I'm sorry for what I've been saying! And you must go to her at once. You mustn't leave her to sit alone."

He put a hand against the wall on each side of her, holding her captive, and bent his head so that his lips were only inches from her cheek. "I wish it had been different, Anitra."

"Then so do I!" Her voice was low, husky with passion. "But what does it matter? You married Josefa."

She ducked under his arm, whirled through the gate and back into the golden glow of the lanterns.

There was no pleasure in the beauty of the scene now, and no pleasure either when Vicente drew her into his arms, saying, "There you are, my cousin. I wondered where you had disappeared to."

She shrugged.

"You spoke a long time with Matthew," Vicente went on.

She raised her eyes, their green glinting dangerously through fans of black lashes. "Why not?" she demanded. "Matthew and I are old friends."

"No reason, of course. Except that while you were with him, I longed for you."

"Did you indeed?" she snapped.

A man she didn't know approached them, and Vicente sighed openly, relinquishing her.

After that there were others—so many that she lost count. One spoke of the Governor. "He said, and since we're good friends I believe him, that it's only a matter of months and the Constitutional Convention will ratify a state constitution, and New Mexico will be admitted into the Union." She considered that there were more complications than his optimism suggested, but said nothing. Another said, "My dear girl, how is it that Vicente Vargas has managed to keep you hidden away?" She thought the young man might better blame Don Lorenzo, but didn't bother to enlighten him.

Without conscious direction her feet moved her through the waltz, the schottische, the polka. Her lashes fluttered against her cheeks. Her hands applauded the last of Carlota's new gowns. And as she danced once again with Vicente, she saw Leigh standing just within the gate.

Her expression, which had stiffened the moment Vicente touched her, suddenly changed. Her mouth curved and Leigh understood at once. The moment the music ended, he was at her side, bowing.

Vicente understood, too. A wave of red suffused his face as Anitra, without so much as a graceful apology, went into Leigh's arms and looked up at him, smiling. "I've asked myself for so long where you've been."

She hoped desperately that Matthew was watching. She hoped that it would hurt him to see her in Leigh's arms.

Leigh grinned. "I've been here and there. And a while back I was having a smoke at the end of the garden."

Her throat reddened over the pink of her gown. Her eyes blazed like green fire. "You were listening, weren't you!" She tried to back away, but he wouldn't release her. He held her, forcing her to continue the dance.

"You were charming in your temper."

She tried to remember all that she'd said to Matthew. Then she shrugged. What did it matter?

The dimple near Leigh's mouth became deeper. He said, echoing her thoughts, "It doesn't matter to me. Except I'm glad that you dislike your cousin Vicente. For you belong to me. I want you, and I'll have you."

She had no time to answer, nor did she know what she would have said. She only knew that she would have wanted the dance with Leigh to go on forever. But Lorenzo interrupted.

He touched Anitra's shoulder, drew her deliberately away. Ignoring Leigh, he said, "We leave at sunup for Tres Ríos. Make your farewells right now, Anitra. Then we'll retire."

"So early, Don Lorenzo?" Leigh asked, openly amused.

Lorenzo's mouth thinned within his gray-streaked beard. "It's not early enough," he said, and turned his back on Leigh. "Come along at once, Anitra."

Don Lorenzo's anger had not cooled by morning, but he said nothing until they had left Santa Fe behind and had begun the first long climb up the mountain road. Then, as the sun dyed the ridges a soft rose color, he exploded. "It isn't bad enough that you embarrass Vicente, that you, while dancing with him, flirted with the gringo. Not only that, but at such a time . . . just when I had concluded the arrangements with César. Vicente was about to speak to you when . . . "

"What arrangements?"

"The arrangements for your betrothal and marriage," Lorenzo answered.

She pretended not to understand. "And to whom? Or shouldn't I ask?"

Lorenzo pressed his hand to his temple and Antonio said, "Anitra, now isn't the time . . . "

She cut through his words, "I ask you, my father, my betrothal to whom?"

"To Vicente," he answered in a voice as cold as hers.

"I won't have him," she said.

"But you will." Lorenzo gave her a brief, burning glance, then returned his attention to the road ahead. "The wedding is set at the end of November after your birthday. And meanwhile you'll behave with circumspection in all ways. I've given him my permission to visit you, you'll be glad to know. And I'll thank you to receive him properly."

"I'll not have Vicente Vargas," she retorted, and felt Antonio's fingers tighten warningly around her own.

178

15

"Perhaps you're offended with me, Anitra." Vicente gave her a placating smile. "Forgive me, my cousin. It was something which couldn't be helped. Much important business is afoot in this February of 1893. If I could have avoided the delay after your birthday I would have. But my trip to Washington City was necessary. And now I've returned. So . . ."

"I'm not offended with you," she said coldly. "I've told you already, Vicente. Regardless of what my father says, I don't consider myself betrothed, and I shan't marry you."

"You'll change your mind. I'm confident of that. And I'll cherish you as Esteban cherishes my sister. You'll have even more. For what's Tres Ríos compared to Santa Fe?"

"No!" she exploded. "Why won't you listen to me?"

"If it could be tomorrow, I'd be a happy man," Vicente persisted. "Regrettably I must return East once more. But I'll be back in good time before Santa Semana. And we'll be married then. Your father agrees."

"No," she said again.

But he smiled as he walked across the sala to the stone fireplace and held his pudgy hands out to the blazing piñon fire. "We'll talk another time."

She left him there alone and found Carlota in a small

179

back sitting room, no doubt directed there by Vicente himself so he could privately harass her with his unwanted
attentions. "That brother of yours, Carlota—is he mad?"

"Dios, he's in love with you," Carlota said, as if that
explained his stubborn behavior.

"I haven't asked him to be," Anitra retorted.

Esteban glanced up from the papers he'd been examining under the hanging lamp. He was glad of the distraction. The figures with which he dealt were disheartening.
Every day brought worse news. And he had thought all
would go well.

This house, for instance. With its papered walls and
linen window shades and damask drapes, that he'd
bought from Leigh for a good price—surely he should
have been able to meet the payments. It hadn't worked
out that way. Of course Leigh hadn't pressed him, and
wouldn't. Still, Esteban would have preferred more peace
of mind.

His glance settled on Carlota. How pretty she was,
and what a glow had come into her face with her pregnancy. It was glorious to think that in another four months
he'd become a father. He shoved the papers away from
him, got to his feet, smiling at Anitra. "I think Vicente
presses his suit too hard. I think, too, you'd be unhappy if
he hadn't come to see you."

"Oh, would I?" She drew a deep breath. She could
be, she thought, no more bitterly unhappy than she was
at that moment. The small freedoms she had had were
gone now. Her father watched her, and Antonio, once her
beloved brother, watched her, too. She was allowed only
those grueling visits to Josefa, during which Josefa continued to try to use her to keep Matthew from a boredom
she herself wouldn't allay. But Anitra was an unwilling

conspirator. What sustained her was the knowledge that Leigh loved her, and that his love might provide her with an escape.

Aside from her trips to the Diaz ranch, she was allowed these visits to Carlota and Esteban. She enjoyed them, for she and Carlota often spoke English together, and read aloud to each other, and in general, Carlota made a pleasant companion. But when Vicente appeared, trailing her like a lovesick puppy, Anitra said quickly, "Esteban, my father insisted I come, and I have . . . I want to return to the ranch now, however. You'll take me, won't you?"

"You won't wait for Antonio to fetch you as arranged?"

"He'll be hours yet, being in league with my father on this. I'd like to go at once."

Esteban hesitated, and Carlota cried, "Dios, you can't keep her here if she wants to go!" Then Esteban said, "My dear Anitra, of course. I'll just get my coat."

The air was biting but sweetened with the scent of burning cedar. The windows of the big white house glowed, leaving a trail of light as she walked down the path beside Esteban and passed through the white picket fence.

"You enjoy living in town?" she asked.

"It has its inconveniences, of course. But the ranch was no fit place to bring Carlota. I never even noticed until I began to think of marriage. But then . . . "

Leigh looked at the glow of the windows, watched the two silhouettes pass between the tall white columns, and when they reached the carriage, he stepped out of the shadows.

Esteban said, "Oh, Leigh," startled and not overly

pleased. "Good evening. I was just about to drive Anitra home. Were you coming to see me?"

"I was." Leigh smiled down at Anitra. "A small matter of business."

"Oh, then . . . "

Leigh said quickly, "I'll ride along with you and we'll talk on the way back."

Esteban continued to hesitate. Don Lorenzo had made his feelings about this man quite clear many times. And yet, how was Esteban to dismiss him without hurting his feelings?

Anitra decided the matter for him. "Please," she said, do come along for the ride."

Leigh grinned to himself and helped Anitra into the carriage, allowing his hands to linger at her waist. When they were all settled, he slid a hand under the lap robe and clasped her fingers. "I hear that your cousin Vicente has come to see you."

"For all the good it'll do him."

"You remain firm on that?"

Esteban cleared his throat uneasily.

She looked into Leigh's eyes, nodded, then lowered her long lashes.

"That's what I wanted to hear, Anitra."

Esteban asked hastily, "What business did you have in mind, Leigh?"

Smiling at Anitra, he answered, "I've completely forgotten now."

That night Esteban didn't reach out to embrace Carlota. He lay staring at the fringes of the canopy through the long, dark hours.

His loyalties were with Lorenzo. They'd been friends

all their lives. And there was Vicente, his own brother-in-law, to consider as well. But he was beholden in so many dangerous ways to Leigh. It had begun with a few friendly loans to help him in desperate moments. He'd paid those back, but the burden of lawyers' fees and bribes given in Santa Fe in an effort to prove the title to the land that had always been his had continually drained him. He had borrowed from Leigh again. And now it was likely that he'd have to go to Leigh once more.

It was dawn before Esteban drifted into uneasy sleep.

Leigh rode away from the Delagado house warm with elation. He hadn't known the good use to which he would put the white-columned house when he bought it from the Americans who had built it. They'd been unwanted when they came, unmourned when they left, and Leigh had received the place at a bargain price. But if he had planned it then, it couldn't have been more suited to his purpose.

He went slowly around the plaza, the white plumes of his horses's breath drifting before him.

Each summer since the first one in 1887, he had made his three-day trips into the mountains at carefully irregular intervals. Each time he had followed Jake Heimer's procedure. He crossed his own tracks, doubled back. He watched the trail before and behind. A new Cora and Cal ran with him now—dogs as well trained as the old. He had shot the first Cal as soon as he was certain the new litter would survive; the first Cora when she began to refuse her young. He had chosen two of the litter, a male and a female, and worked them with belt and bloody meat, until they were as obedient as he wished. The cross-breeding had made them even meaner than their parents.

With these two running beside him, he had no need to concern himself with anyone's interference.

He worked the stream, sweating, counting. Afterward he rode to Albuquerque, and, in more recent years, sometimes to El Paso, where the nuggets were sold and turned into cash, most of which went into the bank in Santa Fe.

It was on those trips away from Tres Ríos that he found women to suit him, and each time he lay with them he imagined he held Anitra in his arms.

The gold had brought him the scattering of acres he owned beyond the town. Aside from his bits and pieces, there were the three great ranches he coveted: the Diaz, now owned by Matthew Britton, the Delagado, and the Martínez y Escobedo. The Delagado was very nearly his, though Esteban didn't know this yet. But Leigh wasn't quite ready to move against him. Because of Anitra. He planned the winning of Anitra as carefully as he had planned the taking of the valley.

He'd waited a long while for her, thinking to give her father time to accept slowly the idea of having a gringo son-in-law of wealth and position. But he'd wait no longer. He would begin his courtship and let Don Lorenzo say what he would.

He was certain of Anitra now, and could make his move.

It was Sunday of that same week when Dora opened the door and gasped to see Leigh Ransome on the threshold.

"Don Lorenzo, if you please," he said smiling.

"Don Lorenzo?"

Leigh said no more, only waited, still smiling.

She edged away, disappeared through a door, then came back on the run. "Don Lorenzo's occupied," she panted, and moved to close the door.

But Leigh held it with his boot and said, "He'll see me, I think, occupied, or not."

She pressed her plump body tight to the wall as he passed her. Afterward she shuddered as though a blazing fire had swept by.

Lorenzo sat in a chair by the hearth talking to Porfirio.

Leigh said, "Don Lorenzo, I'm sorry to interrupt you, but I have business that won't wait any longer."

Lorenzo stared at him silently, his face reddening with mounting blood. At last he jerked his head at Porfirio, and the foreman left the room. Later he would tell Felicia in the kitchen, "I thought Don Lorenzo would explode."

When Lorenzo spoke, it was in a hoarse whisper. "What do you want, Señor Ransome?"

Leigh seated himself, knowing that there would be no invitation forthcoming. He unbuttoned his heavy riding coat, crossed his long legs, and leaned back, looking slowly around the room. His eyes fell on the words carved into the wooden roof beam.

He smiled faintly. There was Don Lorenzo's pride. After all, the words meant the same thing to him as El Castillo meant to Leigh.

"What do you want?" Lorenzo repeated.

"Your house is impressive," Leigh said. But he thought it wasn't nearly as pleasant as his own, nor as modern, and the feeling was expressed in his tone.

Lorenzo tapped his fingers on the carved arm of his chair. "Señor Ransome . . . "

"Don Lorenzo, I'm here to ask your permission to court Anitra. I know that she's willing. I want to . . . "

Lorenzo got to his feet, the veins swelling in his temples. "No. No. No. How can you ask it? She's betrothed to her cousin, and has been for nearly six months. No, Señor Ransome, we'll not even speak of it."

"She doesn't care for her cousin."

"It's arranged," Lorenzo said coldly.

"I love her," Leigh continued. "I'll be good to her, and I'm a man of substance. There's nobody in Tres Ríos who would say a word against me."

"No—and I won't hear another word, I tell you. Even if Anitra were not betrothed to Vicente, even if there was no one, and you were the last man on earth to want her, the answer would still be no."

Leigh rose, too, but when he spoke, it was softly. "I mean to have my way, Don Lorenzo, and you can't stop me. No one can stop me. I'll court Anitra and marry her, with your permission or not."

"Get out," Lorenzo roared. "Get out of my house, and get off my land."

Leigh buttoned his coat slowly, drew on his gloves, bowed, and left Lorenzo without a word.

He went directly to Esteban, who took a quick look at his stony face and poured him a large whiskey. Finally he asked, "My friend, what troubles you?"

"Don Lorenzo troubles me."

"Oh?" Esteban asked cautiously.

"You know how I feel about Anitra, Esteban. I've just asked Don Lorenzo for his permission to court her, and he has refused me."

Esteban was silent. He felt a coldness in his chest.

Leigh said evenly, "I'll not have him stop me. And you're going to help."

Esteban had known for some time that this was coming and tried to stop the sudden trembling in his legs.

"When Anitra visits you, as she's bound to, I want to

know. I want to be invited at the same time. We'll arrange a few dinners. I shall be seen with her. I shall make certain that everyone in Tres Ríos knows of my intentions."

"My friend, is this wise? Don Lorenzo . . . "

"Don Lorenzo can't stop me. And Anitra wants it."

"Still . . . "

"Esteban, it's a very small favor that I'm asking of you." His tone said, "And I've done you many large favors. And could possibly do more."

Esteban forced a smile. "It will be as you wish, Leigh. And I want you to know that I hope only the best for you, for Anitra."

16

Anitra's eyes kept going to Matthew. The pallor of his face was almost like Josefa's. He was restless, his usual sober stillness dissolved by some acid that burned in him, she thought.

Josefa yawned, then coughed into her handkerchief, saying, "I must have my rest now."

"Yes," Matthew said tonelessly.

"You'll forgive me, Anitra?"

"Of course." Anitra rose. "Antonio will be coming soon, I'm sure. I'll wait for him in the courtyard."

"Oh, no. It's too cold. Matthew, don't let her go out. Keep her company beside the fire, and I'll lie down in my bedroom."

"Matthew surely has things he must do," Anitra said, and, turning to him, "You mustn't think you need entertain me. I'll just sit here and read."

From the door, Josefa blew them both a kiss.

When the door closed behind her, Matthew said, "It's kind of you to visit. I know it's a chore for you. We're not the most entertaining company, are we?"

Anitra stared fixedly into the fire. "She's worse."

"So it seems."

"I'm sorry, Matthew."

"I know you are."

"But it's for Don Cipriano that I come," she whispered. "I promised him."

"Ah, Don Cipriano thought of that, too, did he?"

"He was concerned for you both, Matthew."

Matthew didn't answer. The look in his gray eyes was thoughtful. Then he turned away. "I've seen you a good many times lately with Leigh Ransome, Anitra. And I've heard that you're allowing him to court you."

She was pleased, though she didn't permit herself to show it. She had wanted Matthew to see Leigh holding her arm, whispering to her. Always, always, when she was with Leigh, she hoped Matthew would see her and feel pain.

Esteban and Carlota had arranged it. They had given two small dinners, and Matthew and Josefa had come, and Matthew had watched as Leigh bent over her hand, kissing her fingertips.

She remembered that Carlota in her pregnancy was beautiful in red velvet, and that Leigh, as he bowed, had asked, "Is it all right at home?"

She had shrugged. "No worse than I thought. He heard that you took me for a ride around the plaza, and then to the hotel for chocolate. He was furious, of course."

"Is it too hard for you?" Leigh asked.

"No, no," she had said quickly, and watched Matthew's pale eyes flash.

And now Matthew was asking, "Is it wise, Anitra? Do you know what you're doing?"

"I don't want to discuss it with you, Matthew." Her voice was sharp, the glance she sent him bright with warning.

She no longer wanted his jealousy. Suddenly she no longer wanted to hurt him.

"Leigh Ransome's making a great show of it. Do you know, Anitra, that the town's divided? Half for him to have you, half supporting your father?"

"You're ridiculous," she snapped.

"I only wish I were. But it's true. And it's what he wants, though I'm not sure why. I only know he hopes for popular approval of the marriage, regardless of your father."

"Leigh doesn't care," she said stiffly.

"You know better in your heart," Matthew said soberly. "You just don't want to hear it. Perhaps it's because he's a gringo . . ."

"And you?" she jeered. "What are you?"

He grinned. "It may be that I'm a gringo, too. But I hardly qualify when you consider how I was brought up. Anyway, perhaps because Leigh is an outsider, he feels it necessary for the town to be with him. I don't know. But I'm sure you should consider carefully before you think of marriage with him."

She turned on Matthew, her cheeks flaming. "I'll thank you to look after your own affairs, hombrecito! You've no right to advise me. None at all," she said in a harsh whisper. "I begged you not to marry Josefa, but you turned your back on me and chose her. And perhaps I was fortunate. Now you pretend to be a man. But what are you? What true man would live as you do?"

He made a small sound of protest.

She heard but she could no longer stop herself. "Do you think I don't know the truth?" She laughed contemptuously. "But I do, dear Matthew. Josefa confided in me. She's been troubled that . . . that she doesn't share your bed. She fears you'll become restless and bored. And that's why she leaves us together so often. She believes I can interest you. But I see that no woman could. I pity your poor Josefa her marriage. I suppose I must pity you, too."

He was suddenly close to her, color surging into his face, then falling away swiftly, leaving the earlier pallor. "You don't know what you're talking about." At the same time, his hand came up, lashed at her face.

An ember in the fire crackled, and they both started.

"Anitra! Anitra, forgive me!" His words were soft, so soft that they were barely more than thought. "Please . . . " He took her fingers from her cheek and pressed his lips to the bruise, then with a groan gathered her in his arms.

She clung to him, trembling, while he kissed her eyes, her throat, and then buried his head at her breast. She clung to him even as they sank together to the settle before the fire, and then to the floor, bodies and hearts linked in love.

And later, when he sought to rise, she clung to him tightly and searched his face for a further sign of the love he had already given her.

What she saw was regret. Regret and shame. He drew away from her, took her arms from his neck, and held her hands tightly. "Forgive me for this, too," he said at last.

She stared at him in shocked disbelief. She had yielded to him the ultimate proof of her feelings. Nothing could change what they had shared.

"Forgive me, Anitra," he said again.

"Matthew," she cried. "Matthew, what are you talking about? How will forgiveness change what we are to each other? Josefa doesn't need you as I do. We can leave here. We can live our own lives. I don't care what happens if I can just be with you!"

"I gave Don Cipriano my word, Anitra."

"And what did you give me?" she demanded hotly.

The bright points of light in his eyes seemed to have gone out. He didn't answer, only tightened his fingers around her hands.

He didn't truly want her. Their shared passion meant nothing to him. Her very flesh trembled, but she said nothing more. She freed herself, feeling as if she left a part of herself with him.

She didn't speak until Antonio arrived, and then it was only to say, "Goodbye, Matthew."

He nodded, his gaze not meeting hers, so that she would not see the tears burning his eyes.

17

The snow packs were still thick, blazing white on the mountain peaks that Good Friday, but each day during Santa Semana, Holy Week, the sun had bathed in cold brilliance the varied religious processions around the morada. Only partly shielded from the chill, the Brothers had spent the week in prayer, sleeping for short periods on the hard-packed floor.

Now the brilliance of the sun was fading. The surrounding hills became pink, then red as blood, red as the blood of Christ, for which they were named Sangre de Cristo. The three rough wooden crosses leaning against the morada wall took on the changing hues, and slowly the prayers within faded away into exhausted silence.

Antonio drew a deep breath, feeling the burn of the yucca cuts on his bare back. He was exultant. The moment for which he had been preparing himself had come at last.

This time Porfirio hadn't refused him.

He wore only loose white trousers. His feet were bare. The scar at the base of his throat was dark. When Porfirio handed him the black hood, he nodded.

It had taken long hours of pleading discussion to convince Porfirio that Antonio be allowed to be one of the three who would carry the two-hundred-pound crosses to Calvary in the reenactment of the Crucifixion. When his determination and sincerity had prevailed against Porfirio's unwillingness, Antonio had kissed the older man's hand in the deepest gratitude. In the slow walk, in the offering of his pain, he'd prove himself a man worthy to be his father's son.

He put on the hood, and through the eye holes he saw Porfirio's signal, urging him to move outside and take a position near one of the crosses.

There was silence as the three men picked up their heavy burdens. Porfirio raised his hand in a signal, and the group slowly made its way across the fields, past wind-scoured red rock into an isolated canyon.

Praying, wailing, to the accompaniment of the pito, a handmade flute, the Brothers stumbled through the fading twilight, while an armed guard of four men peered into the shadows, watching, and strained their ears for signs of interlopers who would defile these holy moments.

Once such precautions wouldn't have been necessary. The whole of the village would have participated. But with the coming of the Americans, the Mother Church itself had begun a persecution of the Brotherhood, forbidding ancient practices. What started with the Frenchmen priests was continued by the new Archbishop. Only a few years before, some three hundred of the Penitentes had been brought, by various means, to recant their oaths before receiving the Blessed Sacraments.

The men carrying the crosses moved slowly, each step a dragging effort. Sweat poured down their faces, down their self-lacerated backs. They fell, rose, fell again. They struggled up and moved on. Behind them, yucca lashes rhythmically applied to their own backs, the fifteen others followed.

In step with them, grunting and gasping with strain, two men pulled the old solid-wheel wooden cart. It was loaded with stones now, and among them stood La Santa de la Muerte, whose other name was Doña Sebastiana. The red-tipped arrow in her bony hands seemed aimed directly at the backs of the men ahead.

Antonio's elation grew more intense as his breath quickened and the weight of the cross grew heavier, his legs weaker. The lights of the village had disappeared into a misty distance below. The canyon was hushed, as if all living things had come to a pause.

The men stopped, and with them Antonio, struggling to remain upright.

Three men set to work digging holes in the hard rocky earth, shovels scraping, breaths rasping—sounds that only underlined the stillness.

A whispered prayer began as the crosses were set up.

Antonio was the first of the three to step forward. When the other two took their places, Porfirio nodded again. Each man was gently lifted against his cross and then tied with leather thongs that bound him at the throat, arms, knees, and ankles.

The wail of the pito rose higher, thin and sweet on the chill air. The Cantador sang words passed on from generation to generation: " 'Look, oh sinner, on El Cristo / Jesús nailed to the Cross / Look on the Son of the Eternal / Expiring for love of you.' "

The voice of the Cantador was deep and strong as he went on, chanting words of praise to the Virgin, honoring the Passion.

Porfirio waited until, finally, there was a hushed silence. Then he stepped forward, raised his head. He spoke slowly, and as he ended, "My God, why hast Thou forsaken me?" his voice broke, and as it faded slowly away into the stillness, the pale moon rose.

The celebrants drifted away, leaving the three alone on their crosses, enwrapped in darkness and ever-increasing cold. The guards also withdrew, unseen as before, vanishing into the night.

Antonio raised his eyes to the bitter white diamonds in the sky, the hard cold silver of the moon.

Slowly, slowly, the leather thongs tightened as the hours passed. He dreamed of the scent of lilacs. He dreamed of Anitra, her hair flying like black silk, riding toward him over a golden meadow. He dreamed that his father smiled at him and opened wide his arms. His pain faded with the sinking of the moon.

The men on either side of Antonio spoke, but he didn't hear. It was done. For those that he had wronged, for Patricio Sánchez, for Anitra, for Mundo Segura, for his father, he had mounted the Cross. It was done.

The morada was dark except for the light of a single white candle signifying El Cristo, and twelve yellow ones representing the disciples.

The ceremonials commemorating the flight of the Apostles and the death of Jesus—when darkness descended, and rocks split, and the earth trembled, and the temple veil was torn—began late that Good Friday night. Las Tinieblas, it was called.

The window was covered, the door shut. One candle after another was blown out. The white one was hidden away. Sudden explosive sound filled the dark. The beating of tin pans and drums, the cry of the pito, cries, screams, and prayers, sounded in the heavy air as the Brothers joined together in flagellation for the last time during Santa Semana.

In the pink dawn, the Brothers returned together to the still canyon.

It was in dense shadow as yet, only a rim of sun at the high white ridges. The thin air was scented with piñon and sage. Birds fluttered in the trees. A squirrel chattered from a low-hanging limb.

Two of the men raised their weary heads and, with their hoods withdrawn, smiled with glowing joy from the crosses.

The third man, Mundo Segura, was motionless. His hood had fallen back to expose his gray face. The leather thong at his throat was buried deep in his flesh, showing clearly how he had died.

Porfirio cried out, wept, then went on his knees to pray. Much later he walked from the canyon alone and went to the morada. He took from it the shoes Mundo had left there before he set out on the long walk to his Calvary.

As Porfirio made his way to the small hut in which Mundo had lived, a prairie dog barked annoyance at his intrusion and scurried to a rocky ledge.

"Sea por Dios!" Porfirio whispered, stopping before the door of the hut. "God's will be done," he repeated, gently setting down the stained and broken shoes, so that those within who loved him would know that Mundo was dead on the cross.

Later, the velorio, the wake, in his name, would be held. The mirrors would be turned to the wall, black crepe would be hung from the lanterns. But for the next twelve months Mundo would lie in secret in a place known only to the Brothers in the Penitentes. During the next Santa Semana, his body, the shell which had once contained his soul, would be returned, and he would be buried among his own.

"God's will be done," Porfirio murmured for the third time as he hurried back to the morada.

He found Antonio resting, his young face at peace, and he took the boy's hand. "You're blessed, my brother. You're blessed of God, my little Jesús," Porfirio whispered.

18

At the end of the month Vicente, newly returned from Washington City, came to Tres Ríos again.

He stopped Anitra, putting a hand on her arm, as she was going toward her room in the hope of evading him. "My cousin, a word with you."

"Now, Vicente?"

"Better now than later."

She led him into the courtyard and seated herself on a stone bench. He watched her. There was a brightness in her eyes, a richness in her mouth. He sought for a graceful way to broach the subject, but the heat in him made him clumsy. He blurted, "I want to set the date for our wedding."

She rose, small trembling hands clasped into the blue silk of her gown. "I won't marry you. I've said so, and you ought to have listened."

He sputtered, "What? What's that?"

"I'll not marry you, Vicente. Not now. Not later."

His cheeks slowly reddened with anger. "You don't know what you're saying."

"I know I'll never marry you."

The heat within him died, but pride made him say, "The dowry is arranged, let me remind you. The agreements are made. So we'll marry, and you'll soon learn that I'm right in all things."

Her laughter was sudden and harsh. "I see already that you're wrong in all things." She turned, fled into the house, her silken skirts floating like a blue cloud.

Moments later, Vicente complained sourly to Lorenzo, "She's adamant. I didn't think she'd dare speak so to me."

But Lorenzo was more determined than ever that the marriage take place. He felt the shadow of Leigh Ransome hover over the hacienda. Anitra must wed Vicente and leave Tres Ríos as quickly as possible.

Vicente was saying, "I can't return to Santa Fe without knowing."

"Do you look for a way out of your promises?" Lorenzo demanded.

"No, I'll have her, though she has offended me." And when he did, Vicente thought, Anitra Martínez y Escobedo would learn new manners.

Lorenzo went to the door, bellowed, "Anitra! Come here at once!"

The girl came in softly, with so light a step that she seemed to float above the floor. "Yes?" she asked.

"We're discussing the plans for your future," Lorenzo said.

"I shan't marry Vicente." She said quietly, "You made the decision, not I. I never agreed. I won't agree now."

"Then be damned to you!" Vicente shouted. He turned to Lorenzo, "Forgive me, my cousin. The betrothal must be considered at an end. Your daughter's future is no longer any concern of mine."

Lorenzo waited until the door slammed shut, the angry sound of Vicente's boots fading away down the hall. Then he said heavily, "And what's to become of you?"

"I don't know," she answered.

"You can't stay here, flaunting your will before the valley."

She shrugged.

"I'll send you to the Sisters in Santa Fe. Perhaps the convent is the best place for you," he went on.

She flashed him a coldly defiant look and returned slowly to her room.

The heavy carved chest was in the back of the cart. Porfirio stood waiting.

Anitra slipped out, closed the thick door gently.

She crossed the courtyard without a backward look, and climbed up to the seat. A breeze rustled through the peach trees and brought down a shower of pink blossoms. Some of them caught in the rebozo over her head.

Porfirio swung up beside her, took the reins in his calloused hands. "Are you sure of this, Anitra?" he asked. "Is this how it must be?"

She nodded, and he flicked the reins.

Dora watched from the window, tearful but silent.

The cart rolled and jolted under the big curved sign that read "Martínez y Escobedo," crossed the small wooden bridge, and bumped into the track that cut through the valley toward Tres Ríos.

What awaited Anitra there, Porfirio didn't know. He wasn't privy to her secrets, though he knew more of them than she guessed. What awaited Porfirio when he returned to the ranch, he did know. Lorenzo would storm about, blaspheming, threatening, while Antonio tried to make peace. But Porfirio had weathered such storms before and he'd somehow survive this one. In any case, Anitra was a woman now, one who knew her own mind as most women did not. And she had a strength in her, too, that most women had not.

She was silent when he pulled up before Doña Carlota's house. Then she smiled. "If you'll bring the chest in, Porfirio?"

He hesitated, then said, "At once. And God be with you always, niña."

As if he knew, she thought, her smile growing warmer. As if he knew what she planned.

She watched Porfirio unload the chest and remembered how it came to pass that she stood here before the Delagado house on the Tres Ríos plaza, her heart hammering against her ribs, and her throat tight with excitement....

Carlota whispering behind her fan, "I must speak to you privately, Anitra," her eyes on Don Lorenzo, and then in the bedroom, "Leigh asks me to tell you. He's heard that your father will send you to the convent. He wants to come to you, but it will cause an ugly scene if he does. Leigh feels that would be wrong. But he . . . he sends you his love, Anitra."

Anitra nodded, said nothing. She felt a pulse begin to beat quickly in her throat.

"Anitra," Carlota still whispered, though there was no need for it here, "He loves you. Why, if you could see him! He's like a man possessed and speaks only of your plight."

"Tell him I thank him for the message."

"And that's . . . that's all?" Carlota took Anitra's cold hand. "Come to me secretly, Anitra. Speak to no one. Just come, and before your father sends you away, which will be very soon, I think."

"Yes," Anitra breathed. "Yes, yes, I will. And thank you, Carlota." Suddenly her green eyes were aglow. She was going to the man who wanted her.

Porfirio had carried the chest as far as the big veranda when the door of the big white house swung open. Leigh stood there smiling, and then with a shout, he leaped down the stairs and raced toward her, his long legs covering the yards between them as if they were nothing. And suddenly she was running, too, her skirts flying around her.

His arms caught her and he swung her up in a wide circle, her feet off the ground. "Finally, my Anitra, finally," he chanted.

"Leigh, put me down," she said laughing. "Let me breathe!"

"There'll be time for that later," he said, lowering her to the ground and leading her into the house.

Carlota and Esteban were there, waiting, and after a quick exchange of greetings, Carlota took Anitra upstairs.

"It's all ready," Carlota was saying. "Leigh insisted I pick the best."

The gown lay spread on the quilt, a traveling costume of green, braided at the throat and shoulder and sleeves. A small hat of matching fabric crowned with golden feathers rested beside it.

Carlota asked anxiously, "What do you think? Did I do nicely?"

"Ah, it's a beautiful gown, and you know it," Anitra cried.

"Then let's show Leigh. He's waiting."

He was alone when she came downstairs, for the others had delicately left him. He turned slowly and looked at her, while the fringes of the window shades cast strange black lines on his face. She shivered momentarily. It was as if a stranger peered suddenly at her from his pale-blue eyes. At last he drew a deep breath. "I've thought of this for so long, Anitra. And now . . . now I don't know what to say. Except that I love you. I've loved you since I first saw you, I think. I told you I was going to have you . . . and I want to . . . " He grinned, a boy's grin, mixing hope and excitement. Then he drew a plain gold ring from his pocket and held it out to her.

She took the hand that offered the ring and kissed it, and then she kissed the ring itself.

Laughing, he caught her to him, pressed his lips on hers, drawing her body tightly to his.

Then, releasing her, he said, "We'd better get started, Anitra."

"Get started?"

"I promised you, remember? That I'd take you on your first train ride? Well, we're going to Tres Ríos Junction right now."

"And then?" she asked softly.

"Santa Fe, Anitra. I've made all the arrangements."

They were at a bend in the track high above the river gorge when they saw in the distance a horseman pounding toward them across the mesa.

A faint frown touched Leigh's brow but when he recognized Antonio he motioned to the driver to pull up.

Antonio ignored Leigh's greeting and Anitra's silence. He said, "Don't do this, my sister."

"We shall be married in Santa Fe," she said softly.

"You mustn't shame our father this way," he pleaded.

"Listen to me. He has already promised me to think again of his decision. I know he'll change his mind about the convent. You needn't do this. Think a while, Anitra. Wait a while."

"There's nothing to think about and nothing to wait for," she answered. Once she would have listened, she thought. Once the old closeness between them would have compelled her to listen. But he had gone his own way and had left her, as Matthew had left her. She put her hand on Leigh's arm. "We must go on," she told him.

Without a word he jerked his head at the driver and the rig jolted on the track.

Antonio was quickly left behind.

Tres Ríos Junction was at the bottom of the gorge, close to where the river ran green and deep.

They waited near the tracks until with hooting whistle and cindery smoke the train jerked around a curve and stopped. There were two passenger coaches attached to the small locomotive, and behind them a freight and baggage car. It was called the Chile Line because in the autumn it would be packed with chiles grown in the bottomland of the river and shipped out, north and south, for sale in the markets. More formally, the narrow-gauge railroad was known as the Denver and Rio Grande Line, and for part of its route it skirted the mountain chain in a roadbed cut out of rock over the river.

She listened to the clack-clack of the wheels and the occasional hoot of the whistle and looked at the red of the mountains slowly changing color as the hours passed. Once she and Antonio had chased the sound of this very train, racing across the meadow to the gorge, where the shining track gleamed in the sun. Now she and Antonio had become strangers. She put the painful thought aside.

This was her wedding day. She would know only happiness.

The river, swollen by the melting snow packs in the mountains, was in full flood. It sucked at the red banks below the tracks, drained them away. Giant cottonwoods were uprooted and flung aside like kindling wood. Willows bent low and silently drifted into the boiling current. As she watched, a huge boulder rocked gently in the tide, bearded with white spume, and then, in a shower of rising red spray, it shot down the bank, taking mountain and mesquite with it, to churn in the cauldron that now ran dark as blood. A tremor touched her. Her hand crept to touch Leigh. But the train whistle sang out and the wheels clacked on, and soon they were past the danger.

At Espanola they changed to another train, and then they moved swiftly across the broad rich valley and climbed high again, so that she had a brief glimpse of the red-tiled roofs of Santa Fe far below before they rolled downward once more.

The sun was high and bright, the sky blue and cloudless, when they reached the city. Leigh found a buggy, and they drove across the river, past where women knelt and scrubbed their clothes still using soap made from amole root as in the old days, and through the blocks where the poor were huddled in their jacales in resigned misery. She noticed none of that now, for her eyes were fixed on Leigh's face. She wasn't surprised when the buggy stopped before the old parish church of San Miguel. She had the feeling that nothing Leigh did could surprise her any more.

He helped her down, stood silently for a moment, his arm around her waist, then led her inside.

The padre, who was plainly expecting them, came bustling forward. "Ah, Señor Ransome, you're just on time, aren't you?" Small black eyes peered at her, examined her from the golden feathers on her tiny hat to the tips of her slim black slippers. His eyes narrowed in unspoken disapproval. She understood. Now he saw why special arrangements had to be made, why there were no relatives as witnesses and to give her away. She was Spanish and marrying a gringo. The padre shrugged mentally. He'd given his word. His personal disapproval was meaningless. At last he said, "And this . . . this is your bride."

He put on his vestments and softly, reverently, spoke the words of the marriage ceremony, while around them the lights of small candles flickered and danced and swallows cooed in the bell tower.

Afterward, under the trees in the churchyard, Leigh took her into his arms and said hoarsely, "You're really mine now, Anitra."

The high walls of El Castillo blocked the corner and stretched away at right angles, one to disappear in the shadow of the trees in back of the house, the other to the courtyard gate.

Anitra had been within these walls only once before. But a curious revulsion shook her as Leigh helped her down before the front door. Then, waving the servant away, he drew her into his arms and the unpleasant feeling disappeared. There was no reality but the pressure of his hard muscles holding her and the hunger of his mouth against her own.

He saw her look admiringly at the house. "I've made some changes for you, Anitra. I wanted it to be right. Not that anything came easy. The workmen are used to their long siestas, but I finally got what I wanted. You'll see."

She glanced around the courtyard. Except for the

row of fir trees planted just within the walls, it was bare red dirt, pocked with broken adobe brick.

It should have had peach trees and willows and lilacs, she thought. It should be lush with greenery. She had a moment's memory of the courtyard at the ranch . . . blossoms floating down. . . . Her fingers tightened on Leigh's arm.

He said, smiling at her, "I know it's too bare, Anitra. We'll put in whatever you like. Your favorite trees and bushes. Your favorite flowers. Maybe some yellow roses, and you . . . " His voice dropped. " . . . And you can wear them in your hair for me."

"You indulge me, my husband," she answered softly. "But I promise you it will be beautiful when it's finished."

Still holding her, he took her to the door. She had a brief glimpse of a whitewashed wall, a tiled floor, a high gunrack and then Leigh swept her into his arms. "This is how we do it," he said, carrying her over the threshold.

Tinita, the serving girl, stood waiting, dark eyes cast down, her face expressionless. "A meal is prepared," she said.

Leigh, laughing still, set Anitra on her feet. "This girl has worked for me for years. You tell her what you want and she'll do it."

Anitra smiled warmly. "And what's your name, niña? Though we met before once, I don't remember it."

"Tinita, señora," the girl answered, ducking through an archway.

Leigh smiled into Anitra's eyes. "Hello again, wife," he said softly. "We're finally alone. It seems to me I've been waiting all my life for this."

"Yes," she breathed. "Yes, my heart," and opened her arms wide to him.

The wild baying of the dogs awakened her.

It was a chilling sound, echoing from the very walls of the room, as if the beasts were close and ravening with hunger. There was a single breathless instant when she didn't know where she was, or recognize the sound, and she felt sudden terror. But then she felt Leigh's warmth beside her, and memories of love came flooding back.

The passion of his kisses on her mouth and breasts had brought her to a fever pitch of half-fainting desire. His weight on her body as he made her his own had been all sweetness and final satiation. But it was only a temporary satisfaction. Looking at him as he slept, she felt the warm sweet yearning begin again.

He smiled as he opened his eyes, and once more the wild baying of the dogs echoed through the room. "Did they wake you up?" he asked.

She shivered involuntarily.

"You'll get used to them."

"They don't sound friendly, Leigh."

"I'd shoot them if they did. They're not here to be friendly."

El Castillo was his fortress, the dogs his sentries. Nothing could breach the walls of his castle. It was the safe center of the kingdom that would soon be his.

He turned and drew her into his arms, and she saw that his eyes had darkened to a midnight blue. Forgetting the wild baying of the dogs, she gave herself to the enchantment of his love.

19

The bells rang for Sunday morning mass. Anitra raised her head, listened, and turned back to the cage.

"Cora?" she said tentatively. "Cal?" She put her fingers through the wire and saw the sun gleam on her wedding band. "Cora? Cal?"

The dogs' ears lifted and snapped forward. They gave deep-throated barks and made long leaps, tongues lolling and eyes glittering, to hurl themselves at the fence.

Anitra dodged back, her heart suddenly pounding. Each day, for the five since she'd come to El Castillo, she'd made a tour of the two courtyards, deciding what she would have planted there. At the west were to be great bushes of Chinese lilacs, framing the view of the mountain peaks above the wall. At the east, within the sentinel firs, she'd have rows of roses in raised beds, and then poppies. The well house would be trellised for morning glory or honeysuckle. She saw it all in her mind as she walked slowly through the red dust—a garden warm and bright with color, perfumed with scent, where humming-birds would hover over nectar-cupping blooms.

The tour completed, each day she went to talk to the dogs, to make them familiar with her voice and scent. But they were strange animals, she began to see. They knew no playfulness. They understood no soft words. They accepted only one master and would respond to no one else.

From across the courtyard there came a familiar whistle. The dogs yelped and streaked through the small entry door into the room where Leigh awaited them.

She went inside quickly, knowing that within moments Leigh would leave his office. When, the day after their marriage, he had shown her through the whole of the house, he had paused before the door and said, "This is my office." From within, she had heard the lunge of the dogs. "They look after things for me when I'm not here. So don't go in without me, Anitra. And don't open the door."

She had thought nothing of it then, and he had led her away to see the big room for guests that was next to their bedroom. But now she wondered fleetingly why, in his absence, the dogs guarded the office, and why Tinita was permitted to clean it only when he was there.

She forgot that when he met her in the hallway.

"You look perfect," he said.

"Perfect for what, Leigh?"

"For a drive," he answered, laughing.

They set out a few minutes later, the dogs running ahead, much to Anitra's surprise.

As they entered the plaza, the sound of the church bells died away. When only moments before there had been silence and emptiness, there was now a sudden surge of movement.

The road was crowded with people in their Sunday clothes. The women wore bright skirts and bright rebozos on their shoulders. The children running before them were scrubbed and clean. The men had on black coats and brushed hats; here and there a few swung canes.

For a single instant, Cora and Cal seemed diverted by the excitement. Their hackles rose and their eyes gleamed, but Leigh gave a harsh command, and they subsided. Suddenly blind, suddenly deaf, they moved sedately before the carriage.

Leigh smiled, and his blue eyes shone as he looked about him, and then at Anitra. He saw the faint beginnings of a frown on her face as they rolled out of town, and knew she had noticed the particular road they were taking. He held her hand and said, "Yes, Anitra, you've guessed it. We're going to see your father and Antonio."

"I never thought I'd go to the ranch again," she answered stiffly, a cold dread welling up in her. She had thought she was finished with her past. She had thought she had put it behind her forever.

Leigh went on swiftly, "I know how you feel. And that's one reason I think we must go. We've done no wrong, Anitra. I want your father and Antonio to accept our marriage."

"They won't, Leigh. I know them too well to pretend otherwise."

"Perhaps not. Still, I'd feel better if we tried. I'd feel better if we went to them and told them that we're married, and asked for your father's blessing."

She clutched hard at Leigh's fingers, turning to look into his eyes. "Leigh, you can't really think . . . "

"Listen for a minute. We've fallen in love and married. I want him to see that so you'll be free of him, Anitra. I don't want your father's disapproval making you unhappy. I'm a proud man, and I've friends in Tres Ríos. I can't have my wife afraid to walk across the plaza lest she meet her father or her brother and have them insult her. I can't have even a small part of the town believe that if your father disowns you you must have done something wrong." He searched her face anxiously, waiting for her answer.

How young he looked in that moment, she thought. And how good of him to concern himself with her feelings —even if such concern was useless. And it was. She knew her father too well to expect him to change. She said unwillingly, "All right, Leigh. We'll try, if you like."

When they rode into the courtyard, Porfirio was there to hand her down from the carriage. She drew a deep breath, allowing the familiarity of the place to touch her.

"Doña Anitra, welcome," Porfirio said.

"Is my father at home?"

Porfirio nodded, his eyes sliding sideways to look at Leigh as he leaned over to caress the dogs and say, "Now you sit and be good, and don't let anyone touch you."

"Your Felicia?" Anitra was asking.

"Well enough, but not getting younger."

"And Dora?"

Porfirio grinned. "Doña Anitra, you've been gone only five days."

Doña Anitra . . . the first time she'd been called that since she and Leigh were married. It was a title of respect not used much any longer, except in places like Tres Ríos where the old ways still prevailed.

She went to the door, but it opened before she reached it.

Dora gave a cry of pleasure and welcomed her with a quick embrace. "Anitra, niña . . . "

"Will my father receive me, Dora?"

Dora's mouth firmed. She wouldn't ask him. She turned quickly and led the way into the sala.

Lorenzo looked up from the papers he held on his

213

knees. "I suppose you want your clothes, whatever you left behind of your life here," he said harshly.

Antonio rose from the settle where he'd been sitting. "Papa, please . . . " And to Anitra, "I'm glad to see you, my sister."

She forced a smile for Antonio, then turned back to her father. She had known from the look on his face, even before he spoke, that it was no use, but for Leigh's sake she forced herself to say gently, "I've not come for my things, my father. I . . . you've probably heard . . . but I wanted to tell you myself that Leigh and I were married five days ago in Santa Fe."

"Married? Is that what you call marriage? You ran away like some slut of the village and said your vows before a gringo filled with whiskey, who made out a paper for silver. Is that marriage?"

"It was in the church of San Miguel," she said quietly. "And whatever you think, my vows were made before God and man."

"And what do you want?"

Before she could speak, Leigh said in a voice edged with anger, "I'll answer, Don Lorenzo. We came here for your blessing." As he went on, Anitra took his arm, feeling his deep surge of anger. "I love Anitra, and I'll make her happy. I'm a wealthy man, and I don't want anything you have for her. Except your good will."

"Papa, listen . . . " Antonio began softly, seeing the distress in Anitra's face. He had never liked Leigh. He believed Anitra was wrong to marry away from her own people. But Antonio wanted her happiness. "It's done, Papa . . . "

Lorenzo got to his feet, roared, "Get out of my house, you damnable gringo! And take with you that accursed girl who has meant nothing but trouble and heartache to me since the day she was born. Get out! Leave me!"

Leigh put his arm around Anitra's shoulders. He drew her with him. His eyes were a dark blue and his dimple was gone. He shot a single murderous look over his shoulder and led her outside.

Lorenzo heard the slam of the heavy door and fell back into his chair, the dim shadows gathering around him. His breath came hard, labored. He tried to see the words on the roof beam, but a gray cloud hung before his eyes. He pushed himself to his feet, pain thrusting like spears through the back of his head. Antonio cried, "My father, what is it?"

"I'm sorry," Leigh said quietly, as they rode away. "I'd never have asked you to go back if I'd imagined . . . "

"I'll never go back," she answered. "No matter what happens, Leigh." She meant what she said, but they were hardly beyond the acres of the ranch when Porfirio came pounding and shouting after them.

"Doña Anitra, your father . . . you must come."

Leigh reined in. "What's the matter?"

"He's very sick, Antonio says." Porfirio looked into Anitra's face. "Believe me, niña. You must come."

Leigh made the decision. He turned the carriage, and, with the dogs following, they returned to the ranch.

The courtyard was filled with grim-faced men and frightened women. They watched Anitra hurry inside. Eustacio Rivera was among them, and as she passed, he thought, Pobrecita! I'll make for her a bulto of the Virgen de Guadalupe, and she'll look upon it and be soothed in her grief.

They found Lorenzo lying on the floor of the sala

with Antonio kneeling at his side. His face was gray and his breath came slowly and harshly.

"He can't speak," Dora whispered. "He can't hear or see, I think."

Anitra knelt. "Papa?"

His body convulsed and she drew back, but his hand crept along the floor toward her and found her gown, drawing her closer. His other hand inched slowly toward Antonio and touched a sleeve and clung to it.

A few minutes later the harsh slow rasp of his breath was stilled.

20

Leigh smiled at Anitra across the length of the table, his eyes as bright as the flame that danced over the white tapers beneath.

Watching, Antonio forced his gaze away. A twist of discomfort burned through him, stoked a restlessness in his long legs. He crossed them at the knee, and felt the tip of his boot hook in the thick floor covering.

"More wine?" Leigh asked quickly, reaching for the decanter.

"No, but thank you," Antonio replied.

It was a good vintage that Leigh served. Not for him the slightly raisiny wines of the grapes grown in the valley. His were brought up in casks from Santa Fe. And where those casks had been filled, only God in His Heaven knew, Antonio thought, with a mental shrug.

The meal had been a good one, too. He supposed that Leigh's table was always thus, covered with a white damask that seemed never to have been used before, and the china thin and hand painted.

Automatically Antonio adjusted the collar of his shirt and made sure the scar at his throat was covered. He was, he supposed, accustomed only to ranch life and ranch food, and that was what suited him.

He hardly remembered those years of misery when

he had struggled against his father's will. He understood now that only the need for manhood had oppressed him. He had found what he sought in the Brotherhood and had become again his father's son.

And now the ranch was his life.

But Leigh had known faraway places and had different tastes, as well as the wealth to enjoy them. And enjoy them he plainly did. His pleasure in his possessions was blatant. El Castillo—the very name chosen for his house bespoke the pride of ownership. It was the same for the objects with which he had filled the place. And the look he bent upon Anitra, too . . .

Antonio carefully unhooked the tip of his boot from the floor covering and uncrossed his legs. He caught Anitra leaning sideways to watch, and their eyes met, and for an instant it was the same as when they were children together. He grinned. She burst into laughter.

Leigh said, "Then if you'll have no more wine, we'll take coffee and brandy in the sala."

When Tinita had served them, Leigh said, "Tell me, Antonio, do you know well any of the politicos in Santa Fe?"

"No. I don't."

"Don César does, of course," Anitra put in.

Smiling, Antonio said, "I feel that the less those politicos hear of Tres Ríos, the better."

Leigh laughed softly. "Antonio, surely you must realize that our valley is a part of the world."

The brandy burned Antonio's throat. Finally he said, "It is our world, Leigh. And we want no other."

"Pay no attention to him, my husband," Anitra said, smiling, though her voice was serious. "Antonio is another one of those who refuses to accept progress."

"I accept it," Antonio protested quickly. "But only if it doesn't mean losing everything I care about."

"It means just the opposite," Leigh retorted firmly.

When he spoke of progress he wasn't thinking of the benefits of outside investment in the valley or the benefits that statehood would bring. To him it meant only his increasing ownership of the valley.

Antonio saw the darkening of Leigh's eyes and was certain that he didn't know the man his sister had married. Then he wondered if she knew him, if she knew him as a woman should know her husband.

"And how are things at the ranch?" Anitra asked, hoping to break the silence.

Antonio adjusted the black mourning band on his arm. "All's well, my sister."

"Whatever help I can give you . . . " Leigh offered.

Antonio finished his brandy, rose. "Thank you, but I need none. And now I must go. I've an errand or two."

The Penitentes, Anitra thought. Always it was the Brotherhood that occupied him. The old irritation was sour in her throat, a bitterness she couldn't swallow. How was it that Antonio refused to look forward, and that she refused to look back?

She considered that same question the next day as she sat sewing in the courtyard. Why did men like Antonio fear the changes that must inevitably come as the territory moved ever more surely in the direction of statehood? Why did they oppose men like Leigh, who welcomed, even brought, those changes about?

A clatter near the wall distracted her. She raised her head to look.

Tinita's brother, Eloy, was knocking at a half-buried adobe brick. The clearing out of the courtyards, both front and back, was nearly finished. Soon he would begin the first of the plantings. The evergreens would go in at the end of the month. Next spring she would start with the flowers.

As she watched, he turned his head to shoot a sour look at the dogs inside their wire cage. He disliked and feared Cora and Cal as much as they disliked him.

A shiver touched Anitra. She bent her head, took a careful stitch. She could hardly blame Eloy for feeling as he did. Leigh's animals were not endearing.

She drew the silken thread carefully through the fine fabric and paused to examine it before taking another stitch. This baptismal dress, she told herself, must be perfect. Those hours sitting unwillingly at her grandmother's side suddenly had meaning. Anitra and Leigh had been asked to be padrinos, godparents, to the new Delagado son, their infant Felipe.

She shook the dress out and studied it. It was of the finest linen she had been able to locate in Tres Ríos, long and beruffled so that the tiny body would be quite lost in it. But the shirring and tucks and lace inserts were exactly as Doña Lupe would have done them herself.

She felt restless. All through the past summer months she and Leigh had gone out together each day. She marveled at his never-failing interest in the valley. He was fascinated by each arroyo, by every track. By now she supposed he knew every canyon, every stand of cottonwood and willow thicket, every trail that led to or from Tres Ríos. She had begun to realize that his feeling for the land was akin to his feeling for her, and somehow it frightened her. Though he offered her every freedom, she had a sense of being constricted within the bounds of his love.

In those first days after her father's death, Leigh had

not left her alone. It was as if he wanted to protect her even from the memory of those awful moments when her father had lain between Antonio and herself, blind eyes glaring into her face, once again binding brother and sister together.

Leigh was with her when Josefa and Matthew came to pay their condolences at the velorio. Anitra sat with Antonio near the candle-banked coffin out of respect, not love.

Josefa's cold bony hands clasped hers. Her pale lips pressed Anitra's cheek. "I'm sorry for this, Anitra. I know how you must feel. I'll visit you soon at El Castillo."

Anitra thanked her dryly and wished the formalities done.

Matthew took her hand, bowed over it formally. "My regrets," he said, and his eyes searched hers, asking, Are you happy with Leigh? Is all well with you?

"My thanks," she answered stiffly, responding only to the spoken words, while she shivered at his touch and reached out blindly for Leigh's arm.

Leigh was with her, too, when Dora came, saying, "Anitra, Antonio sends me to take care of you."

Anitra had seen the faint darkening in his eyes and answered quickly, "But who will take care of Antonio then? He's alone at the ranch now. How will he manage?"

"He has Felicia. And Porfirio. Be sure they will see to him, niña."

"And I will see to Anitra," Leigh said firmly.

Dora gave him a blank-eyed look, returned her gaze to Anitra. "You mustn't send me away."

"Ah, Dora, how can you say that? I'm not sending you away, yet I'd feel happy to know you were with my brother."

"You don't want me here," Dora answered. Anitra

heard the open relief in her tone. She knew that the older woman didn't like El Castillo.

"I'm concerned only for Antonio," Anitra answered.

But it wasn't so, she conceded to herself. It would have been good to have Dora with her. Yet she had seen a flicker of displeasure in Leigh's eyes. He wanted her completely to himself. He wanted nothing in El Castillo to remind her of the past. "Antonio will need you," she said firmly.

"Don Antonio is proving himself to be a good patrón," Dora said softly.

"And we'll do all we can for him," Leigh assured her, seeing in his mind the wide, rolling, sunlit acres of the ranch.

But Dora didn't respond. She drew forth two wrapped objects from the straw basket she had brought with her and opened them slowly. They were bultos, one of La Virgen de Guadalupe, the other of San José. "Eustacio sends you these, niña. He wants them to be with you always, that they may watch over you."

"You must thank him for me," Anitra answered, taking the two carved statues into her arms.

When Dora had gone, Leigh said softly, "If you really want her here with you, Anitra . . ."

In this, too, he offered to indulge her, though he preferred otherwise, she was certain.

She smiled at him. "Dora was with me always when I was a child, but I'm a child no longer, my husband."

He left her only three times during those summer months. Business in the South had taken him away, and though she had teased him to take her with him, he had been surprisingly adamant. These were the only times he had said no to a wish of hers. Perhaps for that reason she was curious about those trips and the business that they involved.

He told her nothing of the hours of backbreaking labor with pick and shovel and sieve, when his clothes were dark with sweat, and his hands toughened with callouses, and he looked more like a mountain prospector than a man of ease and wealth. He told her nothing of his trips to deliver the rough golden nuggets that enriched his steadily growing bank accounts, which to him represented only another acre, another section of that land to which his passion was devoted.

She wore, without knowing it, the symbols of these successful forays into his hidden source of power. For each time, on his return, he had presented her with a gift.

Once he placed around her throat a strand of small, perfectly cut emeralds and said, smiling at her, "The color of your eyes, my dear. I couldn't resist them, could I?"

Another time he led her into the courtyard, and she found awaiting her a small buggy, black and gleaming with silver emblems on its doors, the mark of the Martínez y Escobedos, and below it written the words, El Castillo.

A third time he brought her a gown of purest Chinese silk, the color of the yellow roses of July, and a Spanish shawl embroidered with the same yellow roses on a black silk ground.

He was, she thought now, as she began the careful stitching again, a most complicated man, this husband of hers. Though he smiled often and spoke softly and moved with graceful ease, she had begun to see that there was a granite-like quality beneath. She remembered watching him handle the dogs. He wouldn't give way to them. He would destroy them first. He would give way to nothing, she thought suddenly. Not unless it suited him.

Deep in consideration of these things, she was unaware of his approach. Suddenly his shadow fell over her and she looked up, smiling.

"Will you be finished with that frippery in time, do you think?"

"Of course I will. To be invited to be padrinos is an honor. To make the gown is an honor, too."

His big hands touched the white linen gently, and she noticed the callouses on his palm. Always, when he returned from his business trips, he had them. But they were soon smoothed away. It was one more thing that she wondered about.

"You do beautiful work, Anitra. Who taught you?"

"My grandmother. And I assure you, I wasn't a very willing pupil, though I'm glad now that she was insistent I learn."

He grinned. "You'd rather have been riding with your brother, of course." Then, teasingly, "And being rude to the strangers who crossed your path."

"Rude?" She laughed. "If you thought me rude then, you should have heard me when I was really tart."

"I have, my dear. Don't you remember?"

She felt a flush stain her cheeks. His grin broadened to cover a deep thrust of jealousy. She had wanted Matthew first. Perhaps she still wanted him.

Anitra was saying, "But if I'd known how soon I was to lose my grandmother, I'd have wanted to spend more time with her. She was all the family I ever had except Antonio."

She knew that Leigh understood why she didn't mention her father. He knew everything about her—except for Matthew, of course. Quickly she thrust the thought away. Matthew was nothing to her now. He was married to Josefa, and she to Leigh. And it was what they both wanted.

She said quickly, "Do you know, Leigh, you've met all my family, seen into my life, and I suddenly realize, I know nothing of yours."

"I've no family to know," he said, and as he spoke, the dogs bayed angrily, and Leigh felt a certain pleasure touch him. Cal and Cora were, in a sense, his real family.

"But you had people once, Leigh," Anitra protested. "Your mother and father—where did they live? Where were you born?"

"Far away from here. In another country and in another time—at least that's how it seems to me. And what difference does it make?" He took her hand in his. "There's only you now, my dear. And that's how I want it." His voice deepened, became harsh as his fingers tightened around hers. He thought of Matthew again, saying, "I'll never let you go. Never, Anitra."

She knew how deeply he meant those words, and later, with terror in her heart, she was to remember them.

But now she only laughed as she freed herself. "How shall I finish Felipe's baptismal dress if you distract me?"

Small Felipe wore the lavishly trimmed gown.

His mouth yawned wide and pink as the padre said over him the traditional words, and Anitra and Leigh, in the sight of their fellows and God, made the traditional vows to see to the baby's religious upbringing, to provide him with home and shelter should he be orphaned.

Anitra, holding the soft squirming infant, stepped forward finally, and said to Carlota, "Receive this loving jewel, who from the Church comes, with the Holy Sacraments, and the holy water received."

225

Carlota took him joyfully, but with awe, too, and responded, "I receive thee, loving jewel, who from the Church comes, with the Holy Sacraments, and the holy water received."

Afterward there was a feast, and Leigh presented to the infant three five-dollar gold pieces instead of the usual one offered by the padrone, and Carlota cried, "Dios, you're already spoiling my son," and stretched on tiptoe to kiss Leigh's cheek.

Three weeks later the Bishop arrived in Tres Ríos, and all the infants born in the two-month period since his last visit were brought to the village church for their confirmation. As the Bishop proceeded with the ritual, there were screams of rage and fear, but he smiled into each tiny face, lightly striking the soft cheek, and murmured that the child must be ready to accept any pain for his religion.

It was the evening after this confirmation ceremony, a cold one, that Esteban came to El Castillo, but it wasn't the chill of early autumn in his bones that made him shiver. Esteban was troubled, more troubled than he had ever been in his life. His debts pressed him from all sides. This, as opposed to the happiness he felt at having a son, made his days and nights miserable.

He had, even when younger, looked more than his years, and now that he had turned forty-three, this quality was even more noticeable. His thin black hair had become webbed with white and had receded, leaving him very nearly bald. His small paunch had rounded, and his shoulders, too. In addition to his moustache, he now wore a beard, but it was thin, his sallow jowls showing through its sparseness. By contrast, his step was still jaunty when Tinita admitted him to the house and brought him to the sala.

226

He greeted Anitra affectionately. "Carlota sends you her love."

"Ah, but she didn't come with you. I'm disappointed, Esteban."

He managed a smile. "She had the feeding of Felipe to attend to, I think. And my visit this evening is of business matters, which would only bore her." They would frighten her, too, he thought. He had no intention of allowing her to know the true state of his affairs and he hoped that Leigh hadn't spoken of them with Anitra, as he followed the American to his office.

He had been there several times before, of course, but each visit brought him a new uneasiness. It was a small room, with thick walls and two high, barred windows. There were only two chairs, hard and straight, with no ornamentation; the desk, too, was plain and workmanlike. In the corner squatted a large black safe.

But for that safe, which seemed to emanate visible waves of wealth, the place was like a monk's cell. Esteban lit a small cigar, puffed at it. He took a deep breath and began. "Even in this backwater," he said, "even here in Tres Ríos we feel the ripples of currents of the East. The crash of the New York City Stock Exchange this summer, the panic that ensued, the . . . " Esteban stopped himself. "Ah, the summer of 1893 will be remembered for a long time. But that's not what I came here to talk about. It's a proposal I have to offer you, Leigh."

Leaning back in his chair, Leigh nodded. He had been awaiting this moment for some time, knowing it would come, for he had himself arranged it. "I am always interested to hear of proposals, as you know, Esteban."

"Thank you, my cousin," said Esteban. "You see, I'm in severe need of cash. If you could lend me some ten thousand, I'd pay you whatever interest you ask as soon as the spring wool is sold at the end of March."

"We're kinsmen," Leigh said softly. "And became so through your aid. You must know that I'd do anything to help you."

Esteban held his breath.

"Of course I'll let you have the money."

Esteban breathed again. "Thank you, Leigh. You won't regret it, I promise you."

"Of course I won't." Leigh smiled faintly. "But you know, Esteban, it's different now that I'm a married man. I have Anitra to think of. She must be protected, and if, like you, we were to have children . . . "

"Yes, yes, my cousin, and may God bless you with that most marvelous joy soon."

"I hope so. But that's why I don't dare take the risks I once took. The interest on such a loan means nothing to me, nor do I need it, but for Anitra's sake, I must have some security. After all, if something should happen to me . . . "

"What security?" Esteban asked quickly, a rasp in his voice. There was so little that he owned outright. The house on the plaza was already mortgaged to Leigh.

Leigh smiled reassuringly. "It's only a formality, of course. We both understand that. You've nothing to worry about, have you? Your return on the spring wool will be excellent."

"The security?" Esteban asked again.

"Your ranch, Esteban. It's all you have that you can offer me."

Esteban coughed on the cigar smoke. It was, he realized, just what he feared Leigh would say. And the ranch had been in Delagado hands for nearly two hundred years. Early Delagados, young and fearless, had marched with their people three times around the boundaries of the grant, declaring it theirs in the name of God and the King. Other Delagados had died to keep it so. His own father, he himself, had struggled for years to maintain what was theirs. What Leigh proposed was a frightening risk to take. In the past six years, much gold had gone into Santa Fe pockets, and still his title was not safely cleared. Mounting expenses due to accident and misadventure had drained him, almost as if a malevolent intelligence was planning his ruin. He couldn't hide from himself what might lie ahead, should the ill luck of the past dog him into the future.

Yet Leigh was his kinsman, through Anitra's cousin-hood with Carlota, and a compadre now as well. Even if something did happen and he found that he couldn't repay the loan on time, Leigh would surely extend it for as long as necessary.

Finally Esteban allowed himself to face the truth. He had no choice. If he was to go on, there was simply no choice.

He said aloud, "Very well, Leigh. If you'll prepare the papers, I'll sign them at the bank tomorrow."

21

Some small sound beyond the window awakened Anitra. For a moment she lay still, aware only of a pale finger of moonlight touching the brocade of the canopy overhead. But then she realized that she was alone.

She sat up, shivering. The dying embers in the fireplace were no more protection against the midnight chill than was her long-sleeved, high-necked white gown. She lit a lamp on the bedside table, and as its quick light wavered across the white walls, she heard the faint sound again. It came from outside.

She slipped from the bed, hurried to the high window. By stretching on tiptoe, she could see through its ornamental bars into the courtyard below. A black shadow, horse and man, moved quietly toward the gate, where two dogs waited, still as black statues.

Leigh, with Cora and Cal . . .

She tried to open the casement-window catch, but it stuck, resisting her suddenly shaking fingers. By the time she had freed it and pulled the window ajar, he had gone through the gate, his shadow huge and ominous, and it was silently closing behind him.

She looked at the ormulu clock he had brought .her from one of his trips to Santa Fe. The golden leaves in which its face was set gleamed through the dimness. Its hands said half after twelve, an odd hour for him to go out.

She shivered again. A strange silence, which at first she couldn't identify, enwrapped El Castillo. Then, slowly, recognition came to her. What she missed was the sound of the dogs. All was still in the courtyard below. All was still in the office she had never seen.

She sank down on the edge of the bed, wondering where Leigh had gone. The clock sang sweetly at one o'clock, then at two. By then she had snuggled beneath the quilts. Still her ears strained for sound of his return. She heard nothing, but she was wakeful when he finally came, as silent as a shadow, into the room. She sat up, asked anxiously, "What is it, Leigh? Where did you go? I heard something, hours ago it seems to me, and when I looked from the window, I saw you . . . " Her words trailed away.

A trick of the faint lamplight seemed to have wiped his face clean of all expression. He had become a stranger, a man she had never seen before. But even as she watched, her heart suddenly pounding, his mouth began to curve into a faint smile, his dimple deepened.

"I'm sorry I disturbed you, Anitra." He sat beside her, slid a warm arm around her shoulder, and hugged her close. "It was nothing for you to worry about."

"Nothing that you went out in the middle of the night for two hours or more, Leigh? I ask you—how can I believe that?" It was only because she was leaning against him that she could feel the stiffness in his long body, could sense his withdrawal.

His voice was mild, half-laughing, when he said, "If you must know, I thought I heard something. I got up to see about it."

"But . . ."

"You were still sleeping then, and I saw no reason to disturb you. I went into the courtyard to have a good look around."

"Did you find anything?"

"There was nothing to find. So I rode around the walls, just to be certain."

She thought, but didn't say, that nothing could climb the walls of El Castillo. For the first time she wondered why he had troubled to build those walls so high, as if he had expected attack. And then she asked why he had taken the dogs with him.

"For safety's sake. They see far better in the dark than I do, you know."

"And there was truly nothing?" she asked, still troubled.

He shook his head. "If there was, I didn't find it." He rose then. "Let's go back to sleep, Anitra. It's a long while until morning."

The next time she awoke it was to the sound of tolling bells. She listened for a little while before she rose uneasily and went to the window.

There was a red glow against the pale dawn in the sky. Her breath frosted the windowpane. She smoothed the mist off and stared through the bars, blinking as the glow spread over the mountain slopes just above the village.

A horseman rode wildly past the outside wall. There was the thud of hooves on the hard earth, the jingling of spurs and harnesses.

The dogs below barked in rising excitement.

She bent over Leigh and awakened him, saying

urgently, "Leigh . . . Leigh, there's a fire, I think. It looks . . . I'm very nearly certain . . . Esteban's hacienda is burning."

Leigh yawned, stretched, bronze curls disheveled. "What makes you think it's Esteban's place?"

"Look out and you'll see for yourself."

He rose without hurry, went to the window. "Yes," he agreed at last. "Yes, I'm afraid you're right, Anitra." He added in a deep, soft voice, "It's too bad, isn't it?"

"It's terrible, terrible," she cried. "Oh, I'm sorry for him, for Carlota, too. What will they do now, Leigh?"

"Why, they'll rebuild the place, I suppose."

"But that will take a great deal of money, Leigh. And I doubt that they have it."

Even as she spoke, she began to dress. A warm woolen gown, thick stockings, her riding boots. She swept her long hair back, tied it at the nape of her neck with a ribbon.

Leigh said, "They've the house in town, you know. They'll be all right."

But she ignored that. "Hurry, we must hurry. Perhaps there's still something we can do." She looked one last time at the red pall that hung over the mountain, then caught up a shawl. When she saw that he was still not quite dressed, she said stiffly, "We here in Tres Ríos have always answered the fire warning. We care for our neighbors, and our neighbors care for us."

He moved more quickly then, but still with the same graceful ease. "I'll go alone."

"No, Leigh. I must be with the Delagados." And as they hurried down the steps together, she went on, "Perhaps there'll be some way you can help them, Leigh."

She didn't notice then that Leigh didn't answer her. But later she would remember that, too.

It was the second time that night that Leigh had ridden out. Earlier he had been accompanied only by Cora and Cal, and, cutting a wide route around the dark and sleeping town, he had approached the old hacienda from above. No light flickered behind its dusty windows. No movement stirred the shadows. In the distance there was the single bleat of a sheep.

Though Esteban lived in the house on the plaza, it was from here that he ran his ranch. Here his records were stored, his books and tallies and bills of sale. From here the provisions were distributed, the equipment handed out. In these ancient rooms the shepherds played cards and told each other tales. The old hacienda was the heart of Esteban's land and it was at the heart that Leigh had struck.

The kerosene-dampened hides he had carried roped together on his back were heavy, but he hardly felt their weight. His eyes moved in constant search through the dark. His ears strained in constant suspicion of the silence.

When he eased the door open, its rusty hinges squealed a complaint. He sent the dogs in, saying softly, "Find them, Cal. Get them, Cora."

They surged over the cracked threshold. Snuffling they went from room to room.

The place was empty, as it should have been at that time of the year. The shepherds had still not come down from the higher country with their flocks.

He waited a moment more, then followed the dogs in. He went quickly to the four corners of the oldest section of the house, the central square onto which, over the generations, new rooms had been added as the Delagados multiplied.

Here, in the odors of manure, rot, and long-spoiled food, he squatted down, his hands busy, the damp hides loosened on the moldy floor beside him.

It was the work of only a few moments. Then, calling the dogs, he rode away.

Now, hours later, he returned with Anitra at his side.

The trail was crowded with horses, with shouting men, all eerily lit by the glow that spread over the sky.

He leaned toward Anitra and said in a regretful tone, "I'm afraid there's not much to be done here."

Her face was strained, almost haggard. Her black curls, escaped from their ribbon, hung to her shoulders, loose and free-flowing. She was beautiful even in her distress. She said, "Perhaps they can save something."

"I don't think so." He was fairly certain there would be nothing to salvage. The fire would have burned slowly for a long time before it exploded into the hungry flames that would consume the walls, the frames, the furniture, and all the records and papers, as well as what had caused it.

He had planned that the fire would burn slowly while he returned to El Castillo and lay once again beside Anitra.

"There's nothing to be done," Esteban muttered to Matthew, who stood beside him.

Matthew nodded, but didn't speak.

"It's all gone," Esteban groaned. "What am I to do? What shall I tell Carlota?"

Anitra, hearing the last, cried, "Ah, Esteban, no, you'll see by daylight, when it's possible to go in, you'll see it's not as bad as it seems now."

The men said nothing, but Matthew looked at her and then at the smoking ruins, and her eyes filled with tears.

She clung to Leigh's arm and whispered, looking up at him, "Leigh, what can we do?"

The crowd surged around them and there was a great shout as the last heavy beams of the house collapsed and a huge red tower of dancing red made a hungry leap for the sky.

Still Anitra clung to Leigh's arm and waited for him to answer. But then, across the space between them, her eyes met Matthew's. She remembered another fire, another night when the bells tolled over the valley. She remembered the intensity in Matthew's smudged, unhappy face as he drew her into his arms.

"But he blamed me, Hermano Mayor," Don Esteban's foreman had told Porfirio indignantly, while his eyes, ringed with fatigue, were anxious. "Me, who has been with him since . . . since . . . " A shrug. "Who remembers, Hermano Mayor? I don't know any more how long it's been. But I was a child of the ranch, I was born here. And he said to me that I must have been less than vigilant. I, he said, I had been careless. But it's not so. How can it be?"

Porfirio remembered now the look of the man's eyes, the sound of his voice. There had been no guilt in either—of that Porfirio was certain. The man knew he had been careful. There had been no smoldering embers behind him when he left the old hacienda that evening. He had left no candle burning, no lamp aflame. He had done nothing that could account for the total destruction of the place. Yet it had been destroyed.

Porfirio was filled with unease. Slowly he turned his head, surveying the trampled land around the broken and blackened walls—all that remained of the venerable house. There was nothing to see but the imprint of hooves, the deep ruts left by wagons, the heel marks of the boots dug in by men who had come to offer aid. With a shrug, Porfirio turned away.

He stepped carefully over the cold earth to the still-smoking ruins. He threw a leg over a jagged wall and let himself down cautiously near what had once been a corner fireplace. The split cone was warm to the touch of his fingers. He sniffed, sniffed again, a frown deepening between his heavy brows.

He spent two hours moving slowly through what was left, grunting as he squatted in crushed debris, sifting through it. He stuffed into the pocket of his sheepskin coat small bits of charred leather that he had painstakingly gathered, carefully noting in his mind the corners in which he had found them.

As he rode away, he saw Don Esteban. The man was seated on his horse, head bowed, hands limp at his sides.

It crossed Porfirio's mind to go to him, to offer comfort, to say, "Sea por Dios! God's will be done! All will be well, hombre."

But it was an impossible thing to do. Instead he rode on thinking, Something's wrong. There's something wrong in the valley.

Later, when he met with Antonio in the morada, as arranged earlier, he thought the same thing. But he kept his own counsel. He wasn't yet ready to speak.

Antonio said, "There's no doubt of it, mi hermano? You're absolutely certain?"

"I'm certain. I have no doubt at all," Porfirio answered. "But I heard of it just today, after I returned from the Delagado ranch. When it happened, I'm not sure, my brother. But it was in the bank that it occurred. Don Esteban signed a paper and Señor Ransome gave him a stack of gold."

"And was the paper read carefully?"

"Very carefully, mi hermano."

"And understood accurately?"

"I'm sure of it."

Antonio looked into the heart of the candle flame. He remembered how, at his own visit, Leigh had sat in his sala with his head against the carved high back of his chair. He remembered the sense of discomfort it had given him. He felt the same now.

He looked up at Porfirio and saw reproach in the older man's eyes. It was for this. Leigh had taken a mortgage on the Delagado ranch, and now the hacienda had burned to the ground. Porfirio had known nothing of the arrangement between Leigh and Esteban. But he believed that Antonio must have known it.

"Mi Hermano Mayor," Antonio said softly, emphasizing the words by repeating them, "mi Hermano Mayor, I assure you I knew nothing of it."

The title thus stressed indicated that Antonio spoke only as a Brother, and not as patrón. His position by birth and wealth were to be dismissed.

Porfirio nodded. "Perhaps they both wished it to be a secret."

"There are no secrets in Tres Ríos," Antonio said.

"I believe there may be." Porfirio turned his head to look into a shadowed distant corner.

The carreta de la muerte was there, dusty now, tipped forward on its shafts. Within the cart of death stood La Santa de la Muerte, the Saint of Death, her bony face enwrapped in a black shawl as always. She waited in her place for spring, for Santa Semana.

"Well, we shall see," he said at last.

But Antonio couldn't leave it at that. He believed the suspicion of a connection between these two separate events was unworthy of Porfirio, and surely unworthy of himself. He said, "Porfirio, I think that we are wrong and ugly in these thoughts."

A gleam appeared in Porfirio's dark eyes, his mouth turned down in a faint smile. "It's surely ugly. And possibly wrong."

"Then what do you think I should do, Hermano Mayor?"

"Do? Why, nothing. We must wait, of course. I only wanted you to know about this. It's not necessary to speak of it with anyone else."

Antonio's eyes clouded. "With whom would I speak of such matters?" And then he burst out, sounding like a boy again, "But we must be wrong. I can't believe any connection. The Delagados have been good to Leigh, my brother. And Don Esteban was his only friend in Tres Ríos for a long time. And he is godfather to Felipe."

"Yes, yes, I remember," Porfirio replied, once more glancing sideways at the Saint of Death. "I hope Señor Ransome remembers it, too."

He leaned forward to blow out the candle and rose.

Together he and Antonio left the morada. When they had locked the door behind them, they crossed the shadows of the clearing and mounted their horses. At the wooden bridge they separated, each taking a different path through the dark to the ranch.

22

It was a few days before Christmas.

Anitra stood in the kitchen doorway, checking to see if all was prepared. The huge barrel of sand that Eloy had brought in, the long rows of thick white candles, the bundles of brightly colored papers, and the large buckets of candies.

Yes, all was as it should be.

A further glance assured her that Tinita had finished the refreshments—a tall silver pot of hot chocolate and small cakes filled with caramel custard.

It would be a good few hours, the padre would be pleased, and the children of the church joyful. She looked at the watch pinned to her collar. It was well after noon. Carlota should already have arrived.

Anitra was anxious that she not be alone when Josefa came. She wanted to avoid the possibility of any confidences. Although they had performed this holiday task together for so many years, Anitra wouldn't have invited Josefa except that she had been virtually forced to it.

Leigh had just driven her to the plaza, insisting that she must not walk because there might be snow. As he helped her from the carriage, Matthew and Josefa pulled up behind them, and Josefa called in her high piping voice, "Wait, Anitra. I want to talk to you."

It was impossible to flee, and Anitra reluctantly went to speak with her.

"You haven't come to see me," Josefa said reproachfully. "You said you would." Her face within the crescent of gray fur was as small as a doll's. "Ah, we did have fun once, but it's dull without you, Anitra."

"I've been busy," Anitra said. "So much to do—so much—" There was false apology in her voice, and beneath the hem of her gown her feet did a small impatient dance.

Matthew recognized both. He had known her too long to be deceived. She would struggle for courtesy and yearn to be away.

Josefa turned her sad eyes on him. "And Matthew," she said, "he always has some excuse for why we must stay at home."

Matthew could have taken her by her small bony shoulders and shaken her. She knew perfectly well that he was seeing to her health so that she might live.

Leigh cut in, smiling, "Well, now that we've met, let me suggest that you come to El Castillo tomorrow. Carlota will be there. They're going to make farolitos and piñatas for the church."

"As we always used to do," Josefa said softly. "Oh, Matthew, Anitra, do you remember?"

Anitra kept annoyance from showing on her face, as she quickly seconded the invitation. There was nothing she could do but pretend an enthusiasm she didn't feel.

Now she hoped only that Carlota would arrive quickly.

But when Tinita came to tell her that her guests had arrived, she sensed that it was Josefa and Matthew who were here first. Clasping her fingers in the thick velvet folds of her gown, she went slowly into the sala.

Matthew took off his hat, bowed a wordless greeting.

"Josefa," Anitra said, "come to the fire. You look like an icicle."

Indeed, Josefa did resemble an icicle. She was so pale and thin in her light-brown frock. Even her lips seemed white. But her eyes were aglitter with excitement.

She said hoarsely, "Ah, I do like this house, Anitra. It's . . . it's full of love." Matthew thought, She might as well have said outright that there was no love in her own. The home that Don Cipriano had made was no more. His spirit was no longer there to warm it.

When Josefa tried to speak again, she coughed, and she couldn't stop. Her body was wracked by hacking explosions until her eyes streamed tears and her white lips turned blue.

Matthew scooped her into his arms, carried her to the settle, and sat down, holding her against him. Even so as Anitra ran for Leigh's brandy, he was aware of her grace, the shimmer of her hair against the ivory of her cheek.

She brought him the brandy, and he fed it to Josefa, forcing it drop by drop between her lips. At last she lay still.

"All right now?" he asked in a quiet voice.

She smiled faintly. "I'm sorry, Anitra. I can't think what happened. I've never done this before. But it's over now, thank goodness."

Never done this before, Matthew thought. Once, twice, three times a day, she had these seizures. Did she lie intentionally or did she forget?

"It was too cold for you to be out," he said, then looking apologetically at Anitra, "But she did insist, you know.

And I hated to spoil her fun. Being with you and Carlota . . . "

"Carlota hasn't yet arrived," Anitra answered.

"Oh? Then you haven't yet begun," Josefa cried. "I'm so glad. I was afraid you had."

Matthew released her and rose quickly. "I'll return for you in a few hours, Josefa. You'll be careful, won't you? If you tire, you'll rest?"

"I'll be careful," she said sulkily.

It was, Anitra thought, just like when Don Cipriano had looked after Josefa. But was that a task for a young man, a man with his life before him?

She managed to smile a farewell at him but avoided his eyes.

When he had gone, Josefa said softly, "It's warm in El Castillo, Anitra. Snug and warm, even though it's so big a house. You have all that you want, haven't you?" But the question was only a courtesy. She was about to go on, and it was with relief that Anitra heard Carlota's voice. "Dios, it's cold!" Then her cousin was in the doorway.

"I'm sorry, Anitra," she said, breathing hard. "I know that I'm a bit late. But it's been such a day!" And, "Hello, Josefa. How are you?"

"As always," Josefa answered, sighing.

Anitra looked at the window. It had begun to snow and soon the mesas would be white with it.

"Have they begun work yet on the old hacienda?" Josefa was asking.

Carlota held her hands out to the fire. "No. No, they haven't."

"It'll be soon," Anitra answered. Then quickly, to forestall further discussion, "Shall we go to the kitchen? The materials are set out there, and we'll have more space to work."

Settled at the big table, with the chocolate and cakes served by Tinita, they began to assemble the farolitos, filling bags with sand, fitting in the thick white candles, then folding back the rims of the brown paper bags. These would light the walls of the church and mark the path to it.

Later, when they had finished the farolitos, they made the piñatas, weaving colored papers into animal forms, and stuffing the insides of them with candies and tiny carved animals.

Josefa said, "What happened was terrible, Carlota."

"And worse that they've not yet begun to build after all this time," Carlota said. "There are so many problems. I don't understand it—no matter how Esteban explains it. And I don't know what he'll do either. Today he's gone to Santa Fe to see my father and to talk to Vicente. Her voice shook and she looked at Anitra, dark eyes veiled. "Leigh visited the place the other day again. I think Esteban was glad."

"Matthew was also there," Josefa put in.

"It's frightening," Carlota whispered. Her slim hands were still, clasping strips of colored paper, blood-red against the white of her fingers. "Piñatas for the children of the church . . . piñatas . . . But what will my Felipe have? What will become of him?"

Anitra said quickly, "You mustn't think that way, Carlota. You'll see that it will be all right. Leigh will help Esteban rebuild the hacienda. I'm sure of it."

Later that same night, she and Leigh sat before the fire in the sala. The snow whispered steadily against the window and the piñon logs hissed on the hearth.

She said, "When Carlota was here today, she spoke of Esteban's troubles. It was terrible to see how her hands trembled, and the look in her eyes. She's very frightened."

"She has reason to be," Leigh said softly.

A chill touched Anitra, as if the very blood in her veins was suddenly cold. "But . . . but I don't understand, Leigh. It's only a matter of money, and you . . . surely you have that. Esteban will repay you, of course. If he can rebuild the hacienda and restock what has been lost over the past summer, then in the spring . . . "

"He can't restock his luck that's lost, Anitra. Esteban's luck has gone."

"Luck changes," she cried. "And these things do happen. If he has enough time . . . "

Leigh slid an arm around her and drew her head down to his shoulder. "My dear, if you could only hear yourself. You argue just like a woman. And I like that, I truly do. But you must allow me to deal with business. It has nothing whatever to do with you, and I don't want you to worry your pretty little head about it. That's what I'm here for, to deal with such things. So just let me do it as I think best."

She looked at him through her lashes. From that angle his jaw looked square and stubborn, his mouth thin, even cruel, belying the softness of his voice. She moved her head a little and looked again. The stony expression frightened her, but she said quietly, "I thank you for the compliment, my husband. It's nice to be told that I'm pretty. But I'm not a child. What I don't know of business I can surely learn, and I want . . . "

"There's no reason—no reason, Anitra. I'll give you all that you'll ever want."

"I'm concerned about Carlota and Esteban," she cut in firmly. "They're my kinsmen, and they've been good to me—to both of us, in many ways."

"I'll do whatever I can," Leigh said, smiling. "You can be sure of that. And I'll postpone collecting what Esteban owes me until I can't possibly hold off any longer." His voice dropped. "But you must remember, Anitra, I have you to think about now. And you'll always come first with me."

23

The pale sun of mid-March lit the mountain slopes.

Long columns of sheep trotted in brown waves, over the meadows, shouted on by the shepherds. The pens were ready, the shearing crews waited.

The first big chore of the spring was about to begin. Esteban watched from a ridge, his spirits rising. The panic of the summer before was fading. The year 1894 held promise. Soon, with the help of God, there would be mounds of thick brown wool, and the work of baling would begin. Soon the Delagado wagons would be loaded and on their way to the Santa Fe market.

He would recoup his losses, pay his debts and be able to breathe again as he hadn't been able to since he signed Leigh's notes.

"A beautiful sight, eh, Don Esteban?" his foreman said, smiling.

"A beautiful sight indeed," Esteban answered.

That night the sky was clear, but there was no moon. The stars were pale and far away and the Delagado ranch was dark.

Leigh moved silently, with Cora and Cal beside him. In the distance he heard the occasional bleat, the rest-less surgings that marked the herd. A few small fires showed where the shepherds huddled for warmth, drowsing through the night hours.

He grinned faintly, drew on heavy gloves, and went to work.

Anitra gazed past the ornamental bars into the courtyard. The morning sun was warm on her face. It would soon be time to begin the new plantings. There would be flowers and velvet-green grass, and the well house would be covered with morning glory. And the following spring, the shrubs would be rich with leaf and branch.

Suddenly she heard a bustle beyond the walls.

Leigh!

She jumped to her feet in a swirl of skirts and hurried to the front door. He had been gone for two days, two nights. The unnatural silence of the house had troubled her, and now her heart lightened at the thought of seeing him.

But it was Antonio who came riding in. Even in her disappointment she was happy to see him. He visited El Castillo rarely and she suspected that he blamed Leigh for Lorenzo's death.

As soon as she saw him she knew he had not come to pay a casual call. He was gaunt and pale, his dark hair disheveled. And then she noticed the horrible brown stains, stains that could be nothing but dried blood, that streaked his trousers.

"Antonio! Antonio, what is it? What's happened?"

He dismounted and embraced her quickly. "There's been trouble at the Delagado ranch, Anitra."

"More trouble?"

"An avalanche fell in one of the canyons last night. The shepherds went to see, and meanwhile, the sheep . . ."

"Esteban's sheep," she said softly.

"Esteban's sheep. Yes." He went on, "It was carnage. Wolves, it appears. Wolves that came down from the high forests . . . "

"But how . . . when . . . ?"

"Last night. They drove the animals mad with terror and tore out the throats of many." Antonio's green eyes were expressionless.

"I can hardly believe . . . "

"They say there have been no such wolves in these parts for thirty years and more," Antonio said. "The shepherds whisper among themselves that it was the work of Satan. Only the devil could have committed such carnage."

She swallowed hard. "Are many destroyed?"

"Some say two hundred. Some say two thousand." Antonio shrugged. "And it doesn't matter, for Esteban has lost all."

Anitra shivered. The old hacienda had burned down before Christmas. Now this . . .

"Antonio, come into the house. I'll give you coffee. You must rest a little."

"No. I'll go back." His eyes searched the courtyard. "Your husband, Anitra? He's not here?"

"He's in Santa Fe, but I expect him later today."

Antonio didn't mention the dogs, but his gaze lingered on the cage. It was the first time he had seen it empty. "I'd better go back to Esteban," he repeated. "But Carlota . . . she's alone . . . "

"I'll go at once," Anitra cried, and remembered Leigh's saying, "Esteban's luck has gone."

In the plaza she found small groups huddled together against the cold, staring at the white-covered mountain peaks above the town.

"Lobos! Who would believe it?"

"I remember . . . in my grandfather's time . . . "

"But now? Now?"

At Esteban's house the serving girl opened the door and showed Anitra in. A funereal silence hung about the place. Carlota sat in the sala, Felipe squirming in her lap. "You've heard the news, I suppose, Anitra."

"Yes, my cousin. Antonio brought me word only a few moments ago. I came to see what I can do for you."

"You can do nothing but thank you." Carlota sighed. "It's like a bad dream. One struggles and struggles to awaken but can't."

Was this the same girl who had laughed so happily at her wedding? Was this the Carlota who delighted in small subterfuges to get her way?

Anitra asked, "And Esteban? Where is he? Why isn't he with you now?"

"He's at the ranch, of course. They're looking . . . "

"Looking? But what for?" She remembered the dark stains on Antonio's trousers and shuddered.

Carlota answered, "To find the wolves—or their tracks. If there were wolves. For myself, I don't believe it, Anitra. Something inside tells me . . . "

"But if . . . if wolves didn't destroy the sheep, then . . . "

"I believe there's a devil loose in the valley," Carlota said. "He assaults us. I don't know why. I've harmed no one. Nor has Esteban. He's a good man. He *is* good, Anitra. Why should this happen to him?"

"Calm yourself," Anitra said, though her own heart was beating fast. "There'll be a way. Sheep can be replaced, after all."

"Do you know what it would cost to do that?" Carlota demanded bitterly. "Do you know that my father refuses now to help Esteban? He says he can't. And perhaps it's true, but I suspect it's all Vicente's doing. He doesn't want to see what might one day be his come to me now, even though I need it desperately."

"Oh, surely not, Carlota," Anitra protested. But she wasn't as assured as she sounded. She could believe this of Vicente. She rose, "I must go home. I'll come again to see you tomorrow."

Leigh rode in just as she reached El Castillo. She went toward him, but he motioned her back as he ordered the dogs into their cage.

"Go, Cora. Go, Cal." The dogs were excited. Their coats shone as if freshly washed and they ignored the raw and bleeding meat that Leigh tossed into the cage after them.

When she told Leigh what had happened, he took the news calmly. "It was a difficult winter. It can happen. I've heard of it in other places."

"But what can we do for them?"

"I don't know," he answered. "I'll talk to Esteban."

And later, that same day Esteban rode into the courtyard, slumped in the saddle. Antonio was with him.

Leigh said, "I can bring Cora and Cal out. If there are wolves, they'll find them. Believe me, Esteban, they can find anything."

"What good would it do?" Esteban asked. "It would be necessary only if I should replace the herds."

"If you can manage that." Leigh waited.

Esteban sighed. He had imagined the sheep shorn, the wool baled. He had seen it on the scales in the Santa Fe market. For a little while, then, he'd been a free man. But now . . . At last he said, "I can't replace the herds, as you know very well, my cousin, unless . . . unless . . . "

Still Leigh said nothing.

Antonio watched him, green eyes narrowed, the dog cage he had seen empty still in his mind.

Esteban collected himself enough to say, "It's a great deal to ask, my cousin. But if you could manage to give me . . ."

"Wait, Esteban," Leigh cut in, speaking softly. "Wait and think a little longer. You've borrowed a great sum of money from me in the past. Are you sure you want to borrow more? Remember that in only a little more than a month there are payments to be made again. I've always been patient. And I'll be that way now, too, of course. But are you sure you want to increase your indebtedness to me?"

Antonio drew his breath in sharply.

"I'm sure I don't want to," Esteban said weakly after a long moment. "You're quite right, Leigh. It wouldn't be wise."

On a bright spring afternoon, Anitra sat glumly in the courtyard watching Eloy set out the new young shrubbery. It was Martes Santo, Holy Tuesday. All that day she had heard the distant wail of the pito drifting on the wind. She had imagined the figures that would gather by dark in the morada across the meadow.

Behind her the dogs prowled in their cage, filling her with a vague disquiet. At that moment, they began to howl, and Carlota came into the courtyard. She walked slowly, dragging her feet, her young face so lined with worry that the woman she would one day become was already apparent. She dropped onto the bench near Anitra without greeting or comment, but only stared at her with tear-filled eyes.

Anitra said softly, "Tell me, Carlota—what's the matter?"

"We are destroyed." Carlota's voice trembled. She swallowed so hard that Anitra saw the muscles tighten in her throat. "Destroyed, Anitra!"

"Oh, no! What's happened now?"

Suddenly, where the sky had been blue, there was only a long narrow cloud of black. The birds were still and the dust in the courtyard lay motionless.

"You must know," Carlota said quietly. "Surely Leigh has already told you."

"Leigh has told me nothing, Carlota. Please—explain . . . " But already she felt a sick suspicion.

Esteban's luck had gone, Leigh had once said. Though she had begged him, he had never actually promised that he would help.

Carlota was saying, "Esteban had borrowed from Leigh, and in exchange he signed over the ranch as security. Esteban agreed because he couldn't help himself. And he was so certain Leigh wouldn't press him. And now . . . now . . . "

Anitra pressed her hands to her chest. She couldn't speak.

Carlota burst out, "But why did he do it? Is it because he's a gringo? Doesn't he have a heart? We loved you, Anitra. We brought the two of you together and helped you find your happiness. How could you do this to us? We're cousins. We share the same blood. How could you do it, Anitra?"

"I didn't know," Anitra whispered, trembling. "I never dreamed this could happen. I was sure he would help you if he could. He told me . . . " And again, she heard his words: "Esteban's luck has gone."

"But he wouldn't do anything. And then, when he did, it was only a pittance, and for further security. And now . . . now, the payments are due. Yesterday he told Esteban that he wouldn't wait. So we must pack and go at once—to my father's house in Santa Fe. Esteban can stay here no longer. He has lost what has been in his family for one hundred and fifty years. He feels that he has lost his honor. And Leigh Ransome owns the Delagado grant."

An evil spirit abroad in the valley . . . Carlota had used those words herself. Now she was naming the evil spirit: Leigh Ransome.

Anitra said softly, "You're distraught, Carlota. Leigh needs nothing from your Esteban. Believe me, he's a wealthy man."

"Then why has he done this to us?" Carlota demanded.

Why? Anitra asked herself. "I'll talk to him, Carlota. Let me see what he says."

"But will he listen to you? Will he change his mind?"

Anitra rose, touched Carlota's trembling hand. "Wait for me here."

Tinita emerged from the office as Anitra approached it. "He's loco, that one," the girl murmured. "How does a person clean under a man's feet? And the place stinks of those awful beasts!"

Anitra heard but said nothing. She went to the still-open door and saw the small bare room for the first time. Leigh sat at his desk, the sun making a bright halo of his bronze hair. He smiled as she came in.

"Leigh, I must speak to you at once."

"All right," he said, maneuvering her out of the office. "We'll go into the sala."

She sank onto the settle, feeling as if her legs would not hold her up another moment. "Carlota is here in the courtyard. She's half mad with fear of what will happen to her, and to Felipe."

Leigh said nothing.

"You have no idea how desperate she is, Leigh."

He leaned back, crossed his long legs. "I thought she might try it."

"Leigh, you mustn't do this to them! Not to Carlota and Esteban. They're your kinsmen. You're godfather to their son. The ranch is all they have. It has always been in his family."

"They're not my kinsmen," he said softly. "Though they are yours, I suppose. Still, that doesn't matter to me." He smiled faintly, but his eyes were dark. "Business is business, Anitra. I've told you that before. And I've told you that you mustn't concern yourself with it."

"It's been Delagado land since . . . "

"It's Ransome land now," he said softly.

"Were it not for them," she whispered, "we'd never have married, Leigh. You must know that."

He laughed and shook his head. "They only made it easier for me, my dear. I'd have had you no matter what. No one could have stood in my way."

"Leigh, I can't believe . . . it just isn't possible . . . "

He rose and drew her into his arms. "My dear, you simply don't understand. Men's affairs are something you know nothing about. Esteban understood the risk he took. I made it quite clear to him. What I've done is perfectly legal." His arm tightened, drawing her even closer. "And it's all for you, my dear."

"I don't want it at the Delagados' expense. I want nothing! We have enough."

He held her so tightly that she felt like a prisoner in his grasp. "No, Anitra, there's more, much more."

"I still can't believe that you would do this," she said.

"It's finished," he told her. "Go and tell Carlota I said no. Esteban will have no more chances; the Delagados no longer own land in the valley of Tres Ríos."

But the bench in the courtyard was empty when Anitra returned to it.

Carlota had known. She had already gone.

The single lamp burned low on the bedside table.

Anitra looked into the gilt-framed mirror as she brushed her long silken hair.

The strand of emeralds, emeralds the same color as her eyes, gleamed from the top of the dressing table that Leigh had had built for her. She touched them with her fingertips. They must be valuable. If they should be sold, surely the proceeds could help Esteban reestablish himself.

Moments later, she slipped out of El Castillo. When she reached the plaza, three blanket-wrapped Indians watched her as she approached the door to the casino and stepped inside.

It was quiet, the large round chandeliers unlit, the gaming tables empty. She remembered briefly the big red-faced man with whom she had come here years before, and Leigh, walking across the room, tall, square-shouldered, smiling as he came to her rescue. He wouldn't smile if he knew why she was here now. A tremor touched her. She wasn't happy to deceive him. Yet what else could she do?

Rafael came quickly from behind a beaded curtain. He looked surprised when he saw her, then hurried forward to take her hand, to bow. "Doña Anitra, what brings you here at this time?"

"Not gaming, I promise you." She smiled. "I thought to have a few words with you."

"Of course. Why not? I'm always happy to see you, though it's been years since you last came here."

"You're not supposed to remember what a foolish child I was then."

She wasn't far past being a foolish child still, Rafael thought, but he asked, "How can I help you?"

She hesitated for a moment, then drew the emeralds from her reticule. "Is it possible that you could find me a buyer to take these? But it would have to be quickly."

He didn't touch the stones. His gaze was fastened on her troubled face. "Why do you want to part with them, Doña Anitra?"

She didn't answer him.

"They're very valuable."

"I had hoped they would be."

"You need—forgive me, Doña Anitra—you need money, is that it?"

Again she didn't answer him, but she reminded herself that he had been an old friend of her father's.

Rafael said slowly, "I'll take them myself, Doña Anitra. Would six hundred dollars in bills suit you?"

"If that's what you offer me."

"I can give you no more, I fear. At least not immediately."

"Then it's done," she told him. "And when will I have the money?"

"If you'll wait but a moment . . . "

She put the emeralds into his hand, and in a little while he returned from behind the beaded curtain and gave her the sheaf of bills. Carefully folding it, she stuffed it into her reticule and left.

Later that night, Rafael said to Porfirio, "I don't understand it. But perhaps you should know, Hermano Mayor."

"I'm glad you told me."

"But Señor Ransome is rich and would surely give her whatever she wanted. Why did she sell those emeralds to me?"

Porfirio said, "She went from your casino to Don Esteban's house on the plaza. When she left there, her eyes were red with weeping."

24

"I was very careful," Leigh said casually. "I checked and rechecked the records. You can be sure that the information is accurate."

He leaned back in the saddle. "It's something to see, isn't it, Anitra?" he asked, and his smile was a wide boyish grin.

She turned disbelieving eyes away from him, her hands suddenly wet inside her riding gloves, and stared into the valley below.

The men worked quickly. The spaced holes they dug bloomed like roses in the hard red earth. The posts were thrust in, buried. The glittering wire was strung between.

Esteban Delagado's land was being enclosed behind sharp-pronged wire only three days after he had left Tres Ríos for good. But it was more than Delagado land that was being enclosed.

She said softly, "Leigh, you've taken the common grazing meadows. They're not a part of the Delagado grant."

"It's El Castillo Ranch now," he told her. "And I've taken only one third of what you call the common grazing meadows. Antonio will have his third whenever he wants to claim it, and the same for Matthew."

"That isn't claimable land," she answered. "Each grant, when received, marked a certain portion for the use of all. It can't be taken back."

"It has been."

"But what will the people do? They have a few sheep, a few goats. They raise a few cows. The free grazing is vital to them."

"Those acres belong to El Castillo," he told her.

"It's not possible."

"Then let them get lawyers in Santa Fe and prove otherwise."

She turned her horse and rode away at a fast trot, her face flushed with anger. He followed, admiring her carriage, her control. It didn't trouble him that she was angry. Soon she would understand.

She didn't speak when he overtook her. She looked straight ahead, her chin high and her mouth firm. It was wrong. What he was doing was wrong. What he had done to the Delagados . . . what he was now doing to the people. How could she make him see?

"Believe me," he told her, "I'm altogether within my rights. As I say, I made certain of it in Santa Fe when I was there this week."

He had gone down on Wednesday morning and returned around noon today. Already the wire was being strung . . .

"But the common lands have always been just that, Leigh."

"We're finished with what you call 'always,' Anitra. It's a new world now. A new country. The old laws don't matter any more."

"But people matter," she cried.

"Nobody can stop me," he said in a quiet voice. "Nobody."

She felt the force within him, the power that he held in check but that was always waiting, sustaining him.

"Even if nothing can stop you, what you've done remains wrong, Leigh," she said.

"Not if I say otherwise."

"You don't make laws, Leigh."

"Perhaps. But I know how to use them."

It was twilight when they reached the outskirts of town. He said, "I must stop in the casino for a moment. Ride down with me, will you?"

She would have preferred not to go there so soon after her embarrassing errand. But she could think of no excuse.

Leigh dismounted and tied his horse to a post before the casino. When she didn't follow him, he asked, "Won't you come in with me?"

"I'll wait," she said.

"Please," he asked, smiling.

Something in his voice made her look at him quickly, and she was certain that he knew what she had done.

He continued, as he helped her down from her horse, "You don't wear your emeralds any more."

Yes, he knew.

"I no longer have them, Leigh."

"Oh? Did you lose them?"

"You know better," she burst out.

"Come along." He took her arm, smiling down at her.

The large chandeliers glowed. The bar was crowded. The air in the casino was rich with the scent of flowers, ladies' perfume, and cigar smoke.

Leigh shook his head when Rafael started to show the two of them to a table.

"No," Leigh said. "No, we're not staying. I just wanted to ask you—do you buy jewelry occasionally, amigo?"

Rafael sent a quick look at Anitra.

"The emeralds," Leigh asked. "Do you still have them?"

Rafael hesitated.

Anitra said, "Do you, Rafael?"

He nodded unwillingly.

"And you paid six hundred dollars for them? Is that right?"

"How do you know?" Anitra asked coldly.

"From Vicente, my dear. Vicente Vargas. Carlota told him and Vicente told me, since, after all, those emeralds are mine."

"When you gave them to me . . ."

"They remained mine. Let me remind you, lest you've forgotten—you're my wife. As my wife, all that you own is mine." He looked now at Rafael. "If you still have the gems, I'll buy them from you. For the price you gave."

"Now?" Rafael asked unbelievingly.

"Now," Leigh said.

Rafael disappeared behind the beaded curtain.

"It was unnecessary for you to do this here," she said. "Do you humiliate me deliberately? Or is it that you know no better?"

He said, eyes narrowing, "My dear, why should you feel that way? I'm making the only gesture that can save you from the contempt of your fellow townspeople."

"What are you talking about?" she cried. "I did nothing to deserve that."

"What's more contemptible than a husband who allows his wife to sell her jewels in a casino to help her indigent cousins, Anitra?"

"And what more than a man who shames his wife?"

She saw his eyes darken, but he answered quietly, "I love you. You're all that I want in a wife. If you've

262

behaved as a child in this, then I must see you don't do so again. It changes nothing between us."

Rafael reappeared with the emeralds in his hand.

"I'll give you the money tomorrow," Leigh told him.

"When you like, Señor Ransome." But later, speaking to Porfirio, he grumbled, "Hermano Mayor, I don't understand that man."

"Nor do I, my brother," Porfirio answered. "I don't like him either."

"Then what's to be done?"

Porfirio didn't answer. He knew more than he was ready to explain.

When Leigh and Anitra were outside the cafe again, Leigh stopped and put the emeralds around Anitra's throat. "How lovely they are on you. So like your eyes."

She didn't reply.

He said in a quiet voice, "Forgive me, Anitra. But you shouldn't have done it. You do understand?"

"I understand," she answered shortly.

"And you forgive me?"

Now there was no mockery in his face; he was openly pleading with her. She found herself softening, her anger suddenly gone.

She reached out, took his hand. "Ah, my Leigh, you're all that I have, and I'm all that you have. We mustn't be unkind to each other."

He took her by the arm and they walked side by side toward where the horses were tethered. As they passed by the empty house where Carlota and Esteban had lived until only a few days before, Anitra turned her head away. She didn't want to think of them. She didn't want to remember. Leigh loved her and she loved him. That was all that mattered to her.

Suddenly she felt Leigh go rigid, his fingers tightening on her arm. She turned to look. The Delagado house, Leigh's house now, was tipped on its foundations. Its broken door hung open, its shattered windows glared in the dark like angry eyes.

"The Penitentes," she whispered soundlessly, only shaping the words with her lips. "The Brotherhood, Madre de Dios!"

"What?" he demanded. "What did you say?"

She shook her head, unwilling to say more.

But he had read the words as her mouth formed them. He understood.

25

Below, in the courtyard, the dogs howled, and above their noise Anitra could hear the pito, its music drifting all the way from the morada across the fields.

Good Friday. The last day of Lent. The night of the Crucifixion. A shudder touched her. Why wouldn't Leigh listen? Why didn't he see that what he was doing was wrong?

Again the song of the pito rose. She pressed her hands over her ears and collapsed weeping onto the bed.

Leigh lay concealed in the grove of cottonwoods that surrounded the morada. He breathed slowly, lightly, forcing himself to remain still, while his body poured out the sweat of fear. He had known the feeling rarely in his life, and certainly not since he was a child. He was strong, he told himself. There was a power in him that no one could hold out against. He wasn't sweating out of fear—it was anger that made him hot.

They had destroyed what was his. There, on the plaza, in the most public of all places, they had damaged a house belonging to Leigh Ransome.

A faint light shone from within the morada. The thin cry of the pito went on, and the clacking sound of the matracas was like the rattle of bones across a stone-hard floor. Slowly, as he listened, the whispered prayers faded away.

Damn them to hell, he thought. They had finally finished that foolish caterwauling—then why didn't they get on with it, do what he had come to see?

And see it he would, in spite of Anitra's pleas.

They had ridden silently back to El Castillo, he too angry to speak, she in a frozen stillness. He had stabled the horses, flung fresh meat out for Cora and Cal, and then had gone into the house.

Anitra was in the bedroom. She had taken her riding hat off and removed the pins from her hair. It gleamed like black silk as she braided it.

He watched her for a little while, then asked, "Anitra, what makes you think it was the Brotherhood that damaged the house?"

She shrugged, but he saw the quick flash of her green eyes.

"I want to know," he said quietly.

"You'll never know."

"Somebody must have seen it."

"You'll never find anyone who knows about it or saw it."

"Why do you think it happened?"

She shook her head.

"Anitra, I want to know."

"Leigh, listen to me, you'll never know. You'll learn nothing about the Penitentes. The Brotherhood is secret. You mustn't think of it."

"Why should they destroy what's mine?" he demanded. "I ought to know that much."

"Perhaps . . . " her voice became a husky whisper . . .

"perhaps because . . . because of the Delagados. But I . . . I can't be sure. It may be . . . Leigh, it could be the grazing land that you've started fencing. It might be . . . "

He laughed. "Come, Anitra. They wouldn't dare. That land is mine now."

"They wouldn't think so. No matter what your lawyers in Santa Fe have told you."

"But what they think isn't important."

"The house is destroyed, isn't it?"

He nodded. She was right. What was said in Santa Fe was one thing. What was enforced here was another. "Is Esteban a Brother?"

"I don't know. He might be."

"Who that you know is a Brother?"

She turned away from him. "There's no use talking about it, Leigh. Forget the Penitentes."

"But who?" he insisted.

"I have no idea," she said coldly. "I don't want to speak of it."

"Why?"

"It's not safe for you," she said. And then, when he started for the door, "Leigh! Leigh, where are you going?"

"Out for a little while."

The sound of the pito drifted between them. She raised her head to stare at him, then cried, "Oh, no! No, you mustn't! Leave them alone, I say."

He didn't tell her then that he had stopped at the morada many times before in hopes that he would see someone entering or leaving it. But always, before tonight, it had been empty.

Not that he had cared about the Penitentes' secrets. Whatever they did was all right with him. If they whipped themselves to ribbons, tore the flesh from their bones, it didn't matter to him. He had had only one interest in these people—to use them. They represented power. And he wanted that power in his own hands.

Now he had a second reason for his interest. They had damaged something that was his own. More than ever he was determined to learn the Brotherhood's secrets.

He smiled into the darkness as the morada door swung open and a single man came out, holding a lantern. Its pale rays fell on his hooded head, on loose white trousers and shirt. Behind him, within the faint circle of light, was an old, solid-wheeled carreta. Leigh swore, then sucked in his breath. The figure in the cart was gowned in black, a black cowl draped over her bony face, and in her bony hands she held a bow and arrow. The sharp flint tip seemed to point directly at Leigh's heart. La Santa de la Muerte, the Saint of Death, known by some as Doña Sebastiana.

He didn't know her name, but he knew what she symbolized. For an instant he froze, awaiting the stretch of the bow, the bite of the arrow. Then it was over, and he shook with soundless laughter realizing that the thing was a statue of wood.

There was a rustling in the cottonwoods, and then a second man came from the morada. The two moved together into the shadows.

From within the building came the sudden rattle of chains, the slap of bare feet on hard earth, a thud as some heavy wooden object fell heavily.

Now another figure appeared in the open doorway. Leigh raised himself slightly on his elbows. From nowhere, it seemed, a shower of stones rained down on him and he wriggled backward into the shelter of the trees.

He hadn't expected that they would be watching for intruders. But he remained untroubled. They were like children, the Brothers, playing at secret games.

He mopped a small cut over his brow, and as he did, the stones exploded again. He was seen, he knew, and must escape. One retreat wasn't decisive. He slithered away as quietly as he could under the new rain of rocks and waded across the small stream. On the far bank he looked back and saw that the pale light that had filtered from the morada was gone.

He didn't know that a hooded shadow watched as he crossed the field, recognized his gait and his conspicuous height and muttered, "Si, si, as I thought. It's the gringo, Ransome."

Back in his office, confident that he had escaped unrecognized, he poured himself a brandy from the decanter and sat down at his desk.

From the top drawer of the desk he took his map of the valley, moving aside a gold nugget, the first he had taken from the old man's stream, briefly touching with a gentle forefinger a tiny wilted rose that had fallen from Anitra's hair the night he kissed her for the first time.

He sat smiling, the map spread before him. He had colored the Delagado land red, along with all the small bits and pieces of acreage he had accumulated over the years. Now there remained only Matthew Britton's ranch and the Martínez y Escobedo holdings.

He was a patient man. The gold that made it all possible was secure in its cave in the mountain, unknown to anyone but him. For now, there was enough in the stream to support whatever he wanted to do. The plan was worked out in his head. Slowly, carefully, he would begin its execution.

"Your brother Eloy?" Anitra asked. "Is he ill, Tinita? He didn't come yesterday. I see he's not here again this morning."

Tinita shrugged, looked down at her hands. "Perhaps tomorrow, Doña Anitra."

But the following day Eloy again did not appear, and when Anitra asked after him, Tinita replied, "I don't know, Doña Anitra. I think perhaps he's gone to Coronado. I think perhaps he's not coming back."

Anitra recognized the evasiveness but asked no further questions.

She didn't know that someone had come to the small shack in which Eloy lived, and called him out into the night, speaking with him softly for a little while, and that soon after, Eloy had stuffed his few belongings into a straw basket and set out on foot for Chimayo.

She did know that Tinita wouldn't explain.

That afternoon Eustacio presented himself at El Castillo.

"Doña Anitra," he said, "Don Antonio tells me that you now need a gardener and that I must make myself available to you. That's good, isn't it, eh?"

"Very good," she said, smiling. "I'm pleased." And then, "But we must speak to my husband."

Leigh, having given Eustacio a cursory look, was amenable. He didn't care who grew the velvet grass for Anitra or planted the trees. If she was satisfied, then he'd be satisfied, too.

"And truly, Señor Ransome—" Eustacio grinned—"I see that I'm sorely needed. These two courtyards could be the gardens of Eden, and the work is only just begun. I'm a man who loves the earth and it loves me back. I shall grow you such trees, such flowers . . ."

Leigh told him to get on with it and waved him away.

It was not precisely clear in Eustacio's mind why he had been sent, but it had been the Hermano Mayor's wish, and what the Hermano Mayor asked of him he would naturally do.

Watch, the Hermano Mayor had said. Listen.

Very well. He would do that. And meanwhile he would enjoy Doña Anitra's smile and remember his Juana, his daughter whom he hadn't seen for many long years.

"And here," Anitra said, pointing, as she explained her plans, "if we could have hollyhocks, perhaps the hummingbirds would come."

"Si, Doña Anitra. There'll be hollyhocks."

"And at the walls, lilacs, do you think?"

"Lilacs, Doña Anitra. For certain, there'll be those. Great bushes of lilacs dripping their purple blossoms and spreading their fragrance."

"And . . . " She allowed the word to trail away. She couldn't concentrate now. For all her plans, she hardly cared what Eustacio did in the courtyards. She was thinking of the ruined house on the plaza, of the thin strands of wire that glittered like long streaks of flame in the midst of the valley. . . .

The dogs bayed.

Eustacio cocked his head. "They are formidable, eh?"

"They're always in the cage. You mustn't be afraid of them, my old friend."

"In truth, Doña Anitra, I'm glad to hear that." He gave her a wide grin. "I shouldn't like to have them at my back while I dig in the soil."

26

When Anitra rode away from El Castillo an August brilliance lay heavily on the valley. Her face was lifted to the sun, her dark hair unbound and loose on her shoulders, the horse trotting beneath her as frisky with freedom as she herself felt. They ran a mountain trail, where the tall aspen fluttered as they rode by.

Then, between one breath and another, the golden light of late afternoon turned into a terrifying darkness. A quick wind burst through the mountain ring, sent dust devils scurrying and tumbleweed rolling in silvery tracks in the canyons below.

Thunder exploded with a sharp clap that was repeated in a long echoing roar. No sooner was the valley still than another bolt shot skyward and the thunderhead spilled over the ridge, bringing a drenching rain.

Anitra laughed, lifting her face to the cold stinging drops, but her horse snorted and balked, refusing to move. "Silly beast," she grumbled. "There's nothing to fear." But it was hopeless to struggle with the animal, so she dismounted and led the horse to the shelter of a rock overhang.

Wrapping herself closely in her cloak, she sat down to wait out the storm. The rain slashed into the darkness of the lowlands, while higher in the mountains, dry and rocky streams filled and poured down, carrying with them leaf and stone and log, their power always increasing so that when they reached the lower, drier slopes, each had become a battering force, and they hurled themselves into the crusty red earth, washing it away and turning the roads into roaring rivers.

The trail Anitra had ridden only moments before was now a red torrent that would have swept her away if she hadn't stopped.

She had watched the flood rise, and then as the storm faded, she watched its gradual decline until the rain was a thin silver sheet. She decided to wait a little longer, allowing the trail to clear, before she started down into the valley toward Tres Ríos and the big house awaiting her return.

It was three months since she had pressed the emerald money into Carlota's trembling hand and heard her cousin cry, "I take it only because it's a small part of what your husband owes us. I have no feeling of shame for this. Dios, don't you see it, Anitra? The man is a devil. A gringo devil! He cares nothing for any of us. He has used you, and your kinship with us, to destroy us!"

Anitra had not allowed herself to believe the accusation. Leigh loved her. And she loved him. But neither the wish nor the insistence gave her the conviction she hungered for.

Some time in the months since the Delagados had left Tres Ríos, the truth had forced itself upon her. She had married Leigh without understanding her own feelings. What she had called love had been the need to escape her father's house. A marriage arranged by her father could have been very little different from the one she herself had chosen.

273

She bit her lip and rose. She mustn't think any more. The thin rain continued as she mounted her horse and started down the slippery track.

There were lights below—the Diaz ranch. She had no desire to stop there, but the rain suddenly thickened again and she took the familiar trail like one in a dream. "Doña Anitra," cried the serving girl, "how happy I am to see you! But you're wet and cold. Come in. There's a fire in the sala, and I shall tell Don Matthew and Doña Josefa that you're here."

"Anitra," Matthew said softly, entering the sala, "What brings you out in this rain?"

"I've come for shelter."

"You didn't come soon enough, it appears," he said. "Let me have your cloak. It'll be dried in the kitchen."

She gave it to him, careful that their hands not touch, careful that their eyes not meet. "Ah, this is good," she said, sitting before the fire.

"Josefa is always cold," he answered. "We keep the room warm for her all the time."

"Always cold," Anitra echoed. "She's no better then?"

Matthew didn't answer. He left the sala but returned within moments, followed by the serving girl, who brought brandy and a pot of coffee. "Like old times," she said, as she served Anitra a brimming cup.

Anitra looked at the piano, at the dried pampas grass with its dusty silver plumes. She glanced at the portrait of Don Cipriano that hung between the two velvet-draped windows.

"We miss him," Matthew said quietly.

"So do we all," she answered.

In the silence that followed there came the soft cough that always signaled Josefa's approach.

"Anitra—" she smiled over her handkerchief—"how

long it's been." She seated herself at the piano and Matthew winced as he looked quickly away from her.

"You look well," Anitra said politely.

"I wish Matthew would say so," Josefa returned. Then, "Has he told you our news?"

Matthew looked into the fire. "We leave here early next month, Anitra."

"Leave? But why? Where will you go?"

"To Santa Fe. I've bought a house on Cañon Road."

"But the ranch?" Anitra cried. "How can you abandon it? What would Don Cipriano say, Matthew?"

"My words exactly." Josefa's cough was triumphant. "I've told Matthew, but he won't listen to me. Perhaps you can dissuade him from this idiocy."

"It'll be better for Josefa in Santa Fe," Matthew said. "The winters here are too difficult."

"And the ranch?" Anitra asked. "Will you give it up?"

"You know better," Matthew told her. "But my people will run it for me for the time being."

"Anitra, you mustn't agree," Josefa cried. "It isn't my wish. It's Matthew's. A kind idea perhaps, but a foolish one. I know no one in Santa Fe. I shall have no friends. I'll be all alone."

"You'll soon make friends. And there are the Delagados," he told her.

"Don't do this, Matthew." Josefa coughed, and covered her face with her hands. "You're wrong to do this," she whispered. "And no good will come of it."

"You know I've promised you we'll return in the spring," he said.

"Ah, but that's too far away."

Anitra was shaken. She should have been glad that Matthew would leave Tres Ríos, that she need no longer feel his presence close by and remember what they had once been to each other. Instead she felt something that was almost fear.

"And Leigh often has business in Santa Fe, Anitra. You must come with him to visit us," Matthew was saying.

He would do anything for Josefa, Anitra thought, but aloud she said coolly, "Of course I will," and swore to herself she'd never set foot in the house on Cañon Road.

"Ah, you disappoint me, Anitra," Josefa said softly. "I'd thought you, of all people, could make him see how wrong he is."

"If it's best for you ... " Anitra began.

"Oh, yes," Josefa said bitterly. "I know it's for me. It'll be my fault then. Whatever happens, it shall all be on my shoulders."

"But nothing will happen," Anitra said quickly. "How can you think it? All will go on as before. And in the spring, you and Matthew will return."

"Do you really believe it?" Josefa whispered.

"Josefa, I've promised you," Matthew said stiffly.

"Then I'll remind you of your promise when you decide to delay our return," she answered with equal stiffness.

It was with relief that Anitra saw that the rain outside had subsided. She rose quickly, "I must go."

Matthew offered to drive her in the wagon, and when she protested, Josefa said, "Ah, Anitra, at least allow Matthew to pay you the courtesy of a gentleman."

Anitra protested no further. She accepted her now-dry cloak and went into the courtyard with Matthew.

He tied her horse to the back of the wagon and helped her up on the seat. They were silent as they left the ranch behind them.

Ahead the lights of Tres Ríos twinkled through the broad limbs of the cottonwoods.

At last Matthew said, "Yes, yes, it is like old times."

"Do you hear of the Delagados?" she asked quickly.

"I've seen them. Carlota is bitter that all their expectations have come to nothing. And Esteban is changed. I think he's not well."

"Don César? Vicente? Won't they help?"

"Oh, yes, but only grudgingly."

"It's all Leigh's doing, Matthew," Anitra said. "I know that's what you think. I know that's how the Delagados feel."

"It was good of you to help them. Carlota told me."

"Compared to what I wanted to do, it was nothing. Oh, if you only knew . . . I begged Leigh . . ." Abruptly she stopped herself, shocked at what she was saying, but Matthew said only, "Of course, Anitra. I knew that."

She didn't answer, relieved that the wagon had reached the plaza. When Matthew stopped at the gates to El Castillo, she invited him in, but he said he had to hurry back to Josefa, adding, "We'll see you before we leave."

Alone on the path, she stared at the house, which was silent but for the faint sound of the last of the raindrops spilling slowly from its thick beams.

She drew a deep breath, and went inside, pausing at the door to Leigh's office. She knew he wasn't there, for the dogs growled when they heard her and hurled themselves against the sturdy door.

She hurried up the narrow staircase to the bedroom, and had changed from her wet riding habit into a clean gown by the time he came in.

He stood smiling at her while she finished smoothing her hair and telling him about the Brittons' plan to move to Santa Fe.

"It's probably a good idea for her health," Leigh said,

and added as Anitra was about to go downstairs, "Tomorrow we'll ride out to the ranch together."

"The Delagado ranch?" she asked softly.

"El Castillo Ranch," he said, grinning.

She nodded, but didn't speak. With great care, she closed the door between them.

He saw that, and understood, and his eyes turned suddenly dark.

It took little time to reach the outskirts of town. The air was sweet, perfumed by wild flowers and the small cedars that grew in dark groves along the lower mountain slopes.

Leigh feasted his eyes on the wide empty acres that spread around him. This was land that had once belonged to an hidalgo of Spain. It stretched all the way from the very place at which he stopped, reining in, with Anitra beside him, to the dark rim of the river gorge. These acres now belonged to El Castillo, to Leigh Ransome.

"You see, Anitra?" he asked.

She caught her breath. This time she looked at more than the silver strands of wire enclosing the land. It had been torn down and repaired twice, and she knew it would be restrung as often as was necessary. Leigh would never give in.

Within the fencing stood the charred and broken walls of the old hacienda. But beyond that scene of desolation there were new walls going up. Workmen scurried about and fresh adobe bricks were drying in the sun.

"It'll be modest," Leigh said. "Not a house for us, you know. Only a place for storage. Yet just what I'll need."

"Did you need the commons, too?" she asked. "It'll always make trouble for you, Leigh."

"It won't." He tipped back his hat, and a curl gleamed on his forehead. He grinned. "The people are like children. In the first flash of rage, they destroy. But then they'll forget they ever used this land."

She knew he was mistaken. He didn't understand the Penitentes. "They won't give up," she said. "They never do."

He knew she referred to the Brotherhood. But he laughed. "I won't give up, Anitra. I never do either."

He saw it in his mind—the map in his office, all of it colored red. Red for Leigh Ransome's kingdom. The Delagado place. The Diaz place. The Martínez y Escobedo place. The whole of what had once been the common grazing meadows. They were all colored red. They belonged to him, just as Anitra and the soul of the valley belonged to him.

"It's only the beginning," he said, riding under the sign that said El Castillo Ranch.

She waited, as he gave orders to one of the men.

"Anything you find inside the fence, anything, goats, sheep, cows, chickens, whatever you find, you kill," he said. "And I want the carcasses burned. You understand me, hombre? I want them burned."

Anitra winced. No, he would never give up. But neither would the Brotherhood.

Soon he was riding again. She followed slowly, knowing his destination even before he spoke.

When he said, "We'll stop in to see Matthew and Josefa," she wasn't surprised. What did surprise her was the circuitous route that he took, and when he stopped on a ridge, looked down at the wide spread of the unfenced ranch that bordered the wired acres, the look on his face disturbed her.

"Leigh, do you mean to have the Diaz ranch, too?"

He didn't even glance at her. He said, laughing, "My dear, it belongs to Matthew. How could I?"

"If you wanted it you'd find a way, wouldn't you?"

"I would. But I've no such thought in my mind. Unless he should want to sell."

She was suddenly frightened. She was certain that she knew what was in his mind.

"You must forget that idea, Leigh. Matthew isn't another Esteban."

He only laughed again. "If I'd known you'd be so affected by my ownership of Esteban's ranch, I'd never have made the loans that were responsible. And he'd have lost it to someone else. To some stranger from Santa Fe, no doubt."

"Perhaps. But I think not."

Ignoring her, he kicked his horse into a gallop and rode downhill.

At the ranch she listened uneasily while Leigh offered to help Matthew look after things in his absence. Matthew thanked him and refused, saying, "I won't need to trouble you, I hope. Antonio's ranch is closer than yours, Leigh. And my people are the best—they've been with the family for generations."

"A strong hand is necessary," Leigh answered.

Anitra thought, He sounds like my father.

"Don Cipriano had a gentle hand," Matthew retorted. "And he had no difficulty."

"Don Cipriano's dead. And the times have changed."

Anitra said quickly, "Don't worry, Matthew. All will be well here."

Later, riding across the meadow, she said again, "All will be well here, Leigh. I'm sure of it."

"Of course," he agreed. "Why not?"

"As young as Antonio is, he manages."

"I've noticed. No doubt your father looks down from heaven or up from hell, and smiles to see how well Antonio does," Leigh answered dryly.

But when they rode into the Martínez y Escobedo ranch courtyard, Anitra noticed that the garden, once so carefully tended, was neglected.

With Eustacio spending his time at El Castillo, the flowers and bushes had a dry and dusty look, and the sight pained her.

When she mentioned it to Dora, the older woman shrugged. "For whom shall we tend the flowers, now that you're not here, Doña Anitra?"

"Do you reproach me for marrying, Dora?"

"I miss you, niña," the older woman said. "I want you here where you belong."

"I belong in my home with my husband," Anitra answered.

Even as she spoke, she realized that she had not left the ranch behind her as she had thought. She had tried, instead, to reproduce this garden at El Castillo.

"Everything is different now," Dora was saying.

"And why not? Time passes. Would you have everything remain the same?"

"Sometimes I think it would be better so."

Anitra laughed. "Then would you be content to be scurrying after me while I run wildly through the courtyard, refusing to permit you to braid my hair?"

There was no answering laugh in Dora's voice, no hint of humor in her eyes, when she replied, "Doña Anitra, there are many many moments these days when I go on my knees before La Virgen de Guadalupe and pray that it were so. I pray, with tears in my eyes, that those days could be again."

27

The last stop that Matthew and Josefa made before they left Tres Ríos was at El Castillo. Josefa remained in the carriage, swathed in a heavy cloak, her eyes red-rimmed and tearing.

"You'll remember, Anitra," she whispered. "You've promised me that you'll visit us in Santa Fe."

"It won't be long," Leigh told her. "When you're settled, and ready for guests, Anitra and I will be there."

Matthew took Anitra's hand in his. "Until then," he said.

She felt a great wrench of pain as the carriage rattled out between the gates. Carlota and Esteban were gone, and now Matthew and Josefa. Only Antonio remained from her past.

Sighing, she went into the house, and Leigh said, laughing, "Are you lonely already?"

"No." She denied it quickly. "How can I be lonely?"

Later that night, sitting before the fire, she asked herself the same question. How could she be lonely? Yet she was. There was an emptiness within her that nothing filled.

That night, as she slept, she dreamed of Matthew. She saw his tall form riding away from her. She saw his chestnut head, the white streak above his right temple gleaming, as he turned to lift his hand in the familiar salute.

She awakened, with tears still on her cheeks, and thought, turning cold with the shock, I'll never see Matthew again.

But in the first week of the new year, Matthew held her two hands in his and said, "Thank you for coming, Anitra. If Josefa hadn't insisted . . ."

"I understand, Matthew."

No, Anitra thought, he wouldn't have sent for her unless for Josefa's sake, and certainly not asked Antonio to accompany her as well as Leigh.

He hesitated. "You'll find her much changed, Anitra. I want you to know that."

"Whatever I can do . . . " Anitra let the words trail away. Plainly there was nothing. It was why Matthew had sent for her. The white streak above his brow seemed to have widened in the months since she had last seen him.

"Then if you'll come with me, Anitra . . . "

"I'll wait," Leigh said, with a quick reassuring smile.

A few steps down the hall she entered a large room ablaze with light. A fire burned in the corner fireplace and lamps glittered on every surface.

The white bed curtains were drawn back, and Josefa lay against a hill of white satin pillows. Her brown braids, laced with white ribbons, hung to her shoulders, framing her small face with dark shadows.

"Anitra . . . how good of you . . . "

"We should have come sooner," Anitra said quickly. "But Leigh was unable to leave Tres Ríos."

She tried not to think of all the matters that had

283

occupied him. He had supervised the building of a wall across the back of the rear courtyard, with a gate that locked, and a small Judas hole through which he could look at anyone who came there. He had twice more refenced the common grazing lands. He had, himself, with Cora and Cal, made sure that the villagers no longer tried to use it. He had killed dozens of goats, sheep, and chickens, and built of their carcasses a huge pyre, which had for days filled the valley with the odor of corruption.

Of these things Anitra said nothing to Josefa, who, smiling faintly, put out a clawlike hand and motioned Anitra closer.

Matthew drew up a chair at the bedside.

"Leave us," Josefa murmured. "Leave us, Matthew."

He looked as if he might protest, but after a moment he said, "Very well, Josefa. But don't tire yourself."

"Why not?"

"Josefa . . ."

"Leave us," she murmured. "Please, don't waste my time."

But when he had gone, leaving the door ajar, she was silent, except for the harsh and labored sounds that came from her chest.

At last she said, "Anitra, it was wrong." Her eyes shifted to the portrait of Don Cipriano that hung on the wall. "I wanted him with me, always, but he was wrong, too. Between us, Don Cipriano and I, we've done Matthew a great disservice. How is it, that loving him, we could hurt him?"

"You mustn't think of it now," Anitra said softly. "You must rest, and soon you'll be well, and . . . "

"I shan't be well, Anitra. That's why I insisted that Matthew send for you."

"And now I'm here," Anitra said, trying for a lightness that she didn't feel. "I'm here with you, and here I'll stay until you no longer need me."

"It won't be long." Again Josefa fell silent, then she whispered, "He loves you, Anitra. He loves you still."

Heat and color crept into Anitra's face. She said softly, "Ah, Josefa, there's no use to this."

"Life . . . " Josefa murmured. "Life, Anitra. It comes before all. Everything else that we were taught was lies. To breathe, to know joy and desire—to love, that's all there is. And he loves you so. Without you he'll have nothing."

Anitra closed her eyes against the pleading face. What was she to say? That Matthew still loved her could mean nothing to her now. Leigh was her husband. He awaited her return only a few steps away.

"Anitra?" Josefa pleaded.

"You mustn't worry about Matthew. All will be well with him, I promise you," Anitra said finally. "Close your eyes and rest now, and I'll be here with you."

"For a little while," Josefa murmured. "Only for a little while." She sank back against the softness of the pillows, plainly worn by the words she had spoken. Before she closed her eyes, she looked once more at Don Cipriano's portrait and whispered, "He was a good man. Yet even such a one can be wrong."

In the sala, Antonio was asking, "What happened, Matthew?"

Matthew looked at the dusty silver plumes of the pampas grass that Josefa had insisted on bringing from the ranch and said, "It has been expected. But not so soon. I had thought that to be here, closer to the physi-

285

cians, would be a good thing. But now the long-time inflammation of the lungs is complicated by lung fever and there's nothing to be done."

Leigh sat quietly, his long legs stretched before him, his thick shoulders filling the wide chair back. He looked into the fire and saw his map of the valley. Diaz land. Martínez y Escobedo land. Soon Matthew would be coming home. . . .

"And your plans?" Antonio asked.

Matthew shrugged. He had thought nothing of the future. These past months had been the most difficult he had ever known.

Josefa had seen what was coming and had suddenly become avid for life. She had dressed in her finest clothes and colored her pale cheeks. He had watched her, pained and troubled, not knowing what to do to make her happy.

One night she came into his bedroom and sat on the arm of his chair, perfumed and painted, and touched his hair, and he thought of Anitra, Anitra for whose caress he would have given anything. But it was Josefa whispering, "Matthew, Matthew, it's so terrible to die without having known love."

He'd been unable to answer her. It seemed to him that the odor of death already surrounded her.

He said finally, "You'll catch a chill, Josefa."

"I have it now. It's in my bones, my heart, Matthew." And her eyes pleaded with him.

He took her by the hand, led her carefully to her room.

She threw open the window. The bed curtains fluttered. The draperies swayed. She breathed deeply, the mantilla blowing around her, and her curls tore free.

"Josefa! No!" He closed the window quickly, and

built up the fire and settled her in bed with extra quilts. Then he left her there alone.

Perhaps it was that night that had led to today.

Another time, soon after, he'd awakened suddenly. She lay beside him, her cheek against his shoulder, her limbs trembling against his. "I can't die like this, Matthew," she whispered. "I must have life, life, I tell you."

But it was too late, he'd thought then. It was too late for them to become more than brother and sister. When they'd first married, it might have been different. He had been strong with determination then, and what might have begun at the onset would have survived to give them warmth between them now. But now the most he could summon for her was a tired tenderness.

He held her gently and let her sleep in his body's heat, but after that night he made sure that his door was locked against her.

Antonio's voice brought him back to the present. "You must plan to return to the ranch as soon as you can, Matthew."

He didn't reply.

"You must come back," Antonio insisted. "Your life is there, the ranch, your friends. What do you have here in Santa Fe?"

Matthew shrugged. "I won't think of it now. Later . . . perhaps . . . " But he already knew. He had been certain when he welcomed Anitra and Leigh. He wouldn't return to Tres Ríos, though he missed the ranch more than he could admit even to himself. He wouldn't live with the reminders of what he had lost, constantly seeing Leigh's hand possessive on Anitra's shoulder. Anitra's face turned up to his. What he had lost was gone forever. And even now, with his duty near done, he couldn't regain it.

"There's nothing for you in Santa Fe," Antonio repeated firmly. "You must come back as soon as you can."

"Perhaps I will," Matthew said at last. "Perhaps I will soon."

Leigh, aloof and unspeaking, thought that Matthew might be surprised to discover that whenever he returned, it might be too late.

Josefa was sleeping, Anitra at her bedside, when Matthew entered the room. "Carlota has come, Anitra," he said softly.

He saw a pulse flicker in the ivory of her throat, her green eyes grow brilliant with tears.

"It's all right," he assured her quickly. "Go and greet her. You'll see that it's all right."

He took the chair she vacated and listened to the rustle of her skirts as she went slowly down the hall to the sala. The big room was crowded now, and the fire was high. Near it a group of men stood together, Leigh's head towering above them.

The women had gathered at the other end of the room, speaking in whispers. From among them, Carlota came toward her, hands outstretched, a smile on her lips.

"Dios!" she cried. "How glad I am to see you, Anitra!" She kissed her quickly on both cheeks. "Ah, it's been so long."

Anitra clung to her, happy with relief, thinking, Old affection doesn't die. Yet she wondered when she saw with what civility Carlota greeted Leigh.

He came, bowed over her hand, and said formally, "Doña Carlota, I hope all's well with you and yours."

"I thank you," she answered. "We do nicely." And then, smiling sweetly, as she seized Anitra's hand, "You'll

288

forgive me if I borrow Anitra for a few moments. We've not spoken together for so long."

Leigh had no opportunity for a reply. Carlota drew Anitra away swiftly, murmuring, "Truly I must speak to you. Take your cloak and come with me, quickly."

Within moments, they were in the snow-filled patio, and Anitra understood. Carlota had been civil to Leigh so that she could be alone with Anitra. "Come into the street for a moment," she said, leading Anitra to a carriage.

The driver opened the door. Carlota motioned Anitra to get in. She gathered her gown, stepped up, and froze.

Esteban sat in a corner, silent, unmoving. Carlota thrust her forward so that Anitra half fell onto the seat beside him.

He was dressed all in black, shrunken within his clothes, and aged. His hair had receded into a narrow ring at the back of his head, and his hands lay loose on his knees, thick, ropy blue veins thrusting upward from wrinkled flesh.

"Tell her," Carlota said softly.

Memories rose within Anitra . . . Esteban smiling, helping her into the saddle . . . Esteban laughing . . . Esteban always present in time of trouble. . . .

Anitra took his hand in hers, held it tightly. "I've brought you so much grief. But I never meant to."

"Not you," he answered.

"Tell her. She must know," Carlota insisted. "Dios, what do I have to do to make you see it, Esteban? She must know, I say."

His head trembled on the thin stalk of his neck. "It doesn't matter any more."

"She must know," Carlota said. And then to Anitra, "I wormed it out of him. It took me a long time, but finally

I know the truth, and you must know it, too. It was all planned, my cousin. Esteban, speak."

"You were still a little girl," Esteban said softly. "Perhaps you were twelve years of age, Anitra. But already beautiful."

"Never mind," Carlota cut in impatiently. "Tell her about the gringo."

"The gringo . . . " Esteban sighed. "Leigh . . . That was when he first came to Tres Ríos, when you were only twelve. I met him first in Rafael's casino. Looking back, it seems to me that he deliberately jostled my arm, and then apologized with such courtliness that I was taken with him. And then . . . I was his guest at dinner. We had much to talk about, and I was alone, as he was. Then, do you remember? Antonio was lost. Leigh was with me when I heard. He insisted that he, too, would come on the search. I couldn't dissuade him, though later I should have guessed why Leigh, always so proud a man, ignored your father's rudeness that night. But I did not even think of it, Anitra."

"Get to the important part, Esteban." Carlota's voice was sharp. "We've not much time."

But Esteban went on slowly, "We were often together, Leigh and I. He built the house, and I helped him with it. Of course I wondered about his wealth. I'd thought he had little when he first came, but I soon saw I was wrong. And once, discussing my problems, I allowed him to offer me a loan, and I accepted it. There were other loans. They were, of course, always repaid. My problems increased. I lost sheep. My streams were dammed. Each catastrophe was expensive. Leigh helped me. You were grown, and he fell in love with you. I knew your father's feelings, but I could hardly turn my back on Leigh. He used me to court you. I was confused. I wanted you to be happy. I didn't want to hurt Don Lorenzo. Yet . . . yet what could I have done?"

"Tell her," Carlota cried.

"The debt was already large when the old hacienda burned down. I feared to make it larger."

"It was immediately after your marriage, Anitra." Carlota could contain herself no longer. "Esteban asked for a loan, and for the first time Leigh demanded security, a note on the ranch. Esteban gave it to him, believing that it wouldn't matter. Ah, yes, he trusted the gringo devil who was his friend. He was sure he could recoup. But then our sheep were destroyed. You remember. They said wolves came down from the forests. Wolves! Leigh took the house in the plaza, the ranch, and all else we owned."

Anitra said softly, "Carlota, I know most of this. And I'm sorrier than you'll ever realize. But what . . . ?"

"Leigh was always determined to have the Delagado holdings. That's what he set out to win, and that's what he did. I believe he planned each mishap that befell Esteban."

"Planned them?" Anitra's bewildered gaze moved from Carlota to Esteban. "But how?"

"Ask him how!" Carlota said. "Ask him how the hacienda caught fire, how the sheep were destroyed."

"What he did was bad enough," Anitra said gently. "I'm sorry for it, and I'd have stopped him if I could. But to blame him for those accidents . . . "

"Accidents," Carlota scoffed.

A carriage pulled up before the gate. Several men stepped out, tall silk hats catching the pale light.

Anitra drew herself up. "That he wronged you both, I don't deny. But you must be mad to suggest . . . "

Even as she spoke, she remembered. Leigh had been

out the night the old hacienda had burned down. He had been out with the dogs. No, she told herself. These thoughts were only Carlota's obsession affecting her. Leigh had been with her, his body warm against hers, when she heard the church bells toll.

A small gig drew up. A padre climbed down, round as an egg in his cassock, and hurried to the gate.

"But I assure you, I'm not mad," Carlota said softly.

"And from where did he get his wealth so suddenly?" Esteban asked.

"I must go in," Anitra said. "I'm sorry, but I must go in."

"Yes," Carlota agreed. "But be careful. Be careful of that devil, cousin."

Within the house it was warm, and the room was even more crowded. Anitra put away her cloak, smoothed her hair.

Leigh smiled at her across the room. But she didn't go to him. All that Carlota had said echoed in her mind.

She heard only bits of conversation. "The first telephone was installed in the city last year. And now . . . now do you know how many there are? And more and more houses have electric lights. Soon, believe me, there'll be no house without them. We move into the modern world at last."

"We must resolve these problems that impede statehood. It's the only way. Our interests, and their interests, too, depend on it."

"There'll be trouble between the two races, mind you. The gringo wants it all. We must force the Democratic party in the right direction."

Santa Fe talk, Anitra thought. The talk of the politicos.

And then, from the room where Josefa lay, the murmur of the padre.

It was near midnight. The sala was still crowded, but the voices were softer now.

The padre appeared in the doorway.

Into the sudden hush he said, "Sea por Dios! God's will be done."

It was snowing when the party of two carriages reached the heights. Anitra leaned at the window, barely able to see the outline of Santa Fe below. The city seemed lost behind a thick curtain of white flakes.

They had been in the campo santo, the cemetery, the day before, when the first snowflakes had begun to fall. The padre had just sprinkled the holy water on Josefa's grave, on the white stone cut with the words she had left with Matthew. *Here lies Josefa Elena Maria Britton de Diaz Who died in innocence in 1895.*

Josefa's own words, Anitra had thought, as Leigh held her arm and drew her away.

Now the snow drifted heavily across the track, piled high at the ledges, spun like white dust devils. The two carriages labored on.

In the last one, Anitra was bundled in a buffalo robe beside Leigh. In the first one, Antonio sat with Porfirio.

They were on the road the whole of the day, the horses laboring, breaths steaming, hooves slipping. By dark they had emerged from the canyon and made the last long climb to the pass. Suddenly a great sheet of snow high on the mountainside shifted. With a sharp explosive crack it began to move. Slowly at first, and then picking up speed, it crept down the decline, taking scrub brush and tree and loose rock with it.

293

The two carriages had hardly cleared the pass when the avalanche struck. The world seemed to shake with its thunder. The sky was obscured by great clouds of rising snow.

Porfirio put his head out of the window, and looked back, and shuddered. "Maria Santísima! That was close." Then he looked forward into the valley of Tres Ríos, and saw the lights flicker, and he murmured, "It'll be good to be home, my brother."

"It will," Antonio agreed.

But when Porfirio leaned out again to sniff the air of home, a chill settled in his heart. He imagined the odor of brimstone.

28

"I'll work at my books this evening, my dear," Leigh said, smiling at her.

"Again?" she teased him. "My husband, you'll grow to the seat of your chair in that office of yours."

"There's a lot to do," he answered.

"Ah, yes, I believe you." The teasing was gone from her voice when she added, "I wish that I didn't."

It was as if she could hear Carlota saying bitterly, Ah, yes, the gringo devil has much to do now that he has stolen the Delagado ranch from my husband. No matter how Anitra tried, she couldn't forget Carlota's words.

Leigh seemed not to notice her sudden stillness. She heard him walk down the hall, his footsteps light and slow, then the clink of the key in the lock, and his deep voice saying, "Out, Cora. Out, Cal." After that, all was quiet. She imagined his head bent over the papers before him.

At last, sighing, she climbed the narrow iron stairway, the lamp she carried making dark dancing shadows on the walls. Tinita, before going down to her small room at the foot of the courtyard for the night, had laid a fire in the bedroom. Anitra held a taper to it, and when the flames leaped upward, she had an uneasy feeling that someone was watching her.

She turned swiftly. From the nicho built into the corner, ornamented with gold and silver leaf, the bulto of the Virgin of Guadalupe seemed to smile at her. San José watched from the shelf above.

The prickling faded as she knelt before them, folded her hands, and bowed her head. These had been a gift of love from Eustacio, made by hands that had surely been guided by God.

If only They would hear her now. Silently, she asked the saints for peace, for help to forget these sinful suspicions. . . .

She didn't know how long she knelt, but when she rose her spirits were lightened. She took off her dress, hung it away in the trastero. She put on a gown of pale silk trimmed with lace and got into bed. The ormulu clock struck midnight, twelve soft chimes that stressed the stillness in the house, and she waited, thinking that she would soon hear Leigh's step upon the stair.

But he didn't come. At last, with a sigh, she took up the lamp and went down to the office, that room into which he had never invited her, and which, now, suddenly, she was determined she would see.

At the bottom of the door there was a thin line of light. She approached slowly, hearing snuffling and scratching.

She stopped, frowning, called, "Leigh? Leigh? I should like to see you for a moment."

There was no reply, but the dogs barked. Their heavy bodies hit the wooden panel, which shook beneath their combined weight.

Involuntarily she took a step back. "Cora, Cal, be quiet." And then anxiously, "Leigh? Are you there? Leigh, answer me!"

Still there was no reply but the angry barking of the dogs.

At last she turned away and climbed the stairs to the bedroom.

She was alone in El Castillo. Once more she knelt before the bultos and bent her head in prayer.

The cold was bitter. Each breath left its white trail in the air before his face. A high cloud drifted across the silver of the quarter moon.

Leigh smiled, working quickly, his hands adept at the task he had set himself.

The ormulu clock struck two as he entered the bedroom. He warmed his hands at the fire before he took Anitra into his arms, expecting that his touch would waken her.

But she was already awake. She had lain listening for the sound of his boots on the stairs. She yawned, blinking her eyes. "Oh, how late it is, my husband."

"Yes, my dear."

"And you've been at your papers all this time?"

"All this time," he repeated.

She knew that he lied. He had gone out, leaving the lamp lit, the dogs behind. She raised herself on an elbow, leaned over him, and looked into his eyes. "Leigh, tell me truly, do you love me?"

For answer he drew her close, pressed his lips to hers.

Yes, he loves me, she thought.

But in the bright light of morning, she thought once again, He lied.

And in the bright light of morning there was grumbling at the old Diaz ranch.

"If Don Matthew were here it wouldn't have happened."

"If you'd attended to your job, compadre, it wouldn't have happened," the foreman snapped.

"But the roof was in good repair."

"Oh, yes, of course." The foreman was bitter. "I know the roof was in good repair. Perhaps that was when Don Cipriano still lived. And that's why, last night, because the snow melted, the grain is now soaked and spoiled."

"I checked it myself," the man insisted.

"I'm certain of it, amigo. But you had your eyes closed."

A week later, a fight erupted between two of the men. One accused the other of stealing his few coins. The other denied it. The argument ended with the flash of knives. One of the men bore a scar on his cheek for the rest of his days.

The next month, dozens of chickens, a few from each family, were found with their necks wrung. Goats disappeared. Pigs drowned. Men began to look suspiciously at one another.

When two of the deep wells soured, the families that had used them simply moved away.

In the small dim cantina the men gathered and said that now that Don Cipriano was dead and Don Matthew gone, the ranch was cursed. How else to explain the losses, the sounds in the night?

The foreman listened, wearing a worried frown. He had begun by ignoring the annoyances. Now he experienced a certain fear.

It was a matter for Don Matthew, but the patrón was in Santa Fe, and pride kept the foreman from discussing his complaints with anyone else. He was, after all, charged with the care of the ranch in Don Matthew's absence. The patrón trusted him. How could he admit that such small things had begun to give him bad dreams? How could he say that he, who had been Don Cipriano's right hand, was now afraid?

Still, once the talk began, it spread. Eustacio heard of it and spoke to Porfirio, and Porfirio listened uneasily, knowing somehow that there was more to come.

In mid-April he knew that his feelings were justified.

Leigh's black-gloved hands worked at the thick cone of paper. He spread its flared end into a wide mouth and imagined it aflame, sailing through the air.

He took out a match. A whisper of sound made him raise his head. His hat was pulled low, covering the brightness of his hair, his black clothing making him a part of the shadows.

He smiled faintly when he saw the coyote on the nearby rock. It sniffed deeply, hackles rising, then, with a show of teeth, it barked sharply once and trotted away.

When all was still, Leigh moved down, his step as quiet as the single cloud that passed before the moon and hung there, enshrouding the ranch below.

Even nature worked for him. And from nature he drew his strength. He felt the blood pulse in his veins. He knew his power. Below, he saw the lights in the shacks adjacent to the vacant Diaz house and paused to watch the uncurtained windows of the occupied buildings. No figures moved. The women and children slept and the men were at the morada.

It was Good Friday, and for the whole week Leigh had been aware of the comings and goings in the clearing. He had heard the sound of the pito and had seen

Anitra lift her head and tighten her lips in silent disapproval. To her they were the past, her father. She was determined to forget both.

To Leigh, they were nothing. He no longer needed to spy on the rituals they performed. He no longer believed they had power. The tales he had heard of men disappearing never to be seen again made him smile.

He ignored the Brotherhood, except that now what happened in the morada became a part of his planning.

Let the pito sing on the still air, and the matracas clatter. Let the disciplinas cut deep, and the heavy crosses be dragged through mesquite and cactus into the distant canyon. The men were gone from the Diaz ranch. And that was what Leigh wanted.

He moved on slowly, listening with every step.

Porfirio sighed, squinting into the pale sun of dawn. "Such carnage is against God," he said.

"So terrible, Hermano Mayor." Antonio's handsome young face was grim. "I can hardly believe what I see." He turned, looked away from the corral, its gate sagging, to the few yards beyond where the carcasses of dead horses lay.

Porfirio said nothing.

"Why the horses should run so, how it could have happened . . . "

Porfirio squatted down on his heels, let a handful of red earth sift through his fingers. He knew how it had happened. He had seen, and what he had found reminded him of the charred bits of hide he had taken from the old hacienda of the Delagados.

A flaming torch had made a brilliant arc through the air and, still burning, had fallen among the horses. . . .

They reared in panic and charged the open gate. Driven by fear, they slammed into the wire, and their forelegs were shattered. Those behind trampled them, fell. . . .

The wire was withdrawn.

When the foreman came to investigate the screams of the injured, he found some already dead. He destroyed the wounded. Of twenty-five fine horses, only two remained.

Porfirio had found traces of paper ash in the corral. He had found scars on the corral posts.

"What do you think, Hermano Mayor?" Antonio asked, looking into the older man's face.

Porfirio rose, brushed at his dusty knees. "Remember," he said, "that when the troubles began at Don Esteban's ranch, they were small ones. Then they grew larger, and when Don Esteban was backed against the wall, we learned that the gringo held the notes that took the Delagado property."

Antonio nodded.

"And the common grazing land as well. Which made it not only Don Esteban's trouble, but also ours. After all, Antonio, Don Esteban wasn't one of us, and he was a rico as well."

"But now," Antonio said softly, "now, Porfirio, there's more."

"Don Matthew isn't here to protect his own," the older man answered.

"Then I must do it for him."

"*We* must do it for him, and for ourselves."

29

"No, thank you," Anitra protested. "No, no more wine. If I drink more, I may disgrace you, Leigh."

He grinned and moved the candelabra that stood as a barrier between them. "What of it? I'll see you safely home."

"I'm sure of that. But how will it look if you must carry me to the carriage?"

He gave the near-empty dining room a slow and deliberate glance. "What of it? I'll carry you to our carriage if I like. Who's to stop me, Anitra?"

She took up the glass, and holding it to her lips, she studied him through her lashes. Only the day before she had heard from Dora about Matthew's horses. Since then she had thought only of what it meant, and she remembered the intense yearning with which Leigh had gazed upon Matthew's land.

What could she do? At last, she answered Leigh's question. "I suppose there's no one, Leigh, to stand in your way in anything that you do."

She saw his eyes darken, his hands grip the table edge.

Where had he been the night she went to find him in his office? Why had he lied to her then?

302

She went on in the same level tone, "And no one whose opinion you value."

In the huge gold-framed mirror on the wall, she saw the straight stiff line of his back. Her own face was reflected too, eyes glittering as green as the strand of emeralds at her neck. She never wore it now except at his insistence. When she did, she was continually conscious of its weight, as if, instead of an elegant jewel, it were a chain that bound her to memories she would have preferred to forget.

"And whose opinion should I value?" he demanded.

She shrugged, took a sip of wine.

"But whose?" he repeated.

She put her glass down with care and leaned back. "The town's perhaps. There was a time when you did, you know."

He laughed, a short, hard bark of sound that had no mirth in it. "And when was that?"

"When you used Esteban Delagado to court me," she told him quietly.

Leigh laughed again. "Perhaps I didn't care as much as they—and you—thought. Perhaps I had my own reasons."

"No doubt you did. You've reasons for everything you do."

"And would you have it different? Think, Anitra. Would you want me to be another way than I am?"

"I suppose you must be as you are, Leigh."

"For good or for bad."

"Yes," she agreed.

"And which is it?"

She said nothing.

"I've given you everything you want," he told her,

and he leaned toward her, his face intent and his blue eyes dark and bottomless. "And there'll be more. You know that nothing will stand in my way."

There was no need to convince her. She had seen how he moved to get what he wanted. She understood now what he considered progress to be. Power. Power in his hands.

He had used her to that end. She promised herself it would never happen again. When she didn't speak, he drained his glass and quickly refilled it. Time would convince her. When she knew what it was to be a queen, she would understand.

She took up her fork, and though she wasn't hungry, she forced herself to eat. He had ordered this meal the day before. A goose, which Tinita could never have managed at El Castillo. A huge dish of mushrooms, picked only hours earlier near the Río Lucero. Crisp green spinach, chopped and seasoned with the juice of lemons and with cumin. Sliced tomatoes sprinkled with diced green chiles. A large platter of pinto beans provided by the hotel cook, who couldn't imagine a meal without them, and didn't believe they had been deliberately omitted from the menu.

She chewed the mouthful of rich goose knowing that he was watching her. Always he watched her. She would start down the steps in the morning and see him waiting, his eyes raised to observe where she went. She would be embroidering, and he would appear in the doorway to look at her. She would walk in the courtyard and know that he peered from the window.

She had once taken that to be a sign of his love and had been warmed by it. Now she understood that it was a sign only of joy in possessing her. He felt the same joy in owning El Castillo, the Delagado ranch, their house on the plaza.

Leigh made a sound of impatience. "I *have* given you everything. You know there'll be more. Why don't you answer me?"

She looked around the room. The chandelier was unlit as yet. It was dusky with late twilight outside. A great sheaf of the yellow roses of July stood in a vase in the corner, spilling out their scent.

At last she said, "I wish we could leave Tres Ríos."

"What?"

"Yes," she said softly. "Yes, my husband. I should like very much to move away from Tres Ríos. I've the feeling we could be . . . could be happier elsewhere."

"But it's our home."

"It's been mine all my life. That doesn't mean that I must live here forever."

"I'll never leave Tres Ríos," he said coldly. "Nor will you, Anitra. Everything I want is here. I knew that from the first time I saw the valley."

"But the world is so wide. There's so much to see."

"It's not the world you want to see." He looked deep into her eyes. "It's Santa Fe."

"Santa Fe?" she repeated, instantly seeing Matthew in her mind.

"And I know why." Leigh's voice hardened. "It's because of Matthew Britton."

She didn't answer.

"You want him, don't you, Anitra? For all I've done for you, you still want him."

"I'm married to you," she retorted. "You've no reason to accuse me, and no right either. I've given you no cause to speak so."

"I don't need a reason—remember? I know that you wanted Matthew before he married Josefa."

A faint pink spread through Anitra's cheeks. Her eyes burned. She recalled only too clearly the words Leigh had overheard.

"But you married me," Leigh went on. "As you just told me, you're my wife. So forget Matthew Britton, Anitra."

"There's no need to speak of it," she said. She brushed the lace of the mantilla back from her cheek, and then pushed back her chair. "If you're ready to leave . . ."

He rose, threw coins on the table, and took her arm. She felt his fingers bruise her flesh, and drew away.

"I'm sorry, Anitra." He took her arm again, but gently.

Even so, she understood. He would never let her go. As they walked across the plaza the air was warm still, and sweet with the scent of the golden roses.

Two elderly woodcutters, leading burros laden with cords of piñon, passed by.

"Good evening," Anitra said.

Neither of the two men acknowledged the words, but their eyes flashed from under the curled brims of their straw hats. Obsidian eyes, expressionless and empty, rested briefly on Leigh, then on her.

Leigh was either unaware or unconcerned. She thought of what she had told him about the town's opinion, but she knew it was useless to mention what had happened just now. It didn't matter to him that he was hated and that she, being married to him, was hated too.

Later that night she lay at the very edge of the big bed, pretending to sleep. But Leigh knew otherwise. He slid across the wide space she had deliberately left between them, his hand caressing her breast. She remembered when his touch had brought her joy. Now she felt nothing.

"Anitra, querida, you're not asleep."

She didn't reply, but she opened her eyes. He bent his lips to hers. It was a bruising kiss, and it left the taste of blood in her mouth. There had been no tenderness and no love in that kiss, and there was neither in what came after. She endured the weight of his body, the touch that was no longer a caress.

Her face was wet with tears when finally he turned angrily away from her.

She pretended, at last, to drift into sleep. She didn't move when Leigh rose. She listened as he eased the door open, closed it gently behind him.

Quietly saddling his horse, he rode out of town, the thought of Matthew bitter in his mind. She couldn't trick him. She had changed after Josefa's death. Well, now he would concentrate on the problem at hand.

It didn't take him long. Soon he was squatting on his heels, the paper cones he carried in the burlap sack beside him. It was so quiet that it seemed to him he could hear the angry beat of his heart. Soon it would be different. Soon the wild bells would ring. Where there was darkness now, there would be light that flickered and danced, and the Diaz acres would be raw and bare, charred and ruined, by dawn.

Leigh smiled, a flash of white that deepened the dimple near his mouth. El Castillo would stand unchanged, but within months it would double in size, its fence posts and wire stretching farther than the eye could see.

He set a paper cone into the earth and moved on to set another a few feet away. He moved in a zigzag line, avoiding a pattern that could be identified. With the morning wind from the north, all traces of the cones would be swept away. He knelt to place still another when he heard a sound below him. For an instant he froze, head bent, listening. Then he turned slowly.

A horse snorted. A pebble bounced with a soft, clear *ping* and was suddenly silent.

Antonio appeared over the edge of the arroyo and said in a quiet voice, "You're out late, Leigh."

Leigh rose, a stick gripped tightly in his hand. "So are you."

"I found that I couldn't sleep," Antonio answered.

He hadn't slept for many nights. He had been taking his turn, along with each of the Brothers, in riding Matthew's property. His eyes, as hard and green as wet stone, swept the earth near where Leigh had risen. He saw the zigzag pattern of paper cones. He looked into Leigh's face and inquired, "Were you sleepless because you had chores to do?" Even as he spoke, his hand crept to his collar, drawing it up to cover the thin red scar at his throat. Anitra was married to this man. . . .

"Chores?" Leigh asked, a laugh in his voice. At the same time he lunged forward. With his full weight he hit Antonio in the chest.

Antonio fell backward into the arroyo. The gun he had been holding behind his right thigh slipped from his hand and spun away, immediately covered by the dust raised by the two flailing bodies. Silently Leigh brought the heavy stick down hard, and then again.

Antonio felt the pain as a great explosion of heat, and in that same instant, sank into the cold of death.

Leigh was immediately on the move. He had killed out of instinct. It hadn't been what he intended—but

Antonio had stood in his way. Anitra would never know. No one would know.

Antonio's horse snorted, and the sound led Leigh to where the animal was tethered just beyond a bend in the arroyo. He reared but Leigh caught him by the bridle, and, whispering soothing words, led him to where Antonio lay.

Leigh lifted the limp body and placed it behind the saddle. He gathered the cones into the burlap bag and hobbled his own horse in a thicket. Then he mounted Antonio's horse, the body behind him, and rode wildly across the mesa to the gorge.

Now he hobbled Antonio's horse, dragged the body free, and left it where it fell.

He quickly roped himself to a juniper, and, crawling on hands and knees, moved cautiously to the very edge of the gorge. There the earth softened under his weight and crumbled, and a small bush tore away.

He hung by the rope, gasping, his face pouring sweat. He was conscious of the river, the jagged teeth of the rocks, some three hundred feet below. When he caught his breath, he clawed more earth away. Satisfied, he pulled himself up until he reached the heights. Then, on hands and knees again, he crawled to Antonio's body and dragged it as near the edge as he dared, then shoved it, grunting and gasping, until its own weight took it over the rim, and it went tumbling, pulling more earth with it, more bushes, creating a slide that rumbled and roared into the depths below.

He looked down but could see nothing. What was there was sheltered by impenetrable shadow. He freed himself, coiled the rope neatly, and rode back to where he had left his own horse.

It was near dawn when he returned to El Castillo. The dogs barked, and he ordered them to be silent. Inside all was quiet. Anitra didn't speak when he lay down beside her.

30

Leigh watched her over the rim of his coffee mug.

She moved slowly, the watering can tipped just so, a single drop hanging at its spout as she poised it over the pot of flowering red geraniums.

Her hand jerked at the first banging at the gate. The drop at the tip of the spout flew away like a chip of bright glass. The color faded from beneath her ivory skin, leaving it a strange muddy color.

She turned, and he knew that she was holding her breath. Her suddenly pale lips were frozen. "What can it be so early?" she asked faintly.

"I'll see." He set the mug down with careful deliberation. He was in no hurry, nor did he want to appear to be. He wasn't afraid. He knew nothing would happen. What he wanted fell into his hands. With his usual casual grace he walked down the hall to the front door.

He opened it, leaning a hand on the gunrack above it. Eustacio had swung the gate open and Porfirio rode in and dismounted. He was an old man suddenly, with bowed shoulders, but his eyes were black and smoldering.

Antonio's horse had come in soon after dawn. Porfirio had immediately organized a search and the men continued it while he came himself to tell Anitra.

"Good morning," Leigh said. "You're in town early, Porfirio."

Porfirio didn't answer. He looked past Leigh's shoulders into the shadows of the hall. Finally he said, "Don Antonio is lost on the mesa. The men are looking for him now, but I thought I must tell you at once."

Anitra emerged from the house like a small white-faced whirlwind. Her hands clasped Porfirio's arm. "How can he be lost?" she cried. "What do you mean?"

"Niña . . ." He didn't look at Leigh. Somehow she must be protected. He said finally, "Doña Anitra . . . "

"Tell me, Porfirio," she ordered.

"We found Antonio's horse."

"And we'll find Antonio," Leigh interposed. He put a reassuring hand on her arm. "Don't be frightened, Anitra. There's no need to upset yourself. I'll go out with Porfirio at once. We'll find him. What can happen to him in the valley, after all?"

Still Porfirio didn't look at Leigh. He knew what could happen.

Anitra ignored Leigh. She stared deep into Porfirio's eyes and saw anxiety there. Her heart began to beat quickly.

"Antonio . . . " She bit her lip. For a single instant she was immobilized by terror. Then she said, "Wait, wait for me, Porfirio. I'll ride with you."

Leigh said quickly, "Anitra, no. You'll make it too difficult. Stay here, and I'll send you word as soon as we have any."

But she was already moving. She clasped her skirt in both hands and raced past Porfirio into the courtyard.

"Anitra, listen to me," said Leigh. "We can go faster without you."

Her eyes blazed, and for a moment Leigh saw

Antonio's staring at him in the instant before his death. "I'll find him!" she cried. "I must find him."

Eustacio had Leigh's horse already saddled. When he saw her, he raised his hands. "Doña Anitra, you mustn't do men's work. They'll bring Don Antonio back to you."

"My horse," she answered. "I don't need the saddle. Quickly, I tell you!"

He slipped on headstall and bridle in reproachful silence, thinking that she no longer smiled. It had been, he suddenly realized, a long time since she had truly smiled. He must mention that to the Hermano Mayor. That her bright look had disappeared might mean something.

Automatically he linked his hands as a stirrup. He felt the trembling in her foot as she accepted the help and swung onto the horse's back. Outside, she urged her mount forward to ask Porfirio, "When did he go out?"

"Late last night it was."

"And did he say where?"

"No, Doña Anitra." But Porfirio had known where. The two of them had discussed the site many times together.

"Did you ask Dora?"

"Yes, Doña Anitra." But he hadn't. It hadn't been necessary.

"Did the men see him go?"

"Yes, Doña Anitra. But not after." Porfirio had waited, seeing the moon rise, then sink. When Antonio didn't return, he had ridden to the arroyo. He saw nothing in the darkness.

Anitra was silent. Porfirio would have known what questions to ask. He could be trusted to do all he could. Ahead she saw the glint of sunlight on the fences Leigh had installed. The vast spread of the valley was broken. When she and Antonio had roamed together, they had

313

known no boundaries. The three ranches had blended together around the grazing commons.

Leigh saw her mouth tremble. He knew there would be more to come—but it would be all right. Anitra now owned the Martínez y Escobedo ranch, and only Matthew stood between him and what he had dreamed of for so long.

Only Matthew.

Leigh let his body roll with the quick, smooth rhythm of the trotting horse.

"Antonio!"

"An . . . ton . . . io!"

The name floated on the heat of the shimmering air. It drifted down the slopes, slid along the buttes, through thickets of red and green willow.

"An . . . ton . . . io!"

Anitra remembered another time when she had heard such soft echoes. But then it had been night. The flare of torches had spread across the valley, small circles of light against the enveloping dark. The voices had come back in echoes, rising and falling. The drumbeat of horses' hooves had been lost in the night's stillness. And she had found Antonio in the kiva.

She turned her head and looked toward the distant palisades. No. He wouldn't be there now. This time he hadn't fled Lorenzo's anger.

"Antonio! An . . . ton . . . io!"

Ahead she saw a group of men waiting, horses bunched together. She sped on, breathing hard.

One of the men said, "Nothing yet."

"Then go on," Porfirio told him.

As they turned away, spreading out to ride again, Anitra raised her head.

The sound of a distant train whistle came to her on a gentle hot wind. She and Antonio had raced each other so many times, following that sound.

"The gorge," she said softly. "We must go along the rim."

Porfirio nodded. Perhaps it was wise to look where Antonio should not have been.

The river had taken many men and given back only a few. Porfirio remembered a time when he had struggled to heave a body into it, and the body clung to a yucca spike. But once it had fallen, it had never been seen again.

Leigh followed, his face expressionless. He had expected that they would ride this way sooner or later. But it didn't matter. They went on in silence, picking out a path between black boulders.

Here, Anitra thought, she and Antonio had often stopped, looking down into the gorge below, seeing the silver rails shine at them from the other side of the river. Farther on there would be narrow footpaths. One worked its way down the perilous side of the gorge. She and Antonio had climbed down it often, slipping and sliding, laughing and breathless, to pull off their boots and wade in the icy cold of the river.

A shadow skimmed across the ground and she raised her head and saw the black silhouettes of buzzards swinging in slow circles in the sky. Her heart jerked in her chest, and she slid off her horse to the ground, staring.

The earth was dark red, freshly exposed to the searing heat of the sun. A large gouge gaped at the rim here. Mesquite and sage and cedar were broken, broken limbs still spilling sap. Other brush was pulled free, minute roots exposed. There could be no doubt of a recent slide.

Porfirio had already seen. He moved lightly, testing the ground beneath him at every step, until he spied a partly obscured hoofprint and a narrow white line at the base of a juniper. He had seen such a mark before, and he knew where.

He crawled as close to the broken gouge as he dared, then lowered himself to his belly and went closer still. He saw the marks in the earth, the raveling scars where the break had come.

Behind him he heard Leigh say, "Anitra! No!"

Porfirio looked over his shoulder. Leigh held her by the arm. "No! Let him look, I tell you! He knows what he's doing."

She tore away from him, flung herself forward.

Porfirio raised his hand quickly. "Doña Anitra! Be careful."

A black shadow drifted over the ground between them, and then sailed away. He didn't raise his head to look. He watched as Anitra ran along the rim of the gorge, and then threw herself down and crawled to his side. "Antonio's down there, Porfirio! He is, isn't he?"

Porfirio edged closer to the lip of rock. From that angle the marks of the slide were plain—the jagged and broken scar where the earth had first broken away, the long steep path it had taken, the place where it had ended. Raw dirt, piled amid rock, white slivers of trees thrusting up like broken fingers that reached from the grave.

Anitra gasped, "Ah, no! Maria Santísima! No!"

She lunged forward, but Leigh seized her. "No, querida. No, you mustn't. Let Porfirio go down."

"Let me go, Leigh," she cried, her eyes blazing.

"Now, listen to me, Anitra. We'll wait here together. You've no reason to think Antonio was here last night.

The slide is fresh, we can all see that. But it proves nothing. Wait here with me. Porfirio will get help. He'll go down and see."

His soothing tone only inflamed her. She tore one hand free of his grasp, and clawed at his face, screaming, "Let me go. I can't stay here and watch. I must help. Antonio's there. I know it, Leigh!"

He tried to hold her, but she was like a wild thing. Rather than hurt her, he let his arms drop to his sides.

She moved quickly, following Porfirio's trail, using the footholds he left behind. She knew that Leigh was behind her, but she didn't look back. Each time the black shadows of the circling buzzards passed over her she shuddered.

Porfirio stopped suddenly. "A ledge."

He didn't point to his right where the slide had taken a raw bite out of it. But she saw the place, drew her breath in slowly.

When he climbed over and disappeared in a clatter of stones, she paused for an instant to look up. Far above, at the rim, horsemen had gathered. She watched as they dismounted, their figures like small dolls as they began the descent.

The broad brim of Leigh's hat shadowed his face when he caught up with her. "Rest here, Anitra. Let the others go on."

"I must go myself," she said, turning away.

She let herself over the edge of the rock, and reached with her feet, but felt nothing. She kicked and strained and finally found a toehold, but her arms wouldn't hold her, and she let go, tumbling down through brush, the earth sliding away under her and red dust rising, the sky spinning above. She landed on hands and knees, gasping.

Leigh caught up with her quickly and drew her to

her feet, angry now. "Be careful, won't you? You can see how it is."

"I see how it is," she said, and continued her descent.

Porfirio was already there, digging at the earth, clawing it away, flinging off stone, lifting away splintered limbs of trees. She flung herself down beside him, and within moments her hands were torn and bleeding.

Then Leigh drew her away, and the other men came to take her place. She shivered within the circle of his arms, as high above the buzzards still circled and glided.

There was no conversation among the men, but she noticed when all at once they stopped working, and she saw the dull sheen of sunlight on leather. "Por favor, no, no, no."

Leigh turned her head to his shoulder, held her tight, blinded and breathless.

She heard the low murmur of voices, and then dragging footsteps approached. "I'm sorry, niña," Porfirio said softly. "We've found Antonio."

"We'll go back now, Anitra," said Leigh.

She nodded, her temples pounding. "Yes, yes. We must go home."

An arm around her shoulders, he turned her toward the cliff. She moved obediently for a few stumbling steps. Then she stopped. "I must bid my brother goodbye, Leigh."

"Later," Leigh said. "Let the men get on with it."

"Now." She didn't wait for his agreement. She slipped from under his arm and hurried to where the men stood. The circle of their bodies opened at her approach.

She fell to her knees as a shadow settled beside her, then another. Without looking up, she said, "I'll do it myself, por favor."

Very gently, she began to dig, her slender hands scooping away the moist earth. A boot appeared. A flap of trouser leg.

She heard the hiss of Porfirio's breath, drawn sharply through his teeth.

Here is my Antonio, she thought. I must uncover his face.

It took her only moments. An arm appeared. The point of a shoulder.

"Niña, por favor . . . " Porfirio's voice was harsh.

She worked on. Then, beneath her careful fingers, in the crusty, grainy earth, she felt the softness of familiar dark curls.

Suddenly her composure broke. Gasping, she clawed at the earth, while tears gathered and spilled from her eyes, and a silvery flood made tracks down the curve of her cheeks.

Antonio's face emerged. Except for a smear of blood at his mouth, it was untouched. The scar at the base of his throat, which had been thin and red in life, was pale now. She touched it with wondering fingers—the mark of those entangled cords that had bound them together at their birth. He had always made certain that it was covered and she found herself adjusting his collar and heard herself say in disbelief, "My brother is dead!"

High in the sky, the buzzards swung in lazy circles, the shadows of their huge spread wings drifting slowly over the gorge below.

"My brother's dead," she said again, all strength gone from her body. It seemed then as if one of the slowly drifting shadows seized her and enwrapped her in blackness.

Leigh caught her as she fell.

31

Porfirio watched as Anitra's slender, limp body was passed from Leigh to another man, then to another, and so on, up the treacherously steep incline.

He watched as other arms offered Antonio, accepted him, and handed him on with careful tenderness.

Brother and sister arrived at the rim of the gorge within moments of each other. Porfirio watched as Leigh mounted, took Anitra in his arms, and set out immediately for El Castillo.

When he had gone, Porfirio motioned one of the men to his side. "Go to Santa Fe immediately. Tell Don Matthew what has happened. And don't stop for anything."

The man gave him a grim nod and began to pick his way up as Porfirio waved the others off. By the time he had reached the top, the messenger he had sent to Santa Fe had already disappeared.

Porfirio examined the white scar on the juniper limb, and lightly touched the edges of still-fresh earth at the top of the landslide. He felt his age in his bones; yet there was much to be done.

With a sigh, he mounted his horse and headed toward the arroyo. He had seen it by the dark of night. Perhaps the light of day would tell him more. He allowed the horse to pick his own way down the bank of the arroyo, but once in it, he dismounted and allowed the animal to amble along behind him.

Staring at the ground, he walked slowly. Here was a set of hoofprints. Here boot heels. With his eyes he followed them up the broken bank.

Frowning, he went on. But after a few slow paces, he stopped again. Here there were more boot heels, and scuffs, and a scar in the crusty earth where something heavy had fallen.

He squatted on his heels, examining each inch of soil, and gently put his hands on the earth, as if, were he careful enough, its secrets would be yielded up to him. At last, after a long time, his delicate, probing fingers felt out a mound that hardly showed to the eye. He brushed firmly and uncovered a familiar gun, then a long thin splinter of wood. It was stained on one side—a heavy dark-brown stain.

It was as he had supposed and feared. He climbed the bank above and looked slowly around until he saw the neat zigzag row of holes. These hadn't been made by some small burrowing animal; they had been dug by man.

Porfirio turned. The wire fences of the Delagado ranch stood shining in the sun. El Castillo Ranch it was called now, and one third of the common grazing land of the valley now lay behind those fences.

If a man wanted to clear off the adjacent acres—Diaz land—quickly, to build, for instance, or simply to fence, he might make a fire and let nature do for him what it would otherwise require many men and much time to do. But a wise man would be certain that there was a fire break in the right place. That was why those holes were at the edge of the arroyo's widest point. That was what Antonio had come upon as he patrolled the arroyo.

Porfirio sighed. He took no joy in what lay before him, yet he knew what he must do.

32

"Sea por Dios, Doña Anitra!"

"My deepest regrets, Doña Anitra. But God's will be done."

One after another the people of the ranch came to her, spoke the formal words, and passed on to gaze briefly into the candle-lit coffin where Antonio lay. To each Anitra murmured a brief reply, her voice hoarse from long hours of weeping.

Now her eyes were dry. She saw in every face that bent above hers a withdrawal, a concealment of innermost feelings.

It was the same with the people of the town.

All came to the velorio. In a little while they would follow the flower-decked wagon to the church and see Antonio buried beside his mother and father and grandmother. They would sigh as the holy water was sprinkled on the fresh white piñon of his coffin. They would pray for the repose of his soul. They had loved Antonio. They would remember him.

And then they would look at her guardedly.

Beside her, Dora shifted on the straight chair and sighed heavily. There was a moment when the two were alone.

Anitra asked, "What is it, Dora? Why do they look at me like this?"

"It's nothing, niña. What do you mean?"

"You know," Anitra retorted impatiently. "Porfirio, Felicia, even you . . . all of you, stare at me as if I've done something. As if . . . "

"Oh, no," Dora cried. "Not you! You mustn't think so. It has nothing to do with you."

"Then with what?" Anitra demanded.

Dora pressed a handkerchief to her face, hid her eyes. "Doña Anitra, not now. Now's not the time."

"Tell me! I insist, Dora," Anitra cried.

Dora tucked her handkerchief into the black sleeve of her dress. "Don't you see, niña? All's changed now. You are la patrona."

"La patrona," Anitra echoed. "Ah, yes. I see. I see." She was la patrona, but she was married to Leigh Ransome, and Leigh had made himself feared in the valley.

A new group entered the room. The men bowed to her, their heads uncovered, and they spoke softly. The women smiled faintly, huddling together for support.

Even as she greeted each one by name, she considered and watched. Among these, too, she saw the careful and withdrawn look. Dora. Porfirio. Even Matthew. Even these three, close to her all her life, had the same look.

Matthew . . . It had been near midnight when he rode into El Castillo, after hammering at the gate until Leigh had finally admitted him.

From her bed she had heard him say, "I must see Anitra—even if only for a moment, Leigh. I've just arrived from Santa Fe. I want to tell her . . . "

"She's asleep, finally," Leigh said coolly. "I doubt she'd appreciate being awakened. She's had a terrible shock. Perhaps, tomorrow, if she's able . . . "

"I must see her now," Matthew insisted.

She rose, threw a shawl around her, and ran down the narrow stairs.

She knew that both men turned their faces up to her, but she saw only Matthew, a gleam of lamplight in his chestnut hair, and the trapped stars shining at her from the depths of his eyes.

She whispered, "Matthew, you've heard?"

He nodded, took both of her hands in his, drew her close. "I came at once, Anitra. What can I do? How can I help you?"

"I can't believe it," she whispered. "It's not possible, Matthew. What was Antonio doing at the gorge at night? And how could he fall when he knew every inch of the place as well as I do?"

Leigh said, "You can see for yourself how she is, Matthew," and though his voice was cool and measured, his mouth was tight and his eyes had turned dark and angry.

"We'll find out," Matthew told her. "Be calm, Anitra."

"But what's there to find?" she demanded. "I can't believe it. I'll never believe it."

"Rest now," Matthew told her. "We'll speak again tomorrow." She saw in his eyes that closed secret expression. "Sea por Dios, Doña Anitra."

She murmured an answer and returned upstairs.

Now, praying by the coffin, she heard the rattle of wagons and the stamp of horses' hooves. Porfirio and Matthew came into the room, followed by four other men.

"If you'll wait in the courtyard, Doña Anitra . . . " Porfirio suggested.

She hesitated for a moment, looking into Antonio's calm face, and then left, with Dora trailing after her.

Matthew and Porfirio laid the coffin cover in place and sealed it quickly without speaking.

"Yes," Porfirio said. They lifted the coffin to their shoulders and carried it into the courtyard. As they loaded it onto the wagon, the bell over the gate began tolling softly. Soon the wagon moved over the small bridge.

A black carriage with the emblem of El Castillo followed. Inside, Anitra sat straight and stiff-backed next to Leigh, and Matthew's whole body tightened as he watched the gringo put a possessive arm around her, drawing her closer.

She doesn't know, Matthew told himself. She mustn't know. Not until he, with Porfirio's help, made certain that she would be safe.

33

A warm breeze stirred the draperies at the barred window, bringing with it the sweet scent of roses. The flames over the small white votive candles leaped and danced over their flexed wicks.

Anitra watched them, eyes narrowed and breath held. If they were to go out, then she would know she had dreamed. All the sharp bitter images of the past two weeks would have been nothing—but the flames steadied and burned on.

She sighed and looked down at her hands. No. It hadn't been a dream. It was all true. She had stood at the place where Antonio had fallen, and with her own hands had dug the earth from his face. She had stood at his graveside and watched the thick red clods drop on his coffin.

The dogs howled below. She listened, shuddering. Their bark these days seemed to touch her as if their teeth raked her very flesh.

Soon, she told herself, she must begin to think, to live. But just now she couldn't. She hardly knew the words to describe what she felt. There was the fresh and aching grief. But beyond this, she was afraid. It was as if a dark and shapeless beast would at any moment come creeping out to reveal itself and to destroy her.

She didn't turn her head when Leigh spoke from the doorway. "Porfirio is here, querida. He wants to see you."

"No," she said softly. "I'll see no one now, Leigh."

"You can't hide here forever, you know." His voice was quiet, but there was an edge of impatience in it.

"Why should I do that? I just don't want to see anyone yet."

"It's important, Anitra."

"Nothing's important to me at the moment," she retorted. "Tell Porfirio to come another time."

Leigh continued, still at the doorway, "I must insist you see him. Life goes on, Anitra." He hesitated. "You have many people depending on you, as you know. You should think of them instead of yourself. The ranch continues to exist. You can't pretend it doesn't."

"Porfirio is here about that ranch. Is that it?"

A faint smile touched Leigh's face now. "I believe so. Because he refused to state his business."

It would, Leigh thought, take a little while, but not very long, for Porfirio to learn his place. Leigh himself would see to that.

"Then perhaps I'd better see him after all."

"And since you seem to be in no state to deal with these things, Anitra, perhaps you'd better explain to Porfirio that, for the time being, I'll do it for you."

"You?" she asked softly.

"Of course. What do you know about running a ranch?"

"Quite a bit, I think."

"My dear . . . " he was smiling indulgently. "My dear, I don't want you to worry about such things. I've told you so before. I only want you to be happy and beautiful for me."

"I must think of something," she told him.

"Certainly. But remember that I know what's best."

"And what do you think best, Leigh?"

"We'll discuss that later. Meanwhile Porfirio is still waiting for you."

She was thinking of the common grazing land when she entered the sala, picturing the long thin strands of wire that cut across the valley, enlarging the El Castillo Ranch. She saw the Diaz land, and beyond it those vast acres that had come to her when Antonio died.

Leigh would think it best to enclose those acres, and she must not let it happen. For Antonio's sake, and in his memory, Leigh couldn't be permitted to do it.

A wave of fear swept over her. She stood trembling and waited for it to recede.

"Sit down," Leigh said. And to Porfirio, who stood with his hat in his hands, "You can see that your mistress isn't well."

Anitra seated herself, her hands folded on the silk of her black skirt. "I'm not ill." She gave Porfirio a faint smile. "And you, Porfirio? How are you? How are Felicia and Dora?"

"We manage, Doña Anitra."

His voice was soft. He didn't raise his head.

"As we must, old friend." Then, "You wanted to see me?"

"There are the books . . . certain debts must be paid soon. Then, when the wool is shipped to Santa Fe for sale, we must . . ."

From where he stood at the fireplace, Leigh said softly, "You speak only of trivial matters. I can certainly deal with those. You mustn't trouble your mistress any further."

Porfirio didn't reply.

Anitra saw the question in his eyes, saw his fingers clench the brim of his hat.

She had no doubt that he had worried deeply over what would happen now that the gringo Leigh Ransome, and the gringo's wife, Anitra Martínez y Escobedo, owned the ranch. It would be easy for her to acquiesce now, to say, "Yes, yes, Porfirio, in the future you must deal only with Señor Ransome. He'll tell you what to do." But what of the people of the valley?

And what of Antonio? She knew what his feelings had been. It was for him that she said softly, watching Leigh, "Why, no, Porfirio. I'm in no way troubled by your visit to me, and I have a great deal of interest in the ranch and its affairs. I believe I shall deal with these myself." She turned a faint smile on Leigh. "Always asking my husband's advice, of course."

"Whatever you like," Leigh told her. But when he walked from the room she saw that his usual grace had been transformed by the stiffness of anger.

"And now, Porfirio, shall we go on?" she asked, as the sound of Leigh's footsteps faded into silence.

But Porfirio was staring at her, alarm written all over his face. "Doña Anitra, your husband . . ."

"The ranch is mine," she answered firmly. "It's a trust that comes to me from Antonio. And I'll have you to help me, won't I, Porfirio?"

Porfirio hadn't expected this. He had imagined that her very innocence protected her. Her safety lay in her ignorance, in her compliance with her husband's wishes.

"Señor Ransome will help you," Porfirio answered firmly. "That's how it should be."

"Why not?" she asked coolly.

"Then I'll gather the papers, the books and return tomorrow . . . no . . . no, better the next day. Will that do?"

"It will do nicely." She rose and went with him to the door. "Old friend, you've seen Matthew?"

Porfirio nodded. "Don Matthew's here."

"He'll remain in Tres Ríos now?"

"Yes. He'll remain now. I'm sure of it, Doña Anitra."

He waited, expecting that she would say more, but when she remained silent, he asked, "Is there a message for him?"

"No, Porfirio, not at present."

He nodded and slowly left her, feeling her eyes on his back.

Late that night, as he made his customary inspection at the ranch, he felt eyes on his back again. He stopped his horse, remained still, listening, for a long time. The feeling stayed with him when he finally continued his work.

At El Castillo all was silent too. Leigh had paused beside the bed, thinking Anitra asleep before he had gone out. She lay limp and unmoving, listening to the sound of his footsteps on the stairs and then the faint thud of the horse's hooves drifting away beyond the walls.

She was no longer immobilized by grief. What she had to do was for Antonio. She pulled on a light robe and went to open the door. The hall was dark, but a lamp burned on a narrow table so that bars of pale light lay on the stairs. Slowly she tiptoed down.

As soon as she stopped before the door to his office, the dogs sensed her presence. They immediately threw themselves at the wooden panel, raking it with their claws. Once again she shivered, feeling as if they cut through her flesh to the bones.

"Hush, Cora, hush, Cal." She spoke the words without hope. They had never heeded her. Leigh had trained them so. For another moment she listened to the wicked sound of the dogs' claws. There'd be new long white scratch marks in the wood by morning, she thought. Then she turned away.

She was determined to go into the office. She wanted to see the place now—and alone.

That office was his retreat; there he set aside the face of the man he pretended to be and showed the face of the man he was. It was there that she would know him.

She hurried into the courtyard, to the barrel in which Leigh kept raw and fetid meat for the dogs. She caught up two thick, heavy, foul-smelling chunks and flung them over the wire. Watching the low entry door, she waited. It was only an instant or two before it burst open, and the dogs came charging out.

It was less than an instant before she fled inside, raced down the hall, and was in the office, bolting the catch on the dogs' door. Cora and Cal immediately thrust their muzzles against it, howling, but they couldn't get in.

She let her breath out slowly, pressed her fingers to her temples, and then began a careful search. What was she looking for? The bare whitewashed walls told her nothing. The black safe in the corner was locked, and she couldn't open it.

Carlota's thin angry voice echoed through her mind. He's a devil, your gringo husband. He loves nothing and no one. He uses you, just as he used Esteban. Be careful, Anitra. Be careful.

The night the old Delagado hacienda had burned to the ground, Leigh had ridden out. But she recalled clearly that when she awakened to the sound of the bells, he had lain beside her. Still, there had been another time. He had been in Santa Fe when those strange wolves attacked Esteban's sheep. She closed her eyes, seeing Leigh's return. He had ridden in, the dogs racing ahead. She had noticed how clean they were, their coats smooth and shining, even after the long dusty journey from the city.

And the night Antonio died? Where had Leigh gone then? She choked down a deep gasping sob and forced herself to go to the desk. She must know the truth or go mad.

"Maria Santísima," she whispered aloud. "Help me, help me."

She opened the top drawer of the desk. A rough golden nugget gleamed at her, a tiny wilted rose that had once been yellow. She didn't understand the meaning of the nugget, but the small rose reminded her instantly of the day Matthew married Josefa, the day Leigh had first kissed her.

She blinked away sudden tears, drew out a heavy roll of paper and spread it open on the desk. The great red patches leaped to her eye. Red, the color of the earth of the valley, the color of El Cristo's blood.

Slowly the color drained from her face, leaving it as pale as ivory. She sat very still; in the pen outside, the dogs yowled mournfully.

Red for what had once been the Delagado Ranch. Red for the Martínez y Escobedo acres. And long red lines through Matthew's land. He had tricked Esteban, he had married her, and Antonio had died. What would happen to Matthew?

She saw the full dimensions of the black beast she had only glimpsed before. Leigh would do anything, including murder, to possess the valley.

"Did you want something here?" Leigh asked from the doorway. His voice was silky, but his eyes were dark as he took in the map of the valley spread on the desk.

"I found what I didn't want to find," she told him.

He closed the door behind him and looked down at the map. It would be all his. No one could stop him now. He felt his own strength.

"I know it all," she was saying.

He raised his head, a faint smile on his lips. "You know what, Anitra?"

"All that you've done."

There was sudden mockery in his faint smile. She couldn't possibly know what he had done. Old Jake Heimer's body still lay undisturbed where Leigh had buried it eight years before. The gold remained his monument in the mountain. The Delagado ranch belonged to El Castillo now. Antonio was buried in the churchyard, and the secret of how he died was buried with him. The Martínez y Escobedo ranch belonged to El Castillo, too. But there was nothing in this room, or anywhere else, to show how he had come to own so much of the valley. She didn't know. No one knew.

He said softly, "I don't know what you're talking about." And added with cool deliberation, "I do think you should go to bed. You look feverish, Anitra."

She spread her slender hands on the map of the valley. "Do you think I'm a stupid fool not to be able to read this?"

She suddenly saw the thick, hard arrogance of his jaw. "But you knew Delagado lost his land to me," he said gently. "And as for Antonio's unfortunate accident . . . "

"An accident which proved to be fortunate for you," she said sharply.

"For you, Anitra. You are his heir."

"And *you* are mine. And you want the whole of the valley."

"But you always knew that."

"I didn't know you would kill for it," she cried.

He was suddenly very still, looking down into her face. "Do you realize what you're saying to me?"

"You murdered Antonio!" she screamed, her rigid and icy control suddenly gone. "You, my husband, you murdered Antonio. I'm certain of it. And how long before you murder me?"

"What are you saying?" he demanded. "I'd never harm you."

"It was no accident that Antonio died. It was murder. He'd never have fallen into the gorge."

Leigh answered carefully, without anger, without inflection, "If you've spoken of this to anyone, then everyone in the valley knows that you're unhinged by your grief. No one will believe you."

"You can't deceive me, Leigh. I know, I tell you."

"And what do you know, my wife?"

"Your wife . . . your wife . . . how can you use such words to me? Your possession, rather. Call me that. Say I am one more *thing* that you own." She drew a deep breath. "I shall leave El Castillo, and leave you. I won't be your wife much longer, I promise you."

She remembered his saying, I'll never let you go, Anitra. Never. You belong to me.

He said the same words now. "I'll never let you go, Anitra."

"And how will you keep me?" she demanded. "As long as there's breath in my body I'll accuse you."

"Your accusations aren't proof," he retorted. "And there's no proof against me, Anitra."

"I can speak. I can watch. And if anything should happen to Matthew . . . "

334

No one knew, Leigh told himself. The valley was nearly his, and no one could say how he had come by it. Who would believe Anitra's empty words? Matthew Britton. Porfirio, perhaps. The men who looked at him with hard blank eyes and stepped aside when he passed. They would all want to believe her. She would need no proof.

His hand moved from her shoulder along the silk of the robe he had brought her from Santa Fe and settled at her throat. His other hand came to join it. Those hands were hard, calloused from hours of panning for gold. His thumbs dug deeply into her throat.

Her breath was gone. Her heart pounded slowly, falteringly, against her ribs.

A red mist swirled before him, but through it he saw a green fire that singed him to his soul.

"It's Matthew," he said through gritted teeth.

"Yes," she gasped. "It's always been Matthew. I've always loved him, and always will. What I thought was love for you was no more than my own need to be loved."

Once again he willed his hands to tighten into the softness of her flesh. He had struck old Jake Heimer down without thought. He had clubbed Antonio when it had been necessary. He willed one more murder. This time for safety, for the sake of all he was and would become. But his hands wouldn't obey. He couldn't kill her. She was his love, all that he wanted. He couldn't kill her.

He let go of her, and as she backed away, he said hoarsely, "Anitra, forgive me. I couldn't stand hearing the things you said to me . . . I . . . "

"They're all true."

He took a deep breath, waiting for calm. "No, Anitra. None of it's true."

"I'll never believe you, Leigh."

Her hands were at her throat now; between her spread fingers he saw the dark red crescents left by his fingernails.

"I should have understood before. You're not well. It's Antonio's death, of course. I understand. I forgive you. We'll never speak of it again."

"What are you going to do?" she demanded.

"Do? My dear, what can I do? You've accused me unjustly. Do you propose that I confess to something I'm not guilty of?"

"You're lying, Leigh. Just as our life together has been nothing but lies."

He went on evenly. If he had heard her words, he gave no sign. "I'm afraid there's nothing I can do to convince you, so I hope that soon you'll recover your senses."

She shrank back as he came toward her. "No!"

"You mustn't be afraid of me," he told her gently. "There's no reason for it. You're my wife. My love. How could I harm you?"

She saw that at least that was true. He could have killed her, but he'd been unable to bring himself to it. Still, one day he would see what a threat to him she must be. Then what would happen?

"Come, Anitra," he said. "You must go upstairs and lie down. You must rest."

He would pretend to her, perhaps even to himself, that grief had led her to illness and illness to imaginary horrors. But for how long could he maintain that pretense? She didn't know. But for however long he did, then she must maintain it, too. Later, she would find a means of escape.

"Leigh, can I be mistaken? Can this be nothing more than a bad dream?"

"That's just what it is. You'll be over it soon." He drew her to him, and though she shuddered at his touch, she didn't allow herself to cringe.

The lamps were still lit in the bedroom. She remembered the first time she had seen this room, how she had gone so willingly, happily, into his arms. The white of the bed curtains, the white of the draperies at the window— now they seemed to her no more than shrouds, fit only for wrapping the dead. The carvings of the headboard, the grapes and bread and wine, seemed to writhe as if alive. The ornamental bars at the windows were thickened, to keep her a prisoner.

She sank down on the settle before the empty fireplace.

"I think you should go to sleep," he said. "When you wake up, you'll be well again. You'll have forgotten this nonsense."

"Yes, yes, perhaps then . . . " Her voice trailed away. She didn't dare look up at him, but heard his faint sigh, then his slow footsteps. The door opened, closed. As she jumped to her feet, she heard the key turn in the lock.

34

Eustacio stood on tiptoe and peered through the Judas hole into the courtyard. The newly risen sun hung just at the mountain ridges, but the morning glories on the well house looked limp and dusty in the already warm, dry air. Everything would need watering.

For the second time, he pushed the gate. It still didn't open. Suddenly he found himself stepping back. The dogs had come streaking across his carefully weeded grass. He felt sweat break out on his face and thanked God that the gate had refused to open. If it had, those devil dogs would have been upon him.

He backed away another step as they flung themselves at the gate, snarling. It was curious that they weren't in the pen. He couldn't remember ever having seen them run free unless Señor Ransome stood beside them.

He looked through the Judas hole again and blinked into Señor Ransome's face. "Good morning, señor."

"Never mind today," Leigh said. "There's no work."

"No work?" he protested in disbelief. Then, "There's much to do. Doña Anitra suggested ... "

"Not today. Nor even tomorrow, Eustacio."

"But what's wrong then? The flowers will die if they're not watered daily. In the heat of the summer ... "

"I'll let you know." Leigh smiled down at the dogs. "You can't come in today."

Eustacio felt the sag of disappointment. He liked to be at El Castillo. Or rather, he amended thoughtfully, he liked Doña Anitra. It was good to be near her, to see her smile. Though in truth, he thought, as he turned away, she had not smiled often lately.

Porfirio was openly upset when Eustacio said, "Doña Anitra said nothing of it yesterday when I saw her."

"You did see her then?"

"Yes. In the morning for a few moments. But this morning Señor Ransome told me to go away. And not to return until he sends for me."

"And you didn't see Doña Anitra?"

"No. But she couldn't come out, for the dogs weren't penned. You know those beasts. When they're not in their cages, then no one can go into the courtyard."

Porfirio nodded, a gleam in his dark eyes.

"And one other thing, Hermano Mayor. I'm troubled about Doña Anitra. Since Don Antonio died, I have not seen her smile, and even with her grief that seems wrong to me."

Again Porfirio nodded. It seemed wrong to him as well.

The night before, he and the other Brothers had met in the morada. Antonio had seemed to be there, too.

Porfirio told the Brothers in a calm quiet voice what he believed. He showed them the splinter of blood-stained wood and the gun he had found in the arroyo. He charted a course of events that had led up to Antonio's death.

Each of the Brothers had something to say, a small point to add, a suspicion to describe, a moment in time to recall. Porfirio allowed them all to talk out the horror and the hate, while La Santa de la Muerte listened from her shadow-wrapped carreta. But when the time had come to draw straws, he had made sure that he held the odd one.

The books of the ranch were prepared, the papers gathered. He was expected.

But what of Anitra? Why did the dogs run loose in the courtyard now? He said slowly, "Eustacio, you must go back to El Castillo and watch."

"From beyond the walls?" the gardener asked anxiously.

"Watch for whatever happens. And if the gringo should ride out, then you must come and tell me at once. See which direction he takes, then come and let me know."

As soon as Eustacio was gone, Porfirio went to talk with Matthew.

It was twilight that same day.

Anitra stood at the window, her fingers tight around the iron bars. All through the night, while Leigh paced the floor in the adjacent room, she had tried to weigh her position. Leigh would keep her in El Castillo until . . . But she wouldn't allow herself to dwell on what the end must be. Somehow she must get word to Matthew.

Cora and Cal raced beneath the window. That morning she had seen the dogs run free, and she wondered. Then she watched Leigh at the gate and knew he had sent Eustacio away. That was one hope gone. Soon after, Leigh came to her carrying a tray with coffee, fruit, and a single yellow rose. She thought of the flower he had kept all those years in the drawer of his desk as she watched him kick the door shut behind him.

"I've brought you something to eat," he told her.

"I believe I could go down," she answered, thinking

of Tinita. If she could but pass a note to the serving girl . . .

"It's better not," Leigh told her. "I've explained that you're not feeling well."

So her second hope died.

She said only, "Whatever you say, my husband."

"But tomorrow, if you like, we'll have a ride in the countryside, or if you prefer to shop on the plaza . . . "

She said carefully, "If you think I'm recovered by then, I would enjoy a visit to the stores."

"Oh, I doubt that you'll be fully recovered, but an outing would be helpful."

She looked quickly into his eyes and knew he was mocking her. Very well, she told herself. She would be content to play along. For a little while anyway.

The twilight had deepened. Deep shadows lay like black velvet across the courtyard. There was the rattle of wagon wheels beyond the walls.

Cora and Cal streaked toward the gate as Leigh walked toward the Judas hole and looked out. He spoke a few words and then ordered the dogs into their pen. When they had gone, he swung the gate back.

The wagon, piled high with hay, rolled through and came to a stop in the shadows. Porfirio climbed down, both arms wrapped around a thick pile of ledgers. He nodded at Leigh and followed him into the house.

Below, Anitra now heard the faint murmur of voices. She hurried to the door, listening.

Porfirio was here, here in El Castillo.

She must somehow speak to him. He would get word to Matthew.

Below, in the courtyard, the dogs howled louder.

The piled hay in the wagon barely shifted as a shadow detached itself and dropped lightly to the ground. Matthew gave the barred window above a quick look, then moved lightly toward the house. As he stepped inside, he heard the rumble of voices from the office at the end of the hall. He passed quickly by the sala and moved without sound up the narrow stairs.

Porfirio stood beside Leigh's desk, the books and ledgers still clasped in his arms. "Doña Anitra?" he was asking.

"She's not well this evening, Porfirio. But since you are here you may as well go over the material with me. You gave me the idea yesterday that it was necessary to avoid delay."

"But Doña Anitra . . ."

Leigh smiled slightly. "You know women, amigo. She's changed her mind. She prefers that I handle matters after all."

"Her name must be on the papers."

Leigh's smile broadened. "Of course. And it will be. Now then, shall we start?"

For Don Lorenzo, for Don Antonio, for Doña Anitra, Porfirio would have stood. For Leigh Ransome he wouldn't. He seated himself without being asked and put all but one of the ledgers on the floor beside them.

"In what way is Doña Anitra not well?" he asked.

Leigh shrugged. "Grief is a bad thing, amigo." He put out his hand for the papers.

But Porfirio wasn't ready. He must give Matthew all the time he needed.

Porfirio had waited all through the day for Eustacio to come to him. When the gardener didn't, he knew that the gringo remained at El Castillo.

By late afternoon, Porfirio had made his decision. He would go to El Castillo himself. But if his fears were true he would require help. He went to Don Matthew.

He said only as much as had to be said. Don Matthew asked only as much as he had to ask.

Porfirio listened. By now Don Matthew should be speaking to Doña Anitra. Within moments they should be on the stairs. But still he heard nothing.

He gave his attention solely to Leigh. "It's the supplies always ordered. We need the same again."

The one ledger lay on his crossed knees. He touched the knife within its pages and set it more securely on his lap.

Time, he thought. Only a little more time, hombre . . .

The same word was in Anitra's mind as she looked frantically around the room. Porfirio was here and she must free herself before he left. But she saw nothing she could use against the big lock on the door, against the thick ornate hinges by which it hung.

She glanced quickly at her dressing table then slowly swung open the trastero doors. A silver button gleamed at her from the neckline of a black velvet blouse, a silver button with a thin fluted rim.

She ripped the button off, hurried to the door hinge, and tried to work the rim beneath it, but the button shot from her fingers and flew across the room. She snatched it up, and her anxious gaze fell on the trastero once more. Its hinges were smaller, less formidable. This time the button caught under the grooved metal. She worked it back and forth, using all her strength. One peg slowly eased out, then another. The hinge dropped to the floor. She caught it up and hurried to the door. With this trastero hinge as a tool, she went to work.

If she heard the voices again, she would scream and bang her hands on the door. Leigh would tell Porfirio that she was demented—but Porfirio would never believe that.

She listened, but she could hear nothing. She tried to imagine Porfirio standing beside the desk in Leigh's office, the books spread open under the light of the lamp. She tried to think how long it would be before Leigh led the foreman out and let the dogs loose again.

If only she could get the door open. Then she could slip down quietly, hide herself in the wagon until it was beyond the walls of El Castillo. If she were discovered before then, she would shout the truth to Porfirio too quickly for Leigh to stop her.

The hinge suddenly gave under her hand. Just as it did, the door swung open. Matthew's long black-clad arm was around her, his hand gentle at her lips, stifling her gasp.

Until that moment he had only known that he must bring her safely out of El Castillo. Until that moment he wasn't certain that what was between them hadn't changed with the passing of the years.

But he knew when he looked into the green blaze of her eyes. He knew when he felt her body against his.

He couldn't speak. Soundlessly he moved his lips. "My love, we must hurry now."

There was the murmur of voices as they reached the lower floor.

Leigh suddenly rose. "Just a minute, hombre," he said.

"And then," Porfirio went on desperately, "and then there are other considerations, Señor Ransome."

But Leigh came quickly around the corner of the desk. Porfirio moved even faster, his hand sliding into the ledger. He stood before the door, blocking Leigh's way. "One more moment of your time, señor. There's something you should know, por favor."

Leigh reached out, seized the older man by the shoulder. But Porfirio was immovable. His deep-set dark eyes had disappeared into their sockets. He became, as Leigh looked at him, La Santa de la Muerte herself.

Leigh clubbed him with his fist and flung him away.

As he fell, Porfirio shouted, "Murderer! Did you believe Don Antonio would go unavenged? Did you believe that we would all go unavenged?"

His knife flashed in the lamplight, made a long silver lance through the air, and buried itself deep into Leigh's ribs.

He took a step, then another. Porfirio rolled to avoid him, but the heavy weight of Leigh's body fell on him in a loveless embrace.

As the dark closed in, Leigh thought, He's the Brotherhood. Then the dark was gone. Leigh saw only sunlight in the valley, and riding through it, a girl with long black silken hair. "Anitra," he whispered. "Anitra, wait for me." Even as he spoke, he saw the sunlight fading, and the girl, too, and as he reached out to capture her, his fingers hooked in the catch of the small entry door. The dogs snarled, and one last time he said, "Anitra. . . ."

Matthew and Anitra were at the front door when they heard Porfirio's shout and the heavy thud of falling bodies.

"Run, Anitra. It's Porfirio."

"Don't open the door yet," she cried. "The dogs, Matthew. The dogs, they won't let you."

But he raced toward the office. She snatched a gun from the rack over the front door, and hurried outside. It took her only an instant to roll the rain barrel that stood at the end of the wall to a place under the window. She climbed up on it, grasping the bars to steady herself, and then peered through them.

The lamp on the desk had burned low. The room was dim. Cora and Cal prowled and worried at something in the shadows, but when they sensed her presence they flung themselves at the wall beneath her. She saw clearly the bloodstained fur at their throats, the clots of shredded flesh on their muzzles.

Behind their wild, gleaming eyes, she saw Porfirio.

He lay where they had brought him down, only feet from the door. His torn throat gaped like a second screaming mouth.

Then the door inched open. The dogs charged and fell back when it snapped shut against them. They drifted slowly to where Leigh lay on his side, a pool of red around him. His shoulder was clawed, and the bone of one leg from thigh to ankle showed through his shredded flesh.

She closed her eyes, willing the awful sight away. But when the dogs charged the door again, she watched them as she rammed the gun through the window, and the shattered glass tinkled musically as it fell within the charnel room. Behind her the courtyard was full of the whisperings of dried leaves as a cool wind suddenly swept through it.

Now the dogs scented her. They flung themselves at the wall, and she waited until they retreated to gather for another assault. When they had retired as far as Porfirio's still body, she fired.

Cora coughed a gout of blood and fell. Cal lurched sideways, roaring, and as she fired once more, he dropped. The yowling of the dogs was silenced forever.

The door burst open. Matthew knelt beside Porfirio.

She heard the sound of her own breath as she stepped down from the barrel. Dropping the gun, she ran for the house. Matthew met her, barring the way.

"Porfirio?" she asked, knowing what the answer would be.

"It's too late, Anitra. We must send for the padre at once."

"And Leigh?"

"The same."

"Why are you here, Matthew?"

"Porfirio."

"He knew?"

Matthew nodded.

She looked into the depths of his eyes and saw points of light gleaming, points of light that looked like trapped stars. There were other questions on the tip of her tongue, but she didn't ask them. Certain things they would never speak of. Certain things she understood now.

Antonio had been a Penitente, and the Brothers never forgot their own.

Matthew put his arms around her and drew her outside. When they had passed through the gates of El Castillo, she paused. But she didn't look back.

She saw that the rising moon shone bright as day on the mountains above the town, glowing with that ancient red which was the reminder and symbol of the blood of El Cristo.

She thought of Leigh, who had believed that he could own both mountain and valley, never knowing that they had a soul, and a protecting magic, so no man could ever be master of either, and surely never possess either.

This was what her people knew, because they had been born knowing it. And those who came afterward, and refused to learn it, would end by destroying themselves.

She raised her eyes to Matthew, said, "I want to go to the ranch. Will you take me? Will you take me home?"